Praise for Mary Ellen Taylor

"Mary Ellen Taylor writes comfort reads packed with depth . . . If you're looking for a fantastic vacation read, this is the book for you!"

—Steph and Chris's Book Review, on *Spring House*

"A complex tale . . . grounded in fascinating history and emotional turmoil that is intense yet subtle. An intelligent, heartwarming exploration of the powers of forgiveness, compassion, and new beginnings."

—*Kirkus Reviews*, on *The View from Prince Street*

"Absorbing characters, a hint of mystery, and touching self-discovery elevate this novel above many others in the genre."

—RT Book Reviews, on *Sweet Expectations*

"Taylor serves up a great mix of vivid setting, history, drama, and everyday life."

—*Herald Sun*, on *The Union Street Bakery*

"A charming and very engaging story about the nature of family and the meaning of love."

—*Seattle Post-Intelligencer*, on *Sweet Expectations*

The Words We Whisper

"Taylor expertly employs the parallel timelines to highlight the impact of the past on the present, exploring the complexities of familial relationships while peeling back the layers of her flawed, realistic characters. Readers are sure to be swept away."

—*Publishers Weekly*

"A luscious interweaving of a spy thriller and a family saga."

—*Historical Novels Review*

HONEYSUCKLE SEASON

"This memorable story is sure to tug at readers' heartstrings."

—*Publishers Weekly*

WINTER COTTAGE

"Offering a look into bygone days of the gentrified from the early 1900s up until the present time, this multifaceted tale of mystery and romance is sure to please."

—*New York Journal of Books*

"There is mystery and intrigue as the author weaves a tale that pulls you in . . . this is a story of strong women who persevere . . . it's a love story, the truest, deepest kind . . . and it's the story of a woman who years later was able to right a wrong and give a home to the people who really needed it. It's layered brilliantly, and hints are revealed subtly, allowing the reader to form conclusions and fall in love."

—Smexy Books

When the Rain Ends

MARY ELLEN
TAYLOR

Text copyright © 2023 by Mary Burton

Published by Montlake, Seattle

www.apub.com

Amazon, the Amazon logo, and Montlake are trademarks of Amazon.com, Inc., or its affiliates.

ISBN-13: 9781542034531 (paperback)
ISBN-13: 9781542034524 (digital)

Cover design by Ploy Siripant
Cover image: © Alliance Images / Shutterstock; © NikonShutterman / Getty

Printed in the United States of America

Do not squander time. It is the stuff life is made of.
—Benjamin Franklin

CHAPTER ONE
DANI

Outer Banks, North Carolina
Friday, June 2, 2023
11:00 a.m.

Blue.

Describing the colors of the Currituck Sound had once been a complicated business for Dani Manchester. On sunny days, she'd have spoken of navy hues streaked with teal bands. Or traces of cobalt mingling with indigo. Sapphire marbling ribbons of cerulean. On overcast mornings, she'd have searched the greens on her mental color wheel for olives, emeralds, and jades. And then there were the undertones. Black. Gray. Avocado.

Blue was a fine color. Nothing wrong with blue. But as a descriptor of this body of water, it fell flat.

Today as she drove across the Wright Memorial Bridge toward her new life on the mainland, she scrambled through her adjectives, hoping to translate the clear sky and calm waters into the familiar. But today, all the magical descriptors escaped her. And the only word that came to mind was "blue." No vibrant displays, no heart-pounding bursts, no exotic tints.

Just blue.

Light. Clarity. Vision. They were her stock-in-trade as an artist and gallery owner. And they were all fading.

Dani's carefully curated future had been rewritten a year ago by a doctor in Norfolk, Virginia, who'd told her she was slowly losing her sight. Retinitis pigmentosa was what the doctor called it. A genetic disease that in her case had led to the slow narrowing and darkening of her vision. Her doctor had likened her field of vision to the interior of a pipe. For now, the cylinder was almost at full capacity, but it would narrow to the circumference of a straw. It could be years (number undetermined) before she lost her vision completely. Or it might all vanish next fall.

She'd made it through the tourist season last year at her Duck, North Carolina, art gallery because she was so familiar with every turn in the road, all the street crossings and speed limit signs and parking lot entrances. During last winter's lull, for the first time in her life, she'd dreaded the arrival of the spring and summer tourists. The season always brought vacationers who crossed Duck Road without looking, cycled a knife's edge from traffic, or didn't anticipate cars pulling out of driveways like hers.

The air tightened as the radio played the most recent Taylor Swift song. A glance in her rearview mirror confirmed that her daughter, Bella, outfitted with wireless earbuds, was not listening as her head leaned against the window. Bella's expression was lost and forlorn. The last link to her old life was ending. The child was convinced she'd never be happy again. Maybe it would take time, but Dani hoped that at some point they both would look back on this day as a good day.

Sitting next to Bella was their eighteen-month-old dog, Rosie, a shepherd mix who'd been pocket size when they'd picked her out. She now weighed sixty-five pounds. Rosie looked out the window, alert. This was her first trip across the big bridge and the Currituck Sound, and she was, as always, excited.

Bella had a right to believe her world was crumbling. And it had nothing to do with this move.

Her father, Dani's ex-husband, had been killed in a car accident four months ago. A restaurateur opening two new establishments, Matthew Peterson had been working twenty hours a day and doing the work of five. Whenever they spoke, Dani always heard him moving around a restaurant kitchen, clanging pots and pans, and issuing orders to his staff. If he wasn't in the kitchen, he was driving to the other location or a farmers' market. All the scraps of his time went to Bella, and there was never a doubt that Matthew adored his only child. However, the time he cobbled together was often fragmented by tasks on a never-ending to-do list.

Just after 2:00 a.m. on a Tuesday morning, Matthew had been driving home from his Kill Devil Hills restaurant to his flattop house in Southern Shores. The drive was seven miles from end to end. No traffic. No rain. A clear night sky. But the police report assumed he'd fallen asleep at the wheel a mile from his house. The car's black box indicated he'd never hit the brakes, and the car had veered off the road and slammed into a cement wall rimming a utility pole. He was killed on impact.

Bella had been crushed by Matthew's death. The girl had adored her father, and his passing had turned her life upside down. Every day when they drove toward Bella's school in Kill Devil Hills, they traveled through Southern Shores past the spot where Matthew had died. The third time Dani drove by, Bella burst into tears and was inconsolable. Dani had called the school and told them she was keeping Bella home that day.

Though Dani and Matthew had been divorced for over ten years, they'd remained friends. They'd married when he was nineteen and she was eighteen. She'd been four months pregnant with Bella. Neither of them had the first clue how to be married, let alone be parents. Fueled by frustration and fear, their immaturity resulted in a marriage fraught

3

with fights, long silences, and finally separate beds. Thankfully, when they'd split, the distance and space allowed them to foster a friendship that enabled them to parent their daughter and give her a balanced, good life.

Dani had loved their house in Duck and her art gallery located two blocks away. She'd built a happy life for Bella and herself on that thin ribbon of land, and she'd always pictured herself staying until Bella went to college. Then, who knew what she'd do. Maybe explore some of that travel she'd longed for as a teenager.

The best-laid plans . . . as her father had used to say.

The roads on the mainland might have been unfamiliar, but at least they'd be wider, a little straighter, and wouldn't transport heartbreaking memories.

Dani's smile masked her unease as she glanced in the rearview mirror. "This move is going to be great, Bella."

Rosie barked, but Bella continued to stare out her window.

When Rosie woofed again, Bella removed her earbuds. "What?"

"I said, this move is going to be good for us."

"If you say so." Earbuds reinstalled, she shifted her gaze to the waters whizzing past.

Dani gripped the wheel and pressed the accelerator. She hadn't lost her mind. She had *not*.

Six months ago, on one of Dani's frequent trips to the Norfolk eye center, she'd been driving up Route 158 toward the Virginia line. It was a trip she'd made countless times. But on that day, she'd noticed a FOR SALE sign planted in front of three grain silos and the adjoining farmhouse. For years she'd admired the property and considered it a charming nod to the past.

The FOR SALE sign had nagged and distracted her during her eye doctor's appointment. On her return trip home on that cold January day, she stopped and pulled into the long graveled parking lot connecting the storage towers and the house. The wind whipped off the sound as she stared at the grain towers and gray-white house with faded blue shutters. She nestled deeper into her coat and walked the property, peeked into the house's dirty glass windows, and then strode toward the silos, covered with tall vines and weeds.

She felt a connection. She loved the faded lettering painted on the silo, which read **NELSON'S**, and the wide patch of land that stretched to the house and the sound. Her heartbeat accelerated as she rattled the main silo's door, discovered it open, and glanced into dark compressed air that smelled of fermenting wheat. She didn't see ruin; she imagined a new art gallery on the sound.

It made no sense to buy the property. Purchasing the place would require a second mortgage on her house and gallery. Though the sale price could be negotiated down, the renovation costs could easily spiral out of control. Stupid idea. Foolish. Only a fool would leave behind the town of Duck for farmland.

Still, the pull was so strong she called the Realtor, Juniper Jones, who joined her on the property fifteen minutes later. Juniper was a bright young woman with a cloud of red curls framing her round face. Freckles arched over a pug nose. Full lips were quick to smile. Her eyes radiated an infectious excitement.

The farmhouse's hardwood floors were stained, rose wallpaper peeled off plaster walls, the back windows leaked, and jade kitchen appliances dated back to the 1970s. The renovation costs ticked higher.

Stupid idea. Foolish.

Dani made a lowball offer that day, never expecting it to be accepted. But by the end of the week, the buyer agreed to a slightly higher price.

Juniper recommended a contractor whom Dani had never heard of before. And having grown up in her father's construction business, she knew almost all the folks who wielded a hammer near the Outer Banks. Still, she met with the contractor, found him steady and direct, and called his references. Impeccable. Straight shooter. Gifted. The reviews glowed.

She accepted his bid, and suddenly panic, fear, and exhilaration spun into one ball. Her life was turning to an exciting page. Maybe this wouldn't be the big-city living she'd once dreamed of, but it would be a step in a new direction. Managing two properties would be difficult, but she could do it.

And then Matthew had died.

After Bella's meltdown in the car on the way to school, Dani had decided her daughter needed a change as much as she did. They'd move from the Outer Banks to the mainland as soon as the school year ended.

Dani and Bella had both lived all their lives on the narrow barrier island, and there was a time when weeks or months could pass before she "crossed the bridge" to the mainland. At one time, there'd never been a good reason to move away from the Atlantic Ocean's breaking waves.

As Dani neared the end of the bridge, light glittered on the water as if tossing her a final wink. Bella shifted and twisted in her seat. Dani studied Bella's stoic expression in the rearview mirror.

Bella's outward calm worried Dani. A kid that age should be shouting, screaming, and voicing all the things she didn't like about leaving the home she'd known. But Bella had never argued or complained when Dani told her she wanted to sell and move.

"That place is going to miss us," Bella said.

Dani released a breath. Her daughter's silence was more worrisome than shouting or crying. "We're not going that far."

As the crow flies, that was true. If they could sprout wings and fly from Duck to the mainland, it would have been less than five miles. But in a car, the trip in light traffic took nearly an hour.

"When will our furniture arrive?" Bella asked. "The truck pulled out last night, so it should be there by now, right?"

"They had another stop to make." Some other resident leaving the beach would fill the remainder of the truck with their furniture. "Once they pack up and drop off the other people's stuff, they'll find the new house sometime tomorrow or the next day."

"And tonight, we do the camping thing."

Dani had brought two blow-up mattresses to go along with their sheets and pillows. They could've gotten a hotel room, but she didn't want to bump around a strange space with a dog and child when the farmhouse was waiting. Best to minimize the changes to the single Big One.

"It'll be fun." Dani grinned, trying to hook Bella's evasive gaze again. "We can order pizza tonight or get hamburgers. Roast marshmallows."

Bella fiddled with her earbud and settled it deeper in her ear canal. "Yeah, sure. Sounds great, Mom."

The car's tires rolled off the bridge onto Route 158, and they passed a collection of restaurants, gas stations, and furniture stores. Dani kept smiling. "If that food doesn't appeal, then we can do something different."

"No, that all sounds good, Mom." A smile flickered at the edges of Bella's lips. "Seriously. That's perfect."

"I'm excited for you to see the silos. The place has changed a lot since the one time you saw it in January," Dani said.

Dani had been back to the property multiple times since the renovations began, and in the last week, while Bella was in school, she'd driven each day with a carload of items. Wakeboards, a few lawn chairs, kitchen pots and pans, paintings, and the antique cash register from her gallery. All the trips had blurred into one endless car ride.

Dani had tried to talk to Bella about Matthew's death. She'd lost her own mother when she was eight, not to a sudden accident but to a fast-moving cancer. She'd wanted to say that life would go on. That one day she wouldn't cry daily, that she'd be able to pull in a full breath without it hurting, and that she could look up at a bright-blue sky and feel hopeful.

But each time she opened this line of conversation, Bella, with watery eyes glistening, would grin, kiss her on the cheek, and tell her she was okay.

Bella's smile perfectly reflected Dani's grin, refined after her mother's death. Seeing as crying didn't fix or change anything, Dani had reasoned that if she was smiling, she wouldn't see pity reflected back in anyone's eyes or suffer through awkward attempts at conversation. Her father and brother wouldn't look as troubled. Just as her mother had been, Dani was determined to look happy, even if she was scared. Terror hid well behind pleasant expressions, makeup, and killer clothes.

And now Bella was smiling when she should have been crying. Not good. She didn't want her daughter living this bottled-up existence that was getting harder and harder to maintain. So she'd pulled the trigger on the move and also enrolled Bella in a grief camp near their new home. The camp began in two days, and Bella, like it or not, would be going.

The remaining drive was silent except for Taylor Swift's song and the hum of the air conditioner. When Dani saw the silo peaks in the distance, she didn't breathe a sigh of relief. Instead, fresh tension coiled in her stomach. What if she had made a terrible mistake? What if she was doing more harm than good? What if, if she'd just held tight, the storm would have passed, and their old life would have found its way back on the tracks?

What if?

What-ifs didn't matter. If Dani had learned anything, it was that the universe didn't care what she wanted. Like the ocean, it swept in and reshaped the beaches and dunes at will, and it never once considered the destruction in its wake.

Dani slowed the car carefully, feeling the items crammed in the back of her SUV shift and groan. Moving a life looked easy on paper, but in reality, it was messy and disruptive, no matter how many lists she made or how carefully she labeled boxes.

The sun caught Dani's eyes, blinding her for an instant. She tensed and slowed the vehicle before carefully turning into her newly graded gravel parking lot. As the car shifted directions, the sun skittered out of her eyes, giving her a clear view of her new life. She drew in a breath, drove toward the house, and arched around the driveway toward the silos. She shut off the engine, checked her lipstick in the mirror, and then turned toward Bella.

"Ready to explore our new digs?"

Bella removed her earbuds and looked at the three gray-silver silos. The faded **NELSON'S** sign was a charming homage to the past, and the newly constructed rooms and a wide front porch were practical nods to modern necessity. Landscapers were scheduled to be here next week to plant small shrubs and bright, inviting annuals.

Bella looked out the window toward the grain elevators. Her grin didn't reach her blue eyes. "Looks cool."

"How about the grand tour?" Dani said. Her daughter had always been an easy kid, as if sensing Dani was in over her head and knew it would take all hands on deck to keep Team Dani-Bella on course.

"Sure."

"Make sure Rosie is on her leash. She's not familiar with the area."

Bella tucked her earbuds and phone in her pocket and hooked the bright-pink leash onto Rosie's matching collar. Dani rose out of the car, stretching the tightness from her lower back, and opened the back car door. Bella and Rosie tumbled out in a rush of energy, as they always did. Rosie immediately dropped her nose to the ground and began sniffing, pulling a reluctant Bella away from the car. This was a grand adventure for Rosie.

"I'd rather see the house first," Bella said.

"Sure." Dani closed the car door, lingering and shifting her attention to the two-story white clapboard house. When she'd first walked the property six months ago, it had never been her intention to move here. She'd authorized her contractor to renovate the house, believing she'd rent it out to anyone traveling to the area by car or boat on the nearby Intracoastal Waterway near Coinjock, North Carolina. As overnight stays went, it was charming. The best-laid plans.

The white clapboard house was nothing like their place in Duck. It was seventy-five years old, and the 1970s patchwork renovations had been scrubbed clean. No familiar squeaks on the stairs, circuit breaker quirks, or built-in memories. It was a blank, albeit rough, canvas.

Was this going to be their forever home? God, Dani wished she knew. She could only hope that she'd made the right choice and not upended their lives on a foolish whim.

Rosie barreled past Dani. The dog ran up on the front porch, barking and sniffing as she scuttled back and forth.

"Rosie isn't sure about the house," Bella said.

Her daughter had Matthew's thick dark hair, his nose and ears, as well as his olive skin and blue eyes. Her height, however, was all Dani's. "She doesn't seem to hate it."

"She doesn't like it either. She's only known one home."

"Like you?"

Bella shrugged. "I'm twelve. She's only one and a half. Big difference."

"The way I look at it, changing houses is going to be an adventure. How many kids get to say they live next to silos on the Currituck Sound?"

Bella folded her arms. "The lucky ones?"

"Very funny."

"Mom, this is the middle of nowhere. All I see is land, and the cars are all driving past here to the beach. If this is an adventure, it's a weird, sad kind."

Dani could conjure at least a dozen adventures she'd rather be experiencing now. "Want to have a look inside?"

"Sure, why not?"

Dani traipsed fingers over the keys on her keychain, past familiar shapes to the freshly cut, strange one. "Nothing ventured."

Dani climbed the three stairs, opened the screened door, and fumbled with the key. At first, she inserted it upside down and then, correcting, shoved it in properly, and the dead bolt turned easily.

She credited the new lock to her contractor, Jackson Cross. As his references stated, he was a meticulous, careful craftsman. Two weeks ago, he'd been frowning at the reclaimed front door with its original lock. "Locks rust fast this close to the water. This one's sticking," he'd said. "You don't want to deal with that kind of nonsense when you arrive."

She'd taken his word, and when he'd given her the new key last week, she'd been grateful he'd cared about a detail that, in the grand scheme of this project, would've been easy to overlook.

The oiled knob twisted, and the door swung open to polished hardwood floors spanning the width and length of the main room, dining area, and kitchen off to the left. New French doors overlooked a patio, an empty field, and beyond it the sound.

"It smells like grain," Bella said.

"At one point, the silo owner stored milled wheat in the house."

"That's random."

"The house was abandoned, and Mr. Nelson apparently put nothing to waste. I think it adds a little charm."

"Is it always going to be this quiet here?"

"I'm sure it'll be very busy Friday through Saturday during the tourist season."

"I guess counting cars for fun isn't the worst thing," Bella said.

"There'll be plenty to do here. This is going to be a crazy summer."

Bella's phone chimed with a text, drawing her daughter's attention to one of her beach friends.

Dani had always relished the customers in her Duck gallery. They came from all over the country and world, and they gave her small town the bigger-world feel she'd craved for as long as she could remember. There was nothing "big town" about this slice of the world. It was about as small as small could get.

The best-laid plans.

Inside the house, Dani hesitated as her vision adjusted to the lower light. She was still determined to see Bella off to college, and with a little luck this eye disease wouldn't interfere too much in the next five or six years. She could still navigate the roads, as long as the sun was bright, the traffic wasn't too heavy, and it wasn't raining too hard.

Would she have made this move if Matthew hadn't died? Most likely, if she was honest. This was a now-or-never opportunity.

All the practical reasons justifying this move still held true. She just hoped the emotions caught up to the facts sooner rather than later.

CHAPTER TWO
BELLA

Friday, June 2, 2023
Noon

This place sucked so bad there were not enough words to describe just how much it blew. Crappy. Terrible. Foreign. Hostile. Unfriendly. Cold. Distant.

Bella listed off more adjectives as she walked through the house's front door toward French doors that looked out over the wrong side of the Currituck Sound. She might as well have moved across the world instead of one bridge.

She texted her best friend, Finn. House looking good! Was there an emoji that summed this experience up? Smiley face with a teardrop, smiley face with hearts, smiley face with side-eye, or maybe a pile of poop.

At least Finn hadn't pressed for details on the new digs. Instead, she had discussed her new skateboard and her last surf lesson. Same old, same old. Life hadn't changed for Finn. So irritating. Bella wanted the *familiarity* of her old life now more than ever. To rewind the clock. Transport her back to her *real* life on the Outer Banks with Dad and friends. Were there any time travelers who could help?

She closed her eyes, pushing back a tide of raging fear that made her want to scream at her mother, her dad, and even Finn. *Dad, please come back. Please come back. If you come back, maybe we can go home too.*

She squeezed her fingers into tight fists, but when she opened her eyes, she was staring at her mother admiring the wrong side of the sound.

"Which room is mine?" Bella asked.

Her mother turned, smiled brightly. "There are three upstairs. Pick which one you want."

Mom did that when she was worried. She smiled. Put on makeup. Picked out her favorite outfit. And today she was looking fantastic in a midcalf green jumpsuit and gold hoop earrings, her blonde hair twisted into a high ponytail. She wore her wire-rimmed glasses, but she had three different pairs (black, tortoiseshell, and pink), which she selected based on her outfit.

Bella wondered if her mother's face was hurting from all the grinning. Her grandmother on the Peterson side had said once if Bella frowned too much, the scowl would stick. Maybe Mom's smile had finally fused the muscles of her face.

Her mother had to be scared and wondering what the heck she'd done. But the grin only grew a little broader. The display of even white teeth was basically a code red. Mom was just as frightened as Bella.

"Don't you want to pick your room first?" Bella asked.

"No, I want you to have first choice."

How different could the rooms be? A room was a room, right? "Okay."

Bella climbed the stairs with Rosie on her heels. Her hand trailed over the freshly polished banister while the dog's toenails clicked on the hardwood floors. As she climbed, she counted the stairs just as she used to do in her real home. The house in Duck had ten steps. One. Two. Three.

When she reached the top, she'd counted twelve stairs. Two extra steps weren't that big a deal, but it was still wrong. Ten was the correct number.

Rosie sniffed the floor, moving along the clean baseboards toward the last room at the end of the hallway. There were five doors on the second floor. A bathroom, a large closet, and three bedrooms. She glanced in the first room, which was large, but it faced the silos. It had a fireplace and an attached bath. *Meh.* Nothing that grabbed her.

The next bedroom faced northeast, meaning a lot of morning light. Her mother loved the morning light. Bella not so much. The last bedroom at the end of the hall was the smallest of the three. Two windows overlooked the sound, like in her room at home. Morning light would be an issue. Hardwood floors. Big closet (a plus) and a window seat. The room also had another side door that accessed the upstairs bathroom. Not bad. Not home, but if she pretended that she was really just on vacation, then she could also imagine this nightmare life would end soon.

She looked out the window and traced her initials on the wavy glass. A Jet Ski skimmed the sound's shallow waters, moving fast along the coastline. She'd ridden on a lot of Jet Skis in the sound with her mother and sometimes her dad when he wasn't working.

Until last summer, she and her mom had taken their kayaks out and paddled along the shoreline several times a week. Somehow, they'd stopped doing it last fall, and this spring, well, normal life had stopped.

The last few weeks had been about cleaning out closets and drawers, dumping everything into boxes marked KEEP, GIVE AWAY, and TRASH. Bella didn't understand why they couldn't just keep what they already had and recreate their real home here. But Mom had insisted they wouldn't have the same storage space in the new house; besides, it was time to get rid of what didn't work. But Bella had kept almost everything, and her mom hadn't argued.

She wondered if the guy who'd bought her actual house liked her real room's layout. She'd heard him tell her mother he was considering gutting the place. New windows, he'd said. Kitchen counters, bathrooms. She'd stopped listening as he rattled on about unnecessary changes.

Rosie sniffed each corner and then trotted over to the closet. She scratched on the door. Rosie was the most curious dog there ever was, and there wasn't a rock she didn't want to look under, a bed of leaves she missed sniffing, or a blanket she didn't burrow beneath.

Bella twisted the brass knob and opened the closet door. Dangling above was a string, which she pulled. The single bulb spit out enough light for her, but already she was glad her mother didn't have this room. Mom had a thing about darkness. She'd never loved it, but in the last few years, she was always turning on lights even before the sun went down. Bella had asked her mother about it, and Dani had said she just hated to lose the sunlight. The moon, Bella countered, did a good job of glistening on the water and deepening blues. They tended to communicate in colors because her mother was an art gallery owner / sometime painter. But her mother had said she just preferred bright colors. Weird. But then her mom was quirky, different from the other mothers.

Maybe it was because she was so much younger than the other mothers. She was thirty-one (old enough in Bella's book), but Finn's mom was fifty-one, and India's mom was in her forties (she never gave the real number). Bizarre that Finn had an older sister who was only a few years younger than her own mom.

Several of the moms at her school owned or ran businesses on the Outer Banks. Finn's mom ran a bagel shop that was open from 7:00 a.m. to 1:00 p.m. It was why Finn's mom went to bed early and was up by 2:00 a.m.

But those moms looked a little more regular, whereas her mom was always dressed like she was a movie star. Heels, wedge shoes, leather pants, V-neck sweaters, bracelets, perfume, splashy earrings. And if that wasn't bad enough, her glasses created drama around her eyes. She never just showed up in sweats and a T-shirt.

Finn said the other moms were always wondering who Dani Manchester (Mom kept her maiden name . . . weird and cool) might be dating or if she was getting married again. They'd attached her mom to a few men, but Bella had never seen one guy visit their house. Ever. And when she asked her mother about these "boyfriends," her mother laughed and said anyone gossiping about her love life had too much time on their hands.

Bella's fingers traveled along the freshly painted gray walls. This room would not work. *At all.* Her bed wouldn't fit, and if it did, it couldn't face the water, *and* where would she put her dresser, her posters, and her desk? None of this would work. "I'm in hell."

Rosie wagged her tail as she moved inside the closet, sniffing the corners. She settled in one corner, snorting and pawing at the floor.

"You just peed," Bella said. "But if you pee in here, I wouldn't get that mad."

Rosie's tail wagged faster as she sniffed along the baseboard.

"Are you telling me you hate this place, Rosie?" Bella asked. "Because if you do, I'll tell Mom. If we both hate this place, she'll call the man that bought our house, tell him she made a terrible mistake, and move us back home."

Rosie didn't look up as she moved her snorting nose farther along the baseboard.

Bella looked over her shoulder at the sound and toward the thin strip of the Outer Banks. Plump graying clouds formed in the distance. It looked so different from here. It was like being trapped on the wrong side of a big gate that separated her from her old life.

She glanced at her phone and saw texts from three friends. **Where r u? Life in exile? Partee next Friday.** Bella smiled at the familiar names. She texted back. **@ new house. A million miles away. See u Friday.**

The party was seven days away. A week on this side of the sound felt like forever, but she'd survive *if* she knew she had a party waiting at the end of this dark tunnel.

"Bella," her mother called. "Come help me unload the car. Then we can go get lunch before it rains."

Unpacking. One step closer to permanent. Nightmare alert. "Coming, Mom!" She moved to the closet and took Rosie by the collar. "If I have to work, so do you."

Rosie resisted a little and then followed Bella down the stairs and out the open front door. Her mother was tugging a large garbage bag full of Bella's clothes out of the SUV's back hatch.

"The apple doesn't fall far from the tree," her mother said. "You own as many clothes as I do."

Bella grabbed ahold of the bag's twisted top. She and her mother liked to shop, though in the last few months, neither had brought up the idea. She wasn't sure why they'd stopped, because it really was fun. She dragged the clothes bag toward the front porch.

"Don't scratch the walls or the floor," Mom said. "I've just had them painted and sealed."

Bella yanked the bag up the first step of the front porch. "It's heavy. What do you want me to do?"

"Be careful."

"It's too heavy."

"You insisted on bringing all your clothes."

"They are my clothes."

"Some date back to third grade."

Her mother crossed to the porch, grabbed the bag's other end, and lifted. Mom had a long lean body that looked kind of delicate, but she was strong. She said it came from hauling boxes, paintings, and artwork at the gallery. She had employees, but none stayed long. Mom said often, "If you have to go it alone, you figure it out."

Bella grappled with her end, sensing that her mother was carrying the bulk of the weight. They moved up the stairs slowly as each struggled to keep a grip on the unwieldy bag. Once or twice Bella thought she'd lose her hold, but when she looked back at her mother's determined face, she tightened her grip.

At the top landing, her mother looked up. "Where to? What room?"

"End of the hallway." The automatic response surprised her. She hadn't bonded with the room. But she could change her mind. She likely would.

"Perfect. Let's do this," Mom said.

When they reached her temporary room, each dropped her end of the bag. Both flexed cramped fingers. Her mother squared her shoulders and looked around the room. "You like this room?"

"'Like' is a stretch."

Her mother smiled and walked to the closet, inspecting the dimensions. "It's a nice size. Your small dresser will also fit in here. I measured it last week."

"Great."

Her mother didn't turn around. "It's going to be fantastic, Bella. We'll look back on this day as the best decision we ever made."

Mom had made the decision, not her. And her mother's optimism could be a little irritating. For once she'd like to see her mother just scream that sometimes life sucked and it wasn't fair. "I know."

Her mother turned, her trademark smile shining bright and wide. "I'll dig out the hangers from the car, and you can organize your closet."

"Thanks, Mom."

"Sure thing, kiddo."

Her mother moved out of the room with Rosie trailing behind, then paused at the end of the hall before sliding her hand on the rail and disappearing down the stairs. Outside, Rosie's bark echoed as she raced through the open front door and chased a bird in the yard. Rosie, she suspected, liked the place. Back home, she'd had to stay in the small fenced-in backyard because they were so close to the very busy Duck Road. The bird escaped, but that didn't stop Rosie from running behind it, tail wagging.

Traitor. Rosie was Bella's dog, and she was supposed to hate what Bella hated. That's what real friends did.

Her mother delivered a bag of hangers; Bella thanked her and turned to the large bag. She loosened the knot at the top and dumped out the clothes into a colorful heap on the floor. As she stared at the pile, her annoyance grew. Why did she have so many clothes? It seemed really stupid right now. Why had they all been so necessary yesterday?

If she wasn't shopping with her mother, her dad was giving her some new outfit, purse, or pair of shoes. He said he liked to spoil her. But this stuff looked worthless now. Why had she let them buy all this stupid stuff? She'd trade all this for her dad.

She kicked the pile once, twice, and then she scooped up an armload of shirts, pants, and skirts. She threw them across the room, covering the entire floor with clothes.

She sat down in the center of the pile, fisted a handful of a blue shirt that still had the tag on it, and ripped it off. She tossed the top behind her. She lay down and looked up at the ceiling. She saw, under the fresh white paint, a slight crack that ran across what was otherwise a perfect surface. She imagined the crack growing wider, larger and larger, until the ceiling collapsed and crashed on her. If the ceiling blew apart, she wouldn't have to deal with the clothes, the house, or her dead dad.

Her mother's steps sounded on the stairs, and then a garbage bag dropped in the hallway. More footsteps, and then Bella could feel her mother staring. "Everything okay?"

"Great, Mom. Just taking a break." Like lying on a pile of clothes in a weird house was normal.

After a brief silence, Mom said, "Okay, sweetie. Let me know if you need anything."

"Will do."

"I'm choosing the bedroom at the top of the stairs," Mom said.

"Okay."

"If you decide to swap, just let me know."

"No, I'm good. Seriously."

Instead of leaving, her mother moved closer and knelt by Bella. "Am I trying too hard?"

"A little."

"Sorry. The constant cheerleading gets old, doesn't it?"

"Positive is good," Bella said. But some days she wanted her mother and the world to feel as miserable as she did.

Her mom kissed her on the forehead. "I'll leave you be for a while."

"Thanks."

"You're good?"

"Super. *Seriously.*"

Her mother's steady steps retreated down the stairs and out the front door. Part of her was tempted to burrow under the clothes and just lie here forever. Maybe if she fell asleep, she'd wake up, and she'd be back in her real home living her life, not this fake version of reality that had overtaken like an alien invasion.

Get up. The whispered words rattled in her head. *Get up.*

She looked out in the hallway, expecting to see her mother. No Mom. She rolled onto her side and pulled a pile of jeans over her head. Annoying sunlight leaked through the folds and gaps between the fabric.

Get up.

"Why? What difference does it make if I hang up my clothes? My life will still be crappy."

Get up.

Bella slowly sat up, crossed her legs, and checked her phone. More text messages from her friends. Thank God. They were her lifeline to her old existence. She scrolled through the messages, wondering why her friends cared so much about this stupid party.

Get up.

Facing the mess, she scooped up a crimson paisley blouse and a hanger and wrangled the plastic into the collar. She arranged the blouse and carried it into the closet, then hung it on the right side (where it had hung at home). But as she stared at the blouse, she decided she hated it. She'd worn it only once, and even then, it had been tight around her belly. She ripped it off the hanger and tossed it to a far corner. She chose more blouses, threw at least half into the give-away pile, and hung the rest up. She arranged each article of clothing by color, like her mother had shown her. She couldn't recreate home, but maybe she could kind of make something of it.

It took an hour to finish going through the heap. The closet filled, and the give-away pile grew. Most of the discarded clothes hadn't been worn in over six months, and many didn't fit her chest (growing fast lately).

She dragged the bag back down the stairs one thump at a time, careful not to mess up the walls or the stairs. But what was the deal with flawless walls and floors? It was an old house, and nothing was perfect about it. In her real home in Duck, her fingerprint smudges on the walls dated back to when she was a kid. There was also a scratch in the floor made by her mother when she tried to carry a chair up the stairs. And there was the dent in the living room wall from when Bella had accidently whacked it with her surfboard.

In her real kitchen there were the pen marks her mother had made each year on her birthday to measure her height. There were the scratch marks on the back door made by Rosie when she was a puppy. And the faint tomato sauce stains on the kitchen wall when her dad had made pasta sauce for Mom and her on her birthday last year. The walls weren't perfect, but they kind of were.

Downstairs, Bella could see her mother had unloaded a dozen boxes and set them on the living room floor. Many of the boxes were marked KITCHEN. Mom's coffee maker, her favorite coffee cups, and a few pots and pans were in one box; another had their dishes and glasses; and the others contained some of the hand-painted pottery bowls Mom had bought from artists who'd shown in her gallery. Several paintings also leaned against the walls. Dad often joked that Mom would go broke buying the art of new potters and painters. Mom always laughed, insisting she couldn't resist color and texture.

Outside, Bella dragged her bag over the stone walkway to the car and hoisted it into the back.

"What's that?" her mother asked.

"Giveaways."

Mom arched a brow. "You said you needed *everything* from your closet."

Bella shrugged. "Some of it doesn't fit."

Mom brushed off a strand of blonde hair. "Okay."

"I need a stepladder. There's stuff I can put on the top shelf in the closet."

"Sure. In the kitchen closet."

"Thanks."

"Are you getting hungry?"

"Kinda."

"Finish your closet, and we'll grab a burger."

"I'm a vegetarian."

"Since when?"

"Since last week. I told you."

Mom sighed. "Okay. We'll figure something out."

Back in the house, Bella grabbed the stepladder and hustled up the stairs. She set up the ladder in her closet and then hurried down the stairs and grabbed a suitcase full of shoes. She hauled up the cumbersome bag and rounded the corner, and as she moved toward the room now known temporarily as *hers*, she sensed that someone was standing behind her.

Bella turned, saw no one, then, when she looked down the stairs out the front door, saw her mother giving Rosie a bowl of water. She searched in her mother's room, the one next to it, and the hallway bathroom but didn't see anyone. The window in the bathroom was open, and a breeze teased the edges of the gauzy curtains. A shiver slithered through the air.

"Dad?" she said.

She tensed, listening for a whisper, searching for a feeling or any sign that he was close. She'd heard about people feeling the presence of a loved one, but ever since her dad had died, she'd felt nothing. Zip. Zero. Nada. But then that would have been like Dad. He was always bad about remembering to call.

Her eyes teared, and for a minute her chest tightened, like it had a lot since the accident. It took nearly a minute of standing still for her agitated emotions to settle. Finally, like her mom did, she drew back her shoulders, moved into the bedroom, and opened the suitcase, then dumped her shoes on the floor. She sorted the jumble into pairs, found more shoes that she'd never wear again, and tossed them to the side. Using the stepladder, she climbed up and placed the off-season shoes on the north side. As she was arranging the last pair, she spotted a mason jar in the back corner of the opposite shelf.

The dust-covered jar was about six inches tall and painted an odd mix of blues, yellows, and purples. She grabbed it, climbed down the ladder, and tried to screw off the metal top. It was stuck. Gritting her teeth, she leaned into her grip and twisted as hard as she could. The top didn't budge.

She shook the jar, hearing the rumbling of something inside. She banged the jar's metal lid against the edge of her stepladder and then twisted again. It didn't move. Of course.

"Bella!" her mom called up the stairs. "Let's get some lunch. I'm starving."

Bella looked at the jar, shook it again, and then, annoyed by its lack of cooperation, set it down on the floor by her seasonal shoes. When she got back from lunch, she'd take a hammer or a rock to the jar and find out what was inside.

CHAPTER THREE
DANI

Friday, June 2, 2023
2:00 p.m.

After walking Rosie and tucking her in her crate, now set up in the kitchen, Dani and Bella headed out in search of food. They found a small diner on Route 158 that Dani had passed dozens of times in the last couple of years when she drove to her eye doctor in Norfolk. She'd eaten here a few times. The burgers and fried chicken were good, and they had grilled cheese sandwiches on the kids' menu. Cheese was vegetarian, and with luck Bella hadn't become a vegan in the last half hour.

When Dani parked in front of the one-story gray building, Bella sat a little straighter. "Dad brought me here."

Dani hoped the memory was a good one. These days she couldn't tell what her normally outspoken daughter was thinking. "Really? When?"

"We were coming back from that Washington, DC, trip last year." She tucked a curl behind her ear.

"That's right. Dad wanted you to see the monuments and a three-star restaurant." Matthew had asked if he could take a four-day trip with Bella. Seeing as he rarely had that much time to spare for anyone, she'd rearranged their schedules and said yes. "They have great grilled cheese."

"And burgers. Dad said they were cooked perfectly. Medium rare."

Dani didn't point out that burgers weren't vegetarian. "They sure do."

Inside, the smells of fried potatoes, coffee, and burgers greeted them. Dani inhaled, savoring the scents. She was doing that more lately—keying in on her other senses. Whereas she'd always focused on color, now more and more it was texture, sound, and smell. Perhaps that was the way it was. The body was anticipating the loss of her sight and retraining her brain. She glanced at the chrome diner bar and caught the wink of sunshine on metal.

"Do you want to sit at a booth or at the bar?" Dani was trying to give Bella more choices to create the feeling of control. Her father had done the same for her after her mother died, and despite all her moods and tears, choosing the paint color for her room (purple) and her new school clothes (her mixing-plaids-and-stripes phase) and eating pizza almost every night had helped on some level. All her decisions had been harmless and questionable, but they'd been hers.

"Bar is cool," Bella said.

"Perfect."

They sat at the end, grabbed two menus, and ordered: Dani asked for the chicken salad, and Bella opted for the grilled cheese and milkshake. Still vegetarian. The waitress set a coffee and a vanilla milkshake in front of them.

"How's the closet organization going?" Dani asked.

"Not bad." Bella took a long pull on her straw.

"An edited wardrobe is the most effective."

Dani doctored her coffee with cream and then poured in extra sugar. She stirred, the spoon clinking against the stoneware mug. "We'll drop the give-away bag off after lunch."

Bella nodded. "I found this jar."

Her normally babbling, outgoing daughter had been silent for months, and the mention of the jar was an unexpected attempt at conversation. "What kind of jar? I thought the place was cleaned out."

"It's a painted mason jar." She slurped on her vanilla milkshake. "I can't open it, but there's something inside."

"A mystery." Dani sipped her coffee. "I do love a good mystery."

"It's a jar." Bella stabbed her straw into the milkshake. "No big deal."

"So, you can't open it or see inside?"

"Nope." *Slurp.*

"Aren't you curious about the contents?"

"Maybe. I don't know. Finding it was so random."

Dani sipped her coffee. "Want me to try to open it?"

"Nah, I'll figure it out." More slurping, straw swirling.

"I know you will. What do you think is inside?" Dani was grateful to be conversing with her daughter. There'd been too much quiet.

"Don't know."

Their meals arrived, and each shifted focus to the food. Matthew's style of parenting focused on the big, splashy moments: trips to DC, new clothes, and making pasta with a visiting chef at his restaurant. Dani's time with Bella had always centered on the mundane: getting to school, homework, simple nightly dinners that weren't restaurant quality. They had fun. Paddleboarding had been their thing, but in the last year Dani had been hesitant to get on the water. She'd been limiting herself even before her sight forced changes. But this move was her way of grabbing ahold of life, taking control, and going forward regardless.

The bells on the front door rang, and the customers arriving didn't have the harried look of tourists who'd spent hours cutting through summer traffic.

"I'd like to stop by the contractor's office on the way home," Dani said. "Why?"

"He has a few more details to wrap up at the silo, and I want to make sure we're on the same page."

Bella's head dropped back. "Can you just drop me off at the house first?"

"His office is on the way, Bella. You'll have to grin and bear it."

"But Rosie needs us. You know she's not a fan of the crate."

"We've been gone forty minutes. And this is her nap time."

Bella made a loud gurgling sound as she sucked up the last of the shake. "Fine."

Dani set the saltshaker on top of a twenty and the bill. "You've got to be excited about the camp next week."

Bella pushed the empty milkshake glass away. "The camp for broken kids."

"All the kids have lost someone they love, just like you. But they're not broken."

Bella arched a brow. "So, we all sit around and look sad?"

"The program is the first of its kind in the area. We're lucky it's so close to us." After Matthew died, Dani had mentioned to her contractor that she had to reschedule a walk-through because of the funeral. Later, when Dani met up with Juniper, the young woman had mentioned she'd recently earned her PhD in psychology with an emphasis on grief. (Word traveled fast in small towns.) Juniper had said she was trying to put together a camp for children who'd lost a loved one. Dani didn't think twice before she offered to sponsor the initial camp. She'd cover the costs for all the children. Juniper had promised to make some calls and get back to Dani. Three days later Juniper had a plan for the camp.

"How long is this?" Bella picked up her phone and typed out a message.

"Two weeks, Monday through Thursday." Dani stood. "Put the phone away, we need to get going. Finn can wait."

Bella's scowl reminded Dani of a moment when her daughter was two. Dani caught Bella on the kitchen counter, her arm elbow deep in a cookie jar. Bella had denied she was eating cookies even as Dani wiped the chocolate from her chubby face. "How do you know I'm texting Finn?"

If not Finn, Dani could rattle off three more of the usual suspects. "Are you?"

"Yeah, but how do you know?"

Dani waited for Bella. "You'd be amazed what mothers know."

Bella followed her through the now-crowded diner to the car. A mile before the silos, she took a right and followed a winding road that hugged the sound. She drove past several small houses to the one at the end of the street. It was white with black shutters and had a neatly trimmed yard filled with a round mulched bed surrounding a tall oak tree. Monkey grass, the perfect plant for a man who didn't want to fuss, ringed the tree's base.

Dani pulled into the graveled driveway behind a large black pickup truck. "There's a workshop behind the house. Jackson, Mr. Cross, is in his shed."

Bella squinted against the bright sun. "How do you know?"

Dani stood a little straighter. "I texted him about an hour ago and told him we were coming."

Bella's head rolled back. "Why didn't you just leave me at home if you knew we were coming here?"

"Because I don't get to have lunch with my girl every day."

Bella shook her head. "We eat together all the time."

"Not all the time. Besides, I want you to meet the man who's transformed old grain-storage towers and our new home."

"That house is not our new home," Bella said.

"Of course it is."

"I'm thinking of it as an extended vacation until you come to your senses, and then we can move back to the Outer Banks."

There was no going back for them. Dani didn't have a choice. Bella needed a new life free of sad memories of her father's death, and Dani needed to take this life shift while she still could. She moved around the side of the house toward the large shed.

She'd met Jackson Cross at the diner where she'd taken Bella for lunch. It was overcast that day, and she was driving slower and therefore running late. Normally, she'd have put off a meeting on a low-light day, but the desperate need to change had outweighed her fear.

Jackson Cross wasn't what she'd expected. He was tall and lean, and his thick blond-streaked hair framed rawboned features. In his late thirties, he had crow's-feet that feathered from his eyes and deepened when he smiled. He extended his hand to her, and long calloused fingers engulfed hers as he shook her hand. He introduced himself.

"When he's not renovating houses, he's building boats and ferrying them from the north to the south along the Intracoastal Waterway," Dani said. "That's kind of cool."

Bella drew in a breath. "What kind of boats?"

"Apparently all kinds. He's a jack-of-all-trades."

Bella glanced at her phone. "Awesome."

Dani cleared her throat. "Put the phone away or lose it for two days." She'd been lax about the phone rules the last couple of months, and as a result Bella's face was glued to the screen too many hours a day. And that certainly wasn't helping.

Bella shoved the phone in her back pocket with a dramatic flourish Matthew had been known for. When he was annoyed with Dani for calling him out on his no-show dates with Bella, he never let a sigh or an eye roll go to waste. *I'm working. Putting food in our daughter's mouth.*

During their eighteen-month marriage, the eye rolls had been aggravating. Barely out of her teens, she was scared and overwhelmed, and she needed him to be an adult. But he used work as an excuse to run away, leaving her with an infant to care for. When Bella was three months old, Dani went to work for her father. Her dad insisted she bring Bella. Uncle Dalton and Grandpa Pete had spoiled the child rotten, but 90 percent of Bella's care fell primarily to Dani. She juggled phone calls while feeding a baby, carried Bella in a backpack while showing properties to clients, and stayed up late doing the company's invoices while Bella slept. It wasn't that Matthew hadn't loved Bella. He did. Desperately. But day-to-day wasn't his thing. She never could convince him that that's what a kid needed.

When Dani and Matthew decided to separate after Bella's first birthday, they'd both been relieved. He could go back to being a kid, and she could figure out how she was going to carve out a real life for Bella and herself within the confines of the Currituck Sound and Atlantic Ocean.

After the divorce, Dani's father, Pete Manchester, had given Dani their family house in Duck. He said he'd been waiting for a reason to move, and he'd found it. He'd packed a few bags and boxes and trucked them all to her older brother Dalton's house the next day.

The sound of metal striking metal echoed from the open shed that Dani had visited several times since Jackson started work on the grain towers. He'd hired crews to do the bulk of the work in the house and barn, but he'd overseen it all.

When they approached the large metal shed's open double doors, she saw a collection of newly minted sundials, crafted out of different varieties of scrap metal. She paused and ran her hand over the smooth metal, the pointed dials, and the raised numbers. These were new.

"He's an artist too?" Bella asked.

"I suppose he is," Dani said. Jackson was a man of few words in many respects. The sundials, like Jackson, were simple, sturdy, and effective.

The hammering grew louder, and as Bella readied to march into the shop, Dani stopped her. The interior was dim, and it took her eyes time to adjust. There were hazards in a workshop that she might not see coming.

Jackson brought a hammer down on a bright-red strip of metal that he'd draped over an anvil. He hit the metal a dozen times before he lifted it and then plunged it into a bath of cold water. Steam hissed and spit. He looked up, and when he spotted them, his gaze lingered on Dani before dropping briefly to Bella.

He set the hot metal aside, tugged off his thick heat-resistant gloves, and removed his safety goggles. As he moved closer, the sweat beading on his brow glistened. His muscled forearms were covered in dirt and flecks of ash.

From the moment she'd first met Jackson, she'd noticed details about him. The scar on the right side of his jaw; the calluses on his thick, weathered hands; the way he frowned when he stared at a project that wasn't going well; how his voice softened when he talked about sailing; and the word *Endurance* tattooed on the inside of his right forearm.

What she hadn't told Bella, or anyone else, was that Dani and Jackson had been . . . dating for five months. Dating. It was such an antiquated word, suggesting romantic dinners, walking hand in hand, and an emotional intimacy they hadn't really achieved. That was not them. Basically, they had been sleeping together.

Their first time hadn't been planned. They were in the silos, and she was inspecting the space where the rounded staircase would be installed. He mentioned the boat he was repairing. She asked to see it, grateful for the warm day and the extra time she had until she picked Bella up from volleyball practice.

He showed her the boat, and when they slipped below deck, she stumbled in the dimmer light. He caught her, and the skin-to-skin touch ignited something in them both. Gray eyes stared at her as her heartbeat butted against her chest. She kissed him on the lips. He raised his hands to her face and deepened the kiss. It had been so, so long since she'd felt a man's touch. In fact, the last man had been Matthew, who she'd slept with a few times after their divorce. She'd cut that off when she realized four-year-old Bella had started noticing his extended visits.

With Jackson, as with Matthew, there'd been no talk of the future, past, or really the present. The first time with him, she was too overwhelmed to think beyond the sex. But each time they slept together, she grew more curious about him. However, digging into his past meant opening a window into her life. Her looming loss of sight was something she still could not discuss.

But her time with Jackson had changed since Matthew's death. She'd been distracted by Bella and the rush of details that came with selling the house in Duck. To Jackson's credit, he'd been patient, willing to give her all the space she needed.

"Jackson," she said.

He reached for a rag and wiped the dirt from his hands. "Dani, it's good to see you."

He'd dropped back behind his trademark wall of reserve out of respect. He knew Dani had not told Bella about them.

She laid her hand on Bella's shoulder. "This is my daughter, Bella."

He nodded to Bella, taking a longer look at her. If he was looking for any evidence of Dani, he'd find little. Except for her height, she was a carbon copy of Matthew. "Nice to meet you."

"Yes, sir," she said. "Nice to meet you."

"No sirs here," Jackson said. "Just call me Jackson."

"Okay. You can call me Bella."

A faint smile tipped the edges of his lips. "Touching base about the final punch list at the silos?"

Dani smiled. "We are."

Jackson nodded slowly. "I'll be by in the morning, and we can go over it. Figured with this being your moving day, you'd have your hands full."

"It's been busy," Dani said.

"Bella, how do you like the house?" Jackson said.

"It's weird."

"Big change," he said with understanding.

"Not the worst," Bella said.

"Bella chose the room overlooking the sound," Dani said. "The one at the end of the hallway."

"Good choice," Jackson said.

"I guess."

"Your mom says you two are staying at the house tonight," he said.

"Camping out," Bella said.

"Blow-up mattresses," Dani added with more cheer than was probably necessary. "I'm thinking we'll also roast marshmallows like we used to do."

Bella's grin didn't reach her eyes. Dani could almost hear her daughter straining not to remind her that kids who roasted marshmallows were little, not fully grown twelve-year-olds. Her baby was growing up. Faster than she should. And Dani suddenly felt the loss of the little girl who loved to snuggle.

Time had never been her friend. When she was younger and rocking a colicky infant, time had seemed to stop. The days and nights were endless. And now time was spinning faster, turning to dust all around her.

"I didn't know you made sundials," Dani said.

"A friend asked me to make one, but I'm not happy with the first few versions."

"If what I saw outside are castoffs, then I can't wait to see the final," Dani said. "What're you going to do with the ones outside your shop?"

"Melt them down, I suppose," he said. "It's good metal."

"You should let Mom sell them in her new gallery," Bella said.

"Think so?" Jackson said, looking amused.

"Mom says most artists aren't as good at selling their work as she is," Bella said. "They undervalue their products. Like you."

"Like me?" Jackson said.

"You want to melt those sundials down. They look decent."

Jackson's expression softened. "Maybe I know I can make better ones."

Bella shrugged. "Maybe you're not the best judge."

Dani cleared her throat. "Bella."

"What?" Bella asked. "You say all the time that artists are not good at judging their own value."

"I'm not an artist," Jackson said. "Just doing a favor for a friend."

"I'd love to buy one of those sundials out front," Dani said. "It would be pretty in our backyard. How much?"

He studied her a beat. "I'll give you whichever one you want."

His gaze triggered an unwanted rise of heat. "You can't give me one. I want to pay."

"I won't take your money," he said.

"See?" Bella said. "Just like I was saying. If Mom sees value, then it's there."

Jackson grinned. "I'll keep that in mind. Which dial do you like the best?"

"The one closest to the door. I love the textures," Dani said.

"That one is the roughest of the lot," Jackson countered.

"That's what I like about it," Dani said.

Jackson regarded her. "I'll bring it in the morning."

"Thank you." There was so much she wanted to say to Jackson right now. So many unspoken words. She missed him. Touching him. But with Bella standing here, she couldn't kiss him on the lips or hold his hand. Maybe the forced distance between them wasn't so bad. Whatever she and Jackson shared had been great, but given all the baggage she now carried, their fledgling relationship wouldn't endure under the weight. Better to end it as friends. Besides, he was set to leave for Norfolk soon to ferry one of those big boats to Florida, and he had several other trips planned for the fall to the Caribbean.

"See you ladies in the morning," Jackson said.

Dani laid her hand on Bella's shoulder, a subtle reminder to say her goodbyes. "Thank you."

"It was nice to meet you," Bella said.

"And you as well, Bella." He seemed to remember something. "And don't be quick to judge this part of the world as boring."

"I didn't say it was boring," Bella countered.

He grinned. "All newcomers do. At first glance, there doesn't seem to be much happening, but it has a way of drawing you in."

Bella looked at him pointedly. "I haven't seen much yet."

"You haven't been here that long. There's plenty. You're living on the water, and that's worth more than anything. And of course, there's the ghost haunting the property."

"Ghost?" Bella laughed. She wasn't one to be easily fooled.

"I've felt it a few times myself," he said.

"What does it look like?" she asked.

His left shoulder hiked into a shrug. "Hard to say. I've only caught glimpses in the corner of my eye. But there's definitely something there."

"Does it come into the house?" Bella asked.

"It does," Jackson said. "The two properties are connected."

Dani knew her daughter loved all tales about ghosts, wizards, witches, and elves. A ghost on the property was a plus for her kid. Had she mentioned that to Jackson?

Bella shook her head, her brow knotting. "I don't believe in ghosts."

"Neither did I, until now."

"When did you first see it?" she asked with a slight edge of curiosity.

"About six months ago."

Bella nodded. "I don't see why any ghost would want to haunt grain-storage towers and an old farmhouse. I can think of better places."

He laughed. "You might be right."

"You never mentioned a ghost." Dani searched his gaze for signs he was teasing.

"Didn't seem that important. It hasn't gotten in the way of the work. And you said once your daughter liked them."

So, he did remember.

"You actually haven't seen it," Bella countered.

"Like I said, movement in the shadows. No pictures or hard evidence."

"Does it speak?" Bella asked.

"I thought you didn't believe in ghosts," Jackson said.

"I don't. But you do."

"It didn't say anything to me. But if it should talk to you, let me know. I'd be curious to know who I've been dealing with."

"If you're trying to freak me out, it's not working," Bella said. "Ghosts don't bother me."

"That's good to hear," Jackson said easily.

He'd drawn out her moody daughter into a dialogue about spirits. "Bella," Dani said, "have one more look at the sundials and let me know if I've chosen right. I'll be right behind you."

"Let's hope a ghost doesn't get me." Sarcasm dripped from the words.

"If I were a ghost, I'd be too afraid to tangle with you," Jackson said.

"That's exactly right," Bella said.

When the girl left the shop, Dani said, "If she wakes up tonight screaming about seeing a ghost, you'll get the first call."

"Call me anytime." His voice deepened, taking on a smoky quality.

She felt the heat warming his words. Her mouth suddenly felt dry, and her stomach tightened. "I wish I could."

"You can, you just choose not to."

"I've wanted to call, but it seems the quiet moments now are in the middle of the night. It's been a little crazy."

"I don't sleep much."

"I'll remember that."

"Your lives will settle down, and pretty soon, you'll have your new normal."

"'New normal.' I have no idea what that means anymore."

He glanced past her and made sure Bella remained out of earshot. "You don't have to do it alone."

She'd always been alone. Even when she was married to Matthew, even when her brother or father lent a hand, even when her friend Ivy helped at the gallery, she was alone. She'd been navigating life by herself ever since her mother died. She wasn't sure she knew how to do it any differently.

"I hear Juniper's holding her first camp. Assuming Bella is enrolled."

"She is." Dani's deal with Juniper was that her donation would remain anonymous.

"Starts Monday, right?"

Dani felt heat radiating from his body. "It does. Bella's not excited."

"It'll be good for her," he said. "Better not to bottle it all up." His stare bore into her as he spoke the last few words.

"Pot calling the kettle black?" she asked. As closed off as she'd been, she sensed he also reserved a big piece of himself.

"Maybe," he said.

His secrets made her feel less guilty about her own. "See you tomorrow."

"First thing." He looked as if he'd lean in for a kiss, but Bella's shout through the open door stopped him.

"Mom, the one you picked is the best."

The tension fizzled in Dani as she tore her gaze from Jackson. "Good to know, honey."

Bella didn't quite smile, but she seemed pleased. "We need to let Rosie out."

"I know." She'd never left Jackson without kissing him on the lips. She liked touching him. His smell. The touch of his calloused fingers on her arms.

Bella, silhouetted by the sun, stood in the doorway, hands on her hips.

Dani smiled at Jackson as she stepped back. "See you tomorrow."

"Will do."

Dani followed Bella outside into the light, where her vision was most clear and sharp.

Bella piled into the front seat as Dani slid behind the wheel. She looked back toward the shed, but Jackson had vanished inside. Yes, it was better they were forced to back away from each other now. The connection between them wasn't so strong that breaking it would be devastating.

The drive back to their house took less than ten minutes, and when they opened the front door, they found an agitated Rosie jumping up and down in her crate.

"Get her outside," Dani said. "I'll check the crate for accidents."

"She hasn't had an accident in a long time."

"New house. New life. We're all a little on edge."

Rosie bounded past Bella outside, and her daughter followed the dog, close on her heels. Dani set her purse on the kitchen counter and, after confirming there'd been no damage, stood at the back door and stared out over the lawn and the water.

In her old home, no matter what kind of day she'd had, she felt welcomed when she walked in the front door. But she'd earned that comfort. It had taken Dani years to strip away the old wallpaper, tear up the fading carpet, and paint the walls a bright white. Slowly she'd swapped furniture dating back to the nineties for newer, more comfortable pieces. Eventually, she'd made the house their home.

She could also walk around in the early-morning darkness and navigate without turning on a light. She expected the creak when she stepped on the fifth stair, the whistle of the wind through the front-porch windows on breezy days, and the squeak of the back-door hinge. She and that house were old friends, and as she stood now in this strange new place, she didn't feel any excitement at the possibility of this grand new adventure. She felt slightly adrift, lost.

Time would help her become acquainted with this old house. One day she hoped they'd share a similar familiarity and kinship. But for now, they were barely acquaintances, like two strangers stuck together on a long flight and forced to make the best of it.

Dani closed her eyes. As much as she wanted to wish away the next few months and the inconvenience of finding a fresh routine in this new life, she didn't want to lose any moments in her life with Bella.

Time was simply too precious.

CHAPTER FOUR
JACKSON

Friday, June 2, 2023
4:00 p.m.

Jackson stood in his workshop, hammering the red-hot metal until it was paper thin. When he plunged the molten edge into the water bath, the steam whistled upward, heating his arm and fogging the window of his welder's mask.

When he pulled the blade out, he realized immediately he'd overworked the metal. Experience said if he allowed it to fully cool, it would be brittle and snap at the slightest impact. He dropped the thin strip in the scrap pile.

Frustrated, he reached for the water bottle, realized it was empty, and tossed it in the trash. He focused on his breathing, in and out. He'd known Dani was bringing her daughter, but for some reason seeing her in the flesh had added a layer to whatever they shared. One thing to hear about a child, another to see her.

He sighed. He liked Bella. She had her mother's spark. The kid had taken one hell of a hit when her father died, and yet she was still showing up.

He shut off the equipment and retreated to his house. The interior design amounted to one large great room. Half was a living room / den, and the other half was his home office. The small kitchen had the basics, including a white retro refrigerator and a small round table where he ate most of his meals alone. Beyond a coffee maker, the countertops were bare. He liked things simple. Less to get broken. Less to lose.

Three years ago, he'd vowed as he was signing his divorce papers that he would never, ever get too attached again. Love, as strong as it might seem, was ultimately delicate. A man could nurture and care for what was his, but he couldn't predict or protect from rogue storms that blew out of nowhere and destroyed like a bomb cyclone.

As far as love went, he'd stayed true to his word. He lived alone, worked alone, and sailed alone. Easy. Simple.

And then he'd gotten a call from Juniper on a remodeling job, and as a favor to her had agreed to meet the client in a local diner. When he walked in, it was just before 10:00 a.m.; the breakfast crowd, except for a couple of old-timers nursing their coffees, had gone, and the lunch crowd's arrival was still an hour away. He didn't see his client. Juniper had said to look for a tall blonde with glasses. So, he sat in a booth. As he drank coffee, the clock ticked. Fifteen minutes late. His annoyance grew. She couldn't claim traffic on this cold January day. He'd tossed a ten-dollar bill on the table and readied to swallow the last of his coffee when Dani Manchester entered the front door with a cold gust of wind.

He froze, his cup below his lips. Carefully, he set it down. Her blonde hair was swept into a high ponytail, and she wore jeans, a black turtleneck that hugged her in all the right places, and a leather jacket. Juniper had told him to look for a blonde with glasses. But she'd said nothing about high cheekbones. Full lips. Long legs.

When Dani spotted him, she smiled and approached the booth. Every coherent thought scrambled away.

He rose and found enough sense to introduce himself. When she looked up at him, he saw the bluest eyes staring at him from behind those glasses that made her look sexy as hell.

He'd forgotten all about his monk's life.

Jackson shook off the memory. He opened the refrigerator and grabbed a beer. He popped the top knowing 4:00 p.m. was too early for a beer but justified a liberal sip because he only had one per day. The malty liquid rolled down his parched throat.

Jackson sat at his desk and clicked on his laptop, and the screen saver he'd been looking at for five years popped up. It featured Jackson and his ex-wife, Cathy, huddled around their seven-year-old daughter, Cloe, whose face was painted with a butterfly design. They were all smiling and holding pumpkins. That had been a fantastic day, and he remembered thinking he had the world by the tail.

He drained the last of the beer, annoyed he'd used up his daily allotment.

He typed in his passcode, the screen saver vanished, and a desktop filled with carefully arranged project files appeared. He opened the folder holding the details of his next ferrying job. In ten days, he'd drive to Norfolk and pick up a sailboat and sail it down to the Florida Keys.

He'd been away from the water too long. On the ocean and canals, he could breathe. It had been his refuge for years. It saved his life.

However, for the first time, he wasn't excited to escape. And that was not a good sign.

CHAPTER FIVE
BELLA

Friday, June 2, 2023
4:30 p.m.

Ghosts weren't real. When she was younger, she'd thought maybe they could be, but now she knew different. If they did exist, she was certain her father would've made contact by now. It had been four months. Four months. And though he could flake for work, he'd never been gone from her life for more than a week.

In the last four months, she'd received no sign from her dad. Not a ringing bell, a slamming door, or any kind of spooky text. Nothing. Nada.

The sun caught her eyes as she looked toward the three silos. They were quiet today. No workers. No customers. That would all change within the next two weeks. When the season opened, Route 158 would fill with tourists heading to the beach.

Rosie ran up to Bella and dropped a dirty tennis ball at her feet.

"Where did you get that?" Rosie was expert at finding anything that could be thrown and retrieved. Bella picked up the slobbery ball and tossed it toward the silos. The sun spilled light down over the treetops. Shadows pooled under the front awnings by the silos' central door.

She followed Rosie toward the grain towers, scooped up the ball again, and tossed it toward the main entrance. The ball bounced against the center silo's black front door and rolled back down the pathway toward Bella. Rosie scooped it up.

Bella twisted the front doorknob, half expecting it to be locked. When the door opened, she released the knob and stepped back. A glance over her shoulder confirmed her mother was inside the house. Mom wouldn't be crazy about her being at a construction site alone, but she hadn't seen the inside of the silos, which were almost finished.

Mom had first mentioned the grain towers back in January. She'd been super excited and wanted to show Bella, so they'd made the trip across the sound. Bella remembered feeling sorry for anyone who lived near here.

On that cold January day, they'd walked around the dusty, dirty storage towers covered in vines that twisted around the rusted metal. There were no doors or windows inserted in the curved walls, but she did see a hatch used for maintenance and cleaning.

"You bought this place?" Bella asked.

"I did." No traces of humor sparked in her mother's gaze.

Bella shook her head. "Why, Mom? It's the ugliest thing I've ever seen."

Mom laughed. "That's because you can only see with your eyes. I see what will be. I'll renovate the structures, add a second floor in each one, build rooms connecting them, grade the land for parking. I'll lease the parking lot space to a food truck vendor who sells burgers and hot dogs, maybe ice cream. Ivy has expressed interest."

"Well, Ivy's food will be good, but no one will buy art from a grain elevator when all they really care about after eating is getting to the beach or home after vacation."

"They'll stop. This will be a hit."

"Who's going to live in the house?"

"I'll make it an Airbnb. It's so close to the Intracoastal Waterway and the beach."

Her mother was excited. And Mom, for all her faults, was pretty good at seeing possibilities. Up until now.

"You're serious?"

"I am."

Bella shook her head. "I hope you didn't pay too much," Bella said.

"Please, not my first rodeo. I negotiated a great deal." *Her mom looked so pleased.*

"Well, there is that." *She didn't know anything about fixing places up, but grain elevators and house screamed expensive fixer-uppers.*

Her mother laughed. "I hear your doubt, daughter."

She ran her finger over a rusted rivet securing two metal panels. "It's a little crazy, Mom."

"That's what your dad said when I bought the art gallery in Duck. He said I was going to lose my shirt."

"Why would he say that?" *Her dad loved the gallery.*

Mom's smile dimmed a fraction. "Didn't have faith in my choice."

"Why?"

She smoothed a strand of hair from Bella's eyes. "Who knows?"

"He takes risks. And I guess if anyone can make these silos work, it's you."

"I know." *Her mother turned, hiding her expression.* "These grain elevators were built in 1920 and were a part of a larger grain-processing center. The property stayed in the Nelson family until two years ago, when the last manager passed. It was only on the market a few hours before I put in a bid."

"Waiting for you?"

Her mother turned, and her grin was bright, broad, and for the first time in a long time reached her eyes. "Yes. Destiny."

She glanced at the tall weeds circling the lackluster steely metal. "How is this going to be a place?" *She stopped short of showing too much disbelief, like her dad had.* "Seriously, Mom, how?"

Mom wrapped her arm around Bella's shoulders. "You'll see, grasshopper."

They walked the lackluster, run-down property, and when she'd glanced at the farmhouse next door, it looked so sad and lonely. Who would ever rent it?

Now, inside the silo, she flipped the switch and watched as large industrial lights flickered, slowly warmed, and spilled light on the wide pine floor made from reclaimed barnwood. Five large windows gently conformed to the contours of the room's curves. There were no display cases or art, but the raw space was kind of cool.

As Rosie barked outside the door, her footsteps echoed in the space as she walked toward a staircase that spiraled to a newly installed second floor. She climbed the stairs and found the old cash register in the space that likely would be her mother's office. Tall slim windows allowed sunshine to spill in, and she imagined her mother's long desk she'd bought from an antique store facing toward the staircase. Mom's desk had belonged to a ship's captain and was salvaged from a vessel that had crashed on the beach near Nags Head about a hundred years ago. It was in terrible shape when she bought it, but now its mahogany glistened, the brass knobs sparkled, and all the desk drawers worked. Mom was good with broken things.

Outside, the wind blew off the sound, wrapping around the building, which swayed slightly, as many did on the shore. She felt a finger of tension trace up her spine. For an instant, she had the sense that someone was standing right behind her again. She stilled, drew in a breath, and fisted her fingers. Turning around would be easy enough. Just face whatever the heck was there. And if it was her dad, she'd give him a hug and then get mad at him for leaving. But Jackson had said the ghost had been here when he'd started renovating six months ago. It couldn't be Dad. And if it was someone else . . .

Tingles danced up her spine. She sucked in a breath and turned quickly, hoping to catch whatever was behind her. No one living or dead stood there. Dust danced in the beam of light streaming in from one of the windows.

Bella's heartbeat thumped in her chest as nervous laughter bubbled. "Good one, Jackson. Tell the kid a story and get her imagination hopped up on ghosts. Won't fool me again."

She moved down the stairs, a little faster than maybe was needed. When she reached the first floor, Rosie stood on the other side of the glass doorway, the ball at her feet.

Bella opened the door. "Hey, girl."

Rosie stared toward an empty corner. The hair on her back rose, and a growl rumbled in her chest.

Swallowing, Bella looked toward the corner and found it empty. "There's nothing there."

Rosie barked but did not enter the silo. Bella switched off the lights, picked up the dog's ball, and joined Rosie in the afternoon heat. The sun felt good on her chilled skin as she closed the door.

"What do you think of the place?"

Bella startled at the sound of her mother's voice. Her mother had changed into forest-green shorts that showed off her long legs, a fitted black T-shirt, and white Vans.

"It's cool. You've done a lot," Bella said.

"That's Jackson's handiwork," Mom said. "He and his crew worked six days a week over the late winter and spring."

Jackson, the ghost maker-upper. "Tell him there are no ghosts here."

Mom grinned. "I thought you liked ghosts."

"Sure. Real ones. Not the fake made-up kind."

"We've only been here a half day, so cheer up, kiddo. You might see a spirit before it's all said and done."

Bella knew her mother was teasing. "Very funny. How did you meet Jackson?"

"The real estate agent, Juniper, recommended him. Juniper and Jackson have been friends for years."

"And how did you find her?"

"She was the listing agent for the property. I saw her number on the sign and called it."

"Isn't that a little dangerous? What if she was a serial killer?"

Mom shook her head and chuckled. "Thankfully, she wasn't."

Bella stared at the curving walls of the structures. "That's kind of random."

"I did my homework on both the land and the Realtor," Mom said. "Remember, I grew up in the construction-and-real-estate business."

"Yeah. I guess."

"Did you walk all the way through the three silos? They connect now."

"No. But I went upstairs in the first. Is that going to be your office?"

"It is."

This place was feeling more and more permanent. First it had been her closet; then the furniture would arrive, and then roots would spring from her feet and burrow into the ground, trapping her here forever.

"I unloaded the blow-up mattresses," Mom said. "Do you want to sleep in the living room or up in your new room?"

A four-month-old knot twisted tighter in her belly. "I want to sleep in my old room in Duck."

Mom's gaze did not stray. "That option is off the table."

God, this sucked. "I'll take the mattress up to my room."

They'd slept on the blow-up mattresses last night, after the moving company had packed up their bedrooms. Mom had originally said they'd leave yesterday, before the furniture, but it had been raining, so their departure was delayed. Lately, Mom had gotten weird about driving in the rain.

"Do you remember how to blow it up?" she asked.

Such obvious questions. "Yes."

"I put snacks, paper plates, and plastic glasses in the kitchen cabinet. We can order pizza for dinner if you want."

Not the pizza from *her* pizza place in Duck. "Okay."

"Take Rosie with you."

"Rosie!" Bella shouted as she headed toward the house (not her house, *the* house). When she reached the front porch, Rosie ran past her and jumped up as she fumbled with the lock. Inside, her footsteps echoed in the empty great room, and she crossed to the kitchen and checked the cabinets. Mom had loaded up on energy bars and bags of baked potato chips. This was as close to junk food as Mom came. Mom had gotten weird about her diet in the last year and now insisted on eating "clean." A.k.a. vegetables. A.k.a. stuff that rabbits ate. Lately, she'd started to see the sense of that kind of diet.

With Rosie on her heels, she climbed the main stairs and rounded the corner toward the bedroom currently assigned to her. Inside she saw a jelly-rolled mattress along with the electric pump that came with it and the green plastic garbage bag filled with her sheets and pillow. When she unfastened Mom's neat knot, the mattress immediately unfurled into a wrinkled rectangle.

She shoved one end of the pump into the mattress's corner and the other into the wall's electrical outlet. After hitting the red inflate button, she stood back, watching as the machine hummed and the creases slowly filled like the rising swells of the ocean.

When she reached for the garbage bag of bedding, she glanced back toward the closet and noticed that the jar she'd left by the seasonal shoes was sitting on the closet's threshold.

Bella walked over to the jar, picked it up, gripped the top, and then tried to twist it off. Nothing. Energy shivered through the air. And suddenly, she wasn't keen on holding the jar. She put it back on the top shelf.

"You're lucky. I forgot to bring my hammer."

CHAPTER SIX
DANI

Saturday, June 3, 2023
4:00 a.m.

Dani's air mattress had deflated. The gradual flattening prompted a dull throbbing in her left shoulder, now pressing against the living room's hardwood floor. Her muscles ached from moving boxes yesterday, her body hummed with the constant rush of adrenaline, and her head throbbed from endless second-guessing. All she wanted was to sleep. She rolled to the mattress's more inflated side, where a plump pocket of air remained, and tugged the covers up over her shoulder. The mattress appeared to hold. A minor miracle. Sleep. Just a few more hours of sleep.

She had to pee.

"Damn it." Last night's third cup of tea had been a mistake. She sat up and stared into the room's inky blackness. Her fingers fumbled over the smooth hardwood floor for her glasses and flashlight. In the disorienting darkness, her minute-long search for her glasses kicked up her heartbeat as she sampled her future. Finally, her hand grazed the metal flashlight and then the wire-rimmed glasses. Glasses on, she clicked on the light and rose up.

Bella had opted to sleep in her room, but Dani had felt being downstairs might be better. If something were to go wrong and she was disoriented in the night, better to be running up a flight of stairs than potentially falling down one.

At her old house, she hadn't needed her light or glasses. Every corner, stick of furniture, threshold, or creaky step was automatic. Here she was out of her element. She blinked, rubbed sleep from her eyes. Why hadn't she left the bathroom light on? Rookie mistake.

She walked toward the wall, and with fingers running along the smooth, freshly painted plaster, she followed it to the first corner. Downstairs bathroom should be twelve to fifteen steps due east. As she made the turn, she ran into two unpacked boxes hiding in her periphery. Pain throbbed in her knee. "Damn it."

Her eyes adjusted as much as they could, but if not for the flashlight's beam, she would've been swallowed in darkness. Moving around the boxes, she shuffled her feet and closed the distance to the bathroom. Ten steps later, her feet skimmed over the tile threshold. She fumbled for the light switch and flicked it on. Bright light threw her off for a second, but slowly her eyes readjusted. She quickly peed.

She flushed, washed her hands, and opted to leave the light on. When she safely reached the air mattress this time, she lay down gingerly, hoping to maintain the air pocket. Covers pulled up, glasses removed, she rolled on her back and stared at the shadowed ceiling.

"Dani, you've lost your damn mind."

Her heart jackhammered against her ribs.

Panic slid through her body, and her breathing shallowed. Who gives up the life they knew so well when the ground was shifting under their feet?

She'd sold a perfectly good business and a wonderful house and left *everything* familiar behind. If she'd been a Viking, her boats would be smoldering on the shore.

Her mind lingered in that odd space between awake and asleep where dreams, regrets, and worries flourished.

This house, this new business, was not going to change her medical prognosis. She was slowly losing her vision, and this move had robbed her of her fragile independence. Add to that, Bella hated it here.

Okay, maybe she'd made a mistake. But there was no taking it back. No selling this property, let alone buying back the old house and business. Choices were simple at the point of no return.

And even if she could have taken back the move, there was no safe harbor. No place where her sight would be fully restored, and Matthew would be alive.

The mattress hissed air very softly.

It's okay.

The words floated in the back of her mind.

It's okay.

She drew in a deep breath and slowly released it. "You've gotten out of worse scrapes. You'll make this happen."

Finally, she drifted off to sleep. What seemed like seconds later, she woke to Rosie's feet scrambling over the hardwood. The sun was rising. The dog trotted into the kitchen, and Dani tossed back her covers, slid on her glasses, and rose. She stretched the tension from her lower back and rubbed her shoulder.

Out the French doors toward the sunrise, bright oranges and yellows peeked above the horizon, glistened on dew-soaked grass, and backlighted cumulous clouds.

Dani, grateful to end this tug-of-war with sleep, pulled the elastic band from her wrist and swept her long hair into a ponytail. Rosie came up to Dani, tail wagging, and jostled her leg with her nose. The day had started. Now the grind of the move and setup of the business would take over her thoughts. All the cracks in time would fill, and there'd be no empty reservoir to store worry or doubt.

Dani reached for the pile of clothes she'd laid out last night, moved to the kitchen, and switched on the coffee maker. Machine setup had been a must since the day she brought baby Bella home from the hospital. She ducked into the bathroom, rethreaded back her hair, and refastened it with a hair tie. She dressed in tan shorts and a white T-shirt.

Dani filled her favorite mug, doctored the coffee with sugar and powdered creamer, and opened the door for the dog. With no sign that Bella was stirring, she slipped on flip-flops and walked outside as Rosie sniffed. She sipped her coffee.

The warm air brushed her face and relaxed some of the tension in her muscles. The glowing sun rose higher, reaching toward an emerging cobalt sky. Cotton ball clouds drifted slowly, as if they, too, weren't quite ready for the day. The app on her phone promised ninety degrees and sunshine. That she could definitely work with.

She walked to the water's edge and stared out over the sound. Bella had been right. This side felt wrong. She should be looking over the Currituck Sound into not the orange glow of the sunrise but instead the sun's reflecting misty pinks and blues that washed over the morning sky. But this sunrise was stunning. Foolish to debate if this was the right or wrong side of the shore.

After finishing her coffee, she went to the side shed, where she'd stowed her paddleboards on her run here last week. She twirled the combination lock until it released and opened. She grabbed the board and paddle used almost every day two summers ago. The last two years, filled with life chaos, had kept her off the water. It was a shame because she loved the sound and the feeling of dragging her paddle through the smooth waters. Foolish not to be out in such perfect conditions. Paddling here was a kind of inauguration for the new house.

The board was lightweight and tucked easily under her arm. She crossed the yard as Rosie ran alongside her, tail wagging. The dog watched Dani settle the bright-yellow board on the smooth water. She wouldn't go out far, but just a small spin along the shoreline would be nice.

She kicked off her flip-flops, and paddle in hand, she stepped into the cool water. Rosie barked.

Kneeling, she adjusted her glasses and angled her body onto the board, then carefully stood. When she was a kid, she could paddleboard or surf for hours. She'd spent most of her childhood in and around these waters. Out here, she was at home.

She glanced up toward the rising sun and, squinting, wished she'd worn her sunglasses. Angling the board away from the rising sun, she moved north along the shoreline with the current, paddling slowly. The sound was about three miles wide from this spot to the barrier island on the other side, but the water wasn't more than three or four feet deep. Back in the day, handcrafted flat-bottom boats and skiffs were a hallmark of the Currituck Sound's watermen, who transported fishermen, duck hunters, and goods. Over time, wood had given way to fiberglass, but the trademark shallow shape still navigated these waters.

The lingering stiffness in Dani's shoulders and back eased as she pushed the paddle through the water. The weights of the last few months momentarily lifted. Whenever she was on her board, she thought about her mother, who had taught her how to surf and paddle.

When her mom had met her father, she'd been a single mother with a two-year-old son in tow. Mom had traveled to the barrier island to take a job in her father's fledgling Outer Banks construction company office.

Her father often said the minute he saw her mother, Becky, he'd forgotten how to string words together in a sentence. Becky wasn't immediately wowed by her father. Becky was a serious woman who had only two priorities: Dalton and work. Dad said he'd asked her mom out at least a half dozen times before she'd finally agreed to a lunch date. He often laughed as he recounted how he had to work hard to impress her. He'd known what love looked like, and he wasn't going to give up easily.

They were married a year after they'd met in a simple ceremony on the beach, with three-year-old Dalton serving as their father's best man. She was born six months later.

Their lives had been golden. And when Mom got sick, she clung to her independence, surfing and paddleboarding up until she became too ill to carry her board. That's when Dad hauled her board to the sound, and as she sat on it, he slowly pushed her along the shore as she tipped her face toward the sun. She'd been so painfully slender then. Her hair was thinning, and she had almost no energy. But her mother kept squeezing what she could out of life. She'd never complained. Always smiled. Putting one foot in front of the other. Dani only hoped she had half as much courage.

Sudden tears glistened in her eyes and blurred her vision. She blinked. She'd done her best to ease Bella's loss of her father, but she knew there was no perfect fix. "God, Mom, what do I do? Forget about me, how do I help Bella through this?"

Rosie barked, distracting Dani for a split second. She turned too quickly, and the simple movement threw her off balance just enough to tip the board to the left. Adrenaline rushed, and she tried to auto-correct, but the more she struggled to stay upright, the less control she had. Finally, momentum tipped her off the board and into the water.

Her shoulder struck the side of the board hard, and when she hit the shallow sound's silty bottom, her glasses flew off her face. She sucked briny water into her mouth and nose. Long water grass brushed her skin, and for a moment she was confused and disoriented.

She pushed off the bottom toward the water's surface and shoved upward. She staggered and braced her feet in the silty bottom. Mud squished through her toes. Shoving hair strands out of her face, she sucked in a full breath. The current had caught her glasses, but the floating lenses reflected the morning sun. She quickly snapped them up. These damn things cost a fortune, and losing a pair would've been a terrible waste.

Rosie barked and ran along the shore.

Immediately, she felt foolish. It'd been years since she'd fallen like that, and she was glad Rosie was the sole witness. She pushed through the water, grabbed her board and paddle, and turned toward the shore, to find Jackson running toward the water. He was reaching for his shirt, ready to strip down and save her from herself.

Dani held up her hand as she pushed through the water toward the shore. "All good."

"Are you sure?" He stood, hands on his hips as he watched her move closer.

"Wounded pride. Which I deserve for being so out of practice."

When she reached the shore, he took the board and paddle and set them down. He extended his hand, and she took it. His muscles flexed, and he pulled her up as if she weighed nothing.

She swiped a smear of mud from her face and grinned because what else could she really do? "Not my best look."

"Are you really okay?" he asked.

"I'm fine. Seriously. I've been on that water a million times in my life. I was just a little distracted today." She removed her glasses and tried to clean the film from them. Her wet shirt moved the silt around but didn't clear it.

He took the glasses and wiped them with the edge of his dry T-shirt. He angled them up to the light and, evidently deciding they were clean enough, held them out to her. "Do you want to talk about it?"

She accepted her glasses back and settled them on her face, grateful to sharpen the blur. "Talking rarely fixes much."

"That's not always true."

She squared her shoulders and plucked at her T-shirt, now clinging to her breasts. "It's never solved much for me."

Jackson's gaze dropped, lingered on her breasts, and then met her eyes. "You can always bend my ear."

She kissed him on the lips, something she'd wanted to do ever since she saw him yesterday. "Maybe another day."

His hand came to her side, and his fingers slowly fisted as if he was trying to keep his thoughts from straying too far. But that was the point. She wanted those thoughts to wander down sensuous pathways. When they were in bed, there was no past or future, only the present.

"You're doing that on purpose," he said.

"Doing what?"

His hand relaxed and settled on the curve of her hip. He deepened the kiss. She leaned into him, savoring the warmth of his body. "I'm wet."

"Is that so?" he teased.

She chuckled. "I'm covered in sound slime. I can't imagine that I smell great."

"Not too bad." Jackson kissed her on the lips again.

Rosie ran up to them and barked.

"It's a matter of time before Bella gets up." She sighed. "I haven't told her about us." She looked up, meeting his concentrated stare. "I've thrown so many changes at her."

"You don't have to explain. I get it. The kid needs time to figure out this new life." A grin tipped the edges of his lips. "She reminds me of you."

"Does she? Everyone sees Matthew."

"She has your spirit. She's not afraid."

That startled a laugh. "I'm terrified all the time."

"Why?"

She sighed, wondering why she'd been so candid. "I've been operating on pure adrenaline ever since I found out I was pregnant with her."

His stare didn't stray. "It's okay to be afraid. We've all been there."

Calm and steady. In the five months she'd known him, she'd never seen him flustered or frustrated. "I don't picture you afraid."

"Get to know me a little better, and I'll tell you about it."

The salty scent of his skin and a challenge lay between them. He wanted them to keep seeing each other. He wanted her to tell Bella about them. He wanted more.

"How about I get into the shower and get this grime off me."

"I kind of like the wet T-shirt look."

She laughed. "Glad you do."

"I brought the sundial. Tell me where you want it."

She slipped on her shoes, and her long legs easily matched his pace as they rounded the corner of the house to his black pickup truck. He lowered the tailgate and pulled the dial toward the edge. She ran her fingers over the smooth edges and the rough raised letters.

"You really do have a knack for this," she said.

"It's a hobby. But if I get serious, I'll hire Bella to be my rep."

"She'd have your inventory sold out in a day. But she'll charge a substantial commission. My girl knows how to earn a buck."

"I have no doubt." He hefted the sundial. "Where to?"

"The back patio." She led the way, retracing their steps to the stone patio she'd had installed last month. She glanced at the sun, considered its path, and then chose a spot at the far-right corner. "How about here?"

He set it down. "You sure?"

"For now. If I change my mind, I'll move it."

"Call me instead. It's heavy as hell. I'll be mad if you don't."

"Fair enough. Listen, let me shower and change, and then I'll meet you in the silo with coffee."

He glanced up toward the house, confirmed Bella wasn't watching, and kissed her. "Deal."

CHAPTER SEVEN
BELLA

Saturday, June 3, 2023
7:00 a.m.

Bella was in the kitchen with her father at his new restaurant. Standing at a stainless steel table, they'd each created a mound of flour, burrowed out a well, dropped in a single egg, and poured in a splash of water. As her father had shown her, Bella mixed the egg and water and then slowly grabbed flour from the sides of the well until she'd mixed all the ingredients together. After she kneaded the pasta dough, she rolled it out and fed it into a sheeter machine several times until it was thin. A tomato sauce bubbled on the six-burner gas stove.

"You have a talent for this," Dad said. "A chip off the old block."

She looked at her oblong section of dough with jagged rough edges. "I cook like Mom."

"Not even close, kid." He chuckled as he took a sharp knife and with four swipes squared off the edges. "Takes practice. Mom never had patience for mixing and stirring. But that woman can sell ice in a blizzard."

"Why don't you two work together?" She'd always harbored the hope they'd reunite. "She can sell, and you can cook."

A half smile reflected resignation rather than mirth as he dusted a whisper-thin layer of flour onto the dough. "Mom and I do best if we focus on raising you together. And we're doing a fantastic job, if I do say so myself."

Bella smoothed her hand over the even, lightly floured dough. "I don't get you two. You act like friends."

"We are friends. We like—no, love—each other. But we don't do married well."

"Why not?"

He shrugged. "Maybe if I could slow down a little. Focus. Not good at either. Maybe if your mom could open up a bit more."

She watched as he pulled a knife tip through the dough, creating straight, even strips. "You look focused. And Mom is pretty open."

A smile flicked the edges of his lips as the sunlight burned brighter into the kitchen. "Your mother is open with you. Not so much with the rest of us. And the food and the restaurants steal all my focus. That's your mom and dad's problem in a nutshell."

Light streamed in through the kitchen window. It grew hotter, brighter, until holes pierced the walls and the floor. The gaps grew wider, consuming the table and then the pasta. The stove, refrigerator, and walk-in freezer vanished until only her father remained. She glanced up at him, panic tearing at her as she reached out. Her fingers locked with his, but the light was so strong. Finally, his grip slackened as he vanished. Bella lunged for him, but her fingers caught only air.

"Dad!" Bella sat up on her air mattress, breathing quick, sharp breaths that didn't fill her lungs. Her gaze ripped around the empty room. Where was her bed, her dresser, her posters? Everything that summed up her life had disappeared, like her father. Where was Rosie? Mom?

She jumped to her feet and ran to the window. She saw her mother walking beside a man who tossed a ball for Rosie. The dog ran after the ball, her tail wagging, before she scooped it up and returned it back to him.

"Dad?" she whispered.

And then she remembered. Her dad was dead. That man with her mother was Jackson. This was the new place. On the wrong side of the sound. Could her life suck any more than it did?

Tears tightened her throat. But instead of allowing them to fall, she curled her fingers into fists. A scream built in her belly and scraped up through her airways, inflaming her lungs. Anger clawed at her insides. But she held the fury close, trapping it and condensing it into a tight ball. The ball dropped back into her belly, joining all the others. She figured if anyone opened her up now, thousands of brightly colored little angry gumballs would fall out and roll onto the floor.

A soundless puff of air leaked over her lips as she ran fingers through her hair and drew in several breaths. In and out. In and out. Just like Mom did when she didn't think anyone was watching.

She crossed to her closet, where she'd hung today's clothes on a hanger. She glanced at the black shorts and purple T-shirt. If she were still in Duck, she'd have fretted over which set of earrings or bracelet she'd accessorize with. But here at the end of the earth, jewelry didn't matter.

She stepped into the adjoining bathroom and found her shampoo and soap and purple towels on the side of the white porcelain tub. The tile was black and white, the pedestal sink looked vintage, but the toilet was new.

She looked in the mirror over the sink; as she did every morning, she categorized all her father's traits. Her eyebrows were his, as were the shape of her lips and ears. She'd looked more like Dad before he died, but since his death, her cheeks had hollowed, creating sharp angles and shadows. Her eyes and ears looked huge. It was like the universe had broken her into pieces, and a cosmic force had clumsily reassembled her with superglue.

Bella bathed, washed her hair, and then lay back in the tub. She inched lower and lower, to the water's edge, and then finally slipped beneath it. All the lights and sounds vanished. It was peaceful here. She wished she could hold her breath forever.

Finally, lungs screaming, she sat up and gulped in air. She rose, toweled off, and dressed, finding calm as she tugged her purple (really lilac) shirt over her head. She brushed back wet hair and fastened it in a ponytail.

In her bedroom she glanced back at the air mattress covered with rumpled, twisted sheets and blankets. In her old, real home, she made her bed every day, like Mom. It set the stage, as Mom said, for an organized day. But as she looked at the rumpled sheets and blankets, she didn't see the point of straightening anything. This bed was temporary. And hopefully this version of life wouldn't last either.

She glanced up at the closet's top shelf and was relieved to see the jar was where she'd left it. She climbed up on the stepladder, grabbed it, and tried the lid. It still didn't budge. She gritted her teeth, adjusted her grip, and tried again. Nothing.

"Why won't you just open? Why is this such a big deal?" If she had a trash can, she'd throw it away right now. She set it down hard on the shelf. "I'm getting that hammer."

She left the jar and her unmade bed behind and moved down the stairs, absently running her fingers down the white wall.

In the kitchen the smell of fresh coffee lingered as she opened the fridge and studied the assortment of energy bars and bottled waters. She grabbed an apple-cinnamon-raisin one and peeled off the wrapper. Finding no trash can under the sink, she tossed it on the counter.

The back door opened. "Bella!"

"Mom." Her mother was dripping with water. "Why are you wet?"

Mom tucked a damp strand behind her ear. "Fell off the paddle-board into the sound."

"You never fall," Bella said.

"Guess I was a little distracted."

"By what? There's nothing out here."

"Rosie. My to-do list."

"The list that never ends."

"That's the one."

"Do we have any real food in the house, Mom?"

"Just the energy bars and snacks. Making a grocery store run today."

Bella groaned. "I need bagels and cream cheese."

"We'll get them this morning."

"Where?"

"Don't know, but that's part of the adventure, isn't it?" Mom's dripping clothes were creating puddles. "I need a quick shower."

"Did you really fall off your board?"

"I did. There's a first for everything." She sounded breezy, chipper. Code red.

"You never fall. Are you okay?"

"Of course I'm fine. Just distracted. Let me get these wet clothes off."

Before Bella could follow up with more questions, Mom dashed upstairs and closed her bedroom door. Bella set down her energy bar, grabbed a paper towel, and wiped the puddles and footprints off the floor. She tossed the paper towel in the sink. Rosie barked from somewhere outside. Where was Rosie? Right. Playing fetch with Jackson.

At the front window, she spotted Jackson with her dog. He was still throwing the ball for the dog, who looked like she was having too much fun. Her dad had liked Rosie, would pitch the ball for her when she was a puppy, but he wasn't around much to ever walk her or feed her.

Drawing in a breath, she went outside to reclaim her dog.

Jackson tossed the ball, which Rosie again gleefully chased. "Good morning, Bella."

"Hey."

He ruffled the dog's ears and, when she rolled on her back, scratched her belly. "How was your first night in the house?"

"Weird."

"How so?" The dog rolled over and barked, and he sent the ball flying again.

"It's not my home."

He nodded slowly. "I felt that way when I moved into my house two years ago. Took me forever to get comfortable with it."

He wasn't grinning or telling her everything was going to be okay, like grown-ups did with kids. A plus in his column. "How long did it take to feel at home?"

His brow knotted as he considered the question. "A few months before it didn't feel like a stranger's house. But I still have days when I wake up and wonder where I am. It doesn't happen as often anymore." Rosie ran straight toward Jackson, and again he handed the ball to Bella.

"You might as well throw it for her. She doesn't want me."

"Sure she does."

This time, when Bella threw the ball, it again smacked the tree and fell flat. Rosie ran past the tree and then, not finding the ball, began sniffing and retracing until she found the lost missile. The dog brought the ball directly to Jackson.

He offered Bella the ball.

She took it, tossed it hard. It barely missed the tree but still fell short. "Do you know anything about the silos or the house?"

"I've been all over both in the last six months. What do you want to know?"

"How about the history?" She wanted to ask about the ghost but didn't because she still believed he had been teasing yesterday.

"Not too much. It was owned by the Nelson family for over a century. The original Nelsons had ten children. The six surviving girls married local guys, and the three boys took over the business. By all accounts they did well."

"Which girl died?"

His brow knotted. "I don't know her name."

"Was she young?"

"About ten, I think. It was an accident."

She flinched. "Car?"

"No. I hear she drowned."

Bella looked toward the sound's calm waters. "That's terrible."

"I imagine it was." His voice sounded heavier.

"Are any of the surviving brothers and sisters left in the area?"

"A few." He eyed her. "Did you see a ghost last night?"

Okay, he'd brought the ghost up, making it fair game. "So how does the ghost fit into all this?"

He shrugged. "Like I said, I spent a lot of time in all the buildings. I got a vibe that something was standing behind me. Like a shiver under the air. But when I turned, no one was there."

Her eyes narrowed. "Do you mean that? Or are you kidding me?"

"I'm not kidding." His solemn, steady gaze held no hint of a joke or trick.

The skin on her spine prickled. "Did you see anything?"

"No, can't say I ever saw a ghost." If this was a joke, he was playing it through to the end.

Bella's head cocked. "Maybe you're just a nervous kind of guy."

He laughed. "Not usually."

Bella raised her chin. "I'm not an anxious kid."

"I can see that." He raised a brow. "Did you see anything that looked like a ghost?"

"Not really."

His voice deepened a note. "What's that mean?"

"Stuff just seemed to keep moving around."

His head cocked slightly, as if considering a problem. "You think it's the ghost moving your stuff?"

"I'm looking for a logical explanation," Bella said. "Maybe Mom moved it. Maybe Rosie knocked it around."

He glanced down at the dog, who was wagging her tail, her tongue hanging out as she panted. "Rosie? Was it you?" The dog barked. "I don't think it was her, which leaves your mom."

"She's always straightening and organizing, especially these days."

"These days?"

"She hasn't said, but she's worried about the move. When she's nervous, she cleans, organizes, or shops."

"You should ask her about your missing items."

"It would be one more question to worry her."

"Your mom's habit of cleaning makes more sense than a ghost. You wanted a logical explanation. There you have it."

She wasn't sure why she wanted to believe the house was haunted. "Logical explanations are the best kind. But sometimes, logic doesn't figure in to a situation. Sometimes weird stuff happens. But I've discovered most things can be explained."

"True."

"If you're trying to rattle me with ghost stories, you're doing a terrible job. I'm not afraid of a ghost. I just want to figure out why it's messing with me." She considered asking him if he could open the jar. He looked strong enough. But she opted not to. She'd figure out something sooner or later.

"If you ever need help, let me know."

"Thanks. I've got this."

"Fair enough."

She didn't mind talking to Jackson. He spoke to her like a person. He didn't look at her with pity or treat her like she was broken. *Poor Bella, she looks so sad.* She'd heard versions of that so much this year, she could scream.

Rosie yapped and ran toward the house and her mother, who was freshly showered and wearing white shorts, a black T-shirt, and sandals. She'd washed her hair, but it hung loose and damp, curling around her shoulders. She also wasn't wearing makeup, earrings, or bracelets. What next, an earthquake or a rogue wave?

"What're you two up to?" Mom asked.

"Talking about the property," Jackson said easily. "Bella was asking about the history. But I only know the basics."

"You're interested in the history?" Mom asked.

Fresh-faced Mom looked younger, reminding Bella that her mother was only eighteen when she was born. God. Bella would be eighteen in six years. No way was she having a baby.

"Just curious," Bella said. "Might as well learn what I can while we're here."

Her mother's brow raised. She'd caught the inference that this setup was temporary. It was a matter of time before her mother came to her senses.

"Juniper knows all there is to know about this area," Jackson said. "Be sure to ask her."

Bella worked hard to stifle a groan. "She runs *the* camp."

"It'll be fun," Mom said.

"You always say that," Bella said. "I'm not looking forward to hanging around with a bunch of sad kids."

"It'll be more than just standing around," Mom said.

"Juniper will plan lots of fun activities," Jackson said.

"How do you know her?" Bella asked.

"We're kind of related," he said. "I've known her since she was a kid."

"And she just started a camp for kids who had someone die?" Bella asked.

Jackson stilled. "Her parents died when she was young. She understands there's a need for kids to talk about their feelings."

Bella and her mother didn't talk about their feelings beyond "I love you" and stuff. When they were feeling off, they picked nice outfits, fixed their hair, and put smiles on their faces. "Jury's out on her."

Jackson chuckled. "I'll be curious what you think of Juniper. My money says you'll like her."

Like she was going to talk to Jackson about all this. She'd already said too much. "Right."

"Is there a half-eaten energy bar in the kitchen?" Mom asked.

"It didn't taste great."

"Then pick another flavor. We have a big day. The moving van driver texted. He should arrive in the next couple of hours, which means the afternoon is going to be crazy."

"I thought we were going to the grocery store."

"We will. But not this morning."

Bella wasn't hungry anymore, but standing here felt weird, and for some reason annoyance churned in her belly along with all the marbles and gumballs. There were days she wanted to break everything and scream.

"Okay, Mom," Bella said.

Bella picked up Rosie's ball and threw it, and as the dog ran toward it and the house, she followed. Rosie snatched up the ball in her mouth, but instead of following Bella into the house, the dog turned and ran back toward Jackson.

"Traitor," she mumbled. "See if I share any of my energy bar with you ever again."

When the dog ran up to Jackson and dropped the ball, sadness washed over Bella. Rosie didn't understand that Jackson wasn't going to be around much longer. Bella sure wasn't going to bond with him.

Her mother and Jackson walked side by side (a little too close if you asked her) into the silo. Mom really was excited about the new house and gallery. Which was great, but everyone was moving on with their life. *Everyone* but her. She was trapped in this new house, and if Mom thought moving could outrun sadness, she was wrong. Her unhappiness was sharper and tighter than it had ever been.

Her phone dinged with a text. Finn. Thank goodness. Her friends were about the most normal thing in her life right now.

Finn: Surf's up. Miss you.

Bella: Miss u 2.

Finn: When r u coming back?

Bella: Don't know. Currently trapped in hell.

Finn: Ha-ha.

Bella: Seriously. Hell.

Finn: Let's go shopping.

Normally, that would've excited her. But like everything else on this planet, it was one more thing she couldn't do right now, and it made her mad. She shoved the phone in her pocket.

Back in the kitchen, her energy bar was just as she'd left it. She took a bite and stared out the kitchen window toward the water.

The mason jar was sitting on the kitchen windowsill. What the heck?

It looked exactly the same. The outside was still a medley of colors, even though the sun shone right on it; the light did not penetrate the paint. With her teeth clamped on the energy bar, she tried to twist off the top again. Still stuck. She shook it; the unknown thing still rattled inside.

She tapped the edge of the jar on the counter. Another twist, and nothing. "Seriously?" she said. "This is getting a little weird!"

The AC hummed, and the wind outside brushed against the house. A shiver loitered in the air.

With the jar in hand, Bella shoved open the back door and marched toward the sound. At the water's edge, she tossed the jar, which splashed into the sound. For an instant, it sank under the surface before it bobbed up as if grabbing a breath. Caught by the current, it floated south along the shore.

As the jar grew farther and farther and farther away, a sense of panic arrowed through the anger and jabbed her insides. What if it got swept away in the current? So what if it did. Who cared about a stupid jar?

"Good riddance."

The words didn't have enough punch to ease the panic as the jar floated farther away. If it stayed on its course, it would travel through the Currituck Sound and on to the Albemarle Sound. Eventually, if it didn't get mired in the reeds, it would travel to the Atlantic Ocean. Maybe it would end up on the shores of England one day.

Bella walked along the shoreline. At first, she didn't keep pace with the jar, because she really didn't care about saving it. But as it moved a little faster, she quickened her pace.

It bobbed, dunked under the surface, and popped up like a drowning swimmer.

She scooped up a long stick and then, running past the jar, waited for it to get closer. When it was just drifting past, she used the stick and guided it back to the shore. When she reached for it, it skirted out of her grasp.

"I'm trying to save you, stupid jar!" Bella groaned her frustration. "You've done nothing but stalk me, and now you want to play games?"

She hurried down the bank and again extended the stick. This time the bent branch stopped the jar's southward journey, and this time when she guided it toward the shore, she leaned in and grabbed it. A sense of triumph washed over her as her fingers wrapped around the slick glass, now dripping with water.

As she held the jar up to the light, the cold water trickled down her arm. She shook off the jar and headed back toward the house.

She stomped across the back deck, past the new sundial (Jackson was everywhere!), and through the back door. She grabbed a wad of paper towels and wiped off the jar. She'd thought maybe cleaning it would give her a better look inside, but the painted interior held its secrets close.

The top refused to turn. She gritted her teeth and put her body weight into her arm. Nothing. Outside, she beat the jar's metal lid harder against the sundial's forged iron. It dented. She tried to open it again. The top refused to move.

"Ah, why won't you just open? What is the big secret?"

It was like everything else in her life. Stuck, broken, irritating. Sudden tears glistened in her eyes as she returned to the kitchen and set it down hard on the counter. She swiped the tears away, wondering why she cared so much about a stupid jar.

Bella pointed her index finger at the container as if it knew exactly how crazy it was making her. "I swear, there's a hammer with your name on it, pal. Just wait."

CHAPTER EIGHT
DANI

Saturday, June 3, 2023
8:00 a.m.

"How did Bella seem?" Dani asked.

Jackson flipped on the silo's lights. As the large industrial bulbs salvaged from an old lumber mill warmed, he walked into the shadowed edges of her blind spot and slipped into obscurity. She no longer panicked when this happened, so she stood in the doorway, waiting for the lights.

"She looks like she's doing fine," he said. "I know she's got a tough road ahead, but I think she'll come out on the other side."

His assessment seemed to carry the weight of someone who'd walked a similar path. "How can you tell?"

"She's a fighter."

"That's good to hear from someone else." She shifted her gaze, zeroing in on him in the growing light. "I know she's tough, but I'm her mother, and I think she's amazing."

"Are you okay?" he asked carefully.

"Me? I'm fine." She smiled. "Big changes. Lots to juggle, but that's standard. On a scale of one to ten, I'm an eleven."

Brow arching, he studied her as if trying to peel back a few protective layers. "No, really, how are you?"

"Okay, maybe not an eleven. Closer to a five or six." The fissures in her resolve were widening. "But hanging tough."

"It's okay if you're not."

It wasn't okay. She was Bella's only parent now, and she couldn't afford to stumble.

As if reading her thoughts, he moved to within inches of her. "You can lean on me if you need support."

"You barely know me."

"Well enough to lend a hand."

She suspected he would step up if she asked, but depending on him would set a dangerous precedent. "Thank you."

"I think you're pretty fearless."

That startled a laugh. "Not even close."

"Don't sell yourself short." His hands skimmed down her arms, sending a sizzle snapping over her skin. "You look nice," he said.

"Nice?" She felt naked without her makeup. "I just stepped out of the shower."

"I like the natural look." He captured a damp curled strand between his fingers. "It's always pulled back. Always perfect."

When she was in bed with him, she loosened her hair and let the ends tumble over her bare shoulders. She cleared her voice. "Business, Mr. Cross. Business. The art gallery needs to be up and running in two weeks."

He nodded slowly, releasing her hair. "Two days of work, and I'll have the final details complete."

"Shelves arrive tomorrow. Once they're up, I'll be that much closer. Two potters are stopping by next week to look at the space, and I have five others committed."

His gaze roamed the spiral stairs coiling toward the second floor. "I never would've pictured this. When you first told me your idea, I thought you'd lost your mind."

"You hid it so well," she quipped. "I caught some of your side-eye."

He chuckled. "I tried to be subtle."

"Your jaw was clenched throughout our first walk-through."

"I was processing what you were saying. You were speaking a mile a minute."

"And now here we are."

He nodded. "Your vision for this place has come to life, and you're putting down new roots."

"Speaking of roots, you'll be uprooting soon to travel the waterways. Quite the adventure." Matthew's death had been a stark reminder of life's frailty, but she couldn't admit to herself that she worried about Jackson on the water alone.

"Not sure it's an adventure. Delivering a boat isn't as glamorous as you think. I have two to deliver in the fall."

"Sounds like business is good."

"I have a wait list. I'll be building another boat this winter."

"That's great."

His head cocked. "Maybe you and Bella should come with me. Bella might get a kick out of sailing."

The muscles in her body tensed as if she were bracing against a charging bull, a.k.a. the future. "As I proved this morning, I've lost my sea legs. So, let's get this place up and running first. One step at a time."

He eyed her closely. "Are we even taking steps toward a future?"

She wanted to say yes. But advancing to the next level would mean having a discussion about her dimming vision and then the letdown when he broke things off.

Matthew certainly had reacted badly to the news. She'd called him, hoped to set up a face-to-face, but when he begged off for work, she blurted it out in a moment of frustration.

"What are you talking about?" Matthew had demanded. *"Are we talking about going blind?"* he asked.

"Low vision."

"Is there a difference?" he challenged.

She gripped her phone, staring at a bright-yellow arrangement of sun-flowers on her desk. "There's a tremendous difference."

Silence stretched between them. "When? When will it happen?"

"I don't know."

"Someone must know. Are you seeing a doctor?" In the background, pots clanged and banged.

"Of course I'm seeing a doctor."

"Right."

The weight of his sarcastic tone snapped her temper. "Are you saying I'm not? I'm reliable. I keep my appointments and my promises."

"I'm also reliable," he shot back. "And if this is about the child support payments, I'll get you your damn money."

"Sure you will."

"Ask yourself how dependable you'll be when you go blind."

Fury crackled up her spine. "What did you say to me?"

A heavy stillness radiated between them. "Dani, I shouldn't have said that. I'm just stressed."

"Aren't we all."

Bitter anger and betrayal had burned through her as she hung up. When he'd phoned back immediately, she'd let the call go to voice mail. She'd refused to take his call the next hour, and the next. And then he was dead.

It might not be fair to hold Jackson accountable for Matthew's reaction, but the wounds were still fresh.

"I like you a lot," she said.

He shook his head. "But . . ."

"No buts. It's impossible for me to make any promises right now. It's been so long since I was in any kind of relationship."

He regarded her a long moment. "Okay. Fair enough. But unless you tell me otherwise, I'm not going anywhere."

A palpable relief washed over her. "Good. I like having you around."

He kissed her gently on the lips. "Good."

A Jeep pulled up outside. A horn beeped several times.

Dani turned toward the parking area and watched the short red-head step out of the vehicle. She wore a peasant top, cutoff jeans, and cowboy boots.

"Juniper." Dani stepped outside. "Realtor and camp director."

Juniper grinned, holding up her hands as if cheering a touchdown. A collection of silver bracelets rattled around her wrist. "One and the same." The woman's grin was vibrant and genuine. "Good to see you again, Dani. Jackson, you're looking fit."

"Hanging tough," he said, sliding his hands into his pockets.

"How's the house working out?" Juniper asked.

"We're settling in," Dani said. "The renovations are great, and I see real promise for a bright future here."

"This property has good energy. Good karma." Juniper winked at Jackson. "So that contractor I recommended worked out?"

Dani felt Jackson behind her. "He did."

Jackson moved around Dani and hugged Juniper. "Where have you been the last week?"

"I was at UVA Medical Center finishing up my postdoc work. I'm officially finished with school. I've spent the last day or so getting settled on my houseboat."

"Real estate and PhD. How do you do it?" Dani asked.

"I know this area and the houses here like the back of my hand, and selling homes comes easy to me. Perfect way to pay the light bill while I was in school."

"Are you giving up real estate?" Dani asked.

"Not quite yet. I have a few properties I'm trying to sell. After that, we shall see."

"Can I get you anything? The house isn't really stocked yet, but I have a few snacks, water, and a bathroom if you need it," Dani said.

"No, I'm good." She reached in her large purse, pulled out a bottle of champagne, and handed it to Dani. "Welcome to your new home."

Dani accepted the bottle. "Thank you."

"Every new ship deserves to be christened with a bottle of champagne, and I don't see why houses are any different. Though I'd suggest you drink it and not break it on the side of the silos."

"Don't worry. This won't be wasted." Dani regarded the woman, realizing she didn't know much about her. "You live on a houseboat?"

"It's docked near Jackson's house."

"You sail too?" Dani asked.

"Hard to know Jackson Cross and not fall in love with the water."

"Juniper and I have known each other since I was in high school," Jackson said.

"Elementary school for me," Juniper amended.

Dani hadn't realized their relationship went back so far. It was a reminder of how much she didn't know about Jackson, or he about her. "That's terrific. I'm grateful you're here and holding your camp."

"I'm looking forward to it," Juniper said. "I have eight kids registered."

"Eight? All in this area?" Dani asked.

"A few live locally, like Bella. But most are driving in from as far as a hundred miles away. A few social media posts, and the word spread quickly."

"I'm grateful your camp is local." Even if Juniper's camp hadn't been close, she would've found a way to get Bella there. It would've meant cooling her heels in a hotel room for a couple of weeks, and the Silos by the Sound opening would be delayed, but she would have done it.

"I'll send out an email today to all the families with directions. We're meeting in Jackson's waterfront warehouse."

Jackson had land. A warehouse. Another surprise.

"Maybe one night we can have dinner," Dani said. "Furniture arrives later today, and I'll be up and running soon."

Juniper smiled. "Moving is a crazy time. I've done it enough to know it's a hassle. How about I have you and Bella over to my place next weekend?"

"Either way would be fantastic. Are you doing any other camps?" Dani asked.

"Maybe. If this one goes well, I'll set up a website and see what happens."

Jackson nodded toward Juniper's car. "How's your car holding up?"

"It's great. And you'll be proud, I had the oil changed right at three thousand miles."

Jackson didn't look impressed. "And your boat?"

Juniper shrugged. "Trouble with the electrical system."

"Want me to look at it?" Jackson asked.

Juniper grinned. "I thought you'd never ask."

"I'll come by now."

"Bless you. Electricity makes life so much easier." Juniper kissed Jackson on the cheek. "Dani, it was great seeing you again, and I'll see you and Bella on Monday."

"Will do," Dani said. "We're looking forward to it."

"Be back in an hour," Jackson said.

"No rush," Dani said.

As the two drove off, she found herself envying the familiarity they shared. She'd never enjoyed that kind of easy understanding with a man beyond her brother and father.

Her father, Dalton, and Ivy were the only three people who knew about her eyesight. Ivy had been pressing Dani to tell her friends and clients, but Dani had resisted. She liked her independence, and she didn't want people second-guessing her or, God forbid, feeling sorry for her.

She walked back to the house, ready to organize what she'd brought with her and prepare for the moving van. Inside, she kicked off her shoes.

"Who was that?" Bella was sitting on a blue blanket spread out on the floor in the kitchen, eating an energy bar and an apple. Rosie was beside her, licking vanilla energy bar from her lips.

"Juniper Jones."

Bella rolled her eyes. "The Realtor-slash-grief-camp lady."

"That's right." She moved into the kitchen, set the bottle of champagne in the refrigerator, and poured herself a fresh cup of coffee.

"She just came by to give you the champagne?" Bella asked.

"And to ask Jackson to look at the electrical system on her boat."

"She lives on a boat?"

"That's what she said."

A brow raised. "She knows Jackson?"

"Since she was in elementary school."

"She's the one that mentioned the camp, right?"

"Not a camp so much, ideas to help kids."

Bella frowned. "And all this came together around the time Dad died?"

"That's right. I knew she was getting a PhD in psychology, which is why I told her about Matthew's accident. As we talked, she said she'd been considering a grief camp. Next thing I know, she had it set up."

"Funny how things come together." Bella fished a bottled water from the refrigerator. "Who are the other kids in this detention camp?"

Dani studied her daughter. "It's not a prison camp."

She twisted off the top. "I don't want to go, but you're making me. Feels like prison."

"It can only help."

Bella took a bite of energy bar and slipped another bite to Rosie while Dani cradled the stoneware cup in her hands.

"Dad would've hated a camp like this," Bella said.

Bella was right. Matthew couldn't deal with any emotion that went too far beneath the skin. "I think it will help, and that's what's important."

"You don't know everything, Mom."

"You're correct. I don't. But in this I do know exactly what you're feeling. You keep forgetting my mother died when I was younger than you."

Bella didn't respond for several seconds. "You better not die."

"I don't plan on it."

Bella's eyes widened a fraction. "You're the end of the line for me. Next stop is Uncle Dalton."

Years ago, Matthew and Dani had agreed that if they should both die, her older brother, Dalton, would raise Bella. Dalton was a bachelor then, and he had just taken over the family construction business. Raising a small child would've been a challenge for him, but he'd readily agreed. Now he was dating Ivy. If the worst should happen, Bella would be in good hands.

But she didn't explain any of this to Bella. The last thing her daughter wanted to hear about was custody agreements in case of her death. "Not going anywhere, kid. But you're going to camp."

"Don't I get a vote?" Her tone ratcheted up several notches. "God, I'm twelve years old!"

"No vote for you on this one. Playing the Mom card, kiddo."

Bella flushed. "But I should have a say in my own life!"

"When you're eighteen and paying your own bills, you can make all the decisions you want."

"Ahhh! That's not fair!"

Dani wondered if Juniper had a camp for parents like her. She'd like nothing better than to hang out by the water for two weeks, sit in circles, and talk about feelings. She had a boatload to share.

The wheels of a large truck rumbled in the front driveway, prompting Dani to walk to the window. The moving van had arrived. Something else to handle instead of her daughter's messy feelings that she didn't know how to untangle.

"Looks like we're in business, kid. The furniture has arrived."

Bella didn't move or look toward the window. "I like the floor and air mattress."

Of course she did.

Dani moved to the front porch, a barking Rosie on her heels, and welcomed the movers, who greeted the pup with a dog treat. Rosie gobbled the little bone, happily chewing as her tail wiggled back and forth.

Another gulp of coffee, and Dani set down her mug. "Showtime."

She spent the next several hours playing traffic cop. The guys set up the kitchen table, chairs, and an armoire Dani had used for dishes. To her relief, it all fit, and she was glad now that she'd asked Jackson to remove a pony wall separating the dining area from the kitchen.

The men set dozens of boxes labeled **KITCHEN** on the counters. Dani had wrapped everything carefully and been diligent about marking. Organization was her go-to in stressful times, and these days her anxiety was off the rails.

Next came the living room furniture. She'd measured the rooms and pieces a dozen times and was certain each would fit like a well-constructed puzzle. That confidence held until the movers set her gray couch in the center of the living room. The couch seemed to balk and resist the house, just like Bella. Suddenly, she was unsure of her decisions.

But this ship she was piloting had crossed the point of no return, so she decided it was all going to be fine, because it had to be.

She wasn't sure when Jackson returned from Juniper's boat, but when he stepped into the front hallway, he looked at Dani standing in the center of controlled chaos. "Can I help?"

"Maybe later." Her head pounded. "Right now, it's strictly triage. I'm not sure what I was thinking. Half this stuff doesn't want to fit."

"You've done some decorating, right?" he asked.

"Sure. A lot."

"And you had clients with pieces that didn't fit?"

"Oh, sure."

"Then take a deep breath, do what you'd do on a work project. Get everything in sight, and start from there."

"Right. Doesn't have to be overwhelming." How many times had she told a panicked client that?

"Exactly."

The movers appeared with a white four-poster bed. "Where does this go?"

"That's Bella's bed," Dani said. "Follow me."

Jackson stepped back as the men angled the heavy piece up the stairs. She might have caught a grimace on his face as she turned. Yes, Bella's bed was an extravagance, but she'd found the bed frame at an estate sale when Bella was three and had fallen in love. She had spent several months removing layers of emerald-green and then baby-blue paint. After the bed was stripped, she'd whitewashed it. When she'd first put three-year-old Bella in the center, the mass of bed and bedding had swallowed her child. But Bella had loved the bed.

"Bella!" Dani said. "Your bed is here."

Bella appeared at the top of the stairs. "It's not going to fit."

"It will. I measured." Numbers didn't lie. The couch might have been off, but not the bed.

Bella folded her arms over her chest. "Bet it doesn't. Jackson doesn't think it's going to work either."

Dani glanced back at Jackson, who lingered at the bottom of the stairs.

He held up his hands. "I didn't say anything."

"I saw the look on his face," Bella said.

Jackson chuckled and turned to leave. "Call if you need me."

Dani directed the men to Bella's room. They tried the headboard on the main wall, facing the windows. "Good, right?"

Bella frowned.

Dani sighed. "Do you have another suggestion?"

Bella looked at the wall with the window. She shook her head no. When she studied the opposite wall, her frown deepened.

"I'm open to suggestions," Dani said.

"That's the only spot."

This was one of those little, but empowering, choices she was giving her daughter. "I know."

"It just looks wrong there. It didn't look wrong at home."

Dani pushed aside her frustration, crossed to her daughter, and wrapped her arms around her. "It'll look like it belongs. Maybe not today or tomorrow, but one day you'll walk in here and just know everything has found its new and right place."

Bella's body stiffened, but Dani held her until her daughter slowly relaxed. "I don't want it to be different."

Her daughter's rattled words silenced all her own frustrations. "I know. But the universe doesn't care about what we want, no matter how much we scream or cry." How many nights had she lain awake in bed, crying for her mother? Or as an adult, bargaining for her diagnosis to just go away, for the shadows to fade? The universe could be a real bitch. "But I'm here. And like it or not, you're stuck with me."

Bella tightened her grip around Dani's waist like she had when she was a toddler. For a moment it was just her and her little girl.

"Mom, you smell like sweat," Bella said.

A chuckle rumbled. "I know."

The thud of footsteps on the stairs hearkened the arrival of more furniture. As Bella pulled away, she turned and wiped her eyes. The men entered with the bed's baseboard and side rails. Once the foot and headboards were joined with the rails, the bed did look big. Maybe even a tad too much for the room. "My room is a little bigger. We can move you in there."

Bella sniffed. "No, this will work."

"You sure? I don't need as much space."

"Yes, I'm sure." Standing in the center of the frame, she looked out the window. "I'll need my curtains, or the sun will burn a hole through me each morning."

It was a concession, and at this point, Dani would take anything. "They're on the truck."

Dani hurried down the stairs as Jackson spoke to one of the movers. The two shared a laugh, as if they knew each other. But that was Jackson. He knew no stranger.

Spotting her, Jackson shook hands with the mover and strode toward Dani. "I'm going to work in the gallery. Unless you need help."

"I have it under control-ish."

He smiled. "You've got this."

"Thanks."

As he strode toward the gallery, movers returned with Bella's box spring and mattress. Next came the dresser and her oval mirror. Dani left Bella to make her bed while she directed the movers into the spare rooms and her own. The morning buzzed past, and by the time she stopped to grab a glass of water, she realized it was nearly three.

"Can I order a pizza?" Bella asked.

"I'm not sure what's close."

She pulled her phone from her pocket. "I found a place. They deliver."

"Yes, pizza sounds great."

Dani found her purse, made the call, and ordered two pizzas, knowing they could very well end up being dinner or lunch tomorrow.

A half hour later, when the doorbell rang, Bella grabbed a few bottles of water as Dani set the pizza boxes on the newly placed wrought iron front porch table. "Mind if I invite Jackson?"

"Why?" Bella asked.

"It would be a nice thing to do," Dani said.

"Sure." No enthusiasm, but no eye rolls either.

"Can you grab another water?" Dani asked.

"Yes."

Dani fluffed her T-shirt, trying to dry some of the sweat on her body as she crossed to the silos and peeked her head inside. The iron railings on the stairs were installed all the way to the second floor. As her eyes adjusted, she slowly climbed, her hand trailing over the smooth black metal. She found Jackson collecting his tools.

"It looks fantastic," she said.

"Thank you."

"We ordered pizza. Join us?"

He lifted his toolbox and stood in front of her. "Bella okay with that?"

"Are twelve-year-old girls okay with anything?" Sweat mingled with his scent, creating a heady male fragrance.

He chuckled. "Not as a general rule."

"Then you'll come?"

He shook his head. "I'd like to, but I promised Juniper I'd take her to dinner."

Before she could temper her curiosity, she asked, "You've known her since you were in high school?"

Jackson stood silent for a moment. "Twenty-plus years. She was a scrawny kid with braces when I met her."

Dani waited, hoping he'd tell her more, but he went silent. "She has a good energy. I liked her from the minute I met her."

"One of the best people you'll know."

She sensed there was so much more he wanted to tell her, but maybe, like her, he was afraid one tug of the thread would unravel the entire tapestry. And she was in no position to push. He'd been more than patient with her, and so she would be with him. "Sounds good. Tell Juniper I said hello."

He leaned in and kissed her softly on the lips. "See you tomorrow?"

His deep tone bolted through her. "I'll be here with bells on."

CHAPTER NINE
BELLA

Saturday, June 3, 2023
6:45 p.m.

With Rosie sleeping beside her on the bed, Bella texted Finn. She didn't mention Juniper or the camp but focused on TikTok videos (kittens were so cute), their friend Blaine's new highlights (looked terrible), and the party Finn was having next week. Bella had assured Finn she'd be there (one way or the other).

She stared out over the water and the softening light saturating the sound. How could she feel so different and basically look the same? How could her bed feel right but look wrong in this room? How could life get so messed up?

She glanced at Finn's response to Blaine's new hairstyle and realized she suddenly didn't care. "Rosie, why am I talking about stupid things when Dad is dead and Mom has lost her mind and moved us to the end of the earth?"

Rosie looked up at Bella, her head cocked.

She rose, walked to the window, and stared out toward the dock. The water always made her feel normal. Problems floated away on the current. She changed into her bathing suit and headed out the back door with Rosie trotting behind her.

At the dock, water lapped against the pylons as the waning sun glistened. Rosie barked.

"Come on, girl. It's okay."

Rosie stepped onto the pier but glanced between the slats toward the water. She backed away.

"You can't fall in."

Rosie didn't budge.

"It's okay. Stay on dry land."

Bella sat on the end of the pier and listened as the wind pulled the current past. On the other side of the sound, her life had been so good.

Until it wasn't.

"Dad, why weren't you more careful? Mom said you were burning the candle at both ends before your accident."

Bella lay back on the pier, staring at the clouds meandering across the sky. She closed her eyes, hoping the lingering sun would warm her chilled bones.

Her mother was acting weird. And the nuttiness had started before Dad's accident. Sometime last year, Bella had started catching her mother staring out over the sound, as if she were trying to memorize every detail. She'd stopped her painting, and then she'd bought this property.

Whenever Bella pressed Mom for details, she morseled out plausible reasons that explained the small changes away. So, Bella just figured whatever it was, her mother was dealing. As long as Bella could remember, her mother had fixed everything. She'd never once said there was a problem she couldn't handle.

Then Dad had died, and Bella became very aware that death was a problem that nothing could repair. No one could do anything to roll back time.

But if her mother died . . .

"Hey!"

Bella sat up and saw a girl about her age walking past a sleeping Rosie down the pier. Balancing irritation and curiosity, Bella rose and met the girl halfway. She glanced toward Rosie, who still slept soundly. All the day's chaos had exhausted the poor dog.

The girl had a shock of curly black hair twisted into a ponytail. She was dressed in a white dress and old brown shoes.

"Hey," Bella said.

"You're new around here."

"My mom and I moved in yesterday."

The girl looked back at the farmhouse. "You live in the Nelsons' old place."

"That's right." Bella couldn't figure out where the girl had come from. "Where do you live?"

The girl smiled. "Nearby."

"Where?"

"In a house," she said, giggling. "How do you like it here?"

"Trying to find the love."

"This place grows on you. In the end, it's kind of hard to leave."

"If you say so."

"I know so."

"What does anyone do around here?" Bella glanced down the barren shoreline.

"All kinds of stuff."

Bella waited for details. "Like?"

"I don't know. You'll figure it out. Maybe Juniper will have an idea."

"How do you know Juniper?"

"Who doesn't know Juniper? She's everyone's friend."

"She's not my friend."

The girl's expression turned curious. "Why do you say that?"

"I don't know her. I don't know anyone here."

"You going to her camp?"

"How do you know about the camp?"

"The one for broken kids? Everyone knows about it. Get ready for lots of sadness." The girl knuckled her eye as if she were crying. "So many tears. Major waterworks."

"I won't be crying," Bella insisted. "Crying doesn't help anything."

The girl nodded. "Boo-hoos are a big, big waste of time. Just like the camp. I wouldn't go if I were you."

"I don't have a choice."

"Everyone has a choice."

Rosie's agitated barking startled Bella. She blinked, realized she'd been lying down. She rose and turned. She didn't see the girl, only her dog standing at the end of the pier. How had the girl just vanished?

"Did you see her, Rosie?"

Bella searched the water below the pier and then the shoreline but found no trace of anyone. No way she could disappear that quickly. What the heck? She glanced back at the beach towel where she'd been lying. Maybe she had dozed and dreamed up the girl? That would make more sense than a disappearing girl or, even better, a ghost.

"Great. I meet one person, and she's not real."

CHAPTER TEN
DANI

Saturday, June 3, 2023
7:15 p.m.

As the sun eased lower in the sky, Dani's body ached in a good way. Unpacking, setting up the kitchen, getting the rugs down, placing and repositioning furniture had been very satisfying. It'd been months since she'd felt as if she'd really accomplished anything of value beyond simply drifting rudderless. Sure, she'd bought the property, but Jackson had brought her vision to life. In many ways, she'd been a bystander.

But today, she had angled the ship into the wind, and for the first time in a long while, she felt a flicker of hope.

When the front doorbell rang, she fished the cash tip out of her pocket for Pizza Delivery Guy. Bella had requested another pizza, with pepperoni this time. Dani didn't mention this wasn't vegetarian or that it was their third pizza for the day.

She opened the door to find a young woman wearing distressed paint-splattered jeans, a ruby-red pizza-shop shirt, and white sneakers. Olive skin and dark hair swept into a ponytail set off sharp hazel eyes.

Pizza Delivery Gal smiled. "Manchester?"

"That's right."

"When I first read the address, I thought it was a mistake. I didn't realize you'd moved in yet. We've all been watching the renovation. Big news. I hear the silos are going to be an art gallery."

Dani smiled, liking the girl's energy. "Silos by the Sound. That's going to be us. We should have the sign up in the next week and be open the following Monday."

The gal shook her head, her expression skeptical. "Nobody around here buys art that much."

Dani took the pizza. "The tourists driving back and forth will. And we're within an hour of plenty of cities. It'll take time for word to spread, but it will."

"Tourists almost never stop here unless it's for gas or maybe the fruit stand down the road."

"Now they'll have a reason. I'll not only have the art, but we're going to have a food truck."

"Sell food?" She nodded. "Good idea. But don't make it too healthy. No one on vacation wants super-healthy food."

Dani chuckled. "That was my thought. Burgers, fried chicken, ice cream. All fan favorites. The food truck should arrive at the end of next week."

"If you're looking for help in the gallery or the food truck, I'd like to apply."

"Really?"

"I'm Naomi Hansen. I've lived here all my life, moved away for a while, and now I'm back. I know everyone."

"Naomi, I'm not ready to take applications now, but could you come back in a week?"

"I sure can."

"How long have you been delivering pizzas?"

"Just started. I love the idea of your gallery. I'm kind of a potter."

"Really?" That explained the glaze and bits of clay on the woman's jeans.

"Nothing fancy."

"We'll set up an interview, and you can bring a sample of your work."

"Seriously?"

She never discouraged an artist. Even when she couldn't represent the work, she cheered it. "Making no promises, but I'd like to see it."

"Awesome."

Dani was certain the gallery and the food truck would be a destination. She handed Naomi thirty bucks. "Keep the change."

"Wow, thanks. See you soon, Ms. Manchester."

"Call me Dani."

The young girl nodded, shoved the tip in her back pocket, and crossed the gravel driveway to a red mid-2000s Toyota.

Dani closed the door. "Bella, pizza!"

Bella was on the dock, no doubt texting or FaceTiming one of her friends. Dani had known many of these girls since they were in preschool. They'd shared birthdays, summer vacations, surf lessons. There'd been divorces within the families, businesses that had failed, job transfers, and of course deaths. As much as she wanted Bella to have her friends, she also understood that their twelve or thirteen years on the planet weren't enough to guide Bella through this time.

The back door opened and slammed closed. Bella's feet thudded across the kitchen floor.

"How's Finn?" Dani asked.

Bella flipped open the box and grabbed a slice of pizza as she sat at the kitchen table. Dani felt a faint spark of normality. This table, which she'd found secondhand in a thrift shop ten years ago, created a sense of home.

"She's fine. She says there's going to be a party next Friday. Can I go?"

"You have camp next week."

"But not on Friday, right? You can drive me to Finn's. It's not that far from here."

It wasn't far. But Dani had hoped more time would pass before they returned to the Outer Banks. "Let's revisit this later in the week."

Bella stilled the slice of pizza aimed at her mouth. "What does that mean?"

"If all goes well, then sure, you can go for the night. Is the party at Finn's house?"

"No, Chelsea's house. She's got the biggest pool."

Chelsea and her family were new to the Outer Banks. The father was a dermatologist whom Dani had met once. Dani had helped Chelsea's mother with design choices during the renovation of a house they'd bought at Martin's Point. "Who else is going to be at the party?"

Bella rolled her eyes. "Just the usual friends, I guess."

She guessed. Which meant she really didn't know. "I'll call her mother."

"You don't have to do that."

She did. She liked Chelsea's mother and wasn't super worried. It was the late-evening distance that troubled her. Two years ago, Dani wouldn't have thought twice about the drive in Friday-evening traffic. She could still make the journey, provided there was no rain. But what if Bella needed her help in the middle of the night or it was raining? A call to Dalton or Ivy would equal a new, higher level of dependence.

"Like I said, we'll talk about it later. Who knows, you might make friends in camp."

"Not likely." Bella bit into the slice.

"You never know."

She picked off a piece of cheese and coiled it around her finger before popping it in her mouth. "I met a girl on the dock. She doesn't seem to like the idea of the camp."

Dani thought about the land around them. The closest house was a mile away. "Where does she live?"

"She said around. She said the camp will be filled with tears and sadness."

"She said that?"

"Yep."

"Did she say anything else?"

"Nope. I look away, turn back, and she was gone. Poof. Vanished. Weird."

"And you said her name was?"

"She didn't say. Seemed okay except for the vanishing act."

Dani couldn't imagine a child walking down the highway alone. Or a child sharing Bella's opinion about a grief camp that was completely new to the area. "Maybe she had to be somewhere."

"Whatever."

"If she comes again, I want to meet her. It's not safe letting a child run around here alone."

"She's my age. Not a child."

Dani avoided the challenge. "Like I said, I want to meet her."

"Sure."

"Maybe Juniper knows her. It's a small town."

"Small. Very, very small."

"That's not a bad thing. The Outer Banks is a small town." Few realized the year-round population was less than thirty thousand residents.

"But that's different. I knew those people."

"And you'll make more friends."

She picked the pepperoni slices off and dropped them on the pizza box. "I don't want more friends."

"Can't have enough."

Bella eyed her mother. "You don't have a lot of friends."

Dani shook her head. "I have friends."

"Just Ivy."

"She's a good friend." She really didn't have time for evenings out.

"When's the last time you had a girls' night out?" Bella asked.

Eight, nine months, no, a year? She and Ivy shared the occasional glass of wine, but Ivy was newly in love with Dalton, and both were consumed with opening the gallery and the food truck. Spare time was a rare thing for them both. "I don't need a girls' night out when I share a roof with the best girl in the world."

Bella rolled her eyes. "That's not healthy, Mom."

That teased a smile. "And when did you become a registered psychologist?"

"I'm smart, Mom." Her pointed, direct gaze was wise beyond her years. "And I keep saying, I'm not a little kid anymore."

She was a kid, and she deserved to enjoy what remained of her childhood. Life came at you fast, and Dani would shield Bella from as much heartache as she could.

"Ivy is coming by in the next couple of days. And she's bringing the food truck next week. Soon, I'll see her all the time."

"That's for business. Not fun."

With the summer season ready to explode with tourists, she well knew life wouldn't slow until late September or October. That suited her just fine. "But that's the way it is here. We work hard in the summer."

Dani had drawn away from her friends, other than Ivy, since her sight had gone on the blink. Maybe the secret was isolating her. It certainly was holding her back from Jackson. But she wasn't in a mood to be analyzed or scrutinized.

"Promise you'll have some fun," Bella said. "If I have to meet new people, then so do you."

Dani cringed. "I'll give it my best shot."

"What's that look mean?" Bella challenged.

A hesitant smile tugged the edges of her lips. "It means yes, I will meet new people."

Everyone coped in different ways. And hers was to draw inward, put her head down, and work. Sure, she'd lost friends and social opportunities along the way, but she'd kept it all together. Would continue to do so. One way or another. Regardless of the cost.

CHAPTER ELEVEN
DANI

Monday, June 5, 2023
7:45 a.m.

Bella, her very intelligent, insightful daughter, was sulking. She wasn't sure if it was hormones, grief, or just being twelve. But as she drove down Route 158 toward the site of Juniper's camp, a heavy silence reverberated in the car.

"It's a beautiful day," Dani said.

Silence.

"Juniper seems like a nice woman."

Nothing.

"I wonder what activities she has planned?" Dani asked.

Nada.

"Maybe space aliens and sea monsters will attack the shores tonight, and we'll fight them off with energy bars and bottled water."

Bella shifted and stared out the window. "Very funny."

Dani slowly released a sigh. At least her daughter was listening. "None of this is funny, Bella. You're not having fun, and I know I'm not. We've both been through some very big changes, and it's going to take time to adjust. But like it or not, we need to make the best of our life now."

Bella tugged at a silver bracelet on her wrist. Matthew had given it to her several years ago, but at the time it had been too big to wear. "I'm not complaining."

"Not with words. But your attitude this morning cuts through joy like a knife through butter."

Bella raised a brow. "It's not that bad, Mom."

"Really?" She'd been tap-dancing around this kid for weeks. Grief was certainly normal, but it had never stopped Dani, and she didn't want it to trap Bella.

Maybe if she'd slept better the last two weeks, or if it hadn't taken so long to find shorts and a shirt after she showered this morning, or if she'd had her second cup of coffee, she might have been able to joke or think of a fun distraction. But with so much to get done in the next two weeks and tension snapping at her like an alligator, she was struggling. The grief books she'd read for Bella could've included her picture at this moment under "What Not to Do."

"Okay, maybe I'm a little moody," Bella said.

"Maybe?" Dani asked.

"I don't want to go. That girl says there'll be crying, and I don't want to cry."

Dani had called Juniper about the girl, but Juniper had never heard of her. "There's a lot I don't want to do, Bella. But we all have to try, okay?"

A sigh shuddered over her lips. "How long is this stupid camp again?"

"The camp is two weeks. Monday through Thursday. Not even full weeks."

Her eyes widened, and she sat straighter. "But what if it's so awful that I break down in tears, or I fall and shatter my arm, or my hair catches on fire?"

"Hair on fire?" Dani nodded. "I would definitely pick you up if your hair caught fire."

"And if I cry?" She ringed her finger under the bracelet.

Dani gripped the steering wheel, wanting to look at her daughter, who was now hidden by her shaded peripheral vision. This camp was going to dredge up difficult emotions. There would be tears. And the idea that her child was going to cry broke her heart. But maybe tears were a good thing. She'd heard they were cleansing.

"You have your phone, Bella." Dani slowed and spotted the gas station that signaled the next left-hand turn. "If it's that terrible, call me."

"Seriously?"

Dani slowed for the upcoming turn and glanced at Bella, who eyed her as if waiting for a "but." "You know I'm always here for you. If it's too much, I'll come get you."

She took another left onto a partly paved road covered in gravel, which popped and crunched under her tires.

Bella's frown softened a fraction, and she eased back into the seat. She shifted her gaze toward the window and stared at the Currituck Sound's waters rushing past.

Had she just caved to her kid? Had her determination to show a little bit of tough love crumbled? Or was her mother's instinct wiser than all the advice books?

"Did you ever cry?" Bella asked.

Dani looked ahead to the long road for signs of the camp. "When?"

Bella tugged at her bracelet. "After your mom died."

Dani remembered the days after her mother's funeral. She was eight. Her father and brother were devastated, and the three of them could barely function. She'd figured out that if she smiled, both her brother and father looked happier. So, when emotions got too much, she washed her face, brushed her hair, and pretended she was okay.

"I've never once seen you cry," Bella challenged.

"I have. I'm just private about that."

Bella twisted toward her. "When did you cry? I mean in the last five years."

"I don't have specific times." After she'd been diagnosed with retinitis pigmentosa, she'd waited until Matthew had picked up Bella for a weekend trip before she'd opened a really good bottle of red wine and polished it off. She'd expected tears to flow, but she couldn't produce one. She drank more. Nothing. No tears. Just a roaring headache when she woke up the next morning. By the time Bella bounded in the back door two days later, she'd masked the lingering headache with aspirin, washed and dried her hair, applied makeup, and dressed in designer jeans, heeled boots, and a camel cropped sweater. In truth, she couldn't remember the last time she'd really cried. Maybe some people just couldn't.

"Why don't you go to the camp?" Bella challenged.

"I have work at the gallery," Dani said. "I have two weeks to get it up and running."

"Seriously? I mean, the work is not going anywhere."

"The clock is ticking. The season opens in less than two weeks. You know I make most of my money during the summer."

"The season will be around until Thanksgiving, Mom. Sounds like a dodge."

Dani spotted the turnoff toward the campsite. She slowed, double-checked for oncoming traffic, and turned. "I'll make a deal. If they give you a homework assignment, I'll do it with you."

Bella's laser attention didn't waver. "No matter what they ask?"

"If you do it, I do it."

"Promise," Bella challenged.

"Promise." She spotted a collection of rainbow-colored balloons tied to a sign that read **CAMP** and followed the arrows to the left.

Gravel turned to dirt at a lot filled with a collection of seven cars. Dani parked, unhooked her seat belt, and got out of the car. Bella lingered in the front seat; then, shaking and muttering, she got out. She crossed in front of the car but stopped short of joining Dani.

"Do you want me to hold that bracelet for you?" Dani asked. "I'd hate for you to lose it."

"I'm not going to lose it," she said. "I'm not a baby."

Pick your battles, Dani. "Okay."

Dani glanced toward the collection of kids, all about Bella's age, give or take a couple of years. There wasn't the kind of excitement she'd seen at Bella's fall soccer camp. The kids weren't grinning, chatting with each other, or running toward the coach, a.k.a. Juniper.

Juniper wore cutoff jeans, a sapphire-blue T-shirt with a peace sign, and sandals, and her red hair pulled up into a riotous ponytail. Her smile was warm and welcoming.

Dani took Bella's hand and, after a firm tug, pulled her toward Juniper. "Juniper. Good to see you again. This is my daughter, Bella."

Juniper grinned at Bella. "Hey, girl. Welcome."

"Hey," Bella said.

Dani looked out toward the blue-gray still waters of the Currituck Sound. Along the shore were a collection of paddleboards. "Looks like you're going to have fun."

Juniper's demeanor was relaxed, joyful almost. "Going to be a terrific day. Bella, are you ready to meet some of the other kids?"

Bella looked back at the children huddling close to their adults. "No one wants to be here."

"I'll change your mind by the end of camp," Juniper said.

Bella shrugged but had the good grace not to utter one of a dozen quips likely rattling in her head.

"I'm off." Dani kissed Bella on the forehead. "See you at two."

Bella tensed and looked as if she'd reach for Dani. But Dani stepped back. It broke her heart, but Bella needed to do this alone.

Bella grabbed her mother's hand, holding it in a white-knuckle grip. Her expression was a mixture of fear, anger, and longing. "Don't be late. Be here at two o'clock sharp."

That face would haunt Dani forever. "I will."

She kissed Bella and turned and walked past the other kids and adults, smiling, shoulders back, and slid behind the wheel of her SUV. She started the engine, turned the radio up, and backed out. Only when the camp faded from the rearview mirror did she stop the car. Tears threatened, but she tipped her head back and willed them away. She raised her sunglasses and carefully dabbed her eyes and the melting mascara under them. Why hadn't she chosen the waterproof brand? She should've seen this coming.

"I'm sorry, Bella. I'm trying to make it better. I'm trying."

Dani retraced her route toward the main road. She hoped a little distance would ease her worries. But as the tires rolled along gravel and then asphalt, the anger and fear she'd long managed clawed at the underside of her skin.

Dani drew in a breath. "It's all going to be fine. It's all going to be fine."

The well-worn mantra frayed badly at the edges, and for the first time in a long time, she wasn't sure if she could actually pull this one off.

Dani drove to the grocery store, knowing they couldn't live on take-out pizza, energy bars, and bottled water forever. She grabbed a cart, swapped sunglasses for her indoor pair, settled her purse in the front seat of the cart, and angled toward the produce section. She'd never shopped here before and discovered, once she was past the produce and meat sections, that it was a bit of a scavenger hunt for the other items. She found Bella's favorite brand of crackers and cookies, but her cereal wasn't on the shelves. After a fruitless second and then third search up and down the cereal aisle, she found a stock clerk and asked.

"We're out of that," the young woman said.

She stared into disinterested green eyes. "Out? As in forever or until next week?"

"I don't know."

"It's important I find that cereal. Does anyone else around here stock it?"

"I don't know."

Of course. "Right. Thanks."

Dani returned to the cereal aisle, picked three other options that Bella might like. She searched for her own brand of coffee creamer, sodas, chips, the makings for sandwiches, and a few frozen pizzas. One day soon, she would get them back on a healthy eating routine, which had always been the norm. But for now, she wanted boxes promising ease and comfort.

Dani loaded up her SUV with her groceries, closed the tailgate, and slid behind the wheel. When she arrived at the gallery, she was grateful she didn't see Jackson's truck. It gave her time to unload and let Rosie out.

She hauled in the bags to the front porch, and as she shoved her key in the lock, Rosie barked. "I'm coming, girl."

The door swung open, and she lugged in the groceries past the dog jumping up and down in her crate. She put the cold food in the fridge and left the rest for after Rosie's break.

Out of the crate, Rosie jumped up and down and followed Dani out the door. At eighteen months, accidents in the house were rare but still very possible.

Rosie peed and then bounded back toward Dani. "What a good girl!" In the kitchen, she fished a rawhide chew stick out of the grocery bag, made herself a fresh pot of coffee, and, as it gurgled, unloaded the last of the supplies.

The shallow pantry had looked suitable before, but as she stacked cans and boxes of cereal inside it, the space vanished pretty quickly. In Duck, she'd had a walk-in pantry. The extra space had been handy, and it also tended to support her habit of buying bulk goods on sale. Unless she considered a major kitchen remodel, she'd need to figure out a different storage system.

She closed the last cabinet, balled up the plastic trash bags, and shoved them in a storage bin under the sink. She poured a cup of coffee into a mug Bella had given her for Mother's Day three years ago, slid out the back door with Rosie on her heels (chew stick in mouth like a cigar), and sat on an aqua Adirondack chair bought from a roadside furniture store. She watched Rosie carry her chew stick around the backyard and then place it down before she dug a hole and buried it in the sandy soil.

She leaned against the chair and tipped her face to the morning sun. Closing her eyes, she soaked up the warmth, hoping to ease the persistent chill in her bones.

Dani and her mom used to sit on their back porch at a picnic table and paint flowers or seascapes. Her mother had been an artist before Dani was born, but two kids, a husband, and a family business left her little time to create.

Long before she'd told Dani about her illness, her mother had quit the job at the family company. She carved out more time for painting, lying on blankets, counting clouds, and watching the evening light sparkle on the sound.

"Time to wrap up for today. We need to put up the paints and get cleaned up." Her mother's voice had softened to barely a whisper. *"Dalton needs to get to a football team meeting, and we need to pick up dinner. Hamburgers or pizza?"*

Those had been the dinner choices for months. Eight-year-old Dani had grown to hate pizza but didn't complain. "Both are good."

Her mother smiled. Dani glanced at her unfinished painting. It was supposed to be the ocean surrounded by sand, and the M's in the sky were seagulls.

"Five more minutes, Mom." She added another M-shaped seagull.

Her mother leaned close to Dani and inspected her work. "It's beautiful. When it's finished, we'll hang it up."

Mom looked pale and tired. Dani should've let her rest, but she didn't want this moment to end. "I don't want to stop. It's almost finished."

Her mother pulled the brush from her hand and dunked it in the mug filled with muddled paint water. "Spoken like a true artist. Never satisfied."

Dani rose, frustrated. "It won't be the same."

Her mother pulled Dani into the half bathroom, grabbed a washrag, and swabbed her face and hands with it.

"I'm fine!" Dani tried to wiggle free. "No one cares if I have paint on me."

Her mother kissed her on the cheek, grinning as she brushed a lock of her hair back. "You look like your dad when you make that face. So determined. Focused. Two peas in a pod."

The comparison made her proud. "I look like you too."

"A little of me is in there, but you're mostly Daddy." Mom smiled. "Like he spit you out himself."

Dani twisted her fingers around a lock of her mother's long hair. "How are you and me alike?"

Her mother winked. "We're survivors, Dani. No matter how many knocks we take, we get up and keep going. You especially can do anything, be anything."

"How do you know?" Her mother's perfume drifted around her. She and Dalton had bought Mom the bottle last year.

Mom took Dani's hand and guided her out of the bathroom toward the back door. She grabbed her purse, pulled her outside, and locked the door.

"I thought you were supposed to be resting," Dani said.

"There's plenty of time for resting later. Now it's time to do some of my favorite things."

Dalton stood by the car dressed in his football T-shirt and jeans. He waved them forward, his face scrunched and impatient.

"We're going to the football meeting too?" Dani complained.

"And then the three of us are getting ice cream afterward," Mom said.

"Before dinner?" Dani asked.

"Before dinner," Mom said as she slid behind the wheel. "Buckle up, kids, this is going to be the best afternoon ever."

Rosie's barking startled Dani from sleep. She blinked at the bright sunshine and realized she'd drifted off.

"Mom," she said.

It had been a long time since she'd dreamed of her mother. In the months after her mother's death, the best part of the day happened in the first few seconds after she opened her eyes. In that tiny fraction of time, she still believed her mother was alive and her life was normal. For a second, the weight of grief lifted, and she could pull in a deep breath. She always lay as still as she could, clinging to the sensation. But the tighter she gripped the past, the faster it trickled through her fingers like water, until she was left holding the emptiness of her fresh grief.

Rising from the chair, she called Rosie, and the two went back inside. She stared at the collection of neatly labeled boxes filled with essentials. So much stuff. How much equipment was required for basic living? She doubted all the cups and plates would fit in the kitchen cabinets, and that translated into more triage.

She dug a roll of cabinet shelf liner out of the top box and spent the next hour carefully measuring and cutting the self-adhesive strips. Smoothing the light, colorless paper was calming, and the small task restored a sense of control. She continued down the line of cabinets until they were all lined. As she reached for the first kitchen box, she glanced at her phone. No call from Bella, which, of course, she would've heard because the ringer's volume was turned all the way up.

A half hour into unpacking glasses, the sound of Jackson's truck rumbled across the graveled lot. Rosie's ears perked up. Dani had always brought Rosie with her when she came to check the work at the gallery, and the dog had grown familiar with the sound of the black truck's engine.

Rosie ran to the front door and barked as she wagged her tail. Dani settled a stack of white plates in the cabinet and checked her reflection in a mirror leaning against the living room wall. She smoothed a mascara smudge from under her eye and, phone in back pocket, let the dog out.

Rosie bounded across the lot toward Jackson as he opened the tailgate of his truck bed. He knelt down and scratched the dog between her ears. "Hey, Rosie. You get Bella off to camp?"

Dani closed the distance between them. "I left Rosie here. I was worried if Bella had Rosie, she'd never get out of the car."

"But she did?" he asked.

"Under protest."

"Juniper will take good care of her."

"She seems very kind."

"She is," Jackson said.

"How do you know Juniper?" Dani asked.

As he straightened, his eyes never left her face as he spoke. "Juniper has an older sister my age. I was married to her."

Jackson had had a wife. Not a crazy notion, but still the bit of information made her a little jealous of Juniper and very curious about the life Jackson had lived before this one.

"Cathy and I divorced two years ago," he said. "It's a long story, but we parted as friends. She's living in Raleigh, remarried and expecting a baby."

Did his voice shift a little when he said "baby"? Was that a sore point for him? Was he envious of his ex-wife moving on?

She was more curious than she had a right to be. She'd been open about Matthew and Bella, but her big information nugget remained hidden. "Fair enough. Sounds like she's doing well."

"She is." He stood, straightening to his full six foot two inches. "Juniper spoke to Cathy the other day."

"Nothing like a little sister to share family information. I don't know how many times I tattled on Dalton to my parents."

"Juniper likes to keep me in the loop." His keys rattled softly in his hands as if he were nervous about this discussion.

"Why? Hoping she can reunite Cathy and you?"

"I think on some level, yes." Hints of sadness threaded around his words. "The divorce was as hard on Juniper as it was on Cathy and me. No winners the day we signed the final papers."

She waited a beat, wondering if he'd elaborate; when he didn't, she said, "Matthew's family didn't have any trouble with our divorce. His mother was glad to see us break up."

"Why's that?" he asked softly.

Her throat went dry. "I ruined her son's future."

"Takes two to tango, and Bella looks like a blessing."

"If you ask my mother-in-law, Matthew could do no wrong." She tasted the bitterness rising in her throat. It had never been like her to dwell on the divorce. "I'm not sure what brought that up. Too much information."

His gaze settled on her. "Never. You can tell me anything."

"Good to know." No prizes for Most Open and Honest.

He shifted his stance. "I have another two days' work to go, and then you'll be ready to stock."

"Terrific. I've got a few hours of unpacking to do, and then it'll be time to get Bella."

He held her gaze. "I didn't tell you about Cathy because she's in the past. I would've gotten around to it, but you've had your hands full."

"It's really okay, Jackson."

Wary eyes speared her. "Is it? Because sometimes it's hard to tell with you. You're always positive." Unasked questions skimmed under his words.

Her smile slipped. "And that's a bad thing?"

"It can be if it's masking more. It's okay to let the walls down sometimes, Dani."

Maybe it was. There were times when she wished she'd been honest with him from the moment she'd realized she liked him. *Dani Manchester, divorced, twelve-year-old daughter, major vision loss looming, a Taurus.* But she hadn't. And now the walls were growing so thick around her that she feared she'd never break through.

She kissed him lightly on the lips. "I know."

CHAPTER TWELVE
BELLA

Monday, June 5, 2023
10:00 a.m.

Death by a thousand cuts. Bella had heard that phrase once when her father had been arguing with a banker on the phone. Her father was trying to get a short-term loan so he could hire more waitstaff. He'd complained about the rising cost of shipping, food, and gasoline. "It's a death by a thousand cuts, Sam," he'd said. "These days everything is conspiring to ruin me."

This entire camp experience was depressing. Everyone was quiet and closed off and looked as if they'd like to be somewhere else. Juniper had all kinds of energy, and she was doing her best to cheer everyone up, but how did you make a camp about dead people fun?

The other seven kids were about her age. They'd had to play several name games first thing, so she knew enough about each. Seth, age thirteen, had lost his older brother to leukemia. He'd been a demon on skateboards. Twelve-year-old Reggie's mother had died of cancer last year. Reggie said she liked to bake cookies and loved *American Idol*. Billy, ten, lost the grandfather who had been helping his mother raise him. High school–bound Sara's dad had died last year. He'd had a stroke. Everyone said he was too young, but that didn't stop him from dying. Jenna and Nick, twins, both eleven, said their older brother died of some kind of illness. And Penny, thirteen, reported in a low voice that her aunt, who was more like a sister, had been killed in a car accident.

When it was Bella's turn to tell her story, she sat straighter and squared her shoulders. "Bella Peterson, age twelve. Dead dad."

The kids had stared at her, waiting for her to expand as they all had, but she sat silent.

Dead. Deader. Deadest. That girl had been right. They were a sad, sad lot of kids.

"Would you like to say anything else?" Juniper asked.

"No. That covers it," Bella said.

"Okay, then on to the first exercise," Juniper said.

And now, after an hour filled with miserable stories, it was time for arts and crafts.

They all sat in the shelter at two picnic tables. Juniper handed out paper to all eight kids and then set a jar of multicolored pens in the center of each table. "We're going to write a letter to our lost loved ones."

Bella studied the blank page and then reached for a black marker. She began to draw small circles in the center.

"What are we supposed to say?" Bella asked.

"Anything you want," Juniper said. "Relive a special time together, ask them questions, tell them things you'd wished you'd said before. Anything you want."

What was the point in writing to *dead* people? There wasn't enough postage in the world to reach where the letters needed to go.

Bella glanced at the small circles floating on the huge blank page. She had no idea what to say to her father. "Do we have to share these letters?"

"You do not," Juniper said. "No one will read it but you."

Reggie wrote today's date in neat, swirling script. Reggie had curly black hair pulled back in a ponytail, pale skin, and big brown eyes that reminded Bella of a sad rabbit.

Bella leveled her shoulders, which kept dipping forward. She didn't want to look like a sad rabbit. She wanted to look in charge, brave, like her mom. What was it that Mom said? *Feeling bad just gets in the way of a good day.*

Reggie gripped the ballpoint pen and dropped her gaze to the paper. She wrote in swirling cursive, *Dear Mom.*

Dear Mom.

Bella's chest tightened, and the tight panic balls rattled around in her belly. Losing her dad had been terrible, but to lose Mom would be the end of her life. Her mother took care of everything. She never complained about long work hours or giving up girls' weekend trips so she could be at Bella's volleyball games. She was always smiling (to the point of annoying sometimes). She encouraged Bella. Told her she loved her, not just in words and texts like Dad. She was *there.*

"You lost your mom." Some of Bella's anger thinned.

Reggie nodded as she slowly raised her gaze from the page. "Nine months ago. Cancer."

"I'm sorry." The words carried a hefty weight.

Reggie didn't smile or pretend she was fine as she looked at Bella. "Yeah, I am too. And you lost your dad?"

"Car accident. Four months ago."

"That's bad. Car accidents are sudden and quick. Unexpected. At least that's what my dad says. He's a truck driver, and he's seen a few car accidents. When death comes quick, you don't get a chance to say goodbye."

Reggie wasn't tiptoeing around Bella like everyone else. "Yeah, but cancer is long and slow. Kind of like pulling off a Band-Aid a millimeter at a time."

Reggie drew a daisy in the top-right corner of her letter. She carefully filled in the rounded center and shadowed each petal. "But it gave us a chance to say things. She made a videotape for me, and I can watch it whenever I want. Helps me remember what she looked and sounded like."

"Do you watch the videos a lot?" She had a few videos of her dad on her Instagram page. Making pasta, dropping sliced potatoes into the deep fryer, and folding a napkin into a swan. There was also a brief video in her texts. *"Hey, squirt, I'm in my new kitchen. Love the lights. I'll see you soon."*

Nothing deep or touching, but that video helped her remember the sound of her dad's voice and his smile.

"I watched it once," Reggie said. "I'll watch it again one day, but I need more time."

"Where do you live?" Bella asked.

"In the country, a few miles off Route 158," she said. "Dad needs the space to park his rig."

"My mom and I just moved here. Mom bought the silos and the house next to them."

Reggie's eyes registered interest. "I know that place. My mom loved the silos. Said they were her happy landmark when she drove home from Norfolk and her cancer doctor. And my neighbor, Ms. Nelson, used to live on the property when she was a girl."

"I should tell Mom. She's all into the history of the place. Maybe you could see it sometime. It looks pretty different."

"Thanks. I'd like to see it."

"Did your dad bring you here?" Bella asked.

"No. My neighbor, Ms. Nelson. Dad's driving on a long-haul run. He's got lots of bills to pay and drives whenever he can. I stay with Ms. Nelson at night."

"Is that bad?"

A faint frown furrowed Reggie's forehead. "Feels weird not being in my house and my own bed."

"I've my own bed, but in the new house it feels really weird. I don't know where anything is. Last night, I woke up to go to the bathroom, and I walked into a wall." Her complaint felt hollow. At least she was with her mother. "What're you going to say to your mother in the letter?"

"That I still love her. That I miss her. That I wish we could bake cookies together again," Reggie said. "What about you?"

Bella couldn't put her real feelings on the page because what was simmering in her felt wrong. Ever since Mom had started cleaning out the house in Duck, her anger toward her father had been growing. If he'd just been more careful . . . burning the candle at both ends, as her mom used to say. "I don't know."

"Juniper says to write about what you feel. There are no good or bad feelings."

Bella grimaced. "I'm not so sure she means that."

"I think she does," Reggie said as she dropped her gaze back to her letter. "Sadness is not totally bad. It means the person you lost mattered."

"Who told you that?" Bella asked.

"Ms. Nelson. She's always saying stuff like that. She's kind of weird, but I like her." A smile teased Reggie's lips. "She reads fortunes."

"For real?"

"Yeah."

"Has she read yours?" Bella asked.

Reggie grinned. "She keeps saying I'm going to have a bright and happy future."

Bella decided she didn't want to know her future. The past and present were enough trouble. She gripped her pen and pressed the ballpoint into the paper. Her bracelet slid down her wrist. *Dear Dad.*

She didn't want to tell her father her true feelings. She never did. All the times he texted at the last minute and said he was hung up at work, she'd always told him it was okay. She said she understood when she didn't. This time, she didn't understand anything.

> Dear Dad,
> Sometimes you make me mad. You always ~~make~~ made big promises, and you weren't good at keeping them. You swore you weren't tired when you called that last day. You said you were fine. You promised we would make pasta again. And then you ruined it. You crashed your car and died. And I'm not happy. I love you, but I don't like you anymore.
> Bella

Her heartbeat raced when she set down her pen and quickly folded the paper in half twice. She clutched the small paper square and crunched it into a tight ball. Reggie signed her letter with a balloon heart before creasing the page into three neat folds.

Juniper walked over to their picnic table. "How's it going, Bella?"

"Just fine. I wrote a letter to my dad and filled it with lots of nice things."

"Is your letter that ball of paper in your hand?" Juniper's voice was soft, nice.

"Yes."

"Okay." She held out a big brown paper bag. "Drop it in here."

Heat rose in her face as she thought about anyone looking at her letter. "What're you going to do with it? You said you weren't going to read it."

"I'm not reading the letters. And I'll give them all back to you next week after you write your second letter." Juniper's voice always sounded like a smile.

"We have to write another letter?" In her peripheral vision, she watched Reggie draw a heart on the outside flap.

"Here's my letter, Miss Juniper," Reggie said.

"Thanks, Reggie," Juniper said.

Bella bet Reggie had dotted all her *i*'s with hearts. "What are we going to do with all these letters?"

"I'll let you know later this afternoon," Juniper said.

"Can't you just tell us?" Bella challenged.

"One step at a time." Juniper shook the bag.

Bella dropped hers inside. If anyone read that letter, she would die.

"Are you girls ready to try the paddleboards in the sound? It'll be fun."

"I've never been on a paddleboard," Reggie said.

"I bet Bella could help you," Juniper said.

"I can do that." As long as they weren't talking about feelings, Bella could deal.

As Juniper left to collect the remaining letters, Reggie looked toward the sound's calm waters. "I can't swim very well."

"I can. Don't worry. Besides, the sound is only about three feet deep near the shore. If you fall, just stand up."

"Seriously?"

"Yeah. I got this." It felt good to be in control of at least one thing.

Bella hoisted her backpack, and the two girls walked to the dressing room. Bella changed into a pink bikini with white polka dots. Reggie's suit was a plain navy blue.

Outside, Bella picked a pink paddleboard that had sparkles embedded in the paint. She knelt and unzipped her backpack and pulled out her board shoes.

"Mom said I might need these. What size shoe do you wear?" Bella asked.

"Eight."

"Good."

"Do I put these on?"

"Yes. They'll help you grip the board."

"What're you going to wear?" Reggie asked.

Bella tugged off her sandals. "I'll be barefoot. I've done it a million times."

"Are you sure?" Reggie looked at the thin pink shoes.

"Yep."

Hefting the board and paddle, Bella walked down the small sandy beach to the water that gently lapped over her toes.

"Bella, do you have this?" Juniper asked as she helped Seth choose a board.

"Got it covered, Miss Juniper," Bella said.

Bella laid the board on the water, stepped into the sound, and walked in up to her knees. Mud squished between her toes. She looked back at Juniper and gave her a thumbs-up. "It'll be fine."

"I don't want to stand on the board," Reggie said. "I'll fall."

A memory of her mother teaching her paddleboarding floated up. "Then you can sit on the board. We'll start with sitting."

Reggie waded slowly into the water toward Bella. "You'll hold the board?"

When Bella was on the water, helping Reggie, life felt half-normal. "Don't worry. I got you."

Reggie chewed her bottom lip as she swung her leg over the side of the board. It wobbled once, but Bella steadied it with her grip. "Did I tell you I can barely swim?"

"You did. And if you fall, just stand up. It's not deep."

Reggie looked at Bella's legs, covered only to her knees. "We're not going to go far, are we?"

"We'll stay close to shore." On the water, Bella had all the patience in the world.

"Good."

Bella pushed the board gently forward several yards, and when Reggie tensed and grabbed it, she carefully turned the nose back toward the shore, just as her mom had done with her when she was about four or five. "See, not that scary."

Reggie still gripped the board's edges. "Are you sure it's not too deep?"

Bella held up her hands. "I'm standing, right?"

"What about biting fish?" Reggie asked. "Turtles or snakes?"

"I don't think we have those in the Currituck Sound, and if we do, I'll chase them away."

"Rats can swim, right?" Reggie asked.

"I guess. I never thought about rats. I guess if we're going to borrow trouble, we should also be looking out for sharks, whales, and maybe big snapping turtles."

Reggie's face twisted with worry. "Are you kidding?"

"Of course I am. I'm the one standing in the water. Whose legs are going to get eaten first?"

Reggie looked under the water's surface to Bella's bare feet. "Yours."

"Exactly."

Reggie squeezed the board with her legs. "But . . ."

Bella turned the board away from shore and toward the sound. "Stop borrowing trouble, Reggie. I don't know about you, but I've got plenty of troubles on my plate, and I'm not adding any more."

"Yeah," Reggie said. "But I sure don't want to meet a rat."

To prove her point, Bella dunked her head back into the water and dipped her hair under the surface. The water felt good in the hot sun and cooled her face. As she wiped the water from her eyes, she said, "No missing ears, nose, or lips. Rat bellies must be full up today."

A smile flickered on Reggie's lips. "You might be crazy, Bella. Crazy in a good way, I mean."

"That's probably true." They moved up and down the shoreline, but Reggie was slow to relax. "I met a girl who lives near me. I didn't catch her name. Dark hair. Pale."

"There aren't many kids where I live in the country near you."

"She speaks in a soft voice. She knows Juniper and about this camp."

As Reggie puzzled over the mystery girl, she relaxed into the board. "Did she just move here?"

"She said she's been here for a long time."

"If she's been here a long time, we would've gone to the same schools. I do know an Ann Mitchell. She's fifteen."

"That's a pretty basic name. Maybe it is that Ann girl."

"I can ask Ms. Nelson. She knows everyone," Reggie said.

Her legs moved back and forth under the water.

"Okay. Not a big deal. I was just curious."

Sara stood on her board and paddled by. Her long, lean body was relaxed, just like most of the kids who grew up on the water. Sara smiled and gave Reggie a thumbs-up. Sara must have recognized Reggie from school, though Bella would bet that, given they were in different grades, Reggie and Sara hadn't hung out. Death and Juniper's "Club Broken Kid" had brought them together.

Bella moved Reggie and her board around the sound's smooth waters. She handed her the paddle, and Reggie slowly pushed through the water.

"Do you miss your dad?" Reggie asked.

Sadness tweaked the nerves under Bella's skin, and this short normal moment ended. But she didn't mind Reggie asking. She was one of the few who had the right. "Sure. I didn't spend a lot of time with him, but I miss what we had."

"Why didn't you see him?" Reggie asked.

"He was always working. He owned restaurants."

"My dad works a lot. I don't see him much either. Dad says it's hard to get ahead."

"My dad said the same thing. He was so afraid of falling behind." Bella adjusted Reggie's grip on the paddle and stepped back, not mentioning that she'd let go of the board. She watched as Reggie paddled along the shore. "Looks good, Han Solo."

"What?" Reggie looked back, saw the distance she'd put between herself and Bella, and frowned. "You let go."

"I did. Looks like you're doing pretty well."

Reggie turned the paddleboard around and eased it back toward Bella. "Do I have to stand?"

"Not if you like sitting."

"Promise?" Reggie asked.

"That's a silly promise to ask. Why would I force you to stand?"

"Isn't that what happens next in paddleboarding?"

There was enough in life they couldn't control, but this they could. "Not if you don't want to," Bella said.

"Promise?"

"Promise."

CHAPTER THIRTEEN
DANI

Monday, June 5, 2023
1:00 p.m.

The rain clouds came suddenly, sweeping over the sound in whistling gusts. The app on Dani's phone had warned of bad weather, but not until later today. She'd planned her day around the bright-yellow sunshine icons. Thick raindrops hit the front porch, splashing against the side of the house, and puddled quickly in the driveway.

Dani checked the time on her phone. She wasn't supposed to pick up Bella for another hour, so there was time for the storm to blow through and for the skies to clear.

The narrowing of her sight was annoying, and she had to be careful when it came to her periphery, but if she was careful, she could function pretty well. However, driving in the rain was too much to risk in a new place with unfamiliar twists and turns in the road.

As she turned back toward unpacking the last of the kitchen boxes, her phone rang. Bella. She'd survived five hours of camp. Better than what Dani would've thought this morning.

"Bella, is everything all right?" Dani asked.

"It's raining."

"I know."

"That means no more water sports, and now we're going to sit in the warehouse in a *circle* and talk about *feelings*."

Her daughter grunted the last word like an oath. "What's wrong with that?"

Bella dropped her voice. "That's not what *we* do."

"We?"

"You and me," she said, exasperated. "We don't whine or complain. We just brush our hair and get on with life."

Dani stilled as she thought about all the times she'd been frustrated with tight deadlines, artists who didn't show, or Matthew missing a visitation or a support check. In times like that, she touched up her makeup and brushed her hair. Did she feel better? Sometimes. Other times the knot twisted tighter.

She'd never said anything to Bella about why she did what she did, but clearly her child had been watching. "That's not always a good thing."

"You do it all the time, Mom," Bella said.

Dani cleared her throat. "Well, maybe we both can do better."

"Better does not mean sitting in a sharing circle," she groaned. "Save me, or I'm walking home."

Bella had never given her an ultimatum like this. "You're not walking home."

"Yes, I am." Determination echoed in her voice.

Dani angled her head back and forth, breaking up the growing tension. "Put Juniper on the phone."

"Fine, but you're telling her I'm leaving."

"Bella—"

"Hello, Dani?" Juniper said.

"What's going on?" Dani asked.

Juniper hesitated, and Dani could imagine her walking away from Bella. "Bella had a good morning. She's great when it comes to the physical activities. But she's not a fan of the emotional exercises."

Dani drew in a breath as the rain tapped against the roof. A part of her wanted to swoop in for the rescue and save her little girl from pain. But another, wiser part understood Bella had to stick this out. "What do you suggest?"

"Maybe we compromise. It's raining, and no need to rush out. Besides, camp will be over at two. Maybe take your time getting here."

But would the rain stop in the next hour? "That sounds very reasonable."

"Bella's made a friend, Reggie, and they've had a good morning. Your daughter's situation is not as dire as she makes it out. I don't force anyone to talk about feelings."

Dani pressed fingertips to her temple. "Maybe you can push her a little. It would be good for her."

"I'll get Bella to participate in activities, but I'll go light on the emotional exercises. Maybe we'll do a little karaoke."

Bella could do so many things well, but she'd inherited Dani's tin ear. "Sounds like a plan. I'll be there when I can."

"I'll tell Bella, okay?"

"Deal."

When the call ended, Dani braced for another return call from Bella. But when nothing came through after five minutes, she fully shifted her attention to the weather. The wind and rain were swirling faster.

The drive to camp took fifteen to twenty minutes. That gave her at least thirty before she had to sweat the trip. Shit. This was not good. What if Bella had needed her now? What if she were forced to race out in the rain or, worse, at night?

She smoothed her fingers over her ponytail as she walked to the window and looked out toward Jackson's truck. She could still justify hiding her vision issues. Why create tension in a relationship that was destined to end, right? Jackson likely wasn't thinking long term either.

He had boats to sail. More of the world to explore. No reason to spoil what they had with a problem that was far off in the distant future.

Lightning cracked. The sky blackened.

She couldn't count on Jackson forever, but she could use his help today. What was a small favor between friends?

She dialed his number.

"Dani." He sounded a little breathless, and she wondered if he'd nailed the last bit of shiplap on the wall.

She turned from the window and pressed her fingers to her temple. On the Outer Banks, Ubers were slow, but they were available. Out here on this end of the county, she doubted she'd see a driver in under two hours. "Don't suppose you could do me a favor?"

"Sure, what is it?"

"Bella needs to be picked up at camp." Rain pooled in large puddles by the front door.

"Everything all right?" His tone had sharpened.

"She's balking at the feelings portion of the program."

He chuckled. "The hardest part."

"For her, yes." She scrambled for one of the excuses she'd used when she couldn't drive. "Look, my car doesn't do well in the rain. Would you mind driving me to go get her?"

He hesitated as if untangling why a late-model car didn't perform in the rain. Most people took her excuses at face value and didn't ask too many questions. "Sure."

"About fifteen minutes?"

"I'll pull up front."

"You're the best. Thank you."

Dani's heart squeezed with a feeling she'd never felt toward a man before. She wasn't sure what it was but reasoned it probably had something to do with her being out of practice with men. Jackson had been her first boyfriend in over twelve years, and let's face it, she was navigating uncertain waters.

Dani had mustered a temporary reprieve. Today. Next time, and there would be a next time, she would require another excuse, another story to simply explain away her inability to drive. Maybe he'd think she was a bit of a kook, but that would be better than the truth.

Fifteen minutes later the black truck pulled up, and Dani explained to Rosie she'd be right back before she dashed out the door. Rain droplets pelted her, and her sneakers splashed in puddles as she raced to the truck. Inside, she brushed the rain from her arms.

"Sorry, I'm getting your car wet," she said.

Jackson leaned back in his seat, his arm resting on the steering wheel. He didn't look annoyed or rushed but amused. "This truck has taken more abuse than a little rain."

She clicked her seat belt as she smiled. She'd ridden in the truck a few times. After she'd first kissed him on the boat, he'd kissed her for the first time in this truck. "Thanks, again."

"Happy to help." His gaze lingered a beat, and then he shifted the truck into drive. "Your car doesn't drive in the rain?"

"It slides sometimes," she lied. "And I'm more nervous about driving in general since Matthew's death." That part was true. She was far more aware of the dangers lingering in the shadows edging her vision.

"Have you had a mechanic look at it? I know a guy."

"I will, I will." Piling a lie on a lie was a shaky foundation for this house of cards. "How are the final finishes coming?"

"Almost complete. I'll be sorry to end this project. Juniper said it would be an interesting challenge, and she was right."

"Don't you miss the open water?" she asked. "I would've thought after being tied up indoors on a job, you'd be eager to get back outside in the fresh air."

"Sure, I miss it a little, but for the last few years, I'd been making deliveries nonstop. I needed a break. Having my feet on dry land is a welcome change. But that invitation for you and Bella to join me on a sailing trip is still open."

"It sounds amazing." She'd craved adventure since she was in high school, but parenthood and life kept getting in the way. Now Jackson was offering it. But instead of grabbing this chance with both hands, she was weighted down by the reasons why traveling now made no sense. "I still haven't told Bella about us."

He slowed at a stop sign and looked directly at her. "I'll leave that to you. I know her life has been turned upside down."

"I need to tell her. I would've by now if not for Matthew's death, the renovation, and the move."

"I get it. I do."

She searched for any traces of impatience but heard none. "You're very tolerant with me."

He shifted into first gear and took a left-hand turn. "This is new territory for me too. I've never dated a woman with a child."

She laughed. "I've never made it past the first date."

"You've never dated since your divorce?" He sounded surprised.

"Really ever since high school. Matthew and I didn't date. We had sex, I got pregnant, and we married. And after the divorce, I was swamped with taking care of Bella and working. Having her made it harder for me to stay out late or travel on a whim. And don't get me wrong, I'm not sorry for any of my choices." If this bit of news triggered worries for him, then there was no point addressing the real shark circling in the water.

"She's a great kid, because of you."

"I have moments when I think so, and then I worry that I'm messing up her life."

"Guilt is standard-issue gear for parents."

She smiled. "Thanks for that."

He took the turn onto the camp road, past balloons that had deflated in the big rain. Tires splashed in the ruts filled with water. The rain was slowing, but she was glad now she hadn't driven.

"Juniper said this is your land?" Dani asked.

He shrugged. "I own a good bit of property up this way."

"Any grand plans for the warehouse?" she asked.

Jackson shook his head. "Seemed like a good investment. Land prices were low at the time, and I'm toying with the idea of building bigger boats."

"And then?"

"Keep building, selling, and sailing boats."

Jackson parked in the lot next to the warehouse. It was filling with other cars, suggesting that Bella wasn't the only child struggling the first day.

She adjusted her glasses. "I'll be right back."

"I'll be here."

Out of the car, her foot landed in a puddle. Drawing in a breath, she hurried across the lot and pulled open one of the double glass doors to the warehouse.

She found all the children standing in the middle of the huge warehouse holding a large round parachute. Juniper and the children were waggling their arms up and down as a kickball in the center bounced from side to side.

Bella was on the end farthest from the door, and though she wasn't laughing, she looked mildly amused. The ball flew up in the air, skipped off the parachute, and bounced on the floor. It rolled toward Dani. She picked it up and tossed it toward Juniper. Thankfully, Juniper caught it.

"Mom!" Bella dropped her section of parachute and ran toward Dani. "You took forever," she said in a somber tone. "The camp is almost over."

"The rain held me up."

Bella raised her eyebrow. "Seriously? I had to sing 'Feelings' in front of people because of the rain."

"You have a beautiful voice," Dani lied.

Juniper crossed the shelter toward Dani. "We'll be winding up for the day in about fifteen minutes. Why don't you stick around while we wrap up?"

Dani nodded. "Sure. Go on and finish up."

Bella glared up at her. "Mom, I would like to go."

"Fifteen minutes won't matter one way or the other," Dani said.

"Mommmm."

"Get back to the circle, kid," Dani said. "I'll be right here."

"Not fair."

"Life. What can I say? It's not fair." Dani's mom had used that saying a million times, generally when Dani was complaining about broccoli on her plate, an eight-o'clock bedtime, or a scuffed pair of shoes.

Bella rejoined the circle and sat next to a young girl with black curly hair pulled into a ponytail. The girl said something to Bella, and her daughter actually smiled. A miracle.

She texted Jackson that they'd be out in fifteen, and he sent back, Take your time.

Juniper held up a mason jar. "Tomorrow, we'll be decorating jars. And if you have anything from home that reminds you of your person, then bring it."

A boy with blond hair raised his hand. "Like what?"

"What is important to you and the person you lost? What reminds you of your brother, Seth?"

Seth shrugged. "Baseball cards?"

"If that's what reminds you of him, then it's perfect," Juniper said.

"What about charms?" a girl with red hair asked.

"Charms are good, Penny. There's no right or wrong answer. But take some time this afternoon and think about it. Make it special. We'll talk about our items at circle time tomorrow, and then we'll decorate the jars."

"What if I can't find something?" Bella asked.

Juniper shook her head and grinned. "You'll find something."

"What if I don't?" Bella challenged.

"It's up to you," Juniper said.

Bella rose and said something to the girl next to her. The girls moved toward Dani. "Mom, can we give Reggie a ride home? Her dad is at work, and her neighbor is supposed to pick her up, but she's running late."

"That's okay, Bella," Reggie said. "I don't mind waiting."

"I'd be happy to drive you home, Reggie," Dani said. "Where do you live?"

"On Camden Road."

Fifteen minutes north of the silos. "That's close enough. Text your dad and neighbor and tell them you're riding with us while I talk to Juniper."

"Thanks, Mrs. Peterson."

"Call me Dani." Dani didn't mention that she didn't share her daughter's last name. She crossed to Juniper and explained the situation. "I'll see that she gets home."

Juniper nodded slowly. "Reggie's father is having trouble dealing with his wife's death. He hasn't been as attentive to Reggie. And he's working insane hours to pay the bills. Her neighbor, Ms. Nelson, is quite the character but has a good soul. In fact, if you see Ms. Nelson, ask her what she knows about your silos. Her family used to own them."

"I will."

"Maybe she'll even read your fortune."

"I'm not sure I can take too much future right now. My hands are full with the present."

Juniper chuckled. "Don't be surprised if Ms. Nelson offers some insights."

"Noted."

"Bella has been looking out for Reggie all morning," Juniper said.

Dani's annoyance with Bella eased. "She can be quite the protector. Jackson and I will get Reggie home."

"Jackson is with you?"

"My car doesn't run well in the rain." The lie slipped automatically. One day she would toss out one too many untruths, and it would trip her up.

"I'm glad he's helping," Juniper said. "It's good for him. He can be a bit of a hermit."

"Not today. We've dragged him away from his work."

Juniper laughed. "He'll live."

After Dani had collected the girls, Reggie confirmed with her father, who said it was okay for Dani to drive his daughter home. Dani offered to talk to Reggie's father, but Reggie said he'd already hung up. When they stepped out of the warehouse, the rain had stopped, and the sun cut through the clouds.

"Why is Jackson driving us home?" Bella asked.

"Because I asked."

Bella glanced at Dani, her gaze appraising her closely, but she guarded the thoughts rattling in her brain. She opened the back door. "Hey, Jackson."

"Bella. How was camp?"

"Not terrible. This is my friend Reggie. Can you drive her home too? Her dad can't come get her."

"Sure, I'd be glad to. Seat belts."

Dani slid into the front seat as the girls clicked their seat belts and closed the back doors. "Thank you."

"No problem." He glanced in the rearview mirror at Reggie but said nothing as he pulled out of the parking lot. He took a right on the main road and said, "Girls, how about pizza? I'm starving."

Bella looked at Reggie, who nodded. "That would be great. I don't eat meat."

"I think we can work with that," Jackson said.

Another pizza. Dani would've said something if the girls didn't look so excited. She leaned toward him. "You sure?"

"I'm hungry, and I've never met a kid who couldn't eat pizza even if they were full."

"Let me pay for the pizza," Dani said.

"On me, Manchester."

So far, they hadn't sailed into turbulent emotional waters but had lingered in the port of Friends with Benefits. But for the second time today, something inside her softened toward him. And for the first time ever, she could see herself falling for the guy.

On a scale of one to ten, ten being Terrible, that realization ranked an eleven.

CHAPTER FOURTEEN
DANI

Monday, June 5, 2023
3:30 p.m.

Reggie's house looked lovely. It was a small brick one-story rancher with a graveled driveway that arched by a porch stretching across the house. The grass was cut, and there were flowers sprouting in a small garden encircling a large oak tree. Looked pretty normal. But she knew well enough that no one could judge the well-being of a family based on a front lawn.

"I'd like to meet your dad when he gets back into town," Dani said.

"He'll be back later in the week," Reggie said.

"Is there anyone at home now?" Dani asked.

"No, but that's no big deal," Reggie said. "I let myself in all the time."

Dani handed Reggie the pizza box with the leftovers. "Take this. I can't eat another bite. And Ms. Nelson might like it."

"Thanks."

"Do you need a ride to camp tomorrow?" Dani asked.

"No, Ms. Nelson will take me," Reggie said.

"Let me text you my number in case you need anything."

"You don't have to do that."

Dani pulled out her phone. "What's your number?" Reggie recited the numbers, which Dani quickly typed into her phone. She pressed send. "You now have my number in case you need me. I'm serious. Call me if you need a ride, okay?"

"I will. Thanks, Mrs. Peterson."

"Dani."

"Okay. Dani."

Out of the car, Reggie hurried to the porch. Jackson waited until she'd opened the front door and waved before vanishing inside.

The drive home was a little weird. It was odd to have Jackson behind the wheel (where Bella likely expected to see her father). Just being with another man and Bella added to the strangeness.

Dani and Matthew had officially separated after Bella's first birthday and were divorced by her second. There'd never been any talk of them reconciling, but Bella often talked about the possibility of them getting together. Maybe that's why their family worked so well. Dani, Bella, and Matthew were the original band players in the Manchester-Peterson Trio. No add-ons had mucked up the group dynamic.

And then there was Jackson.

"Jackson, thanks for driving," Bella said.

"No problem, Bella."

"Do you know anything about Reggie's family?" she asked.

"A little."

She unhooked her seat belt and leaned forward.

"Seat belt," Jackson said.

"My dad never minded," Bella said.

"He didn't mind?" Dani knew Matthew hated to play the bad guy, and she also suspected her very smart daughter took advantage.

Jackson's steady gaze didn't alter. "Seat belts in my truck."

"I can't hear as well when I'm sitting in the back," Bella said.

"I will talk louder," Jackson said.

Bella looked to her mom as if to get a little backup. Who was this guy telling her what to do? But when Dani met her daughter's gaze in the rearview mirror, her stare was as unyielding as Jackson's.

Bella's mouth opened as she readied to argue. Her quarrels generally centered on topics most important to twelve-year-olds: phones, bedtime, studying, practice, or chores.

"Fine." Bella clicked her seat belt on and in a loud voice asked, "What do you know about Reggie's family?"

"Her father drives the long-haul trucks," Jackson said evenly. "The family was hit hard by medical bills. Juniper did a community fundraiser to help, and that put a small dent in the debt. But if he's not on the road, he's not making money."

"Reggie talked a lot about her mom today," Bella said, more to herself. "She's not afraid to say she's sad."

"There's nothing wrong with that," Dani said.

Bella looked out the door and watched the grassy fields pass them by. "What good does talking do, anyway?"

"When you speak your feelings out loud, it keeps them from getting bottled up inside," Dani said.

"But nothing changes," Bella countered. "The dead stay dead."

"It might help you to heal," Dani said.

"You never talk about your mother," Bella said. "Is that the way it is? We just forget about them?"

"I haven't forgotten anything," Dani said. But she had lost so many details. The sound of her mother's voice, the way her hair smelled, and the feel of her hand as she brushed back Dani's hair.

"Why don't you talk about her?"

"I don't know. I'll text Grandpa and see if he has pictures to share."

"Did your mom make a tape for you before she died?" Bella asked.

"Why do you ask?" Dani asked.

"Reggie's mom made a tape. She's only watched it once. Says one day she'll watch it again."

"My mom never made a tape."

"You should ask Grandpa. He would know."

Dani and her father rarely talked about her mother anymore. "I'll ask."

Bella was silent for a moment. "Does all the sadness go away?"

Dani drew in a breath, buying a moment's time as she struggled to find the right words. The loss of her mother had been filled in some ways when Bella was born. But since Bella's birth there'd also been a million times when she'd wished her mother was alive so she could call her about random things. The baby's diaper rash. Colic. Divorce. First-day-of-kindergarten mommy blues. Bella's broken arm in the third grade. There were so many moments she'd never share with her mother.

"It doesn't go away," Dani said.

"What happens to it?" Bella asked.

Jackson was silent, but Dani knew he was listening. "It grows smaller and tighter until it is a hard ball that settles in the pit of your stomach. Sometimes, when you least expect it, it twists and hurts."

"When was the last time it hurt you?" Bella asked.

"At your dad's funeral. I could've used my mom." Dani cleared her throat. "That's why you're in the camp. You might learn a few things about handling your pain."

"I'm doing okay."

"Okay isn't good enough," Dani said.

"You said you'd do the homework we do at camp, right?" Bella asked.

"Sure, of course. What did you do today?"

"We had to write a letter to the person we lost."

"A letter."

"Then Juniper collected them. Tomorrow we're decorating mason jars. I don't know how all this crazy stuff is going to fit together. And next week we have to write another letter to the same person, like a lot is going to change in a week."

The art project she could do. But a letter to her mother . . . God, what would she say? "Of course I'll do it."

"Really? You're going to do *all* the exercises?" Bella didn't hide the challenge.

"I'm not bouncing balls on a parachute or singing karaoke, but all the other stuff I'll do."

"Swear?"

"Swear."

A silence settled in the truck as Jackson easily shifted gears, and they drove back to the silos. When they arrived, Bella thanked Jackson again and dashed off, promising to walk Rosie.

"Thank you," Dani said. "Lots of estrogen in this truck today."

He chuckled. "It was a nice change."

"Bella has been so well contained since her father died. I'm afraid she's turning into me."

He rested his calloused hand over hers. "Then it's good you're doing the assignments. Juniper knows her stuff."

Easy for him to say. "I suppose it can't hurt."

"You look as excited as Bella."

Dani laughed. "Apple doesn't fall far from the tree."

"It's a good tree."

She glanced toward the house and, seeing no sign of Bella, leaned in and kissed him, something she'd done easily when Bella wasn't around. Now she worried about being seen.

He traced her bottom lip with his thumb. "Juniper's camp is a good thing for you both."

"I know."

"You're making good progress."

"Am I? Feels like I'm stuck in quicksand."

"You're not stuck." His phone, mounted on the dash, rang. A glance at the number had him shaking his head.

"Bad news?"

"A client. He has a boat in New York. I've been putting him off, but I need to give him a yes or a no."

"What's the verdict?"

"It's a yes. He's a good client, and he's been very patient with me." He kissed her again. "I should've left two weeks ago but hung around until you were settled."

"Really?"

He shrugged. "Figured you could use a friend."

"You'll be sailing in hurricane season now."

"Weather still looks good. And I've sailed in my share of storms."

Still, it was dangerous. "Don't ever delay on my account. Bella and I will be fine."

"And if it rains again?" he asked.

Better she didn't learn to rely on him. What they had, whatever that was, was about the best she could do right now. "I'll just drive a lot slower."

CHAPTER FIFTEEN
BELLA

Monday, June 5, 2023
5:30 p.m.

Bella was lying on the dock, the evening sun warming her face, her eyes closed. She was more tired than she'd expected and was drifting off to sleep when she felt a presence beside her.

She looked to her right, kind of expecting her mother, but wasn't super surprised to see that girl sitting there. She wore the same dress, shoes, and ponytail.

"You look glum," the girl said.

Bella sat up and glanced at the trinkets she'd laid out on the dock. Each represented a moment she'd spent with her father: shells they'd collected on Carova when they'd driven up the beach to see the wild horses, a recipe card (his super-secret tomato sauce) written just for her, and the charm bracelet purchased in DC on their one and only trip.

"I'm not glum," Bella said. "Just thinking."

"Really? Because you look miserable. The wrinkle in your forehead is going to stick if you're not careful."

Bella rubbed her forehead and sighed. "Don't worry about me."

"What's got you in such a mood?"

"I have to bring something to camp tomorrow and talk about why it's important. Then I have to do some stupid art project."

"I don't like art projects," the girl said. "Feels like a waste of time."

"I know, right?"

"Writing letters, making jars, and talking about keepsakes aren't going to fix anything. You can write all the letters you want, and your father will still be dead."

"Tell me about it."

The girl looked at each item laid out on the deck. "Do you feel connected to your father when you look at these?"

What kind of question was that? "Of course. That's why I feel so bad."

"You're a Sad Sally," the girl said.

Bella fingered the recipe card and traced the small tomato stain on the upper-right-hand corner. They'd spent an afternoon making a huge pot of sauce for an event Dad was catering. They'd told stupid knock-knock jokes and laughed a lot.

"I liked cooking with Dad."

"Cooking is hard work."

"Dad could be a little flaky in life, but in the kitchen, he knew everything. He was at home. And I was, too, when I was with him." Bella rubbed the tears from her eyes. "I feel worse than I did before this dumb camp. Juniper says worse comes before better, but she never said when."

"And then after the sunshine, the rain returns. You can always count on tough times."

"When did you get so smart?" Bella asked.

"I wasn't always smart. Did a dumb thing. But now I know for sure dead is forever." She spoke casually, as if she truly meant it.

"You're a kid. You can only know so much about death."

"You're a kid too. You know more than most about dying," she said.

Bella's phone dinged with a text from Finn. It was the third one she'd sent in the last ten minutes. She left the message unanswered and shoved the phone in her cutoff jeans pocket. "Juniper says most people are clueless about what really matters."

"Does Juniper have all the answers?"

"No."

The girl laughed. "Juniper, Juniper, Juniper. You sure talk about her a lot. She doesn't know everything."

This girl from nowhere was starting to annoy Bella. "Where do you live, anyway?"

"Close by. Down the street. Around the corner."

"What does that mean?"

"Nothing. Everything."

"What's your name?"

Instead of answering, the girl looked toward the tokens. "Which item are you going to take to camp tomorrow?"

"I don't know. They all have good memories."

"And terrible, bad ones. All the camp kids will be in a worse mood tomorrow."

"Yeah." That's one thing she kind of liked about the camp. She didn't have to explain anything to anyone. They all got each other.

"I say pick them all," the girl said. "No reason to choose."

"Juniper said to bring one."

She rolled her eyes. "There you go, talking about Juniper again. Juniper, Juniper, Juniper."

"Do you know Juniper?"

She smiled. "Like I said before, everyone knows Juniper, right?"

Frustration welled in Bella as she carefully gathered her memory tokens. The girl had churned up all the bad feelings Bella guarded so closely.

"How's your mom doing?" the girl asked.

Bella's eyes narrowed. "Fine. Why do you ask?"

"She looks stressed."

"When did you see her?" Bella challenged.

She shrugged. "When I was out walking, I saw her. She didn't see me."

"What was Mom doing?"

"Just staring at the water. A lot of people, like you, stare at the water when they're scared or worried."

Bella's skin prickled. "Mom is fine. Stressed is her normal way."

The girl glanced at her hands and then back up at Bella. "If you say so, but I don't think she's fine."

"I know she is." Bella's irritation doubled. Who was this stranger to tell her how her mother was doing? "Go away. I don't like you."

"Ha! You don't even like yourself."

Rosie barked, and Bella's eyes opened. She was lying on the dock, her feet dangling over the edge. White cirrus clouds streaked over blue skies. Had she dozed?

Bella looked around, but there was no sign of New Girl. Her little buddy had just pulled off another vanishing act. Poof. Gone. Weird girl.

Annoying.

As Rosie ran along the shore, barking and wagging her tail, Bella looked up toward the house just as her mother passed in front of a window. Her mother paused, waved, and smiled. Mom smiled a lot, but the smiles never warmed her eyes. Sometimes her smiles were so tight they looked like they could snap like an overstretched rubber band.

A lot of people, like you, stare at the water when they're scared or worried.

Bella waved back, her grin mirroring her mom's. It's what they did. They didn't wallow. They got on with their day.

Inside the house, Bella went to the fridge and grabbed a juice box. She stabbed the straw in the slot and sucked. The cold sweetness felt good on her dry mouth and throat. The sun had warmed her skin, and without looking, she knew her cheeks were red.

Mom's steady footsteps descended the stairs. "Bella, come to the gallery and help me with the shelves."

Bella's head dropped back, and she shook her head no. She didn't want any more work or projects. She wanted to go back to her old life and maybe see Finn and hang out at her backyard pool. They could talk about Ryan, discuss *Emily in Paris* season two (they'd watched it twice), or argue about who had the best dance routine on TikTok.

Bella drew in a breath, tucking the possibilities in a drawer. Peterson/Manchester women did not whine. When times got tough, they got busy. Her mother had barely sat down. Come to think of it, she hadn't really been still for over a year.

How's your mom doing? The girl's question rattled in her head. *She looks stressed.*

Out the front door, she found Rosie chewing on a muddy stick. The rain had cleared, but the puddles lingered.

Her mother vanished into the building, and Bella and Rosie followed. Inside she found her mother in the center of a dozen boxes.

"They arrived while we were at lunch," Mom said.

"What are they?"

"The display shelves. I need to get them assembled. The first few artists are coming by on Saturday, and I want the gallery to be as pulled together as possible."

Her gaze traveled over wood floors and rounded walls. "How did you decide to buy this place? It's kind of random."

"I was driving by and saw the for-sale sign."

"Why were you driving by? This is far from Duck."

"I was looking at an artist in Norfolk," Mom said.

"And you saw a dumpy property and said, 'Yeah, I want *that*.'"

"I'd been thinking about a second location for a while." Her mother pulled a small retractable blade from her pocket and carefully sliced open the first box. She folded back the cardboard sides and removed the bubble-wrapped shelves.

"When did the second location become *the* location?"

"After your dad died."

"Dad would've never moved me here. This is so far from where we were. It's so random."

"It's a little random. And it's a risk. But it's now or never, kiddo."

"Why? The Duck gallery was doing great. I thought you loved it."

"I did. But I've been craving something new for a long time."

"Something new is a vacation, Mom. Or a new purse or dress."

"This is better than vacations or new clothes." Mom unwrapped the first set of shelves and carefully laid out each, along with the bolts and screws. She unfolded the instructions and frowned. "It's in German."

"We don't speak German."

"Exactly." She adjusted her glasses and narrowed her gaze. "But there are pictures, and that might be enough."

"Get Jackson to do this."

A frown creased her brow. "He told me not to buy these shelves. He said they'd be a pain to assemble."

It was a good sign her mother didn't do everything Jackson said. It meant they weren't a couple, a thought that had nagged her ever since he'd picked her up from camp. It was the kind of move a guy dating a single mom did. At least that's what Finn said. "Then why did you buy them?"

"Because they're pretty. I can picture them displaying pottery and jewelry. And this is going to be an art gallery, so even the shelves have to be nice."

Bella looked at the pieces. It was a puzzle, and she hated puzzles.

Her mother laid out the shelves in a neat line. "I liked Reggie. She seems like a nice kid."

Bella shrugged. "She's okay."

"Are you sure she doesn't need a ride tomorrow?" She surveyed the nuts and bolts.

"She said she'd call if she needed one."

Mom shook her head. "Is she as good at asking for help as we are?"

Bella regarded her mother. "We don't ask for help."

"Exactly."

"I don't know."

"Remind her at camp tomorrow that she's always welcome. And I'll drive her anytime."

That was nice, but her mom had always been kind to her friends. "I saw that girl again."

Her mom met her gaze. "The mystery girl? Where?"

"Down by the water. She's annoying."

"What did she say?"

"Ragging on Juniper and the camp." Telling Mom what the girl had said wasn't really complaining. It was reporting.

"Does she know Juniper? What's her name?"

"She didn't mention it. Said everyone knows Juniper."

A frown wrinkled her mother's brow. "I asked Juniper about her. She doesn't know her."

"Juniper doesn't know everyone."

"She knows just about everyone in this county."

"Are you saying this girl isn't real?"

"I think she's very real to you."

"Like an invisible friend?"

"Didn't say that."

But she had. "It's not that big a deal, Mom. Just forget I brought her up."

When they'd lived on Duck Road, Bella and her mom had known everyone, the history of the houses, businesses, and upcoming projects. There wasn't one thing that she didn't know about that town.

"I don't like not knowing people. I used to know everyone," Bella said.

"That'll change in time." Her attention returned to the instructions.

"What if I don't like anyone here? What if I start the new school and it sucks?"

Her mother frowned at the instructions. "It won't suck."

"It could!"

Mom looked up and smiled. "It could also be great."

"You say 'great' like you know, but you don't have all the answers." Bella could feel her temper rising.

Mom sat back on her heels and looked up at her. "Believe me, I know that."

"Are you still going to write your letter?" Bella challenged.

Mom's chin raised a fraction. "I said I would."

"When?"

"Tonight, or tomorrow."

"Are you going to let me see it?" Bella challenged.

Her mother's smile slipped a little. "Are you going to let me see yours?"

Heat flushed her cheeks. "No."

Her mother cocked a brow. "Why not?"

"It's private."

"Fair enough. I respect that. When mine's finished, you can read it."

"Why would you let me read it?"

"Seems the thing to do."

This felt like a trick. "I'm still not showing you mine."

"Not asking you to."

"What're you going to say?" Bella's curiosity wouldn't let her pretend she didn't care.

"I don't know." She fished an Allen wrench from her pocket and held it up to the screw. It was a little small for the slot. "This is the wrong size."

"Does it have to be exact?"

"I don't know. Maybe we should give it a whirl and see what happens." Mom chuckled. "What could go wrong?"

Bella rested her hands on her hips. "Dad could've put these shelves up for you."

"I suppose. He set up over a half dozen restaurants during his career."

Bella's phone dinged with a text. Finn. Again.

"Why don't you give Finn a call?" her mother said.

"How do you know it's Finn?"

"Is it Finn?"

Bella pouted. "Yes."

"I notice all," Mom joked.

Her mother's smile might as well have been solid steel. There was no seeing behind it. Rosie chewed her stick, leaving bits of bark and wood on the floor.

"You know, you're not the only one who sees things," Bella said.

"What's that mean?" Her mother's tone was mild, just like it was when she was nervous.

How's your mom doing?

She looks stressed.

A lot of people, like you, stare at the water when they're scared or worried.

"You're different." She blurted the challenge but immediately regretted it. If her mother had changed somehow, Bella didn't want to know it. She needed her mother to stay the same.

Mom dropped her attention back to the shelves. She moved a few screws around but didn't attempt to match them up with the other parts. "How am I different?"

"A little weird lately," she said quietly. "Smiling too much."

Her mother's eyes sparked. "Aren't all moms a little weird, according to their daughters?"

"No. Not you." On a scale of one to ten, her mother was the coolest. Reggie had said her mother had started to act odd before she found out she was sick.

"Well, I'm still the same old strange mom."

"Are you dying?" The question flew over her lips before she could muzzle it. It sounded as stupid as it was terrifying. But she needed to hear her mother say she wasn't going to die.

Her mother's gaze softened. "Honey, why would you ask that? Did something come up at camp today?"

Fear rippled through her, stiffening her spine. The little balls of sadness rattled around her belly. "Yes or no, Mom."

"No." Her mother pulled off her glasses and stared right at her. She didn't blink or twitch. "I am *not* dying."

"Reggie's mom died. She wasn't that much older than you."

Mom closed the distance between them. Her perfume wafted. "I'm not going anywhere, kid."

Bella's throat clogged. If she lost her mother, she would die. There'd be no going forward, no matter how many camps she attended or jars she filled with letters. Just the idea of writing a letter to her dead mother made her freeze with fear. "Swear?"

Her mother wrapped her arms around Bella. For a moment she tried to squirm free, but her mother held tight until she relaxed into the embrace. "Swear. Not leaving. You're stuck with your kooky old mom. Forever."

Bella lingered a moment in her mother's embrace, which felt like the safest place in the world. Maybe if she held on to her mother, she could keep her safe and nothing bad would happen. "You're not an old mom."

"True." She hugged Bella tighter. "Still young and hottish."

Bella increased her hold.

"This reminds me of when you were little," Mom said wistfully. "You loved to hug. When you were a baby, you'd wake up about three a.m., and I'd pick you up and put you in bed with me. Every morning I'd wake up, and your hand would be draped across my face. I still miss those little hands."

"I'm not a baby." But she liked the idea that her mom remembered.

Mom rocked her from side to side. "You'll always be my baby."

Bella pulled back, the ground feeling a little less shaky under her feet. "I need to text Finn."

"You okay?"

"Yeah, I'm good."

"Seriously?"

"Yeah."

"Okay."

"I'll be back. I helped Dad enough times."

Her mother adjusted her glasses. "It's okay. I can do this assembly job."

"You sure?"

"I got this. Unless you learn to speak German in the next ten minutes."

"Use Google Translate, Mom."

"Good idea. There might also be a YouTube tutorial. It's all under control. Tell Finn I said hi."

Her mom always made her believe that no matter what, it would work out. "Will do." Rosie followed Bella, leaving the remnants of her chewed stick behind. "Sorry about the mess."

"No worries."

"Can I go see Finn soon?"

"As soon as things settle down here first," Mom said.

"Remember, there's a party this Friday at Chelsea's house."

"We'll talk later in the week." Her mother looked at the unassembled shelves and the empty room.

That sounded like a no, but Bella was good at turning noes into yeses. "I'm going to be in *my* thirties by the time you get all this put together."

Mom laughed. "Hopefully, you're wrong."

CHAPTER SIXTEEN
DANI

Monday, June 5, 2023
7:30 p.m.

Dani had landed in the outermost ring of hell.

She'd thought she was making good progress with the shelves when she realized she'd put them together upside down. It took another hour to carefully undo the elaborate locking bolts not designed to be disassembled.

Her phone rang, and when she glanced, she saw the time. She'd been here for two hours. Shifting her attention to the caller's name, she braced a little before she answered.

"Ivy," she said.

"How's the new house?" Ivy asked.

"It's not bad. We're still placing furniture, but eventually it'll all settle down."

"How is Bella?"

"She's struggling. Doing her best not to show it, but she's dealing with a lot."

"Apple. Tree."

"I'm doing fine. Very different losing a friend versus a parent."

"That's not what I'm talking about." In the background, kitchen equipment banged.

"Do you have an event tonight?" Dani asked.

"We're prepping for one tomorrow. It's the last before I shift all my attention to the new food truck."

"How's Dalton?" Her brother had always been there when she needed him, but he wasn't the type to call and chat. Ivy was now her most direct link to Dalton's day-to-day life.

"He just signed to build six new houses in Nags Head. Excited, stressed, the usual."

"Good."

"You and Bella sneaked over the bridge without telling anyone."

She stepped out the front door, into the dimming evening light. She loved this time of year. Warm air and more sunshine. "Everyone knew I was moving."

"The plan was to follow and help you unpack."

"We didn't bring much with us on the car ride."

"Still . . ."

Fatigue stretched Dani's patience thin. "You'll be here next week with the truck, right?"

If Ivy heard the dodge, she didn't call it out. "Yes. The truck is fully renovated, and I'll stock the pantry this afternoon. But that's beside the point. Dalton and I were supposed to help you move."

"I didn't need the help. I hired movers. Now it's a matter of figuring out where everything goes."

Ivy groaned. "You're killing me. Would it be such a big deal to ask for assistance?"

She pressed her hand in the small of her back and stretched out a cramp. "I'm fine. Bella and I are figuring this out. And I'll invite everyone over for dinner as soon as we're settled. Just a couple more weeks."

"Dalton said you remind him of your mother. He said she could be so stubborn. Never complained. Never asked for help."

Dalton was four years older than Dani, which meant he'd had that much more time with their mother. His memories of her were sharper and crisper.

"He never talks about Mom," Dani said.

"It was the first time he mentioned her to me."

Mom had been the centerpiece of their lives, and now no one talked about her, as if she'd never existed. "What did he say?"

"She was always super positive, according to your brother."

"That's true. I'll take that as a compliment."

"I once worked with a chef who said that the discipline powering me through eighteen-hour days would also be my downfall. I used to laugh, but he was right. I missed my twenties while I was working in those kitchens."

"You were learning a skill." Her twenties had also been sidelined, but she had Bella. "Happy ending."

Pots clanged. "Balance, Dani. Balance. Don't drive yourself so hard. You don't have anything to prove."

Of course she did. Now more than ever. "Bella, Rosie, and I are a little off kilter now, but that'll change as soon as we're settled."

"Will it?" Ivy asked.

"Of course it will."

"By the way, Pete is going to visit you."

"Dad? Why is Dad coming now?" Dani loved her father, but she wanted a little space so she could find firm footing before the family showed up.

"He's worried, and he's on his way. He'll be on your doorstep in ten to fifteen minutes."

Dani scanned the highway's eastbound lane. "Why didn't you tell me?"

"I am. Now."

"A little notice would've been nice." Dani glanced in the glass door and caught her reflection. She smoothed the flyaway hairs haloing her face.

"You would've come up with a reason for him not to see you," Ivy said.

"Not helping."

"He's your father. He cares about you. He wants to help."

"I can take care of myself and my child." She eyed the half-assembled shelf. If her dad saw it, he'd roll up his sleeves and finish all the shelves before leaving. She closed the silo doors.

"Pete's a doll," Ivy said. "You'll be fine. And Bella loves seeing her grandpa."

"She'll worry that something is off," Dani said. "She asked me today if I was dying."

Ivy was silent. "Poor thing. She's scared."

"I know. And she's sharp. She senses something is off with me."

"Your dad is sworn to secrecy, and this meet and greet can be explained away by the move."

"Right."

As Dani followed the path toward her house, her father's construction truck pulled into the circular driveway. Her father, dressed in faded jeans, a white T-shirt, and construction boots, climbed out. Hands on hips, he studied the house and the grain elevators with a contractor's eye for detail.

"He's here," Dani said.

Ivy chuckled. "Tell Pete I said hi. See you next week."

"Right." Dani ended the call and, tucking her phone in her back pocket, moved toward the front door as Bella yelled, "Grandpa!"

Bella raced across the yard, with Rosie on her heels (barking, fresh stick in mouth), and embraced her grandfather. Pete wrapped long arms around Bella and hugged so tight he lifted her feet off the ground. She was his only grandchild, and he adored her.

Bella squealed. "I'm getting too big to pick up."

"Not for me, kiddo," Pete said.

Dani's stomach fluttered. She needed to prove to her father that she had her and Bella's lives under control. Sure, she had her issues, but she'd figure things out.

"Dad." As she moved closer, a genuine smile tipped the edges of her lips. The backup team was here, and despite her need to do this alone, relief eased some of the tautness gripping her belly.

"Pumpkin." He hugged Dani. "How are you doing?"

"Good, Dad." She'd seen him four days ago, when he'd been frowning over the packed boxes in her living room. "We're alive and well."

"I knew you'd be fine," he said.

Liar. He was worried sick about her. But she couldn't fault the guy for loving her. "Would you like a grand tour?"

"Sure. Before I forget, there's dinner in the truck. I grabbed pizza from Bella's favorite shop."

Pizza again. At this rate, her pants weren't going to fit. "Terrific."

"Did you get my favorite pizza?" Bella asked.

"I got exactly what you wanted."

"Great! I'm starving."

Last time her father saw Bella, she'd liked pepperoni on her pizzas. Now that she was a vegetarian, who knew what she'd eat. "Bella, take the pizza boxes into the kitchen, and Grandpa and I will be right there."

"Better start eating," her father said. "It's still warm, but that won't last."

"Thanks!" Bella grabbed the pizza boxes out of the truck's back seat and hurried into the house, with Rosie yapping at her heels.

"They're joined at the hip," her father said.

"She loves that dog, and that dog loves her."

He looked her up and down. "You look okay, but you always do. Just like your mother. How're you really doing?"

That was the second time in the last ten minutes she'd been compared to her mother. "It's a change, but we're doing okay. Furniture is in the house. It'll take me time to unpack all the boxes, but I'll have it all buttoned up in a few weeks."

"I know you will. My girl can move heaven and earth."

"I'll show you the gallery, if you don't remark on the shelves I haven't put together yet."

He chuckled. "Promise not to say a word." As they walked down the gravel driveway, her father's hands slid into his jeans pockets. "How is your vision?"

Dad always cut to the chase. He said he never had time for beating around the bush.

She cleared her throat. "Same as it was four days ago when you asked. No changes."

"The tunnel isn't narrowing?" Her father had insisted on attending her last doctor's appointment.

"Same tunnel."

The lines stretching across his forehead deepened. "You'd tell me if there's a change."

"Dad, we've been through this. Yes, I'll tell you." She tried to imagine how she'd react if Bella ended up with the same diagnosis. "Seriously, all is well."

"How does Bella like it here?"

Dani shrugged. "Good and not-so-good moments. It's a big change, but we haven't driven past the curve where Matthew died in a few days. That's progress. And Bella attended her first grief-camp session today."

"Bet she wasn't happy about that." Sun-etched lines feathering from the corners of his eyes deepened with a grimace.

"She's a chip off the old block. Doesn't like it when life is out of control."

"I can count on one hand the times I really had my life under control," her father said. "And that feeling fooled me into believing I was past the bad times. And then, of course, it all turned on a dime."

"What do you do when the bottom falls out?" she asked softly.

"Bad times are guaranteed. God knows I've seen my share, and so have you. No getting around it. But if you hang in there long enough, the world does turn, and the good times follow."

But her dad had never been the same after her mother died. He'd kept their lives going and grown the business, but he didn't joke around or laugh out loud like he did when she was little.

Dani led him onto the silos' covered porch. "Remember, don't judge me on the unfinished shelves. There's a sharp learning curve on the first one."

He chuckled. "I have my toolbox in the truck."

"I've got this."

He held up his hands. "Not hovering."

She laughed. "I don't mind the offer. But I need to figure this out."

Jackson's truck pulled up. Dani tensed a little as he climbed out and walked up to them. He shook Pete's hand. "This is a nice surprise."

"Jackson," Pete said. "How's life treating you?"

"Can't complain."

"You two know each other?" Dani didn't hide her surprise.

"I may have come out here during construction, just to check it out," Pete said.

"Pete knows his way around a construction site," Jackson said. "He had several good suggestions for the staircase."

Her father and her . . . Jackson had met. "He's the expert."

"As you can see, it's all but done," Jackson said.

"I knew you'd finish it right. Today, I'm just visiting my girls. I tried to stay away," Pete said. "But harder than I thought."

Jackson smiled. "I get it."

The ease of Jackson's comment made her wonder if he had children. He'd never mentioned any, but there was so much she didn't know about him.

"About to give the grand tour," she said.

"Don't mind me," Jackson said. "I'm bringing in the last of the wrought iron rail for the staircase. I'll install them first thing in the morning." As he propped open the silo's front door, he glanced at the unfinished shelf. He shook his head but said nothing.

Pete's curiosity pulled his gaze up the staircase spiraling the wall. Dani had known she'd wanted a second floor but didn't have the construction know-how to pull it off. But Jackson had taken her hand-drawn sketches and designed the circular staircase. The railings were the last piece, and then she could pass next Monday's building inspection. "Looking forward to it."

"Can I give you a hand?" Pete asked.

"I've got this, Pete," Jackson said.

"As you can see, we're almost there." Dani stepped into the brightly lit gallery.

"Looking good, pumpkin." Her father walked across the room and pushed against the curved staircase leading to the loft.

"Thanks."

"I'd still rather have you on my side of the bridge, but if you have to relocate, this isn't bad. Good visibility from the road, and plenty of room for parking."

Jackson entered the room with an armload of metal rungs.

"Still planning on painting the whole place yellow?" Dad asked.

Jackson cleared his throat. "Yellow?"

"Don't look so panicked," Dani said. "I've decided to keep the rustic silver. It adds a charm."

"Good."

"When does Ivy's food truck arrive?" Pete asked.

"Early next week," Dani said.

Pete clapped his hands together. "Love it when a plan comes together. Jackson, we have pizza up at the house. Why don't you join us?"

Jackson glanced to Dani and then back at her father. "I need to get these rails unloaded."

He was trying to give her an out, which she found charming in its own way. And her father's easy vibe suggested Jackson hadn't said anything about their relationship. "You really should join us. We can't eat it all, and there's no such thing as too much pizza, right?"

"If you're sure," Jackson said.

"I am." She was cool with Jackson getting to know her father better. She didn't know what that said about her feelings for Jackson. Maybe nothing. Maybe everything.

The three walked up to the house and found Bella on the back porch with the pizza boxes on the picnic table. She'd set out a roll of paper towels, which in their bachelorette world served as both napkin and plate.

Bella bit into a slice, and her eyes closed as if the tomatoes, onions, and spices transported her back to their old life. Matthew and Bella had visited the pizza shop often on the nights she'd spent with her dad. Pizza was one of Bella's tactile reminders of her dad. For Dani and her mother, it was orange sherbet. How many times had her mother bought her a cone from Ruth's Seaside Resort's restaurant and they'd walked the beach enjoying the sunshine?

"Pick a spot," Dani said. "And grab a slice."

Bella scooted over so her grandfather could sit beside her, leaving the other side for Dani and Jackson. Jackson angled his long legs over the bench, and Dani took what little space remained. Their shoulders brushed. Nothing sexy or sensual, but his touch felt good. She liked having him around the gallery, in her bed, her life. When the day came and it ended between them, she'd be very sad.

She grabbed a small slice and a paper towel. Like the sherbet tasted of sweet memories, the pizza carried the flavors of death and loss. She opened a soda and took a sip.

"You know your craft, Jackson," Dad said. "I'll hire you tomorrow if you ever want a job."

"Thanks, Pete." Jackson grabbed a slice of pizza. His demeanor was relaxed, no hints of unease. "But I'll be leaving soon to ferry a boat from Norfolk to Florida. And if the weather permits, I'll have several more deliveries in the pipeline behind it. Then I'm back to building boats."

"All the sailors I've known couldn't be landlocked for long."

"Guilty," Jackson said.

"You like sailing the Intracoastal Waterway?" Pete asked.

"I do," he said. "Out on the water there's nothing to worry about but keeping the boat on course."

"Are you building a boat now?" Bella asked.

"I've ordered the wood," Jackson said. "I do most of my building in the winter."

"You can build a whole boat?" Bella asked. "Seems impossible."

Jackson nodded slowly. "I used to build several a year."

"Why'd you stop?" Bella asked.

For a moment Jackson said nothing. "Just needed a break."

"A break from what?" Bella pressed.

"Bella." Dani's kid had a talent for asking personal questions. "Eat your pizza."

"What? I'm just asking questions," Bella said before shifting directions. "What kind of boat are you going to build?"

Jackson took another bite. "Think I'll start small with a two-mast schooner, Bella. But I might go bigger. Just depends."

Dani understood the meaning behind his statement. Several times he'd mentioned Bella and her joining him on one of his trips. He had basically put his life in a holding pattern since they'd met. However, he wouldn't delay his life forever.

Pete chuckled. "If a two-mast schooner is your idea of small, then I can't wait until you go big. Dani, how did you find Jackson?"

"My Realtor, Juniper Jones," she said. "She recommended Jackson."

Jackson shrugged. "I'd driven by the grain elevators and the house more times than I could count. I couldn't see past grain storage."

"Dani has a real artist's eye when it comes to design," Pete said. "We're going to miss her at the firm."

"You left the firm?" Jackson shifted toward her, giving her his full attention.

"Dad and Dalton build on the Outer Banks. Driving back and forth right now doesn't make sense, especially with the summer traffic building. And I'll have my hands full for a while here."

"Sounds like you're putting down real roots," Jackson said.

"I am," Dani said.

"Mom, how did you meet Dad?" Bella asked.

Dani set down her pizza slice and wiped the grease from her fingers. Had her very wise daughter picked up the vibe between Jackson and her? "I told you, we met in high school."

"But when did you, like, *like* him?"

What she hadn't told her daughter and didn't wish to revisit in front of her father or Jackson was that she'd never loved Matthew. The best they'd ever been able to manage was great sex and friendship. "I can't remember."

"You must remember the moment?" Bella asked.

Aware that Jackson was listening, she stumbled to find acceptable words that could describe the moment too much booze collided with ovulation hormones. The event itself was not really memorable, and she'd forgotten most of it. However, she could remember the instant she realized she was pregnant. How she'd sat on the bathroom floor, wishing for her mother, and then stressing at the idea of having a child.

She could also remember the first time she'd seen Jackson in the diner, sitting alone. When she'd introduced herself, he'd taken her hand and held it a second or two longer than she expected.

"It's been so long, honey," Dani said. "I don't recall."

"How could you not remember?" Bella asked.

"I'd known your dad for years as a friend."

"But when did you know he wasn't a friend anymore?"

"Dad and I did a good job with friendship."

Bella's brow wrinkled.

"I remember when I first met Grandma," Pete interjected. "We met not too far from here. An old army buddy had called me and asked if

I could give a friend a job. My buddy Frank never asked for a favor unless it was important. I said yes and told him to have her be at work on Monday. The next day, this woman calls me and tells me she's in Coinjock and her car has broken down. I was on a construction site and going in a thousand directions. But before I thought, I agreed to go pick her up."

"I remember you saying you were annoyed," Dani said.

"I was. I was burning daylight. But then I parked by the Coinjock Marina and got out of my truck. I immediately spotted your mother and Dalton sitting on a picnic blanket on a small patch of grass by the gravel parking lot. He wasn't more than two. She had all his toy trucks arranged around him and was feeding him what looked like the last of a peanut butter sandwich. She looked up at me, and I was lost. I knew that very moment, I was in love."

The last time Dani had heard the story, it had been from her mother's perspective. Her mother had been very ill at that point and happy to relive as many past moments as she could.

"While Dalton slept, I made a call from Coinjock Marina to my new employer. I'd smiled, tried to sound relaxed, and said to Mr. Manchester, 'Houston, we have a problem.' To my great relief, he'd offered to come get us. God bless Peter Manchester.

"I hurried to my car, peeked at Dalton sleeping in his car seat, and grabbed a blanket that I spread out under a shade tree. I gathered his toys, a small cooler filled with dwindling food supplies, and a hat for him. He was sleeping so hard until I pulled the truck from his little hand. His eyes opened immediately.

"He smiled, and that gap-toothed grin tore at my heart in the best kind of way. 'Mommy.'

"'Hey, Little D. Want to have a picnic? We can eat a snack and play with trucks.' My boisterous son hated his car seat and cried for the first half hour of our trip out of Greensboro. Finally, outside of Raleigh, he'd fallen asleep.

"*I unhooked his belt and pulled him free. His little back and head were so sweaty. 'All right, big guy. Let's play.'*

"*He ducked his head toward me, laughing.*

"*I lay him on the blanket and quickly changed his diaper. Hands washed with wipes, I spread out my offering of Goldfish, my last two juice boxes, and my last peanut butter sandwich. Dalton took the juice box in chubby hands and sucked on the straw until the box imploded. I handed him the last box.*

"*I arranged Dalton's trucks into a neat circle while he ate. I made truck noises, drove the little excavator over his chubby thigh, and smiled when he giggled. We'd been doing this for a half hour when a large black truck, covered in dirt and mud, pulled into the lot next to my faded red Nova. I brushed my hair and Dalton's and pulled my sleeves over my forearms.*

"*A tall man dressed in faded jeans, worn leather boots, and a black T-shirt covered in drywall dust got out. His gaze settled on us immediately. I picked up my baby, settled him on my hip, and, squinting against the sun, walked toward him.*

"*'Becky?' He removed his glasses, revealing vivid blue eyes. He was lean, fit, and moved like a younger man. But as he stepped closer, I saw the crow's-feet angling from the corners of his eyes.*

"*'Mr. Manchester.'*

"*'Call me Pete,' he said.*

"*'I'm Becky, and this is my son, Dalton.'*

"*Pete grinned at the boy. 'Hey, fella.'*

"*Dalton pointed toward Pete's vehicle. 'Truck!'*

"*'That's right,' Pete said easily.*

"*'Dirty,' Dalton said.*

"*Pete chuckled. 'It's always dirty.'*

"*'Dalton loves trucks. And dirt.' I nodded sideways toward the dozen toy vehicles arranged in a circle.*

"*'He's a man after my own heart,' Pete said. 'Having a bit of car trouble?'*

"'Yes. We almost made it. I think it overheated.'

"'Mind if I have a look?'

"'Sure.' I could be modest and pretend I didn't need the help, but my back was to the wall. And my policeman friend in Greensboro had said good things about Pete.

"I carried Dalton to my car, opened the driver's side door, and pulled the hood latch.

"Pete easily raised the hood and rested it on its support. I came around so Dalton could have a better look.

"'It's definitely overheated,' Pete said easily. 'You've got a busted hose. It's an easy fix.'

"I chuckled. 'For you.'

"He shut the hood. 'I'll make a call and have the car towed. Why don't you load up Dalton in my truck, and I'll drive you both to the Outer Banks?'

"Hot sun on my face warmed my cheeks as I hoped a smile hid my nerves. 'Do you go through this much trouble for all your employees?'

"'Not usually.' His lips tugged into a grin. 'But Frank vouched for you, and that's good enough for me.'

"'You and Frank were in the army together?'

"'That's right. Hope he hasn't told you too many stories about me.'

"'He hasn't said a word. Just that you're a good guy.'

"'I'll catch up with him soon and have a beer.' He nodded to the car seat. 'I don't know much about those contraptions. I'll have to leave it to you.'

"'Sure.' I hustled to the passenger-side back door. When it swung open, I balanced Dalton while I fished for the seat belt behind the seat.

"'I can hold him if it'll help,' Pete said.

"I straightened, hesitated.

"'Does he mind strangers?' Pete asked.

"Dalton knew no strangers. I was the one that worried about them. Pete held out his hands, and Dalton extended his, tipping his bulk toward him. Pete took the boy, and they both stared at each other with great curiosity. I

161

unhooked the baby seat and opened the back of Pete's truck, filled with files, paint sample books, and a file box. I made room for the seat, gathered my blanket, packed it in a shopping bag, and grabbed our one suitcase. I tossed all that in the bed of the truck.

"'I can't thank you enough,' I said.

"'Hungry!' Dalton said.

"'The kid eats all the time. I'm out of Goldfish.'

"Pete nodded to the restaurant. 'Let's grab a bite to eat. Bet this little guy can lay waste to a burger.'

"My smile relaxed a little. It had been a while since I'd felt safe. 'Watch your fingers.'

"He laughed. 'Duly noted. Let's eat.' He kept Dalton in his arms, and my son looked perfectly content to be where he was.

"'I'll pay you back when I get my first paycheck,' I said.

"He opened the restaurant door. 'I got this, Becky. It's all going to be good now.'"

Mom had said she'd been feeling a little desperate and she'd needed a fresh start. But she'd never explained why.

"After Becky and Dalton got settled, I asked her out on a real date," Pete said. "She refused three times before she finally said yes."

"She liked you and was afraid you didn't understand what it would mean to be a stepfather."

"She was right. I didn't know. But no one knows much about parenting when they start off. By the time you were born, Dalton and I were good buddies, and neither one of us knew what we were going to do with a girl."

"Mom, what was your favorite thing to do with your mother?" Bella asked. "Juniper made us answer that question today. I said I liked cooking pasta with Dad."

"We painted," Dani said without thinking. "We'd sit on the sunporch, and she'd show me how to create beachscapes."

"What did she smell like?" Bella picked up another slice. "Juniper has the dumbest questions."

"Like roses," Dani said. Even to this day, when she smelled a rosebush, she thought of her mother. Her visual memories of her mother no longer extended beyond old photos, but the scent of roses brought all the good feelings rushing back.

"She liked the yellow ones the best," her father said. "She carried a bouquet of yellow roses when we got married."

Yellow roses had also been on her casket.

"What other questions did Juniper have?" Jackson asked.

"All kinds of questions that help us remember. 'How tall were they? Did they have a favorite joke? Favorite color, music, or dance.' Some of the kids don't want to remember. Reggie had answers to all the questions right off."

"Which ones did you struggle with, Bella?" Dani asked.

"'What was the last thing you said to your father?'" Bella said. "The last time I saw him was at his restaurant. But I don't remember what we talked about."

"It's okay you don't recall," Dani said.

"Do you remember the last thing you said to your mother?" Bella countered.

Dani remembered that final day. She'd been in a rage. She tore her *Gilmore Girls* and Britney posters off her walls and dumped all her clothes out the window. She'd been wishing that all the sadness and pain would go away.

She was sitting in the corner of her room when her father came in and said she better come quick if she wanted to see her mother. She dried her tears as she walked down the long hallway. By the time she entered her mother's room, she was smiling. Her mother's breathing was so shallow, and her eyes were closed. Dani thought she'd been too late, but then her mother opened her eyes. Dani had taken her mother's slender hands, covered in blue-green veins.

Absently, Dani now rubbed her own thumb over her palm, trying to remember her mother's touch. "I told her that I loved her and not to worry. I would take care of Dad and Dalton."

"What did she say?" Bella asked.

After all these years, these moments had been too tender to handle, so she'd locked them in a box. She only pried open that dusty, dark box now for Bella's sake. "Mom said, 'Don't forget to take care of you.'"

Dani tore off a piece of pizza, but her appetite had gone, and she handed the bit to Rosie. The dog chomped on the dough and gobbled it in two chews.

"Mom, you said no people food," Bella said.

"A little can't be too bad, right?"

"Grandpa, did Grandma make a tape before she died? Reggie's mom made a tape," Bella said.

"No," he said softly. "She never made a tape."

"Do you have pictures of her?" Bella asked.

"I do. I'll scan a few and send them to you."

"That would be great," Bella said.

Under the table, Jackson's leg shifted and brushed against hers. The worn jean fabric soothed the tension snapping in her body.

Jackson checked his watch. "I need to get back to the shop. Dani, if you've got a minute, I've got a couple of questions for you, and then your father can have you right back."

"Of course." Dani looked at Bella. "Don't stuff Rosie with pizza."

Bella looked at the dog. "But she looks so hungry."

Pete chuckled. "Looks like your mama just created a Rosie pizza monster."

Bella tore off a piece, and Rosie devoured it.

Dani normally had a hard-and-fast rule about what the dog ate but wondered now why she'd created such a rule. What did a treat now and then matter?

She and Jackson rose, and they walked toward the gallery, their hands close but not touching, neither saying anything until they reached the silos' awning. "Thanks for the rescue."

"I know how old emotions can bite you in the ass. It's never comfortable, especially when you have an audience."

Unshed tears scratched her throat. After a beat, she swallowed them. "I haven't talked about Mom in a long time. I loved her so much, and I've barely been able to say her name the last twenty years."

"But you did."

"I want Bella to embrace this camp. I want her to develop tools to deal with her grief. So, if I have to answer difficult questions, I'll do it."

"How old were you when your mother died?"

"Eight," she said. Inside the silo's interior, even with the lights on, it took her eyes a moment to adjust as her pupils dilated and gathered all the extra bits of light.

Jackson laid his hand on her shoulder. "I'm sorry."

The tenderness in his tone undid something in her. "It was a long time ago."

Jackson shook his head. "Don't ever say that to Juniper. She'll remind you that time doesn't matter when it comes to grief."

She could barely think beyond his gaze. "You and Juniper routinely discuss grief?"

"We talk about all kinds of things." Jackson shrugged broad shoulders.

Again, her need to know more about him had hit a roadblock. Her questions, sooner or later, would boomerang back, and the inevitable conversation about her eyes would hit.

Beyond Bella, she'd never allowed herself to get close to anyone. Maybe that's why she and Matthew had never made it. He'd tried, but she'd used her pregnancy and then the newborn as reasons not to get emotionally close to him. Maybe if he'd had more maturity, he'd have given them more time. Maybe if she'd had more insight into her own grief, she'd have bonded better. But neither had been enough to make it work beyond the bedroom.

"I like Juniper," Dani said. "She's very kind."

"She is." He took her hand in his. "You look exhausted."

She laughed. "I'm a mess right now, Jackson. I don't know if I'm coming or going."

"Treading water against the current. I know what it's like to paddle so hard because you're afraid if you stop, you'll drown. They say the trick is to stop fighting the stream, to relax, float, and go with the flow."

She arched a brow. "That sounds terrific. How do you do that?"

He chuckled and kissed her lightly on the lips. "I'll let you know when I figure it out."

She wrapped her arms around his neck and kissed him. Something tight in her chest eased. "I wish we had a little bit more time."

He traced her chin with his calloused thumb. "Our timing has been off. But it'll improve."

"Aren't you leaving soon?" A part of her hoped he'd leave so she wouldn't feel this damn pull toward him.

"Next week," he said. "But I'll be back. And the invitation is still open. I'll swing up the waterway and pick you and Bella up."

"Two females on a boat. We would drive you crazy."

He chuckled. "I'm pretty sure I could manage."

She stepped back. "You're kind, but I'll save you from yourself. Get your boat delivered in peace and quiet."

Gray eyes searched her face. "Today's the first time I've heard you open up."

Her protective shield had peeled away, leaving her exposed and afraid. But she quickly pasted it back up. "It doesn't happen often. I can be a little closed off."

He grinned. "Out in the world that's true. When we're alone, you're different. The walls drop."

She blushed, knowing when they were in bed, she was closest to her true self. "That makes one of us. I'm not comfortable with tough feelings."

A faint smile flickered. "No one is. And if they say they are, they're lying." He paused. "You can trust me, Dani."

He was picturing a future with her and Bella that wasn't going to turn out as he imagined. "Right now, I don't trust me."

CHAPTER SEVENTEEN
BELLA

Tuesday, June 6, 2023
10:00 a.m.

Day two of camp sucked more than day one. This day might not have been so bad if Reggie had shown up to camp. But she hadn't made it. Juniper had called her dad's and Ms. Nelson's cell phones, but both calls went straight to voice mail. Juniper had delayed the start of the craft project, thinking the girl was running late, but finally she was forced to start.

Bella and the other kids decorated their jars with paint, glitter, Scrabble letters, and all kinds of random pictures cut from magazines.

At circle time, they'd showed their jars and explained the meaning behind their decoration choices. Reggie would've had a good reason for everything she'd selected for her jar, but Bella had none. When pressed, all Bella could say was that she liked the cutouts' bright colors, now decoupaged to the glass.

Next came the emotional part. Terrible. Terrible. Terrible.

Seth brought his brother's favorite football jersey, which still had grass stains on it from his last game. Billy brought his grandfather's watch. It hadn't worked since the 1970s. Penny held up her aunt's favorite sweater, which Penny had worn all winter. Sara talked about her father's favorite pipe. And Jenna and Nick held up their older brother's favorite AC/DC poster. They giggled when they said he used to play air guitar in front of it.

Bella had the recipe card but didn't have a full-blown story to share. It was just a card. "It's just a recipe."

"Why is there a tomato stain on the card?" Juniper asked.

"The sauce bubbled up," Bella said. "It splashed on everything."

"What did you think about that?" Juniper asked.

"It was kind of funny. Dad said the stain proved the recipe had been used."

"Was the sauce good?"

"All Dad's recipes were good." Each answer poked at unhealed wounds.

"I like the bracelet on your wrist," Juniper said.

Bella glanced at the silver charms. "My dad gave it to me."

Juniper smiled. "Very pretty."

When her mother arrived at 2:00 p.m., Bella was ready to leave behind fake smiles and sharing ragged feelings. God, she hated this camp.

"You look glum." Mom was upbeat. Maybe she'd forgotten this morning's fight about the lame inedible cereal in the cabinet.

"Reggie didn't make it today. And then we had to decorate our jars."

"Why didn't Reggie come to camp?" Mom asked.

"I don't know. Juniper called her dad's and neighbor's cell phones, but no one answered."

"Well then, we'll go check on Reggie. I don't like it that she didn't come to camp today."

Bella sat a little straighter. "Seriously?"

"She doesn't strike me as a kid who skips." Mom's jaw set like it did when she was negotiating a price or dealing with a difficult customer or artist.

"That's what I thought."

The car's engine revved as Mom drove past home toward the side road that led to Reggie's house. "Do you think she's sick?"

"She didn't look sick yesterday," Bella said.

"No, she did not."

"Do you think something is wrong?" Bella asked.

"We'll find out, won't we?" Mom took the right and followed the back road to the small collection of houses where Reggie lived. When Mom pulled up in the driveway, the house looked quiet. There was no car in the driveway, and the shades were drawn.

Mom got out, adjusted her glasses, and gripped her cell phone in her hand as she marched forward. Bella followed, but her mom held out her hand, warning her to stay back.

Mom walked up to the front door and rang the bell, which didn't sound like it worked. She banged on the door. "Reggie, it's Dani Manchester and Bella Peterson. Are you home?"

The house stood silent, and as the seconds ticked, it seemed no one would answer. Mom turned from the door, frowning. "I wonder where she is?"

Bella climbed the three steps and banged on the door. "Reggie, it's Bella! Are you home?"

No answer.

After another minute, the two finally turned and were down the stairs and halfway to the car when the front door opened. Reggie appeared behind the screen door. She was dressed in shorts, a flowery blouse, and sneakers, like she'd been ready for camp.

Bella moved toward the porch. "Reggie! Why didn't you come to camp today?"

Reggie frowned. "My neighbor had to go to work early. I thought about riding my bike, but it's too far."

Mom gripped her phone a little tighter. "Do you usually ride your bike on the highway?"

"Only to the convenience store if we're out of milk."

Mom paused. "Reggie, we're going to lunch. Come with us."

"Dad said to stay in the house."

Mom's expression didn't falter. "Call your father. I'd be happy to talk to him."

Reggie grimaced. "I'll text him. He doesn't like calls when he's on the road."

"Go ahead. We'll wait," Mom said.

Reggie dashed inside, the screen door slamming behind her.

Bella glanced at her mother's tense face. "Mom, you look mad."

"Not at Reggie. But between you and me, I'm not happy with her father or her neighbor."

"I guess her neighbor doesn't think the camp is important," Bella said.

"She's wrong." Mom always had a quick smile, but now it was nowhere to be found. "Reggie needs the camp just as much as you."

"But she seems okay with her feelings and stuff."

"If I had to bet money, I'd wager she's not."

"A camp won't fix everything or anything. Dad and her mother will still be dead."

"It's not a fix, Bella, but it's a tool," Mom said.

"What tools do you have? Maybe you could tell me, and then I wouldn't have to go."

Her mother hesitated. "You're going to camp."

"Did you write your letter?"

"I'm working on it."

Reggie appeared at the door. "He said I could go to lunch."

"And you did contact him?" Mom asked.

"Yeah. I texted." She showed Mom the text thread.

"Text your father and tell him I'll drive you to and from camp for the next two weeks. Ask him if you can spend the night with us while he's gone."

"He'll be home Thursday afternoon," Reggie said.

"Then we'll deliver you home when he arrives," Mom said. "There's no reason for you to stay here by yourself."

"Okay. Thanks." Reggie typed quickly. "Sent." Seconds passed, and then a reply dinged. "He says, 'Sounds good.'"

"Excellent."

"You don't have to do this," Reggie said.

"I want to," Mom said. "Give me your father's phone number?"

"Why?"

"In case I need to call him," Mom said.

Reggie looked at Mom as if the idea of her mother contacting her father was worrisome. "He doesn't like calls."

"If it's an emergency, he'll need to deal."

"Okay." Reggie forwarded the contact information.

"Perfect. Now, Reggie, pack a bag or whatever you need, and let's get lunch. Barbecue or pizza?"

Reggie shrugged. "Whatever you want."

Even though she'd had it twice yesterday, Bella remembered how Reggie had enjoyed the pizza. "I say pizza again. And when we get sick of that, maybe we can get barbecue tomorrow."

"If you're sure," Reggie said.

"Very," Mom said.

Ten minutes later, Reggie had packed a bag, and the three of them were headed back toward the main road. Reggie was quiet at first, but as they drove farther from the house, she seemed to relax. At the restaurant, once the waitress had set the pepperoni pizza in front of them, Reggie almost looked happy.

"What did you do in camp?" Reggie said. "Did you decorate the jars?"

"Yes," Bella said. "But we can do your jar at our house. And maybe I can do another one, because mine looked so lame. And Mom needs to do one for her letter."

Mom sat back and listened as Bella and Reggie chatted. Somewhere along the way, they started giggling, and by the time they'd arrived home, they'd forgotten about her mother and were headed inside. When they reached the front door, Reggie said, "You have the best mom."

Bella looked back and watched her mother walk toward the gallery. She thought about the fight she'd had with Mom that morning over cereal. The argument had been stupid. She'd been in a foul mood because Finn hadn't texted back since yesterday, and she felt blown off. And then she'd seen a text message on her mother's phone. It was from a doctor in Norfolk confirming her next appointment.

"When did your mom tell you that she was sick?" Bella asked.

"She kept it a secret a long time," Reggie said. "She said she thought she was going to get better and there'd be no reason to tell me."

"My mom's mom died when she was young. My grandmother didn't tell Mom she was sick until the very end."

"Why don't they tell?" Reggie said.

"I don't know." Her mother always pretended everything was okay.

"They should tell," Reggie said quietly. "It's not right they don't."

"No. Not right at all."

CHAPTER EIGHTEEN
DANI

Tuesday, June 6, 2023
3:30 p.m.

Dani found Jackson in the gallery installing the last of the wrought iron rails on the curved staircase. He didn't turn from his work but said, "I can hear your thoughts."

"Really? What am I thinking?"

"Don't know. But you're pissed." He tightened the bolt and stood. "And I sure hope it isn't with me."

Dani smiled. "It's not you. Reggie's father. Ronny Bailey. What do you know about him?"

He straightened to his full six-foot-plus height. "He's a long-haul truck driver. Like I said, he stays on the road a lot."

"Reggie didn't come to camp today. She didn't have a ride. Her neighbor fed her an early breakfast and then left her at home alone."

Jackson drew in a breath. "He has lots of medical bills to pay off. And he's still dealing with his wife's death."

"But you just don't leave your kid to fend for themselves."

His gaze softened. "No. But grief can make anyone do crazy things. His wife's death cut him off at the knees."

Dani had never gone crazy after her mother died. She'd pulled herself together and gotten on with her life. As her brain teed up for a silent tirade about self-sufficiency, she caught herself. She didn't want Bella to follow in her shoes, so she had to do all this differently. "What kind of guy is Reggie's father?"

"Good, decent man. Has a lot on his plate now," Jackson said.

If she didn't know better, she'd say he was defending the man. "I don't understand the running. His daughter depends on him."

"Sometimes the weight is so heavy, you have to give up so you can reset."

"Reset?"

"Realize what you were doing isn't working. Ronny didn't abandon Reggie. He left her with neighbors, and she was safe in her house. She's not as lucky as Bella. You're one of the few I've seen manage tough times."

"That's not a bad thing."

"I didn't say it was."

This conversation was headed in the wrong direction. "When did this conversation become about me?"

He shook his head. "It's not. We're talking about Ronny. I'll make a few calls and see if I can find out what's going on with him."

"I have his phone number. I'll call him."

"Let me reach out to Ronny. He's suffering, and he's running scared, trying to keep his bills paid and hold what's left of his world together."

"His daughter should come first."

"Agreed." He moved within inches of her. "Reggie loves her dad. And he adores her. He's afraid that she'll lose her home if he can't bring in the money."

"Money's not the point."

"For a man who's always taken care of his family, it's everything. He can't find words now, but he can work."

The more reasonable he sounded, the more her anger grew.

"I love my father. But I remember how it felt when he took on extra work after Mom died." Her older brother, Dalton, had thrown himself into football practice. She'd had an after-school nanny and then started hanging out at Ivy's house. If not for Ivy and Ivy's grandmother, Ruth, she wasn't sure how well she'd have managed.

"You and your father don't talk much about your mother."

"Last night was the first time we've discussed her in years." She closed her eyes.

"He took care of you in the only way he knew how, even when he was dying inside."

She sighed. "We've never been good at talking about Mom."

"Talk to him more. Ask for pictures. Are there videos?"

"I'm sure there are, but this isn't about me right now. It's about Bella and Reggie."

"From my perspective, it's also about you."

God, she wished Ruth was here now. After mothering two motherless girls, she always knew the right thing to say. When Bella was born, Dani had been terrified, sitting in her hospital room alone. Ruth arrived with a small present and then sat with Dani and listened as she spilled all her fears. Then Ruth had told her to pull herself together and focus on her new baby.

Her head began to throb. "I didn't come here to run down Ronny."

He arched a brow, his sharp gaze keen and uncomfortably piercing. "Why did you come?"

"I don't know. I guess to vent." In a safe space. "To find a solution for Reggie." Her phone dinged with a text. Mom, need glue! "Never mind. I'll figure it out."

"Where's Reggie?"

"In the house with Bella. They're decorating jars."

"Folded her under your arm?"

"Sure, why wouldn't I?"

He laid his hands on her shoulders, tight with tension. "You don't have to do it alone."

"I know."

Her phone chimed with a new text. A quick glance, and she saw: Appointment Reminder: Dr. Malone, 10:00 a.m. tomorrow. Reply to confirm.

Dani had ignored the first message, but the doctor's office hadn't forgotten her. She stepped back, wishing for the time her vision was perfect and Matthew was alive. But wishes were as fragile as the clouds that drifted overhead.

She smiled, maybe a little too brightly. "Thanks, Jackson. I know you mean well. I promise to reach out if I need something."

He folded his arms over his chest. "You're bullshitting us both."

"I am not." She took another step back and turned toward the door. "I'm *not*."

"Takes a bullshitter to recognize another one."

Jackson was the straightest shooter she knew, other than Dalton and her father. She kept walking to the door, not daring to look back. If she did, she might give in to anger, fear, and sadness.

Back at the house, Dani dug the glue gun out of a box she'd marked for crafts and carried it outside to the girls sitting at the picnic table. Bella had grabbed a bag of cookies and two sodas as well as three jars. By their looks, the jars had held mayo, pickles, and olives. "Tell me there are three plastic containers in the refrigerator holding the content of these jars."

"Of course," Bella said. "I didn't waste any food." Her daughter, who'd been in a foul mood since early this morning, was smiling just a little.

Dani set the glue gun down. "If you girls need anything, just shout."

"Thanks, Mom."

"Thanks, Ms. Manchester."

"Reggie, call me Dani."

"Right," Reggie said. "Dani."

"Mom, we've got three jars," Bella said.

Dani's mind had already shifted to the next task. "What?"

"You need to do a jar too," her daughter pointed out. "You said you were going to do everything I was doing at camp."

"I'll do everything but bounce the beach ball." She'd started her letter twice last night but hadn't gotten past *Dear Mom*. Her few attempted openings had ended up as wadded balls in the trash can.

"Did you?" Bella asked.

"I'm working on it." Which was technically true.

"That's a no, right?" Bella winked at Reggie.

"It means I'm getting to it." How could a simple letter be so hard?

"Decorating jars is fun, Dani. Join us," Reggie said, holding up the newly emptied and scrubbed pickle jar.

Dani scrambled for a decent excuse that would satisfy her very sharp daughter. She wanted to run away from the letter, the jar, and all this talk of grief. But that would make her a runner . . . a bullshitter.

Dani sat at the picnic table and grabbed a cookie. She ate it in one bite and reached for the last jar. "I'll warn you ladies, I'm very good at crafting."

Grinning, Bella scraped off a small sliver of label from her cleaned mayonnaise jar. "You can cut pictures from the magazines. Juniper said you can write words, poems. You can put anything on your jar."

She stared at the clear sparkling glass. The emptiness looked vast. How could she sum up her feelings with torn pictures, words, and drawings?

Dani took one of the charcoal-gray pencils and a blank piece of paper. She sketched out an oval face and then covered it with flowing long hair. Next, she drew smiling lips, bright eyes, and a long, narrow nose. This was the healthy, whole version of her mother she'd drawn often as a kid. She could never pin it to a memory or a photo, but this was how she wanted to remember her mother. She tore the edges, liking the ragged border. Next she drew pictures of Bella and Reggie.

"Mom! Why are you drawing us?" Bella asked.

Dani darkened Bella's curls. "Why not?"

"But why us?" Reggie said.

"I don't know. It just feels right. Your faces should decorate my jar."

"Does my nose look like that?" Reggie asked.

Dani studied the girl's long, aquiline nose. "Yes. You both are very pretty." Smearing glue on the front of each picture, she pressed the paper against the inside of the glass, holding each drawing in place until it stuck. Next she cut out flowers, folding several into three-dimensional bursts of color.

"Can I use one of those?" Reggie asked. "My mom loved flowers."

"Of course." Dani pushed her flower pile toward the girls.

"What do you remember about your mom?" Reggie asked.

"She liked to paint. She helped my dad run his business. She was a wizard at math. What do you remember about your mom?"

"My mom baked cookies," Reggie said.

"Mine mastered the slice-and-bake variety," Dani said, smiling.

"You do that," Bella said. "Slice and bake."

"Guilty," Dani said.

"Didn't Ruth try to teach you how to cook?" Bella asked.

Ruth had been Bella's de facto grandmother. When Ruth passed, it had cut as deeply as when her own mother died. "She tried. But she learned quickly that I liked to draw, so she encouraged that. My friend Ivy baked the cookies, while I drew pictures." Dani looked at Reggie. "Ruth was a very talented artist, and she taught me a lot."

She sketched a picture of Ruth smiling, standing on her favorite beach in Nags Head. A breeze teased the salt-and-pepper curls framing her deeply lined face.

"That's Ruth," Bella said.

"That is Ruth," Dani said.

Bella raised a brow. "Ruth wasn't much of a smiler."

"No." Dani grinned. "If she saw the picture now, she would grunt her disapproval. But when she did smile, I thought she was beautiful." She carefully tore the edges around the image and layered it around the other pictures. As tears burned the back of her throat, she picked up a purple marker and drew rolling waves around the top and bottom of her jar. If only the currents could wash away the sadness.

She owed a letter to her mother. And one to Ruth.

Dani texted Reggie's father and told him Reggie was doing well and she was having a good time with Bella. He sent back a terse Thank you as the girls had dashed up the stairs to Bella's room. Tomorrow, the weather was supposed to be clear and sunny, so she'd drop the girls off at camp and then drive up to Norfolk for her eye doctor's appointment. One way or another, she'd be back by two to pick Bella and Reggie up.

Five years ago, a trip to Norfolk had been second nature. She often traveled there to see artists or check out furniture for a client. Now, a trek to Norfolk involved planning that rivaled a military operation. Weather clear. *Check.* Low traffic. *Check.* Bella in school (or camp). *Check.*

What would the trip be like in five more years? Bella would be driving, and she could help. But maybe, just maybe, her eyes would stabilize. The extra planning now was annoying, but she could deal with it if her vision didn't narrow any more. She was still independent. A win all around.

Expecting to find her wine opener where it would've been in the old house, she opened the drawer next to the refrigerator. She rifled through the loosely placed utensils, hoping her online order for drawer organizers arrived soon. No wine opener.

She opened the next drawer. She wanted the house to feel like it belonged to them and they belonged to it. She wanted life to settle down into a lovely predictable routine. No wine opener.

She checked the third drawer, and then in the next, after some rummaging, finally found the wine opener in the back. A flicker of victory soothed her frustration. Two cabinets later, she had a wineglass in hand.

She uncorked the bottle, filled the new stemless (more spill-proof) glass with red wine, and took a sip. Closing her eyes, she savored the taste and this moment of calm.

Eyes open, her gaze landed on the three decorated jars lined up on the counter. She raised her wineglass to her lips. She'd enjoyed doing the project with the girls. Art projects, especially ones involving the tactile senses, were her thing. The tricky part of this exercise was the letters that needed to go inside her jar.

Out the back door, she sat in a lawn chair next to Jackson's sundial. Sipping wine, she traced the raised letters and the roman numerals that marked each hour. As she pulled her fingers counterclockwise around the dial, her mind drifted back to her mother. She had few memories, but the precious few were crisp and sharp, honed to a fine tip. But memory was a tricky thing. It changed with time, emotions, and experience, like the beach did with the tides. After twenty-plus years, she wasn't sure how much her recollections had shifted. However, she didn't dwell on pinpoint accuracy. The feelings they evoked drew her.

In one of those curated memories, Dani was six, and she and her mother had been leaving the grocery store. Dani had scrambled into the van, and her mom had opened the tailgate and loaded the paper bag of groceries into the back.

"Where are we going next, Mommy?" Dani twisted in her seat and grinned at her mother.

"Hardware. Daddy's ordered a few things I need to pick up at customer service. After that, we go home."

Dani wasn't in a rush. She always had to share Mommy with Daddy and Dalton, and this was their day. They'd gotten orange sherbet and then had their nails done. She'd chosen purple with sparkles, and so had Mommy.

As Mommy closed the tailgate, a red car pulled up beside her. A man rolled down his window and called her name. "Becky."

Mommy turned, took one look at the man, and, slamming the back tailgate, hurried around to the front. She slid behind the wheel. "Dani, put your seat belt on. We need to go." Her mother's tone was tight with tension.

"Why?"

"Don't ask why, Dani. Just do it," her mother snapped as she locked the doors.

The man got out of his car and walked up to Mom's side. His tall, lean, grizzled body moved like a spider. He knocked a knuckle on the window. Mommy started and turned the ignition key. The red car was behind them, but the car that nosed against theirs was slowly backing out. Mommy tapped the steering wheel. "Come on. Come on."

"I've missed you, Becky," the man said.

He was smiling, but something about him scared Dani. "Mommy?"

The parking space cleared, and her mother gunned the engine, nearly knocking the man over.

"Who was that?" Dani asked.

"It doesn't matter, honey." Her mother was rigid as she gripped the wheel and glanced in the rearview mirror.

"He looks mean. Are you going to tell Daddy about him?" Dani asked, knowing her father could fix all the troubles in the world.

Her mother rubbed the back of her neck. "Looks like I've got no choice."

"What was your secret, Mom? What did you have to tell Dad?" Her mother was twenty-six when Dad had seen her sitting outside the restaurant on a picnic blanket with two-year-old Dalton. Her brother was proof that her mother had lived a life before she moved to the Outer Banks. "Barely a few years older than I am now."

Dani didn't know what her mother had told her father that day about the mean man. And when Dani asked her mother about him, she'd told her not to worry.

"What could have been so terrible, Rebecca Sullivan Manchester?" Dani sipped her wine. "Keeping secrets is a superpower for the Manchester women."

If her mother was alive, perhaps they'd have had a frank conversation about the life she'd led before Dad, including Dalton's biological father and why they'd split. Who knows, maybe that conversation would have steered her away from Matthew. Knowing how headstrong she was then, doubtful. But she could've had someone to tell about her pregnancy and someone to relate to while in the throes of her divorce.

"Mom, you've seen my choices over the last twelve years. You know it didn't go to plan. I suspect that was true for you."

She traced the **I**, **II**, and **III** on the sundial and read the inscription. **Do not squander time. It is the stuff life is made of.**

This inscription showed Jackson understood time's fleeting nature. Her mother had run out of time. Matthew had. Reggie's mom. The list was always growing.

Time might have distanced Dani from the worst of her past pains, but its *tick-tock* also brought her closer to endless tomorrows bathed in darkness.

CHAPTER NINETEEN
JACKSON

Tuesday, June 6, 2023
7:45 p.m.

Fixing Juniper's boat had required only a battery change. It was a common problem on boats and the first item on his repair checklist. When he closed the hatch to the electrical system and climbed to the cabin, he turned on the starter switch. The motor roared to life.

"You make that look easy," Juniper said as she offered him an unopened cold beer. "Have you had your one beer yet today?"

"No. Thank you." He accepted the frosty can and pressed it to the back of his neck. The cold contact chased away the heat simmering in the boat engine's compartment. He popped the top and took a long sip. His one-beer-a-day limit required he savor every swallow. "Dani's father showed up yesterday, and she invited me to dinner."

"Oh, dinner with the father and daughter. Sounds cozy."

He hadn't told anyone about his relationship with Dani. At first it was too new, fragile, and likely fleeting. But after five months, he wasn't sure he could say that anymore. "I'm dating Dani."

Juniper didn't look surprised. "I had a feeling about her when I suggested you as the contractor."

"Did you? Are you adding 'matchmaker' to your list of accomplishments now?"

"You're my only client." She sipped her beer. "Dani scored points with me when she climbed into the first silo and waded through the rotting grain on the floor. She kept talking about how amazing the space could be."

"I thought she'd lost her mind when she shared her plans."

"I wasn't sure if she could pull it off, but I could tell right off she's a dreamer. And you could use a dreamer in your life."

"You think you know me so well?"

"Dude, you braided my hair before soccer practice, taught me how to drive, and carted me to college my freshman year. Yeah, I know you."

He set his can down and stared out over the water. "And what do you know?"

"You're a bit of a dreamer yourself. If you weren't, you wouldn't create such stunning boats. Dani is the same. Kindred spirits."

He'd thought at one time he'd never dream again. "Maybe."

A brow arched. "Why do you say that?"

"She's amazing. Don't get me wrong. But she's holding back. She keeps herself behind a wall." The only time that wall dropped was when they were in bed. In those moments, he saw strong, loving emotions in her eyes. Once they were dressed and back in the real world, she retreated again.

"She's been through a lot this year."

"I get it. I do. But she was like this before her ex-husband's death."

"She lost her own mother at a young age. That leaves a mark."

"It does." Old losses faded but never vanished. All he could do for Dani was offer his time and patience.

"She's living down the street from you now. Get to know her better."

"She's here, and I'm leaving." His contracts dated back to before Dani was a glimmer in his eye.

"You won't be gone forever."

But the distance would divide them. They might not intend it to, but like water, time apart had a way of seeping into cracks and widening crevices. Over time, gulfs expanded. "How did Bella do in camp?"

"Well enough. Not very open. And Reggie not showing today didn't help."

"Reggie's spending the next couple of days with Dani. She'll be driving her every day to camp."

Juniper's expression softened. "That woman has a kind heart, Jackson Cross. Better hang on to her."

"If I hold too tight, she might not like it."

"Probably. I wouldn't like it." Juniper took a long sip. "I talked to my sister today. She's going in for a scheduled C-section week after next."

Jackson swallowed. He truly wished his ex-wife the best. But he still mourned the life they'd once shared, likely always would. "You going to see her?"

"I am. Figured a little backup couldn't hurt."

"I know she'll appreciate you."

"She asked me about you."

Jackson drew in a breath, wishing he could snap the straps of regret banding his chest. "I truly wish her well."

Juniper shook her head slowly. "A part of me hoped you two would get through it all. I guess any kid wants to see their parents, even the stand-in ones, stay together forever."

"No one's fault, Juniper." If he had to put blame anywhere, it was on his shoulders. As much as his ex-wife had tried to save their marriage, he hadn't wanted to be rescued. He wanted to blow up what remained of his life and be left alone. And that's exactly what he got. For a time, he'd drunk too much and isolated himself. One night, he lay on the couch and was ready to give up. And then he heard the words whispering in his ear. *Get up. Get up. Get up.*

And for some reason, he stumbled to his feet and staggered to the shower. The cold water shocked his system, chasing away the haze and washing away sweat and dirt. As he switched off the cold tap, water dripped from his body as he stood in the stillness. The temptation to reach for a beer had been strong. That need, which had nearly swallowed him whole, still scared him. He wished he could say he'd gone cold turkey. But it had taken another six months to set the one-a-day beer limit.

But on that first day of intentions, a friend had asked him to make a sundial, so he had. After that he kept on giving scrap metal a second life. Time. For a long time, he'd resented the long lonely years stretching out in front of him. Then he'd stopped resenting the future and started searching for moments of joy in the present.

Do not squander time. It is the stuff life is made of.

He'd been content to live his monk's life. And then Juniper had introduced him to Dani Manchester. And all bets were off.

CHAPTER TWENTY
DANI

Wednesday, June 7, 2023
9:00 a.m.

Dani had risen early, made a fast trip to the grocery store, and then, after quickly restocking the cabinets and refrigerator, she changed into a green sundress with an empire waist and a hem that brushed her calves. The scooped neckline dipped to just above her cleavage, highlighting three small gold medallion necklaces. Hoop earrings dangled from her ears, and white wedge shoes added two inches to her tall frame. She finished the look with a wide-brimmed hat and a vintage Valentino purse.

After she dropped the girls off at camp, Dani drove north across the Virginia line toward Norfolk. The sun was bright and the sky clear. Light Wednesday traffic created a quick and much less stressful trip to her doctor's office.

She'd first started seeing Dr. Martin two years ago, when her ophthalmologist became worried after her annual vision test. The loss of peripheral vision had bothered him, but he quickly assured her that a visit to the specialist was the just-in-case type. She hadn't really been worried when she first visited Dr. Martin. Yes, her vision was a little off, but she'd lived through a month of all-nighters as she'd finished several home designs for her brother's construction projects. Surely a few bottles of Visine would do the trick.

She'd been tired and annoyed when she arrived at Dr. Martin's office. Mornings were her most creative time, and instead of working, she'd been driving to see a doctor who would tell her she was fine. Waste of time.

Dr. Martin's office had been sleek, modern, an explosion of glass and light. He'd been charming, attractive enough to remind her how long it had been since she had a date. He ran several tests and then asked her to return a week later. *Return?* The word defused some of her annoyance, and worry flashed for the first time. At the second consult, his partner joined Dr. Martin. The meeting started off light and easy. Weather. Traffic. Life on the Outer Banks.

And then the doctors' gazes had settled on her. Dr. Martin was the one to verbalize what both doctors suspected: retinitis pigmentosa. She'd never heard of it, and then he'd gone on to explain the disease. He'd wanted more tests. Nothing in stone yet. Still, he was fairly certain Dani was slowly losing her vision. She hadn't panicked. More tests would clear up this misunderstanding. The extra tests over the next two weeks had done the opposite. They had confirmed Dr. Martin's initial analysis.

Dani now grabbed her purse and locked her car before she headed across the parking lot. Low vision. Sightless. Unsighted. Different monikers, same ending. Each still caught in her throat whenever she uttered it. All bitter bites that she wanted to spit out but was forced to swallow.

Inside the glittering building, she moved toward the elevator, automatically counting steps. Looking back, she had developed several coping mechanisms because on some level she'd known something was wrong. In Duck, there was the bright-blue planter in her driveway that signaled when she should stop. She'd had extra pot lights installed in her kitchen and den because the house was always too dark. Picking outfits, once a joy, had become a bit of a chore, so she'd arranged all her clothes based on color and potential outfits. Shoes and jewelry were also carefully organized.

She rode the elevator to the fifth floor, checked in with the receptionist. "Hello, Sarah."

Sarah was tall, lean, with a long face. She pulled her brown hair back into a tight ponytail, drawing attention to dark-rimmed glasses and green eyes. Efficient was a good look for her.

"Hello, Ms. Manchester. How are you doing?"

"Terrific."

"You're alone today?" Worry edged her question.

"I am. I was told I wouldn't need a driver."

Sarah's lips flattened a fraction. "It's a beautiful day today."

"It sure is."

Dani's grin challenged anyone who wanted to take her independence.

She sat, grabbed the latest issue of *Vogue*, and flipped through the pages, barely looking at the articles or pictures. She'd complained about the magazines at her second appointment. Judging by the periodicals, you'd have thought that everyone sitting in this lobby was a middle-aged golfer or a medical enthusiast partial to treatises on handwashing. She'd complained to Sarah and then her doctor. At least soften the bad news with pretty fashion and cooking magazines. To their credit, they'd listened.

"Dani Manchester."

Dani set down her magazine and rose. Again, smiling at the nurse in green scrubs, she followed the carpeted hallway to Dr. Martin's examining room. After these appointments her face hurt from all the smiling. She set her handbag down, removed her glasses, and sat.

"How's the vision?" the nurse asked.

"Still firing. Haven't lost any peripheral in the last six months." The edges of the passageway were holding strong. Little victories were a win.

The nurse made a note on her iPad. "That's good news."

"We haven't met," Dani said.

"I'm Clare," she said, smiling. "I'm Dr. Martin's new nurse."

Clare conducted several tests and measurements, noted all in her iPad, and then promised the doctor would be in soon.

Dani rolled her head from side to side as she sat alone in the examining room. Soft voices in the hallway drifted through the door. *Severed cornea. Ocular nerve damage. Vision has dropped.* Colorless fears and worries dripped onto a dark canvas.

Dani cleared her throat and sat up a little straighter. "Remember, Dani, no negative thoughts."

The door opened with a snap, and Dr. Martin closed the door behind him. Blue-gray eyes regarded her with a sharpness that always made her feel like a cell under a microscope.

He wore a light-blue button-down, a dark-blue paisley tie, and black pants. His belt and tasseled shoes were leather, and though she didn't recognize the brand, she guessed they were Italian. Sharp, crisp, sexy.

He shook her hand. Smooth, no calluses. He took a seat across from her. "How are you doing, Dani?"

"Doing well, Dr. Martin." The smile flashed.

"How's life been for you the last few months?"

This was the small talk portion of their visit. She supposed he was judging her overall attitude about life. "My daughter and I just moved."

"Really, where?"

"Across the sound. Closer to the Virginia border. Closer to you."

"Away from your family?"

"They're still nearby. I had the opportunity to start up a new business. We both know my vision is on the clock, and my window of opportunity is closing."

"How'd the move go?"

"Frustrating. We've only been in the house a few days. Moves even under the best conditions are always trying. Par for the course."

"You're able to navigate the new house?" he asked.

"Pretty well. We're heading into summer, and the days are getting longer. Ask me at the December appointment how I'm steering through the shorter, darker days." Impatience snapped. Why the hell did she have to deal with this? Her tolerance for chitchat was lacking today. "I should also tell you Bella's father died in a car crash four months ago."

"Dani, I am very sorry to hear that." His brow knotted. "You're under tremendous stress."

"I thrive on stress." She crossed her legs. "Bottom line, Dr. Martin, what do the tests say?" she asked.

"Have you noticed a slight narrowing of your vision?"

"Slight? No, I don't think so."

"You might not notice it, but we were able to measure it."

"I hadn't noticed any change." That worried her. How do you boil a frog in water? Start in a cold pot and turn up the heat slowly. In her case, start in a bright room and slowly dim the lights.

"It's gradual. Which is good."

She smiled. "Any news on the future prognosis? Any better idea of my timeline?"

"We take it an appointment at a time, unless you notice a real change. Then I want to see you immediately."

She didn't ask how many millimeters of vision the narrowing tunnel had consumed. One problem at a time, and today low vision didn't top the list. "Is that all?"

He studied her a beat. "Have you met with anyone who helps the visually impaired with daily living? Last time you were here, I gave you a few contacts."

Easy to say she was just too busy, but the truth was she'd tossed the list. Any call for vision assistance was next-generation acceptance of a bleak future. "Not yet."

He shook his head. "Do you still have the references I gave you?"

"They're somewhere. The move has upended my organizational system."

"I'll have Clare send you a new packet."

"Great."

"This isn't what you expected, and I know it's easier now to ignore this. But the day will come when you can't. When that time comes, I want you to be prepared."

"Right now, my hands are full." She was fed up and not in the mood for a pep talk.

Dr. Martin studied her. "You owe it to Bella to figure this out."

Some of the wind escaped her sails. "I know you mean well, and you're right. One day very soon I'll have to investigate coping techniques. But for now, I don't have the reserves."

"Okay. But we'll revisit this in December."

"I know."

He knew better than anyone that the disease didn't care about excuses. "Call me if you experience a change in your vision, Dani, or if you have any questions."

"I will." He was smart enough to know when he shouldn't push.

"Have you told your family?" he asked.

"My brother, his girlfriend, and my father."

"No one else?"

"Not until I have to, Dr. Martin. Like I said, my plate is full right now, and I don't have the stomach for pity."

"This is looming over your life no matter what."

She plucked an invisible thread from her skirt. "Only if I let it."

"This disease is not going to give you a choice."

She shifted, uncrossed and crossed her legs. "Unless you have the audio edition of the *Losing Your Vision* operational manual, I'll figure this out, Dr. Martin."

His gaze lingered on her. "You drove here today?"

"I did."

He looked out the window toward the bright sunshine. "And when it rains or it's dark?"

A sigh trickled over her lips. "I've cobbled together helpers." She couldn't exactly claim Jackson as a support team, because he didn't know, but right now he was her go-to. "If you've said your piece, I need to get on the road. My daughter is in her grief camp, and I need to pick her up at two."

"A grief camp?"

"For kids who've lost someone. It's this week and next. It's helping. We're coping. One foot in front of the other."

His brow wrinkled as his frown deepened. "Dani, I'm very sorry."

Was that his third or fourth "sorry"? She was growing to hate the word. "Thank you."

Dr. Martin rose. "Reach out for help, Dani. I mean it. Stress never makes anything better."

"I'm well aware." She picked up her purse and slid the gold chain on her shoulder. "Thank you again."

She walked out of the office, her shoulders straight and her chin up. She wished Sarah a good day and stepped onto the elevator. The doors closed. Even alone, she kept her shoulders back. Posture affected attitude and as an added bonus made the clothes hang better.

In the lobby, she switched to sunglasses and stepped into the bright sun. She tipped her face toward the warmth. The sky was a vivid azure today. No clouds, low humidity. So stunning.

Dani walked to her car. Behind the wheel, she set her hat on the passenger seat and savored the heat that almost warmed her chilled bones. The future loomed around her, swarming like bees, ready to engulf her.

She started her engine and backed out of her spot. A horn blared, and she slammed on the brakes as a small four-door sedan zoomed past her. Heart thundering, she looked left and right before creeping out onto the road.

The drive south took a little longer in the thickening traffic. Pretty days drew people out toward the shores. When she crossed over the North Carolina line, she released a sigh.

At camp, she was glad to see Bella and Reggie waiting together. They were both smiling. A minor miracle. With twelve-year-old girls, it was difficult to predict the mood waiting for her.

The girls piled into the back seat and clicked their seat belts in place.

"How did it go today?" Dani asked.

"Good," Bella said. "Juniper loved our jars."

"I knew she would," Dani said.

"She really loved your jar, Dani," Reggie said. "She kept studying it."

"I'm glad I haven't lost my touch."

"Have you written your letter yet?" Bella asked.

Dani's hands tightened on the wheel. "I had errands to run this morning. I'll get to it tonight."

"Mom, you have to do it," Bella said. "It's way harder than decorating the jar."

Dani hadn't pressed Bella about the contents of her letter but now wondered. What did you say to a parent who had died? "I know. I will."

"We'll all put them in the jars next Thursday, and then we'll put them in the water."

"Into the sound?" Dani asked.

"That's what Juniper said," Bella added.

When Dani pulled into her driveway, she glanced toward the gallery and was disappointed to see that Jackson's truck wasn't there. His work nearly complete, soon there'd be no professional reason for him to visit. And then he'd sail off into the sunset. Not forever, of course, but if she wanted to see him again, it would mean a conversation with Bella.

At the house, the girls ran inside and let out Rosie, who barked as she dashed toward Dani, then paused to pee. "Good girl."

"Do we have anything to eat in the house?" Bella asked.

"I restocked the refrigerator this morning. Make yourself a snack."

"Did you get the ingredients for chocolate chip cookies?" Bella asked.

"I did."

"Can we bake cookies?"

"I can't help you. I have to change and get to work."

"I know what to do," Reggie said.

"Perfect. I'll leave you girls to it." As Rosie dashed back in the house, Dani slipped off her wedge shoes and hurried up the stairs to her bedroom. She closed the door and sat down on the edge of her bed. She tugged off her earrings. The adrenaline that had fueled her this morning flooded from her body. Her shoulders slumped. It was so tempting to slip under the covers and sleep for a week.

Her phone rang, and Reggie's father's name appeared. Her mind staggered away from a long lush nap back toward the life that demanded her attention. "Mr. Bailey."

He cleared his throat. "Ms. Manchester."

"Reggie is here. Would you like to talk to her?"

"No, no, I'll call her later. I wanted to ask you a favor."

"What is it?"

"Can Reggie stay with you while I'm traveling? I mean beyond this week. I'll be home on the weekends, but the weeks are going to be tough. Ms. Nelson has helped, but she can't do it on a regular basis." His voice sounded gruff, full of emotion. Asking for favors didn't come easy for this man.

"Are we talking about Monday through Thursday?" Downstairs she could hear cabinets opening and closing as Bella likely searched for the baking pans and mixing bowls.

"The schedule can change from week to week. I'm driving a lot these days. Bills to pay. And I'd feel better about it, knowing Reggie was with you."

He didn't know her. But she knew what desperation smelled like and how it forced unimaginable choices. "Where are you?"

"Outside of Denver, but I'll be home late Thursday."

"Reggie misses you, Mr. Bailey." She tugged off her glasses and pinched the bridge of her nose.

A heavy silence settled. "I know. And I miss her. But I just need a little time."

Time. That fragile commodity indifferent to people's needs or wants. It moved at its steady, selfish pace, leaving everyone scrambling behind. "Sure, she can stay with us. I like Reggie. She's a good kid."

"She's a great kid. She was really close to her mother. She's handled all this better than me."

"How are you doing?"

"Getting by," he said on a sigh.

"I'm truly sorry for your loss." The words sounded anemic and useless.

"Thanks."

"I'm happy to fill in, Mr. Bailey, but Reggie still needs her father."

"I know. I know. And I'll be home on Thursday, and then we can take it from there."

"Okay."

"Thank you."

She closed her eyes, wondering how much more she could ladle on her plate. "You're very welcome. Call your daughter. My daughter lost her father, and I can tell you she misses him so much. Girls need their dads."

"Right. I know. I'll call soon. Thank you, Ms. Manchester. I have to go." The line went dead.

Dani lowered the phone as she turned toward her dresser and picked up a picture of a grinning Dani, Matthew, and Bella. The image had been taken at the grand opening of one of his restaurants five years ago. Bella was about seven. Right after the picture was snapped, Matthew had run off to handle a problem in the kitchen.

Suddenly she was angry and frustrated with Matthew. How many times had Bella needed him just to be around and simply be her dad?

How many times had Dani rearranged schedules so Bella could see him? Or put off paying a bill because of a late child support payment?

She drew in a breath and slowly let it trickle over her lips. "Don't dig into old wounds. You got plenty of fresh ones to tend, old girl."

When Dani tripped, she'd felt pressured to move faster. Feeling rushed, and maybe distracted, she hadn't been thinking. If she had, she would've been aware of the fading light and been on alert.

But Dani wasn't thinking. She was rushed, distracted, and anxious to join the girls by the firepit on the back patio. The girls were waiting to roast marshmallows and giggling as they poked their sticks into the fire. Normal moments like this had been in short supply the last few months, and she was so ready to enjoy it.

Maybe it was because she was carrying blankets and a basket filled with her s'mores supplies. Maybe she was worried about the "slight change" in her vision. And what about Jackson? Should she call him? Would a conversation like this send him running? Did it matter if it did? She kept reminding herself that theirs likely wasn't a long-term relationship. He had ships to sail, and she had a business to launch.

Matthew always said she could be driven, even unreasonable, when it came to goals. "When you get an idea in your head," he'd said, "you can be annoying."

The automatic comparison between Jackson and Matthew was as unlikely as it was unwanted. The two men were completely different.

Too many thoughts, too little light.

Whatever the reason, she missed the last step as she was exiting the back door, and she stumbled. She took a giant step, hoping to catch herself, but with her arms full and her balance off, she tipped to the right, fell, and hit her shoulder on the stone patio. The blow sent the blankets and s'mores supplies flying, knocked the wind from her, and blasted pain through her body.

"Mom!" Bella shouted.

Bella and Reggie were at her side in seconds, trying to help her sit.

As she sat up, pain shot through her arm. She cradled it as her heart slammed against her chest. "I'm fine, girls. It's not a big deal."

"Mom, you did a shoulder plant!" Bella shouted.

Dani tried to roll the tension from her shoulder. It was stiff, and the skin felt like it had been scraped raw. She wiggled her fingers. Seemed the critical parts were working okay. Not broken, but maybe sprained. "Just a stumble, Bella. I'm fine."

"Not a stumble," Bella said. "You fell hard."

"It's okay. No damage done." She'd have one hell of a bruise on her shoulder, but other than that, manageable.

"That's what my mom said the first time she fell," Reggie said softly.

Dani looked at the girls, who'd both gone pale. "Reggie, I'm okay. It was just a fall."

"My mom said the same," she whispered. "She laughed and told me not to worry."

A frown furrowed Bella's brow. "Mom?"

"I'm not sick like Reggie's mother was. I don't have cancer. I stumbled on the steps because I wasn't looking where I was going. My mind was a million miles away."

"Do you have a brain tumor or some other disease?" Bella asked. "Your mom died young."

"I'm not going anywhere, Bella." She took ahold of both the girls' hands. "I'm not dying."

"You swear?" Bella demanded.

Dani looked between her daughter's panicked face and Reggie's stricken expression. "Girls, it's okay. I bruised my pride and shoulder."

Bella shook her head as she studied her with narrowed eyes. "You've been acting weird for a long time. Even before Dad died."

"Weird?" Dani thought she'd done a good job of hiding her situation.

Bella held up one finger. "You don't drive in the rain or at night." The second finger rose. "You get moody sometimes, like a bad thought is stuck in your head." The third finger joined the other two. "And you don't paint anymore."

Dani rose and gathered up the blankets, the bag of marshmallows, the chocolate bars, and the box of graham crackers. She moved toward one of the lawn chairs with as much dignity as she could muster. She'd been avoiding this conversation for almost eighteen months, and she certainly didn't want to have it in front of Reggie. But the timing was what it was, and if she put this off again, she risked creating distrust in Bella. "I'm having a little trouble with my eyes."

"Your eyes?" Bella asked. "Like cancer of the eyes?"

"No. Let me repeat, I have no cancer. None. But my eyes aren't working as well as they used to. That probably contributed to that little fall."

"That's why you got new glasses?" Bella asked.

"Yes. The glasses help. But you're right, I can't drive in the dark anymore or in the rain."

Bella studied Dani's eyes as if she'd never seen them before. "When will you be able to drive in the rain and dark again?"

"I'm not sure when. But for now, I just have to plan my errands and outings better."

"But you're not dying, right?" Bella pressed.

"Not dying." She smiled and brushed the hair back from Bella's eyes. "Hope to live to be an old woman."

Bella embraced Dani, locking her arms in a tight bear hug. Her tender shoulder protested, but Dani hugged her daughter close. She looked up at Reggie and saw the tears glistening. Dani extended her hand to Reggie, and the girl fell into her arms. Both girls cried.

"It's okay, girls. It's okay." For all the smiles and giggles today, their grief bubbled under the surface. But that's what grief did. It was patient, always lurking in the shadows, ready to spoil a happy moment, sour a day, or prompt unexpected tears.

They stood together for several minutes, and she was content to hold the girls.

Reggie pulled away and rubbed her eyes. "I'm glad you're not dying."

"Me too, honey. How about we roast a few marshmallows now?"

Bella squeezed Dani and then straightened. "When did you find out your mother was sick?"

"She and my father sat me down and told me," Dani said. Most of the details of that day were sketchy, but some moments remained vivid and clear. Her mother's sharp blue eyes, the slight slump of her father's shoulders as if he'd taken a punch, and Dalton's rigid posture and clenched hands.

"What did she say?" Bella asked.

"That she loved me." She hesitated as her voice threatened to break. "And that no matter what, she'd always be close."

"But she died," Reggie said.

"Yes."

"Do you feel her close?" Bella asked.

"No, I can't say that I have or do," Dani said. "There have been a few times that I dreamed about her, but that was a long time ago. I wish I did feel her, but I don't."

"I don't feel Daddy," Bella said. "I keep looking around, thinking I'll see him, a shimmer or something, but nothing."

Reggie frowned. "Sometimes, I think I hear my mother whisper to me at night."

"What does she say?" Dani wasn't sure if she should worry about the girl or be jealous.

"That she loves me. That I shouldn't worry. Be patient with Daddy."

"That's a good thing, Reggie," Dani said. "You know she'd be here if she could."

"Mom, are you going blind?" Bella asked.

"Now, where did that come from?" Dani asked. Her prognosis wasn't great, but no one had been able to put a time limit on her vision.

"You said you had trouble with your eyes. That's blind, right?"

"It doesn't mean that. It means I have to stay current on my eyeglass prescription and see my doctor regularly."

"Does Uncle Dalton know?" Bella asked.

"Dalton, Ivy, and Grandpa know that I don't like to drive when visibility is low."

"Is that why Grandpa came by the other day?" Bella asked. "Is he worried about you?"

"Grandpa has fretted over me since the day I was born. But he came because he really wanted an excuse to see his favorite granddaughter."

Bella wasn't distracted from her course of questioning. "Will you have to carry a cane? Or if you lose your sight, can Rosie be your guide dog?"

Guide dog. Canes. Her doctor had mentioned aids for the visually impaired. And she'd gone out of her way today and every other day to ignore accommodations. "Rosie isn't trained to be a guide dog."

"I could train her," Bella said. "She loves treats, and she can see really well."

Dani smiled as she tucked a stray curl behind Bella's ear. "That's very nice of you, but I think becoming a guide dog requires very specialized training that starts when they're puppies."

"Are we going to get another dog?" Bella asked.

"No," Dani said quickly. "No new dogs. Do you think we could roast these marshmallows? I'm starving for a nice juicy burnt one."

Bella's gaze lingered on Dani as she reached in the basket and removed the marshmallows and sticks. "Reggie, have you ever had a s'more?"

"A couple. But I don't like my marshmallows burnt."

Dani chuckled as she placed a plump white marshmallow on the end of a stick and handed it to her. "You're the chef. You decide how you want yours."

With marshmallows skewered on their sticks, each stuck theirs in the flickering flames.

Sitting back, she realized the full weight of what had happened. She hadn't told the girls the entire truth, which in and of itself was a lie. And the time for a serious conversation with her daughter was coming fast. This wasn't something she could hide forever. Sooner or later even the days wouldn't be bright enough for her, and like it or not, everyone would know. Including Jackson.

CHAPTER TWENTY-ONE
DANI

Thursday, June 8, 2023
9:00 a.m.

Dani dropped off the girls at camp. Juniper had planned more circle time, woodworking crafts, and swimming during the heat of the day. As she strode toward her car, her phone rang. When she saw her ex-mother-in-law's name, she tensed. Inside the car, she turned on the engine and drew in a breath.

"Adele, how are you?"

"I'm doing as well as can be expected," Adele said carefully. "How is Bella?"

"I just dropped her off at grief camp."

"A grief camp? What do children do at a camp like that?"

"They talk about feelings, make crafts, and play in the sound."

"It's got to be terribly depressing for the child."

"I think it's helping. It's got us both talking."

"What will talking change?"

Dani sighed. "Talking is better than bottling up feelings."

"If you say so."

At Matthew's funeral, Dani had stood by a weeping Bella as his coffin was lowered into the ground. Her former in-laws, standing side by side but not touching, were stoic. Dani and Adele had never gotten along. Adele always believed Dani had trapped Matthew into marriage. Though Adele grew to love Bella, she never missed an opportunity to talk (especially when she'd been drinking) about Matthew's successes in spite of so many early challenges. *"If only my boy had a life unencumbered."*

Dani, for Bella's sake, hadn't argued with Adele. When Matthew took Bella to see his mother, her daughter had always spoken well of her visits. So, Dani had let it all go. For the sake of family harmony, and all that crap.

"Is there something I can do for you, Adele?"

"I'd love to have Bella this Friday night. I can pick her up about ten. Seeing her grandparents might help ease some of the shock of your sudden move."

Dani rubbed the back of her neck. "I'll ask Bella and call you later this afternoon."

"Of course she'll say yes."

"I'll call you, okay?"

"Sounds good. Thank you, Dani."

"Of course, Adele."

Adele might not be Dani's number one fan, but she was Bella's grandmother and a link to Matthew.

As she pulled away, she glanced up toward the thick darkening skies promising rain. The county had been in a drought most of the spring, and now, of all times, the heavens had decided to drop monsoons on Currituck County.

While she still had dry roads, she drove to Reggie's house to take in the mail, which Reggie had worried over at breakfast, and make sure there were no issues with the house. As she pulled up to the Baileys' home, she noticed the neighbor sitting on her front porch rocker.

Dani parked, grabbed the mail, and walked toward the woman, who she guessed was Ms. Nelson. As far as this woman knew, Dani was a random stranger.

The neighbor's house was a one-level brick rancher with a dark roof covered with an inch of pine needles. Spiderwebs blanketed unkempt boxwood shoots as high as the windows.

She raised her sunglasses and walked up the path, gravel and twigs crunching under her wedge shoes. "Ms. Nelson?"

"That's right." Ms. Nelson had a petite, full-figured frame and gray-streaked black hair pinned back in a bun. Her sun-weathered skin was deeply lined, and age spots dotted the left side of her face. She wore a blue extra-large T-shirt, jeans, and no shoes.

"I'm Dani Manchester. I bought the silos."

Ms. Nelson nodded. "I've heard about you. Reggie said nice things about you and Bella."

"Reggie is a great kid."

"Her daddy told me she was staying with you."

"She is. In fact, I just dropped the kids off at camp."

"I took Reggie that first day."

"You missed the second day." She was still annoyed about that.

Ms. Nelson shrugged. "And you took Reggie under your wing, just as you were supposed to."

"You make it sound like that was inevitable."

"It was."

Dani grimaced. Reggie had said Ms. Nelson was quirky. "She's wonderful."

"One of the best." Her rocker squeaked as she leaned forward. "I always knew Juniper would end up doing something like the camp. She walks hand in hand with grief, and she's not afraid to go toe to toe with it."

"She's great."

"What are you doing here?"

"I'm grabbing the mail."

"Reggie must have been fretting over it. Her mama was always keen on the mail. Said you never knew what good news could show up in the mailbox. Reggie's a lot like Nancy. That kid does backflips to keep up with all the things her mama did. A shame. I want her to be a kid."

"I'm hoping to keep the girls entertained with activities."

"Oh, I know you're just what the doctor ordered for Reggie. On Monday night, she couldn't stop talking about you. Your buying the Nelson property almost feels fated."

"You see the future?"

"Sometimes."

Dani didn't have time for the future now. "Well, I just wanted to introduce myself."

"Maybe you could ask me about the history of the place. I suppose you heard I grew up there."

"I did hear that." Her mind quickly ticked through her to-do list. Even if she left now, there wasn't enough time in the day to get it all done. "Is now good?"

"No time like the present."

Up the brittle wooden steps, Dani held a shaky handrail. Wind chimes made of bottle bottoms clinked over two mismatched rockers and a green wrought iron table sporting a large glass ashtray overflowing with cigarette butts. She sat in the chair beside Ms. Nelson.

Ms. Nelson glanced out toward the sky. "If you're worried about the rain, it won't come until you get home."

Dani settled her purse on her lap. "Why would I be worried about the rain?"

"I don't know," Ms. Nelson said carefully. "You tell me."

"My car doesn't do well on wet pavement."

Ms. Nelson's eyes brightened with amusement. "That's as good of an excuse as any. Luckily today, we got time before the rain."

Dani's rocker tipped back, forcing her fanny back into the deep seat. She gripped the rocker's arms.

"That one tips. I used to sit in it when I was younger, but it's not the kind of chair for someone with bad knees and a touchy back."

"I hope I can get out of it."

Ms. Nelson chuckled as she reached in her housecoat pocket for a rumpled packet of cigarettes. "What do you think of your house so far?"

"Still feels like someone else's," she said honestly. "My brain still defaults to my old house. I fumble for the right front door key on my ring, or search all the kitchen drawers and cabinets to find a plate or bowl, or when I wake up in the middle of the night, I don't know where I am."

"It takes time. How'd you skin your arm?"

Dani glanced at her red elbow. "Didn't see a step."

"Adjustments are hard."

"I was hoping to skip the unfamiliar phase and jump straight to the feeling-right-at-home part." She'd stayed up until midnight unpacking boxes and arranging and rearranging the kitchen, chairs, and lamps. She'd hung several pictures and installed the curtain rods in the living room. At one point she was on the third rung of the ladder, her hands extended as she smoothed out the curtain. She'd felt someone behind her and looked, expecting to see Bella or Reggie. But there was no one. And then there was Bella's mystery friend, who no one other than Bella had seen.

"There's no skipping the tough parts." Ms. Nelson fussed with the folds of her blouse. "But you've always tried to skip the tough parts, haven't you?"

The truth behind the words was uncomfortable. "Why do you say that?"

"I can feel the walls you've built," she said. "You don't let many behind them."

"There are no walls between my daughter and me."

"There are some, though they're not as thick as the ones between you and the rest of the world. What are you going to do when Bella leaves?"

Dani's chest clenched. "She's only twelve."

"You expect her to go to college?"

"If that's what she wants." That was six years away, which in this moment felt like a lifetime.

Smoke curled around Ms. Nelson's face. "Look back six years. Does it feel like that time flew?"

"Yes." She pictured a gap-toothed Bella on her sixth birthday. The next six years would go as fast. Her baby was already turning into a young woman who was spending less and less time with Dani.

Ms. Nelson's rocker squeaked as she sat back. "In case you're wondering, you're going to live to be an old woman, Dani Manchester."

Dani blinked, surprised by the comment. "How do you know that?"

Ms. Nelson dangled a cigarette in her lips and flicked the flint on her plastic lighter until a flame danced. She held it to the tip. Smoke trailed up around her narrowed eyes. "I have an eye for things like this."

Dani sat very still as she pictured herself as old and totally blind.

"It's going to be a good life," Ms. Nelson said. "Not the one you were expecting, but a good one."

"Really? How could you possibly know?"

"I know things."

Dani cleared her throat. The future scared her. "Tell me about the silos and the farmhouse."

"What do you want to know?"

"Why am I hearing sounds in my house? There have been several times I could've sworn someone was in the room with me."

Ms. Nelson drew in a lungful of smoke. "What kind of sounds?"

"Whispers," Dani said. "Just enough to make me feel insane."

Ms. Nelson stared at the tip of her cigarette. "The body is a magical thing. You lose one sense, and another gets sharper."

"This isn't my sense of smell or touch. It's hearing something in the house that I know intellectually is not there."

"I used to hate it when that happened. Very disconcerting. But after a while you get used to it."

"What if I don't want to get used to it? What if I want my home to house only my daughter and me?"

Ms. Nelson smiled. "You might be out of luck. I don't think you get a vote."

"I paid for it. That should count for something."

Ms. Nelson's throaty chuckle chafed like sandpaper.

Dani tipped her head back. "Are you telling me what I'm hearing is real?"

"I would say yes, but most people think I'm crazy."

"What am I supposed to do?"

"Talk to it."

"Talk to it. You mean sit in my living room and talk to the air?"

"A glass of wine would help."

Dani chuckled and realized she'd lost her damn mind. "Any theories on who it is? You lived in the house, so maybe you have an idea."

"A few folks passed in the house. My grandmother in 1975. And I had an older sister who drowned in the sound."

"That's awful. You lost a sister?"

"She was eleven when she died, but that was before I was born. I never met her. I pressed my mom a few times about her, but Mom didn't want to talk about it." Smoke trickled over her lips. "A renovation does stir things up. Wouldn't surprise me if you've done just that."

"Terrific."

"In your case, I get the feeling someone's trying to get your attention."

"Why?"

"I don't know."

In the distance, thunder rumbled. "My ex-husband died four months ago. Could it be him?"

Ms. Nelson shook her head. "I don't think it's a man."

"How would you know that?"

A smile teased her lips. "I don't know anything for sure. It's all just a feeling."

Right. As much as she wanted a little history on her property, it was time to go. "I better get going. Thank you for your time, Ms. Nelson."

"Call me Kit. Come back and see me anytime. I suspect you'll have more questions. And tell Reggie I said hey. I'm glad she's with you. You're the best thing for her."

"Visit us at the Silos by the Sound. We're officially open on June nineteenth."

"I'll get by sooner or later. Be curious to see the changes."

"Great. Reggie will keep you posted on our opening day."

"Look forward to it."

As she moved down the stairs, Dani paused. "What was your sister's name?"

"Anna."

"Anna? Bella said she met a girl on our dock but didn't get her name."

Kit's eyes grew wistful. "Did she?"

"Is there a girl that lives within walking distance of my house?"

"Not that I know of."

Why was she having a conversation about ghosts and Bella's make-believe friend with Kit Nelson? "It was nice meeting you."

"You too. I'm sure I'll see you soon."

Dani drove home, let Rosie out, and spent the next two hours in the gallery assembling shelves with the dog looking on. She checked her watch. If her luck continued, the rain would hold another hour. By then she'd be back here with the girls.

Rain droplets pelted the metal roof.

A truck pulled up, and the front door opened to Jackson. She patted the sweat from her forehead. "Hey there. I was starting to wonder if you'd left on one of your sailing trips."

"Close. I was in Norfolk inking deals with a few clients. Still leaving next week."

"Looking forward to it?"

"Sure. Not as much as I used to."

"Why not?"

"You." No hedging in his tone. "I'm going to miss you."

A warmth spread over her. "I'm going to miss you too. But you know where to find me."

"You've been fluttering around the last couple of months. Hard to get you to alight."

"I'm standing still right now."

He closed the distance between them, cupped her face with his hands, and kissed her. "I've missed this."

"Me too." She leaned into his calloused hands and pressed against his chest. She wanted nothing more than to vanish into her house with him.

"It's raining."

"Raining? Right."

His eyes sparked with amusement. "Thought you might need a ride to pick up the girls."

"You came here for that?"

"Am I wrong?"

What was the point of making excuses? "I was hoping the rain would clear."

He chuckled. "I'll drive."

In his truck, he easily backed out of the lot and drove the five miles to the camp. As the rain pelted and they waited, Jackson leaned over and kissed Dani.

"What was that for?"

"Just reminding myself of what matters," he said.

Dani looked up toward the shelter and saw Bella staring toward the truck. She was frowning until Reggie came up beside her. The girls dashed across the lot and fell into the back seat.

Bella eyed Jackson as she clicked her seat belt. Dani shifted, realizing her sharp-eyed daughter had seen them.

"How was camp today, girls?" Dani asked.

"Great!" Reggie said.

"Good," Bella said, her tone flat.

"My dad texted me about a half hour ago. He's home," Reggie said. "He made better time than he thought."

Dani looked at her phone and realized she'd missed the text. "That's great. Do you want us to drop you off?"

"That would be awesome. I can't wait to tell Dad about the camp."

"Do you mind?" Dani asked Jackson.

"Not at all."

Dani texted Ronny and told him they'd be at his home in a half hour. As she set the phone down, she could feel her sullen daughter's mood deepening as Jackson drove toward Reggie's house. A big rig was parked in front of the rancher.

As Reggie scrambled to unfasten her seat belt, Dani got out of the truck. She glanced toward Kit Nelson's house, but there was no sign of the woman.

Dani and Reggie were halfway to the porch when Reggie's father opened the front door. He looked freshly showered, though the shadows under his eyes proved he'd been driving nonstop for the last couple of days.

Reggie ran up to her dad, and he wrapped her in a big bear hug. "Hey, kiddo!"

Dani looked back at the truck and saw Bella staring at the two of them. She wondered what fresh wound this father-and-daughter reunion had opened.

Ronny extended his hand to Dani. "I appreciate the help, Ms. Manchester."

"Dani. And we love having Reggie. She's welcome anytime."

"I appreciate that. I'm headed out again on Monday."

"Text me your schedule. Plan on Reggie staying anytime you need us. Will you be back in time for camp graduation?"

"I'm going to give it my best," he said.

"If you can't make it," Dani said, "we can FaceTime so you can watch."

"I appreciate that."

Reggie turned and hugged Dani closely. "Thank you."

"Anytime, honey. Now enjoy your time with your dad. And have a great weekend."

"I will." Reggie looked around Dani and waved to the truck. Bella waved back, but there was little excitement in her smile.

Back in the truck, Dani hooked her belt. "He seems nice."

"Ronny's a good guy," Jackson said.

"I like Reggie," Dani said. "She's a good friend, don't you think, Bella?"

"Yeah," Bella said.

In the rearview mirror, Dani watched Bella fold her arms over her chest and stare out the window. They rode to the silos in silence.

When they arrived home, Bella got out of the truck. As she moved to leave, Dani said, "What do you say?"

Bella drew in a breath. "Thank you, Jackson."

"Anytime, Bella."

She turned and hurried toward the house. Dani got out of the truck and walked to Jackson's truck window.

"I'm sorry she's turned so surly. It's been a roller coaster the last few months."

"It had to hurt when she saw Reggie with her dad."

"I know."

"What are your plans for the weekend? The weather is supposed to be pretty. And I could take you and Bella sailing."

"Bella is going to stay with Matthew's mother this weekend. Her grandparents are going to visit with her and drive her to a party at her friend's house."

"You have the weekend to yourself?"

She nodded slowly. "I do."

"Would you like to go sailing?"

"I have to finish the shelves and get the gallery ready for the new vendors arriving on Monday. But if you wanted to stop by Friday . . ."

"I can put those shelves together while you organize the gallery. That'll leave us more free time."

"You don't have to do that."

"Consider my motives selfish."

She chuckled. "Really?"

"You'll be amazed how quickly I can assemble shelves."

"I'll hold you to it."

The smile brightening his eyes vanished, leaving only seriousness behind. "It's been too long since we were alone. I've really missed you. Us."

"I missed you too."

He didn't pressure her about the future, and she was grateful. Planning ahead to Saturday afternoon was about as far as she could commit.

"See you Saturday."

"Looking forward to it." His voice was pure silk.

She walked away from the truck, sensing he was watching. He'd commented a couple of times that he liked the shape of her behind.

"I never miss a chance to watch you walk away."

He'd spoken those words on a Wednesday morning in February. She'd risen out of bed and leaned down to pick up her clothes. When it came to her business, she was as bold as they came. But personally, well, she was surprised to hear herself say, "You like what you see?"

He was sitting up in his bed, the sheets pooled around his lap. "Very much."

Whatever they had was new, fresh, and exhilarating. Untarnished by life's pressures and demands.

That was changing. No keeping life's complications out forever.

Inside the house, she looked out toward the open back door and saw Bella sitting by the shoreline with Rosie. If only she had a magic pill or spell to make that kid's life perfect.

Dani dropped her purse on the coffee table and stepped out the back door. She crossed the yard and took a seat next to Bella.

"Your grandmother called. She'd like to pick you up tomorrow. Want to spend tomorrow night with her?"

"Can she take me to Finn's party at Chelsea's house?"

"I'm sure she can."

"Good."

Bella continued to stare at the water. Dani knew when her daughter was open to conversation and when she wasn't. Currently she was not. "I'm headed to the gallery."

"Is he your boyfriend?" Bella asked.

"He's my friend."

"You don't kiss friends like that." Bella whirled around.

"I like him, Bella." The beginnings of a headache pounded behind her eyes. "But I don't know what's going to happen between us."

"Why don't you know? You *kissed* him. Doesn't that mean love and marriage?"

She'd never been in love before and had no idea where it led. "Not necessarily. One step at a time."

"For the record, I don't like him." Her daughter was pouting.

"Why not?"

"Because you aren't supposed to have a boyfriend. Ever."

They'd never had this conversation before. More uncharted territory. "Why not?"

"Because you loved Daddy."

"Daddy and I stopped being a couple over ten years ago, Bella. And I don't think we ever gave you the impression we were going to get back together, did we?"

"No, but I thought—"

"You thought what?"

"You two got along so well. I thought that you'd get married again." The words rushed out, leaving her deflated.

"No, Daddy and I were friends. That's it. And you know he dated other ladies."

Bella's eyes welled with tears. "I thought he was being stupid."

"No, he was getting on with his life. I never once told him not to see other people."

Bella blinked. "Why haven't you dated anyone?"

"I don't know. I always thought I was too busy."

"And now?"

"I'm not too busy for Jackson."

"Does he know?"

"Know what?"

"That your eyes are giving you trouble?" Bella's gaze was direct, cutting.

Dani stood straighter.

Bella's eyes narrowed. "There's more to tell, isn't there?"

She hadn't technically lied, and now she had a choice. To be honest with her child or keep weaving half truths that would backfire one day. "Yes, there's more. I'm not dying, so don't get that in your head. But I am losing my sight."

"You're going *blind*," Bella said bluntly.

"It's not going to happen overnight," Dani said. "But eventually, ten, twenty, thirty years, I'll lose most of it."

"A long time from now," Bella said thoughtfully.

At her young age, ten years was forever. For Dani, the next decade loomed so close. "It's not going to change our lives now."

"You sure?"

"Yes," she said honestly.

Bella cocked her head. "And you told this to Jackson?"

Her girl was smart and would keep pressing until her questions were answered. "We haven't had that conversation yet, and I'm asking you not to tell him or Reggie until I do."

Bella's frown relaxed, but her gaze remained piercing. "If you haven't told him, I guess that means you're not that serious about him."

Dani shifted and did her best to remain relaxed. "I'll have a conversation with Jackson very soon."

"And what if he doesn't want to stay when he knows he'll be driving you everywhere forever?"

Hearing her own worries voiced out loud was doubly uncomfortable. A prickly lump lodged in her chest. She cleared her throat. "Then he doesn't."

Bella's anger suddenly melted as if the idea of Jackson leaving was a good thing. She hugged Dani. "Don't worry, Mom. I'm here for you no matter what."

Dani's eyes grew moist. "I know, baby girl. And I'm always there for you."

CHAPTER TWENTY-TWO

DANI

Friday, June 9, 2023
9:00 a.m.

Adele Peterson's white Volvo parked in front of the gallery. She was nearly an hour early, but Adele was always early.

When Bella was six months old, Adele had called for the first time and asked to see the baby. Dani agreed, believing the girl needed to know her only grandmother. Adele had arrived an hour early and found Dani half-dressed and Bella still wearing a milk-stained shirt.

The second time Adele arrived a half hour early, Dani had caught on to the pattern. From then on, she'd always made it a point to be ready well in advance.

Now as Adele crossed the gravel driveway toward the front steps, Dani checked her lipstick in a round silver-studded mirror hanging by the front entrance and opened the door.

Her ex-mother-in-law was six or seven inches shorter than Dani, and her frame was thick and stout. She'd swept salt-and-pepper hair into her trademark twist and wore tan slacks, a blousy sleeveless white top, and beige flats.

Dani grinned. "Adele. How are you?"

Adele looked a little taken aback. "I'm well. And you?"

"Doing just fine."

"You look remarkably pulled together, considering."

Dani heard the censor in Adele's tone and chose to ignore it. "Bella is almost packed and ready to go."

Adele hugged Dani. "Good. I'm excited to have her."

"She can't wait to see the beach. You'd think she'd been gone for years."

"I don't know why you left." Adele had been upset when Dani had told her they were moving. It didn't matter that she was only going to be thirty miles away.

"As you can see, we're not that far away."

"It's not the same."

"Where is Mike?" On pretty days her father-in-law spent all day on the golf course. These days she imagined he was living there, rain or shine.

"Golf, of course. He's joining Bella and me for an early dinner."

Footsteps thundered on the steps. Bella appeared, with Rosie chasing after her. "Grandma!"

Bella hugged Adele as Rosie wagged her tail. "I'm so excited to see you."

"It feels like ages!" Adele said.

"Grandma, I saw you two weeks ago," Bella said.

Adele chuckled. "At my age, a week can feel like forever."

"Adele, you're sixty-three," Dani said. "That's the new forty."

"Maybe for you, but for me it means I'm no spring chicken."

Matthew's parents had offered the garage apartment on their property when Bella was eight months old, but he'd declined. As scared as Dani and Matthew had been after Bella was born, they'd both known having Adele within earshot would be too much. Her father had offered a house he'd built on spec, but Matthew had been too proud, so they'd settled into a very small apartment on the western side of Roanoke Island. Looking back on those cramped rooms, long work hours, and colicky baby, it was a wonder their marriage had lasted a full year.

"I've got a few fun things planned for us," Adele said.

"Like what?" Bella asked.

"Doughnuts, shopping, and hot dogs at your favorite places."

"Cool," Bella said. "Could I invite some friends over to your condo pool this afternoon?"

"Aren't you girls going to see each other at a party tonight?"

"Yeah, but I never see them anymore."

Adele smiled. "Sure, I don't see why not."

"And can I go to Finn's party?" Bella pressed. "It's at Chelsea's house."

"Finn and Chelsea?"

"They've all been friends since kindergarten," Dani said. "If you drive Bella to Chelsea's house in Kitty Hawk and then pick her up by eleven, it's fine with me."

"Eleven is late," Adele said.

Bella regarded her grandmother with angelic eyes. "Convincing people is my superpower."

Adele chuckled. "When you look at me like that, I see your dad at that age."

"I'm like Dad?" Bella asked.

"You're a carbon copy, baby," Adele said.

At first comments like that had annoyed Dani. Nine months of pregnancy, fifteen hours of labor, and a C-section, and the kid didn't look like her. Despite unspoken questions about Bella's paternity after their rushed marriage, one look at the kid silenced them all.

Fast-forward twelve years, and Dani was glad Bella could look in a mirror and see her father. It was comforting, knowing her face was a memento of her dad. When Dani looked in the mirror, she found no traces of her mother. All her memories were based on old photos.

"Chop-chop, kiddo," Adele said. "I want to get across that bridge before the tourists start streaming in. The season is opening, and we all know Fridays can be crazy."

Bella picked up her backpack, and the three walked out to Adele's car. Dani kissed Bella and made sure she had her seat belt secured. "See you Sunday at eight a.m."

"That soon?" Bella said.

"Afraid so. We need to get ahead of the traffic." Dani kissed Bella again. "You two have fun, Adele."

"Are you going to be okay without me?" Bella asked.

"Rosie and I will be fine, Bella," Dani said. "Not to worry."

Bella had been watching her more closely since their conversation last night. "Call me if you need me."

Dani smiled. "Back at you, kid."

"Okay, girls. It's only for a couple of days. Let's get going, Bella."

Dani closed the back door and knelt by Rosie. The dog licked her face. Loss and loneliness washed over her as she watched Adele's Volvo take a left onto the highway and vanish out of sight.

"Rosie, I'm already missing our girl."

The dog wiggled, and Dani set her down. Rosie ran to her dog bed in the corner. Dani had plenty to do, and with Bella gone for the next forty-eight hours, she had the time to do it.

Inside the house, which was far too quiet now, she grabbed a cold soda from the refrigerator and then walked to the gallery. She stared at the five uncrated boxes of shelves.

As she stood in the quiet, she sensed someone standing behind her. She turned, expecting to see Jackson or maybe an artist delivering their art. But there was no one. Just the beam of sunlight streaming through the front door. Dust danced in the light. Outside, cars drove past on the highway.

"Nothing there, Dani. Stop being so skittish."

Dani took the first half-finished shelf apart and reassembled it. That little task took two hours, but her hope was, as she uncrated the next box, that the lessons learned had stuck. "It should be easier this time, right, Rosie?"

The dog rose, pawed at her soft bedding, and circled before she plopped down again.

Dani laid out each piece, lined up the screws, and hoped assembly went faster the second time around. A half hour later, she could honestly say the process was not going any quicker. She'd avoided assembling the shelves upside down this time, but she'd mixed up the right and left sides. You'd think it shouldn't matter, given the two sides looked so much alike, but turned out it did.

An hour into assembly, Dani finished the next shelf. Feeling a sense of accomplishment, she rose and stretched the kinks from her lower back. She half carried, partly walked the shelf to the spot next to the first one. Sweat dripped down her back. She'd chosen these shelves because they had a heavy industrial vibe. They looked awesome. And once they were all assembled, she'd totally love them again. But in this moment, she hated them.

She drained the last of the lukewarm soda, reached for her X-Acto knife, and opened the next box. When she'd been setting up her gallery in Duck, Bella was four. Dani had set up a small television in the corner, told Bella she could watch all her favorite cartoons, and given her a large box of Goldfish. That ploy had worked for a half hour. Then Bella was again mobile and ready to help.

Dani should welcome the quiet. How many times had she wished for a little silence? Now she found it disconcerting, unsettling. Though she considered herself independent, she fed off Bella's buzzing energy.

"She can't live with us forever, Rosie. She'll be on her own so soon."

When she heard the truck pull up, she'd just opened the box and discovered it was missing three key screws. "Damn it."

The front door opened, letting in a flood of hot air. "Making progress?" Jackson said.

Smiling, she looked up. "I was. Until box number three. Someone in the factory is laughing right now. 'Do you think the lady that barely knows what she's doing has realized we didn't put all the screws in the box?'"

A smile tipped the edges of Jackson's lips as he walked over to the inadequate collection of fasteners. "I've got a box of extra screws in the truck."

Dani rose, leaned in, and kissed him. "That's about the sexiest thing I've heard in a long time."

He chuckled. "Just wait. I'm getting warmed up. Be right back."

"Thanks."

When he returned, he carried a box equipped with a dozen little drawers. "It's quiet around here."

"Bella's grandmother picked her up a few hours ago. She'll be back on Sunday. And yes, it's too quiet."

He took the screwdriver from her hand. "Quiet can be unnerving at first. But you adapt."

"I'm not ready to get used to it."

"It's good for Bella to visit her grandparents."

"I know. Adele and Mike are her last connections to Matthew. It's good for them both. I've said this to myself a hundred times. Logic can be very irritating."

Jackson opened the next box and laid out the screws. Identifying what was missing, he dug look-alikes from his magic toolbox. He assembled the pieces with the precision of a true craftsman. The best artists worked with an ease gained only by practicing tens of thousands of hours. "I met Reggie's neighbor, Ms. Nelson, yesterday. She's quite the character."

"Has she told you your fortune yet?"

"She did. Said I'm going to live a long and happy life. But not the one that I expected."

"What did you expect?" His tone dropped a notch.

"At one time I thought I'd be in Duck forever. And now I'm here. Not the life I was expecting. What about you?"

"Ten years ago, did I see myself in a silo assembling shelves for a beautiful woman? No."

She chuckled. "You still haven't told me the story of Jackson. How do you become an accomplished builder and sailor?"

"I grew up in Florida near the ocean. My father was in construction, but he loved the water. I was sailing before I could walk."

"How did you end up in Currituck County?"

"My ex-wife grew up here. After college, Cathy wanted to see the world, and we both landed in the Florida Keys at the same time. Six months later we were married. And when my in-laws died, we became Juniper's guardians. Made sense to stay in this area for Juniper. When Juniper went to college, Cathy and I moved to Norfolk. After the divorce, the Virginia house was sold, and I came back here."

"Why not go back to Florida?"

"Lot of happy memories for me in this area."

This was the second time he'd cracked the door to his past, as if encouraging her to delve deeper. But knowledge was a two-way street.

"You can ask me about her," he said.

When she looked up, she discovered he was staring at her. "Your ex-wife? I'm not sure what to ask."

That was a lie. She had plenty of questions, and most involved comparisons between Dani and her.

"She's smart, like you. She went back to school and earned a master's in engineering. She's remarried and expecting a baby any day."

"How do you feel about that?"

His expression became unreadable. "I want her to be happy."

"I can understand that. I never had ill wishes for Matthew. I would've liked him to be on time and follow through more, but I wanted him to be happy."

"Why did you two divorce?"

"I got pregnant, and when I finally told him, he asked me to marry him. We realized very quickly we'd do better by Bella if we weren't married." She shrugged. "What was your degree in?"

"Engineering."

"Wow."

"Numbers come easy for me." He aligned the two main pieces of shelving and secured them with a side piece. The directions called for a different setup, but he appeared to be making it work.

"Two engineers." College was a dream she'd put aside a long time ago. "How long were you married?"

"Twelve years." He connected another shelf with a few twists of the screwdriver.

"Wow. That's nothing to sneeze at." Other questions fired in her mind, but more from him would eventually mean extra from her.

He set another shelf in place and fastened the screws, finishing the next shelf's assembly.

"How did you do that?" she asked.

"The shelf?" The teasing light in his eyes had dimmed as he easily lifted the unit and set it next to the others. "It's what I do."

"A man of many talents."

"Why don't you ask me about my past?" He wanted her to know him. But when she opened up, their relationship would change. And even if he accepted her now, he would be making a decision that he might one day resent.

"I haven't wanted to press."

"You can ask me anything," he said carefully.

"How about we have an adult afternoon and not worry about the past or the future?" she asked. "This is the first time I don't have a clock dictating where I need to be."

"One step at a time?" Hints of impatience hummed under the words.

"Is that so bad?" She took his hand in hers, rubbing her thumb over his calloused palm. She raised his hands to her lips and kissed them.

He cupped her face. "I like you a lot, Dani."

"I like you, Jackson. A lot." A sly grin tugged at the edges of her lips. "Want to see my bedroom? It's pretty cool."

He chuckled. "You're distracting me."

"Doing my best to keep it in the present."

He traced the underside of her jaw with his knuckle. "Do you always live in the moment?"

Life was full of seconds, minutes, and hours she'd either barely noticed or had forgotten. Others replayed over and over too many times.

This one she wanted to remember. And when she played it back, she wanted to savor it. "Only the good ones."

CHAPTER TWENTY-THREE
BELLA

Friday, June 9, 2023
Noon

It was weird being in her grandmother's house again. The last time she'd been here was for the reception after her father's funeral. The house had been packed with so many whispering adults who all looked at her as if she had three eyes.

Bella looked at the white rattan couch with the aqua pillows, the gray shag rug, and the pictures of her grandparents and father. Many of the framed pictures of Dad looked new. In one picture he was standing in front of an old restaurant he once owned, in another he was making pasta in an industrial kitchen, and the last was with Bella and Grandma standing at the site of the restaurant he'd been renovating when he died.

Bella kinda understood why Dad didn't love it here. It had a creepy museum vibe. A memorial to the past, as her mother had muttered once.

"I made up the spare bedroom for you," Grandma said. "We can sit out by the pool and have sandwiches. Grandpa will join us for dinner."

"That's cool." She let her backpack slide from her shoulder to the couch. "Where's Grandpa?"

"On the golf course, where he now lives." She smiled as if it were a joke. "It's been a long time since we had any time together."

"Life's been crazy." What an understatement.

The wrinkles between her grandmother's eyes deepened. "You poor thing. I know the move must have been jarring," Grandma said as she walked into the galley-style kitchen. She removed tall plastic aqua glasses from the cabinet.

"It hasn't been too bad." Okay, she wasn't bonding with the new house, but there were a couple of cool things about their new life. Reggie. The morning light. Rosie having a big yard. Juniper wasn't so terrible. And the mystery girl, whoever she was, had a way of voicing Bella's frustrations.

Grandma tucked a gray curl behind her ear. "It's beyond me why your mother made such a drastic move. It's not like she's a widow."

Bella fished out her phone and texted Finn. Here! Come sit by the pool with me. Save me.

Finn: On the way.

"Do you mind if I ask a few friends over to sit with us by the pool?"

"I don't mind at all, honey. I want you to have a good time."

Grandma filled each glass with lemonade and ice cubes. She set the glasses on the small round dining table along with a sleeve of lemon cookies. Dad had loved lemons, and Bella liked them well enough, but she didn't want to eat everything lemon. She sipped her lemonade. It was tart enough to make her wince. "Good."

"Your dad always liked lemonade with a bite," Grandma said.

"Savory. He said he liked savory versus sweet." She looked out patio doors to the condo pool. The smooth water glistened a bright blue. The collection of deck chairs was still empty, but that would change as the

229

afternoon went on. It was supposed to be in the low eighties today. A perfect pool day.

"Did you bring your bathing suit?"

"I did." She looked back at her grandmother, smiled.

Suddenly Grandma's eyes flashed bright with tears. "You look so much like him. Have I told you that?"

A million times. Everyone said she looked exactly like her dad, as if that was some kind of positive reflection on her mother. As one mom whispered at the funeral, "Dani Manchester at least trapped Matthew Peterson into marriage with his own kid."

"I look a lot like him," Bella said.

"Do you miss him?" she asked.

"Sure. Of course."

Her grandmother drew in a slow steady breath as if her chest hurt. "Do you talk about him at grief camp?"

Bella didn't want to discuss camp or the angry letter she'd written her father. "Sometimes."

"You need to tell them how much you're like him. I could pull pictures from middle school, and you can show your friends. You'd be shocked at the resemblance. Would you like to see a few pictures of your dad when he was your age?"

"That's okay, Grandma. Maybe later? Why don't we go outside and sit by the pool? It's a pretty day."

"Of course, dear. Whatever you want to do. Do you want a sandwich?"

The last time Grandma had made her a peanut butter and jelly sandwich, she'd pressed the two bread slices flat with her hand and left fingerprints in the white dough. "That's okay. Maybe later?" She took another sip of lemonade. "But this sure is good."

Her grandmother beamed. "I'm glad you like it."

"I invited Finn to sit by the pool with us. She might also bring a friend. They'll be here soon. Let's sit outside and wait for them." The condo was dark, and she imagined the walls had moved a foot closer to one another.

"Of course. Your mom said you might like to catch up with your friends. Though it's only been a week since you moved. I'm not sure how out of touch you can get in five or six days."

The first week after school ended was chock full of stuff to talk about. And the last thing she wanted to do was talk about her grief camp. "I guess."

"Do you talk about your father with your mom?"

"Sure." Please don't ask me about feelings. Please don't ask.

"Your mother and father didn't always get along," her grandmother said.

"I never saw them fight."

"Of course not. Your dad wanted your life to be happy." Grandma studied her closely. "I know you must be sad."

Bella reached for her backpack. "Can I change in the spare room?"

"Of course. I'll get changed too."

"Perfect."

Bella was anxious to get out of the shrinking condo that was quickly suffocating her.

In the spare room there were more pictures of her father. More new frames filled with freshly printed photos. She picked up one taken when her dad was in high school, about the time he'd met her mom. He was grinning and had his arm around Mom's friend Ivy. Ivy and Dad had dated in high school, and then Ivy moved to New York. She always figured that's when Mom and Dad realized they loved each other.

She set the picture down, slipped into the adjoining bathroom, and closed the door. As she pulled off her shirt, she caught her reflection in the mirror over the sink. She didn't like looking at herself anymore because she remembered her father and what she'd lost. Maybe if she dyed her hair blonde, like her mother's? That would be different.

Turning her back to the mirror, she changed into the blue-and-white polka-dot bikini. She slipped on a coverup and slid on red flip-flops before heading back into the living room. Her grandmother hadn't changed into a swimsuit.

"Aren't you going swimming?" Bella asked.

"No. My body hasn't squeezed into a bathing suit in years." She'd refilled her glass to the top edge.

"You don't want to get in the water? It's going to be hot today."

"Sitting and watching you and your friends is enough. I love having young people around. Reminds me of when your dad was little. Go on out and stake out chairs for you and your friends. They're going to fill up fast."

"You're coming, right?"

"I'll sit on my patio and sip lemonade first."

Grandma's patio overlooked the pool area, which made it super convenient if she was swimming and had to use the restroom.

"I'll be right over there," Bella said.

"Perfect."

Bella took her backpack and a few towels, cut across Grandma's patio, and claimed three chaise lounges. She looked back and watched her grandmother settle into a chair. Grandma took a long sip of lemonade.

By the time Bella had laid towels on each chaise and picked her favorite beach playlist, Finn arrived.

Bella's spirits lifted when she saw her friend. It'd been only a week since they'd seen each other, so the distance between them didn't feel so great. But she sensed a small, tiny crack between them. She hated the idea that she and Finn wouldn't be friends anymore. They'd been besties since kindergarten.

"Finn!" Bella shouted.

The girls hugged.

"It feels like it's been a million years," Finn said. "The first week of summer wasn't the same without you. How is it living on the other side?"

"It's not bad," Bella said. "I've met a few cool kids."

Finn peered over the top of her sunglasses. "Not as cool as me."

Bella smiled. "Never. You're the best. Is Sierra coming?"

"She'll be here in a few. Her mother is dropping her off. She can't stay very long. Her family is packing for a vacation. Her dad has decided the family needs a trip to the mountains."

"I thought Sierra wanted to take surf camp with you," Bella said.

"She's going to be a week late." She pouted. "And you won't be there at all. Won't be the same."

"I hate missing it."

Finn settled on the chaise and fished suntan lotion from her beach bag. "Can you put some on my back?"

"Sure." Bella took the bottle and squirted a good amount on Finn's back.

Finn flinched. "Cold."

"It'll warm up." She smoothed the lotion on Finn's pale skin and then handed her the bottle to do the same for her.

Lotioned up, Bella settled back in her chair. She'd sat by pools with Finn a million times, and for the first time in a week she felt almost normal. The bright glittering pool and the laughing people assembling in their chairs looked so positive and happy. It should have been perfect. But she sensed that under the glitter lurked a cave-dwelling, fire-breathing dragon, snorting and spewing flames capable of turning the world to cinder.

"How is your grandmother?" Finn asked.

"She's okay." Bella looked back at the patio and spotted her grandmother sipping lemonade. Grandma waved to Bella. Bella raised her hand.

"How are you?" Finn's voice dropped a notch, like it did when she was worried.

"Good."

Finn rolled her face toward Bella. "How can you be good? Your mother has turned your life upside down."

"It's not as bad as that."

"Don't you miss us?" Finn asked.

"I miss my old life. My dad."

"But not us."

A smile softened her pursed lips. "How can I miss you when we're sitting next to each other?"

"Fair point." Finn smoothed more lotion on her legs.

Sierra breezed through the pool gates carrying a small cooler. She wore cutoff jeans, a teal bikini top covered with a white tank, and flip-flops. "What's up, guuurls?"

Bella had known Sierra as long as she had Finn. "Sierraaa, hey!"

Sierra smacked her hand against Bella's raised one. "Long time no see."

"It feels like I've been gone a million years. I hear you're going to the mountains?" Bella asked.

Sierra sat down, opened her cooler, and handed each girl a canned diet soda. "Don't remind me. Dad's got it all figured out. We're going hiking, and he has a bunch of historical sites set up for us to visit. My dad drives me insane."

Finn nodded. "So does mine. He was grousing about my messy room this morning."

"I hate that," Sierra said. "It's not like they have to live in my bedroom."

Bella had complained about her father a lot. Not about family trips to the mountains but about missing his visits or being distracted when she talked to him. Mom had always made excuses, but in the last year, Bella's patience with Dad had thinned.

But if he showed up right now, she'd jump straight from the silent treatment to hugging him close. Then she'd get mad and demand to know why he'd worked so hard and had fallen asleep at the wheel. Then she'd probably cry because seeing him alive would end this stupid nightmare.

Bella sat silent, letting the other two girls chat about surf camp, Jeff Spencer (the school hottie), and the new surf school for girls in Nags

Head. She glanced at her phone, making sure Mom had not texted. Nothing. Not even a smiley face emoji with a raised brow.

"Bella, I think your grandmother is asleep," Finn said.

Her grandmother's eyes had drifted closed, and her mouth was slightly open.

"I hope no one ever sees me sleeping," Sierra said. "That would be so embarrassing if I drooled or snored."

Finn laughed. "Or bedhead or dragon breath."

As Bella studied her grandmother's still body, a sense of worry crept into her bones. "Let me check on her."

"She's fine. Just sleeping like she does after drinking her lemonade," Sierra said.

"What's that mean?" Bella asked.

"Come on, you know," Finn said.

"What?"

The girls looked at each other. "She puts vodka in her lemonade. My mother caught her doing it at the reception after your dad's funeral."

"That was a bad day," Bella said.

"She's done it before," Sierra said.

Color warmed Bella's cheeks as she rose and strode toward her grandmother. Her dad had once said, "Grandma takes a lot of naps."

At the time, Bella had figured her grandmother was just tired. Inside the patio gate, she jostled her grandmother's shoulder. "Grandma!"

Her grandmother's eyes slowly opened. "Bella?"

"You need to go inside and lie down," Bella said.

"I'm sitting out here with you girls."

"You're sleeping, and you're getting a bad sunburn. Go inside to the couch."

Her grandmother tried to stand but staggered a step and grabbed the wrought iron fencing the patio. "Whoops."

Bella gripped Grandma's arm and steadied her. "Let's go inside."

"I need my lemonade."

Bella glanced at the tall empty glass. "You drank it all."

"Then I'll make more."

"No. You need to lie down." The two walked slowly into the dim living room.

"You're so sweet, Bella. Just like your dad." Bella helped her grandmother onto the couch.

"Lie down. I'm going to text Grandpa."

She breezily waved her hand as if swatting a fly. "Don't bother him. He's on the golf course."

Bella was silent as her grandmother's eyes slowly closed. She texted her grandfather and told him, Grandma overloaded on lemonade. (Smile emoji to soften the news.)

"I want to spend the afternoon with you." Grandma's words slurred.

"Take a little nap first." She smoothed her hand over her grandmother's head just as her dad did when Grandma was tired.

"I'll just rest my eyes for a few minutes."

"That's all you need to do. When you wake up, we'll order pizza." Dad had always fed Grandma when she was tired. Only he didn't order pizza but took Bella to the grocery store, where they bought the fixings for homemade pasta. Back at the condo she and her dad made pasta and a marinara sauce. By the time Granddad returned from golfing, the house smelled of tomato and basil and Grandma was awake and sipping coffee. Dad once said he'd learned to cook so he could feed himself and keep his parents' marriage together.

Grandma closed her eyes. Bella slipped off her grandmother's sandals, spread a purple-and-white afghan over her, and carefully tucked the edges over her chilled toes.

When she rejoined the girls outside, their chatter silenced.

"She okay?" Finn asked.

"She's fine," Bella said. "Just tired."

The girls exchanged glances.

"What does that look mean?" Bella asked.

"Nothing," Finn said.

Bella sat on the chaise, but she found the plastic seat suddenly uncomfortable. Finn was the master of saying a lot with few or no words. A shrug, an eye roll, a raised brow.

Sierra glanced at Finn. "Should I ask?"

"No," Finn said.

Bella pretended she didn't hear and dropped her gaze to her phone and scrolled through TikTok videos. She felt the girls looking at each other and then her, but she continued to study videos that had once made her laugh.

Suddenly irritated by the silly dance routines, Bella closed her eyes. The hot sun beat directly down, burning her skin.

"The party tonight is going to be fun," Finn offered.

"I'm so sorry I'm missing it," Sierra said. "My parents want me home early."

Bella let their conversation drift over her as sweat beaded on her upper lip and under her armpits. She rose and walked to the edge of the pool, and without worrying about her hair, she jumped into the water. The cold blast sent shock waves through her body. She floated under the water's edge in the blissful silence.

She wanted to stay under the water's surface and keep distance between herself and the world, but the pool was colder than she'd expected. And her lungs were running out of air. She pushed through the surface, wiping the water from her face. Imagining the hot sun vaporizing the droplets clinging to her skin, she climbed out, walked back to her seat, and wrapped herself in her towel.

Water droplets landed on Finn's legs. "That water is subzero!"

"Tell me about it," Bella said.

"Why'd you do something so crazy?" Sierra asked. "Your hair is messed up now."

Bella pushed back a damp strand. "I just needed to cool off."

"You're acting a little weird," Sierra said. "You always care about your hair."

She did care about her hair. And her clothes. But not so much today. "Oh, well."

"Something is wrong with you," Finn said.

"Really? How so?" Bella could've reminded them that her father had died four months ago, and she'd just moved to the end of the earth, but she wanted to hear what they had to say.

"You're distant," Sierra said carefully. "You used to talk all the time. Now you're quiet."

"Give her a break," Finn said. "Big life changes."

As Bella wiped off her sunglasses, jumpy energy shook up the gumballs in her belly. She felt like screaming. "Sierra, you look like you have a question."

Sierra sipped her soda, hesitated, and then dropped her voice a fraction. "I heard something, but I'm not sure I should ask."

Finn's eyes widened. "No, Sierra."

Sierra shrugged. "It's just a question, Finn."

"Ask it," Bella said.

Sierra frowned, as if she was super concerned, but the twinkle in her eyes said otherwise. "Is it true your father was drinking the night he died?"

Bella stilled as heat rushed her face. "Who told you that?"

"I heard my mother talking to Finn's mom," Sierra said. "They said he was a little drunk when he was driving home."

"That's crap." Bella wanted to believe her father hadn't been that stupid.

"I mean, your grandmother is drinking today," Sierra said.

"Finn, did your mom say my dad was drunk?" Bella demanded.

Color warmed Finn's cheeks. "She was just talking. I don't think she believed it." Finn had enough sense to look embarrassed. "You know how my mother can talk too much."

"But she said it, right?" Bella pressed. "Who else was talking about my dad?"

"I don't know," Finn said. "Nobody else, I'm sure."

"Yeah, nobody but our moms," Sierra said.

Bella gritted her teeth so hard her jaw hurt. "He *wasn't* drinking."

"How do you know?" Sierra pressed.

"Because he didn't do that kind of thing, Sierra!" Bella shouted.

"But parents do drink and drive," Sierra said.

Bella swung her legs over the side of the chaise. "Not mine."

"Don't get all worked up," Sierra said. "It was just a question."

"It wasn't *just* a question," Bella said. "It was a dig. It was a mean thing to say!"

The girls looked at each other.

"Hey, we're here for you," Finn said. "We didn't mean to hurt you. You know, you can tell us anything."

Could she?

"Let me order the pizza," Finn said. "You like extra pepperoni, right?"

Bella grabbed her phone. "Leave."

"What?"

Bella rose up. "Get out!"

"Why're you getting so ruffled?" Finn asked.

"Maybe she needs a drink," Sierra joked.

Bella walked behind Sierra's chair, pushed upward, and tipped Sierra into the pool.

CHAPTER TWENTY-FOUR
DANI

Friday, June 9, 2023
4:00 p.m.

Dani and Jackson lay together in her bed, the sheets twisted around their legs. They'd barely made it upstairs before each stripped off their clothes and took the other as if starved for touch. Only after the frenzy passed and she lay curled at his side did he break the silence.

"You know I was married." He traced small circles on her arm as he stared at the ceiling. "What I haven't told you is that Cathy and I had a daughter. Her name was Cloe. She was diagnosed with leukemia when she was seven."

"Oh, Jackson." Dani's heart hurt for the child, Jackson, and Cathy. She didn't want to imagine the pain.

He stared ahead. "Cathy and I were devastated, but Cloe was so positive and certain she'd be fine. She gave us the courage during the endless trips into Norfolk for treatment."

Tears burned in Dani's eyes, but she didn't speak. What could she say? *I'm sorry* was woefully inadequate.

"She didn't respond well to treatment. Three hundred and seventy days after she was diagnosed, she died." He stopped breathing for a moment before he drew in a gulp of air and said, "I didn't handle it well."

"Who could? I would've been devastated." She'd gladly give up her sight if it meant Bella lived a good life.

"My ex-wife did. She got herself into counseling, begged me to go, but anger cut me off. I built a wall between us ten bricks at a time. I finally had to leave our house. I couldn't stand seeing Cloe's room, the marks on the wall measuring her height, the pictures on the walls, or her toys in the backyard. The whole house was her, and I was suffocating. I'm not proud of this, but I left my wife and came down here. I spent the next year on the water, delivering ship after ship. I wanted to be so exhausted I couldn't feel."

She nestled closer to him, laying her head on his chest. She tried to imagine the pure pain, but just the idea of losing Bella terrified her.

"Cathy tried, but finally she didn't have the reserves to save herself and me. She filed for divorce."

"My heart breaks for you, Jackson," she said softly. "To lose a child . . ." She kissed his chest over his heart as if she could mend all the pain and scars. "Thank you for telling me."

He cleared his throat and pinched the bridge of his nose. "I wish every day I could've handled it better. I know I hurt Cathy and Juniper."

"Juniper still loves you. And it sounds like your ex-wife still cares."

"And I still love Cathy. Juniper, Cathy, Cloe, and I were a tight-knit family. I'd do anything I could for any of them."

His affection for his ex-wife was natural. They'd shared so much. She also understood how disease and death could fracture a healthy, strong family.

Dani rose up on her elbow and gently brushed the hair from his forehead. She kissed him softly on the lips. "Don't judge yourself. You went through hell."

He met her gaze. "So did Cathy."

"Do not judge yourself. Cathy and Juniper don't."

"They're too kindhearted."

"I don't judge you. And I'm not particularly kind. I can be a bit of a hardnose."

He ran his finger along her jawline. "I was worried."

"About what?"

"How you'd react. You've been a rock for Bella. Christ, you turned a run-down property into a showpiece. You uprooted your daughter and are single-handedly building a new life."

"I didn't lose a child. That's an entirely different kind of grief."

He traced her lips with his thumb. "Thank you."

"There's nothing to thank me for."

"God, I admire your strength and independence."

"Do you have a picture of Cloe?" she asked.

He pulled his phone from the back pocket of his jeans and selected the picture of a beautiful girl with a gap-toothed grin. She had dark hair, fair skin, and gray eyes that mirrored Jackson's.

Dani traced the outline of the girl's face. "She looks like you."

"More like Cathy. She had her mother's brains and my sense of humor. I had to double-time it to keep up with her."

"She's beautiful." Dani handed back the phone.

"Thank you." With care, he closed the screen.

She kissed his neck and his chest and wrapped her arms around him. He held her close as she traced her finger over his belly. His body tensed, a sign he liked it. If death had taught her anything, it was to live fully.

When she moved on top of him, the sheet fell from her naked breasts. He rested his hands on her hips. This round of lovemaking wasn't frenzied but a gentle and slow joining. When they both climaxed, she rolled onto her side beside him.

Dani was nestled in Jackson's arms when her phone rang. She was so comfortable, her body so languid and loose, that she didn't want to answer the call. Just a few more minutes here.

But years of motherhood had her reaching for the phone, even though she was half expecting spam or a new artist.

Through blurred vision she recognized Bella's number and picture, the ease evaporated, and she sat up and cleared her throat. "Bella. Everything all right?"

Jackson rolled on his back and rubbed his hand up and down her back.

"Mom, I want to come home." She sniffed and drew in a breath. "Now."

"What? I thought you were looking forward to having the weekend with Grandma, Grandpa, Finn, and Sierra."

"I hate them all. I hate everything here." Her voice broke. "Grandma drank too much lemonade."

Dani tensed, her heart twisting with worry and anger. Matthew had sworn his mother was no longer drinking like she used to. But her ex-mother-in-law had lost her only son this year, and the lemonade had always made her feel better.

Dani cleared her throat. "Where is Grandpa?"

"He just got home from golf. He's not happy with Grandma. They're trying to be quiet, but I can hear them arguing. Can you come get me?"

"What's wrong? You've only been gone five hours," Dani said as she glanced at the clock on the dresser. "What about Finn's party?"

"I want to come home," Bella said.

Dani swung her legs over the side of the bed, and the last of the sheets slid from her body. The sun still was high enough in the sky, and it would be another five hours before it set. Normally, plenty of time, but with summer traffic and an unavoidable conversation with her in-laws, there was no telling when she'd be back on the road.

She reached for her glasses on the nightstand. Her vision snapped into focus. "Of course I'll come get you. I'll be there as quick as I can. About an hour."

"Can't you come faster?" Bella urged.

"Not this time of year, Bella." Check-in time for most cottages was 4:00 p.m., so traffic was hitting its Friday peak.

"I can call Grandpa Pete," Dani said.

"Nooo," she wailed. "I just want you. No Uncle Dalton. No Ivy."

"Okay. Hang tight. On my way." She ended the call. In spite of what Bella had said, she briefly considered calling Dalton or Ivy. They would drop whatever it was they were doing. But Ivy had her last catering gig today, and Dalton was likely at the office, catching up on paperwork.

"Is Bella okay?" Jackson's tone carried a lifetime of worry.

"Trouble with her friends." She rose and picked up her bra and panties.

The mattress shifted as he sat up and leaned against the headboard. He ran his fingers through his hair. "That's fairly common at that age, isn't it?"

"Not with these friends. They've been her best pals since kindergarten. But they're all girls, in middle school, and they've had some ups and downs this year." She pulled the hair band from her wrist and secured her thick mane in a ponytail.

"I'll drive you," he said.

She slid into her panties and bra and then pulled on her shorts and ruby-red T-shirt. "You don't have to do that. Seriously. You've been more than helpful."

He climbed out of bed and yanked on his jeans. "I really don't mind, Dani." He walked around the bed and kissed her on the lips as she tucked in her shirt. "I like you. I like Bella."

She took his hand in hers. "We're turning out to be more work than you bargained for." Their first few illicit romps had been magical and intoxicating. But even great sex, as she and Matthew had proved, did not sustain a couple for the long haul. That required full honesty, something she lacked.

"I knew you had a daughter from the start. Kids change things, require more effort. I know that. Besides, a drive across the bridge is hardly a lot."

"My daughter is going to be in a foul mood." Dani slipped on her hoop earrings, scooped bracelets off the nightstand, and slid them on. She glanced in the mirror and did her best to smooth out the smudged mascara. "I look like I've had sex."

"Just sex?"

"Great sex. Really great sex." She moved into her bathroom and dug her blush out of the vanity's top drawer. She quickly touched up her cheeks and then smoothed on red lipstick. At least she looked somewhat pulled together.

Jackson leaned on the doorjamb. "You look fine. You don't need to fuss."

"It's what I do when I'm nervous."

"It's going to be okay. Bella's a smart kid." He pulled his T-shirt over his chest and flat abs and reached for his keys, wallet, and phone. "I remember a lot of drama when Juniper moved in with Cathy and me. I was in my midtwenties when I got a lesson in hormones."

She smiled. "You're sure about coming?"

"Grab your purse."

"Rosie needs to go out first."

"Okay, and then we'll put her in the car. She'll help Bella."

"You've always been a natural with the kids," she said.

"Like I said, I learned my big lessons with Juniper, and Cloe taught me patience. Besides, Bella loves that dog. And Rosie likes riding in the car."

Fifteen minutes later, Dani, Jackson, and Rosie were sitting in the front seat of his truck. The beach traffic had picked up considerably, slowing their speed to about thirty miles an hour. However, it was moving, and thankfully there were no accidents to stop the flow.

She'd heard most of the cottages were booked for this summer and into the fall. Great for her business, but traveling anywhere on a Friday through Sunday was going to require planning until after Labor Day.

"What would've upset Bella so much?" Jackson asked.

Dani rubbed Rosie between the ears as the dog held her nose up to the partly open window. "I suspect it has to do with her father's accident. There were rumors that he'd been drinking when he crashed."

Jackson's profile hardened. "Was he?"

"No. I know the sheriff, and even though I wasn't Matthew's legal next of kin, I'm the mother of Matthew's child, so the sheriff was willing to talk to me. I asked about the rumors I'd heard at the funeral. The autopsy report showed no alcohol in Matthew's system. He simply fell asleep at the wheel."

"But the truth never stops the rumors, does it?" A muscle in his jaw tightened.

"Sounds like you've had experience with the rumor mill."

"Ground up and spit out."

A child's death and a separation would've stirred stories in his circle of friends. Since most stories had a good guy and a bad guy, she'd bet he'd been painted as the villain. The tension rippling in his body suggested he didn't want to discuss it.

"I'm sorry," she said. "It's no fun for anyone to be on the receiving end of gossip." Once she went public with her vision loss, she'd be the topic at car pool lines, grocery stores, and restaurants. *Did you hear about Dani? She's so young. I can't imagine.*

Jackson drove across the bridge, and Dani directed him to the Manteo condo that her in-laws had called home for the past ten years. She'd been to the residence only a couple of times. It wasn't that she didn't like her in-laws. They weren't bad people. They'd loved their son. Wanted to protect him.

As they crossed water again toward Roanoke Island, she looked to her right at the sunlight glimmering on the water. A week ago, she'd been unable to marvel at the palette of blues, grays, and greens. Today, they seemed even dimmer.

Jackson stretched his arm over the seat and gently touched the back of her neck. "There's light at the end of the tunnel."

Smiling, she nodded a quick agreement that didn't resonate. "I know. I know."

"Do you? Since the day I met you, you've been going full steam as if something is chasing you."

"I've always been that way." A half smile tipped the edges of her lips.

"Bella and you are going to be okay," he said.

Considering what he'd shared about himself and his own terrible trial, she wasn't going to utter a complaint. "We'll come out on the other side of this. I survived my mother's death. Bella will find her way as well."

Jackson turned right onto South Croatan Highway and twenty minutes later took the turn toward Manteo. Ten minutes later, he pulled into her in-laws' condo-building parking lot. "Want me to come in?"

"Thanks, but I'll spare you the drama."

"I don't mind drama."

She chuckled. "You'll see plenty of theatrics when Bella gets in the truck."

He rubbed Rosie between the ears. "So warned."

She crossed the lot and entered the center hallway that divided the twin banks of condo units. Moving toward the light at the end of the hallway, she stopped at the last condo on the right. She knocked on the door, anxious to see Bella and irritated with life, drama, and the weight that bore down on her shoulders. The door opened to her former father-in-law.

"Hey, Mike," Dani said. "I'm here for Bella."

"I'm sorry it had to come to this, Dani." Mike was six feet and still lean and sported a thick shock of gray hair. She could see so much of Matthew in him. "Adele has not been doing well since the funeral."

"I'm not judging Adele," she said, hugging him. "You've both lost your son. And I can't imagine that kind of pain."

"I hope you never do," he said quietly.

When she stepped into the foyer, the overhead light accentuated the wrinkles etched in Mike's face. He looked as if he'd aged a decade in the last few months.

"Mom!" Bella, backpack hoisted on her shoulder, appeared in the hallway.

"Hey, honey," Dani said. "Did you thank Grandma and Grandpa for having you?"

"Grandma is sleeping." Bella looked up at her grandfather. "Thank you, Grandpa."

"I'm sorry I didn't get more time with you," he said. "I was hoping we'd all have a big dinner at your favorite restaurant."

"It's okay," Bella said. And more out of training than genuine feeling, "We'll do it again sometime."

"And you both are welcome anytime," Dani said. "We should be up and running in about two weeks."

"Still setting the world on fire?" Mike asked.

Dani smiled. "Feels like smoldering kindling right now, but I think it'll be great. I'll text you the time for the grand opening."

"We'd like that."

Bella kissed her grandfather on the cheek and moved past him. Neither Dani nor Bella spoke until they'd reached the parking lot. "Jackson drove me," Dani said.

Bella stopped. "Why? It's not raining or dark."

"He offered, and I don't mind a little moral support."

"I thought it was going to be just you and me. Now I can't tell you about how stupid Finn and Sierra are."

"You can tell me later."

Bella's sigh was long, exaggerated. "He's starting to be around a lot."

"He's renovating the silos."

"And driving me to camp and now picking me up here. It's weird, Mom."

"It's your only ticket out of here, kiddo." Dani's patience was wearing thin tonight.

"Fine."

"Be nice. Please and thank you."

"Fine."

Dani slid into the front passenger seat as Bella climbed into the back seat. Rosie barked and, tail wagging, jumped into the back with Bella.

Bella hugged the dog. "Thank you for the ride, Jackson."

"Anytime, Bella," Jackson said.

Dani clicked her seat belt. Jackson backed out of the spot and was on the road. The Friday-night traffic had thickened more with tourists. Dani was really grateful Jackson had driven. With cars coming in and out of side streets, she would've been a nervous wreck. And if not for Jackson, then what? Maybe Mike could have driven her home, but that would've required a longer conversation she didn't want to have.

"Juniper called today," Jackson said. "She asked if I could bring my kayaks to camp on Monday. She wants to get everyone out on the water."

"That sounds fun," Dani said. "Bella, you can teach some of the other kids a few moves. I hear you did a great job with the paddleboards."

As Bella petted Rosie's head, she stared out the window. "I guess."

"I can take the morning off," Dani said. "I know my way around a kayak pretty well. I can bring ours. What does Juniper have in mind?"

Jackson shook his head. "Supposed to be beautiful weather. Sometimes you just have to stop and enjoy the day."

Bella sighed. "Sunshine doesn't fix everything, Jackson."

"No, it doesn't," he said. "But it's still better than cold and rain."

A sadness echoed from Jackson. If they'd been alone, she'd have touched his shoulder and been willing to listen to whatever he said. But they weren't alone.

She glanced in the rearview mirror. "Bella, you love being out on the water."

Bella didn't respond, and her heavy silence filled the car like a black cloud.

"Well, I'm looking forward to it," Dani said. "I haven't been on a kayak in a year. Maybe we can have a race. I don't think I've lost my touch. I'm sure I can still beat you."

Bella sighed. "I don't want you to come."

CHAPTER TWENTY-FIVE

BELLA

Friday, June 9, 2023
6:00 p.m.

Bella climbed the stairs to her room, not bothering to look back to see if her mother followed. Head bowed, she threw her backpack on her bedroom floor, kicked off her sandals, and flopped back on her bed. She closed her eyes and started to count to one hundred. Her head ached. Her body felt heavy. And she was just so darned tired.

"Doesn't look like you had a very good time," the girl said.

Bella glared at the girl sitting on the edge of her bed. She should've been terrified or weirded out, but she felt totally calm, as if random ghost people just showed up in her room all the time. She could've asked how she got here or how she knew Bella had been gone, but she didn't bother. "Guess that makes you a genius."

"You look mad."

"I'm not mad," Bella insisted. "What's your name?"

"Does it matter?"

"It does."

"Fine. If you need a name, then call me Anna." She rose and walked to Bella's desk. She plucked a pencil from the ceramic purple container and held it between her slim fingers. *Snap.* The pencil broke in half, and she tossed the two pieces on the floor. She grabbed another pencil. *Snap.* Another. *Snap.*

"Knock it off," Bella said.

Snap.

"What's the deal with that guy?" Anna asked.

A groan rumbled in Bella's chest. "Jackson? I don't know."

Anna tossed the pencil halves onto the growing pile. "Looks like he has a crush on your mother. I bet they're dating."

Bella clenched her fists. "They're *not* dating. Mom never dates. It's just Mom and me now."

Anna shrugged, reached for the last pencil. *Snap.* "Times change. And he must be a nice guy. I mean, he drove all that way to Manteo to get you."

"He works for Mom. He's being nice to his boss."

Anna chuckled. "I bet they kiss all the time."

Bella shook her head. "That is gross. Don't talk about that!"

"Don't get mad at me. I'm just calling it like I see it." Anna walked into Bella's closet and pulled out a white peasant top with a yoke embroidered with yellow thread. She threw it on the floor.

"What're you doing?" Bella demanded.

"You don't even like that shirt. Why did you keep it?"

"My mother bought it for me. We had a really fun day shopping, and when I see it, it makes me smile."

Anna snatched a green top with a white collar off another hanger, balled it in her hand, and threw it toward the other blouse. "Baby clothes. Elementary school. You can't wear this now."

Anna chose more shirts and pants and tossed them into a growing pile in the middle of the room. "Get rid of them. I bet those jeans are too short."

Bella sat up and swung her legs over the side of the bed. Her mother had picked out most of the clothes. "Love dressing my baby girl," her mom had said. Bella realized now they were outfits for someone much younger.

"I'm not a baby girl anymore," Bella grumbled. "Mom's got to stop treating me like one."

Anna kicked the clothes and then walked to Bella's desk. She paused and stared at the blotter, magazines, and laptop and the bracelet Bella's father had given her. Anna picked up the bracelet and jerked it so hard it broke.

"Hey!" Bella said.

Ignoring Bella, Anna lowered her forearm to the desk and swiped it over the surface, sweeping everything onto the floor.

"You aren't a baby anymore," Anna said. "It's time everyone saw that."

Footsteps sounded on the stairs, and Bella's door opened. Her mother stood at the threshold, surveying the room, the mound of clothes and the pile of broken pencils, and Bella standing in the middle of the chaos. "Everything okay?"

Bella straightened and blinked, seeing no sign of Anna. Of course. Ghost Girl had vanished. She considered blaming the mess on the missing Anna but realized she'd kind of enjoyed watching her tearing everything apart. "Fine."

"Are you sure? Sounds like something dropped," Mom said.

"Nothing major. I'll pick it up," Bella said. "All is fine."

"I'm fine," Mom mimicked. "That's what I say when I'm really upset. I'm fine. *Fine.* It's just enough to make everyone shut up, isn't it?"

As her mother moved toward the pile, Bella blinked, shocked by the anger simmering in her belly and heating her skin. Rosie trotted into the room, pausing to sniff the clothes. She crawled onto the pile, pawed at it, and then settled in the center.

"Want to tell me what really happened?" Mom asked.

"I don't want to talk about it."

"Tough. Spill it, kid."

Bella rolled her eyes to the ceiling. "The girls were mean."

"Finn and Sierra?"

"Yes."

"What did they say?" her mother said carefully.

"They saw Grandma drinking her lemonade and said she wasn't napping but drunk."

Mom took Bella's hand. Her touch was warm, comforting, and irritating. "Grandma lost her son. It's not right what she did today, but she's hurting."

Tears welled in Bella's eyes, and she snatched her hand away. "*I'm* hurting! My whole life is ruined, and I'm never going to see my dad again."

"I know. You've suffered a terrible loss."

The tears spilled down Bella's face, and she didn't even try to wipe them away. "Is it true? Was Dad drinking?"

"No. Your father was not drinking."

"How do you know?"

"I met with the sheriff's office. I saw the toxicology reports."

"Why would you even ask the sheriff that question?"

"Because I heard the rumors at the funeral too. Daddy had been working one-hundred-hour weeks. He was driving home, it was late, and he fell asleep at the wheel. The sheriff believes he confused the accelerator with the brake. It was a terrible accident."

"Why did Daddy work so hard?" Bella asked.

"He wanted to be a success. He wanted you and the world to be proud of him."

Tears streamed down her cheeks. "I was proud of him."

"I know. But sometimes he had a hard time believing he was a success, which is what made him work even harder."

Bella's shoulders slumped. "Are you going to marry Jackson?"

Mom shook her head. "That's not even on the table, Bella. We enjoy each other's company."

"How long have you been dating?"

Her mother smoothed her hand over the comforter. "Since February."

"Before Dad died?"

"Yes."

"And you never told me! I'm not a child!"

Mom's smile was sad. "I know. You're growing up so very fast."

"Then why didn't you tell me?" Bella wailed.

"There wasn't much to say at the time."

"Did we move here for Jackson?"

"I didn't decide on this move until after your father died. I thought we both needed a fresh start."

More tears burned in her eyes. "He's not going to be my father," Bella said quickly.

"I never said that he would be, Bella. Your father can't be replaced."

"For you he can."

Her mother shook her head. "I've told you this before. Your dad and I hadn't been a romantic couple for a long time. And we never gave you the impression we ever would be again."

"But you two got along so well." How could they not love each other?

"We were friends. And I'll miss him for the rest of my life. But we weren't ever getting back together. You know this, right?"

Bella's mattress sagged when she lay back. She stared at the wave-like swirls in the plaster ceiling. "Why is Jackson being so nice to us?"

"He's a good guy, Bella."

She folded her arms. "I don't have to like him."

"You're old enough to make your own decisions about people. And so am I."

Bella's shoulders tensed. "I hate my life."

Mom knitted her fingers together. "When my mother died, I hated my life too. I was so sad, and then I was really mad."

Bella swiped the back of her hand over her wet cheeks. "Really? You never get mad. You're always smiling."

"Sometimes I get very mad, but I'm good at hiding it."

"Why?"

Mom smoothed her hand over Bella's head. "Because my father was so upset after Mom died. And I didn't want him to be sad. So, I decided if I was happy, I could make him happy."

"Did it work?" Bella asked.

"I used to think so, but I realize now it didn't. He was pretending for me too."

"Why would he do that?"

"Because he didn't want Dalton and me to be sadder than we were." Mom raised her chin. "Dad's never found anyone else. He's been living in Dalton's garage apartment for years. He's just kind of stuck in the past."

"Are you?"

"I didn't think that I was, but maybe I am a little. That's why I signed you up for the camp. I don't want you to be stuck, honey. I want you to feel your feelings."

Bella leaned toward her mother's shoulder. She sniffed. "I don't want to feel bad anymore. When will Juniper's camp fix me?"

"I don't think we ever really repair this kind of sadness. But you can learn to live with it."

Bella plucked at the sleeve of her mother's shirt. "Juniper is pretty nice. And funny."

"I know."

"How did you hear about Juniper?" Bella asked.

"When I told Juniper that Matthew had died, she didn't say much, but a couple of days later, she called me about this camp she envisioned for kids who are grieving."

"And you just said yes? She could've been a serial killer."

Mom chuckled. "She's not. I made phone calls. And when she emailed me her camp flyer, I didn't think for a second. I called her and told her I'd sponsor the camp and cover the tuition of any child who wanted to attend."

"That's how Reggie got in the camp."

"Yes. But she and her dad don't know that. No one does. Everyone believes this is all Juniper."

"I'm glad Reggie is in the camp. And I can keep a secret. I'm not a kid."

Mom winked. "You'll always be my baby."

Bella tugged at a thread on her cutoff jeans. "And I don't want to go back to the beach and see Finn and Sierra ever again. I'll see Grandma again, but not those girls."

"Maybe you could send her a text with a picture. Tell her you're thinking of her. Your grandparents love you."

"Is a picture going to make her feel better?"

"She'll never be who she was, but pictures and notes help."

"Okay."

"For now, let's just focus on this camp and then getting our gallery operational. We've got a lot of great things to do this summer, and I doubt you'll miss Finn or Sierra much."

"I'll never miss them." Her decision was black and white. No going back.

"Never say never, kiddo."

"Are you going to see Jackson again?"

Her mother hesitated a beat. "Yes."

Bella thought about Grandpa living alone all these years. He didn't seem sad to her. "I'm not sure how I feel about that."

"As long as we're honest, it'll be fine."

Bella wasn't so sure about that either. Just because something was true or honest, that didn't make it good.

CHAPTER TWENTY-SIX

DANI

Saturday, June 10, 2023
4:00 p.m.

Saturday was filled with work. The landscapers arrived and spent most of the day planting azaleas, hydrangeas, and monkey grass and filled halved whiskey barrels with bright annuals. Dani's only request was that they be vibrant and colorful.

As the landscapers worked, Dani greeted artists who'd contracted with her to display and sell their work. She'd worked with many before, and a couple were new. Her reputation as a savvy, fair gallery owner was the reason many said they were willing to take a chance on this new location.

Bella stayed close to Dani, content to dust empty display shelves, sweep, and hand Dani nails as she hung paintings around the walls of the gallery.

After last night's meltdown, Bella had woken up in a good mood. But that was the way. Even without grief darkening the kid's life, Bella was almost a teenager. Translation: waves of unpredictable hormones. Dani never knew which version of her daughter's dual personality would be walking through the door.

As she uncrated a painting that she wanted to hang behind her display case and register, Jackson texted. He was driving to Norfolk to inspect another sailboat he'd be transporting down to Florida. She wished him luck but half wondered if last night's drama might have been too much. Taking on Dani was accepting Bella.

Dani slid her phone back in her pocket and inspected a painting that had been created by Ruth Wheeler, Ivy's grandmother and the woman who'd taken her under her wing when she was younger than Bella. It was a seascape featuring two young girls standing on the beach, staring out at a shrimp boat on the horizon. Ruth had scribbled on the back of the painting "Ivy and Dani, 2005."

"The painting is beautiful." Dani cradled year-old Bella as she stared at the vivid painting.

"One of the easiest I've ever painted." Ruth pushed back a strand of curly salt-and-pepper hair.

"Did you have a specific day in mind when you painted it?"

"No. I lost count how many times I saw you girls sit on the beach like that."

Dani had spent so much time with Ivy from third grade through high school. They'd been inseparable until Ivy had packed her bags and left for New York.

"Who'd have thought Ivy would be alone in New York now, setting the world on fire."

"You don't need New York to set your own fire," Ruth said. "I see great things for you, kid."

The memory washed over Dani. How many times had she clung to Ruth's words?

"Mom, I'm going to go through my closet again," Bella said.

"Aren't most in a pile?" When she'd seen the clothes, pencils, and laptop on the floor, she hadn't been mad. This was grief. It wasn't clean or easy, and it had no time limits.

And frankly, seeing evidence of her daughter's anger had been a relief. Bella was finally releasing some of her fury.

Bella shrugged. "Not all of them."

"How's the laptop? I noticed it in the pile of things that fell off your desk."

Bella looked a little sheepish. "It's fine. Still works."

"Okay." Dani turned from the painting and looked at her daughter. "Get rid of as many clothes as you want, but at the rate you're going, you'll be down to a couple of shorts and T-shirts."

"I'm not *that* crazy. I'll maintain a capsule wardrobe."

Dani smiled. "That's my little fashionista. Can you let Rosie out?"

"I will."

"I love you," Dani said.

"Love you too, Mom."

She watched her girl dash out of the gallery. If she could take away her pain, she would, but no one could do that for anyone else.

She moved her ladder to the right spot and climbed with a hammer, stainless steel nail, and hook in hand. She angled her hammer and struck the nailhead. When Jackson drove a nail, the work was done with one or two strikes. When Dani hit the nail for the tenth time, she was glad she didn't make a living as a carpenter. Still, the fastener was secure and straight. Hard to own a gallery and not be expert at hanging pictures.

"Mom, there's a lady here to see you!" Bella shouted as Rosie barked.

She set the hammer down on an empty display shelf and studied the three pictures she still had to hang. Placement in the gallery was critical. Each painting was designed to draw the customer around the room. "I'm in here."

She carried the picture up the ladder, felt for the wire on the back, and then angled it toward the hook. She connected wire with hook and very carefully centered the painting.

"That looks fantastic," a woman said.

Dani turned to see Naomi, pizza delivery girl / potter. Naomi wore her long brown hair twisted in a single braid that draped her shoulder like a seaman's rope, cutoff jeans, a peasant top, and boots.

Dani climbed down and extended her hand. "Naomi Hansen. How are you?"

Naomi's eyes widened. "You remember me?"

"Of course. You're an artist."

Naomi slid her fingers into her jeans pockets. "I am."

Dani liked the girl's confidence. She'd met many talented artists who couldn't admit they were artists. "You said your medium was pottery."

"Good memory."

She'd showcased several potters in Duck, and all had agreed to display their work at the Silos by the Sound. As tempted as she was to tell Naomi that her inventory was full, she never said no to someone who took the time to stop by. "Do you have samples with you?"

Naomi grinned. "I do. In my car."

"Let's have a look."

"Awesome." As Dani stepped into the glaring sunlight, she hesitated as her eyes absorbed the brightness. Absently, she adjusted her glasses.

Bella ran up to her with Rosie right on her heels. "Is the pizza lady an artist?"

"She is," Dani said. "She's a potter. And her name is Naomi."

Bella rolled her eyes but had the good grace not to state what Dani was already thinking.

Naomi paused at the old four-door sedan and opened the trunk. "Naomi, this is my daughter, Bella."

"Hey!" Bella said.

"Nice to meet you, Bella."

From the trunk, Naomi dug a box stuffed with items swaddled in yellowed newspaper. She set the box on the hood of the car, carefully unwrapped the first item, and handed it to Dani.

The tall, thin vase was a vibrant crystal blue with white and purple swirls that spun around it like a wild waterspout over the Currituck Sound. It caught the light, reflecting another layer of colors. The piece was both lightweight and sturdy.

"This is beautiful," Dani said.

"Really nice," Bella said.

Naomi chewed her bottom lip. "Thanks."

"It reminds me of the paintings my mother used to do," Dani said.

"Seriously? Your mom is a painter?"

"Was. She passed a long time ago." Dani peered closer at the vase, which caught her reflection.

She had several existing clients who'd love this. "I'd be happy to display your work for you if you're willing."

Naomi grinned as she ran long fingers through her hair. "That would be awesome."

"I'm still unpacking, but come back on Monday, and I'll have contracts for you to review."

Naomi smiled. "Terrific."

Dani handed her back the vase. "See you on Monday. Say, midafternoon?"

"Terrific. I'll see you then. Do you want to keep this one?"

"I'd love to, but hold on to your work until the contracts are signed. If you're going to be a success, you'll need to understand the business side of art."

"I'm still learning that part of it," Naomi said.

Dani hoped Naomi didn't share that with too many gallery owners. Not all were as protective of the artists as she was.

"We'll go through the basics on Monday."

"That's terrific. I really appreciate it." Naomi extended her hand.

Dani took it, noted Naomi's hand was rough—an artist's hand. "Look forward to it."

Dani and Bella watched Naomi drive off.

"She looks like Grandma," Bella said.

"What?"

"That picture that Grandpa Pete has in his apartment."

She knew the picture. Five-year-old Dani and her mother were standing in front of the ocean. With the backdrop of a bright-blue cloudless sky, they both were wearing matching red bikinis. "Yeah?"

Maybe that's why Dani had felt so at ease with the young woman the instant she'd seen her.

"How many more artists are coming?" Bella asked.

"Three more tomorrow. I'll spend next week arranging the pieces. And then the following Monday, we open."

"Why on a Monday?"

"It's a low-traffic day," Dani said. "It's called a soft opening."

"Dad had those with his restaurants. Need to work the kinks out before the big show."

"Exactly."

"Are you going to run it all by yourself?"

"I'll need to hire help eventually. My former employees don't want to drive this far."

"I can work for you this summer," Bella said. "I know a lot about art."

"You do." The kid had all but grown up around this world. "You sure do." She lay her arm on Bella's shoulder. "That's a fine idea. But you know it can be hard work."

"I like work. Keeps my brain busy."

"What do you think about Naomi?" Dani asked. "If all goes well, I might offer her a job. She could cover while you're in school."

"That could be really cool."

"Great."

This was one of those moments where all the pieces lined up. A perfect slice in time, untarnished by the past or worries of the future.

And if her thoughts should stray to worry, work and tight deadlines kept her mind on track. No time to obsess about loss or a dead ex if you're working sixteen-hour days. "You're a chip off the old block, kid."

"Don't forget, we're going to Juniper's for dinner tomorrow night," Bella said.

"Looking forward to it. Can't wait to see what it's like to live on a boat."

CHAPTER TWENTY-SEVEN
BELLA

Sunday, June 11, 2023
5:30 p.m.

Bella fiddled with her silver bracelet, now held together by a twist tie, as she and her mom parked in the small driveway that led to a blue houseboat docked at the water's edge. Juniper's SUV was parked to the right, giving them plenty of room. The houseboat had a white hull, and the deck was weathered teak. The hardware glistened.

"This is neat," Bella said.

"It sure is." Mom glanced toward the bracelet but said nothing.

Juniper appeared on the deck and waved, wearing a flowing peasant-style dress, her long red hair floating over her shoulders. Silver hoops dangled from her ears. It felt weird to see Juniper outside of camp.

"Welcome!" Juniper shouted as she waved.

"Hello." Mom balanced a bowl filled with a mixed green salad. She couldn't cook, but she could chop.

Bella waved. "Hey!"

As they crossed the yard, Bella went first, knowing if the ground was uneven or there was a hole, she would tell her mother. Her mom had reminded her five times today that her vision was fine, but Bella didn't know if it could break in a blink, like a switch being turned off or a bracelet snapping. And she absolutely couldn't handle losing her mother.

Up close, the boat looked a lot rougher than it did from a distance. The white paint bubbled and peeled, and the varnish on the deck was worn in more spots than it wasn't.

"It's a fixer-upper," Juniper said.

Bella smiled, pretending she hadn't noticed. "What are you going to do with it when it's fixed up?"

"Live here and then sell it. Jackson fixed the battery last week, so I have electricity. He also said he'd help with repairs in his spare time."

"That's really nice." Jackson was Mr. Helpful, but the jury was still out on him as far as Bella was concerned.

"He's a terrific guy," Juniper responded easily.

Juniper came down the gangplank and walked them toward a picnic table and a small charcoal grill. "I hope you guys like burgers. The stove on the boat is on the fritz, so grilling it'll have to be."

"You should've called," Mom said. "I would've had you to our place."

"You've just moved in and are getting ready to open your business. The last thing you'll need is a dinner guest."

"I'm not saying it would've been super delicious," Mom said. "Likely we'd have grilled out too."

"I wanted to treat you. The camp has been amazing, and I couldn't have done it without you."

"I doubt that," Mom said. "You'd have found a way."

In the center of the picnic table was a painted mason jar filled with white, blue, and yellow flowers. Around it was a selection of condiments plus sliced tomato and onion. Paper plates and napkins and plastic forks marked each place setting.

Juniper removed the grill's top and held her hands over the coals. As if deciding it was hot enough, she opened the cooler beside it and removed premade veggie and beef patties. "How's the gallery setup going?"

"Terrific," Mom said. "Always a big push before the opening, but we'll make it."

"Ivy and her food truck arrive on Monday," Bella said. "Once Ivy's on the property, the quality of the food really goes up."

"I'll keep that in mind. What's the theme of her truck?"

"Southern cooking infused with Italian," Bella said.

"So low calorie," Juniper said, laughing as she stirred the coals. Flames danced and crackled.

"Exactly," Mom said. "The food will be fantastic, but budget your calories wisely."

"What can I get you two to drink?" Juniper opened a second cooler filled with iced water and sodas. Mom and Bella opted for colas.

"You know, I grew up down the street from the silos," Juniper said. "The Nelsons owned your property for almost a hundred years. I was shocked when it went on the market and thrilled to get the listing. I think I'd had the for-sale sign in the ground two hours when you called me."

"I met Kit Nelson the other day," Mom said. "She's a character."

"Did she read your fortune?" Juniper sipped a cola.

"She did." Mom grew quiet. "I shall be living a long life."

"What did she say exactly?" Bella asked.

Mom looked at her as if she might not say and then said, "Not much more."

"Did she see Dad?" Bella asked.

"No. There was no talk of spirits, but Ms. Nelson did mention she had a sister who lived and died on the property. Her name was Anna."

Bella's skin prickled. "Anna? That's the name of the girl I saw."

"Really? Funny coincidence, isn't it?" Mom shifted her gaze to Juniper.

Juniper frowned. "Bella, have you seen much of Anna lately?"

"Not lately."

"Tell us about Anna," Juniper said.

Bella saw no traces of doubt in Juniper's gaze. "She's pretty. About my age. She's the one that dumped the stuff off my desk, broke my pencils, and tossed all my clothes on the floor."

"Did she break your bracelet?" Juniper asked.

"Yes."

Mom looked at Juniper. "Bella was pretty upset on Friday."

"It's okay to be mad," Juniper said. "Sometimes anger and frustration just come storming out of us, and we can't stop ourselves."

"Anna was the one that was angry." Bella fiddled with her bracelet. "Not me."

"I'd like to meet Anna," Mom said.

"She shows up when she shows up."

"Do you see her when you're feeling really tense?" Juniper asked.

"Yeah, I guess."

"I had a friend like that after my parents died," Juniper said. "Her name was Rainbow. She kept me company when I was saddest. Very common for us to find friends like that after a loss."

Bella sipped her soda, ready to steer the conversation away from her. "Have you written your letter, Mom?"

"Still working on it," Mom said.

Bella met Juniper's gaze. "Mom's decorated a jar but hasn't written a letter."

Juniper looked so calm. "One step at a time, Bella. We don't rush anyone's exercises. Or chase away their ghosts."

"I'll do it," Mom said.

"I'm so glad you two have moved here," Juniper said. "You're bringing a lot of life to the area."

"Thank you," Mom said. "The move has been a shot in the arm for us."

It sure stung like a shot sometimes.

Juniper sipped her soda. "Bella, how do you like it here? It's a big change."

Bella shrugged. "It's different."

"I like it here," Juniper said. "It's a slower pace, but that can be a good thing. Every time I drive to the city, it feels so busy and crowded. Here, there's time to think."

"What gave you the idea for a grief camp?" Mom asked.

"In my postgraduate studies, I worked with kids who were struggling with loss. I realized healing isn't just crying and sadness, but it also requires living life and finding joy."

Mom raised her soda can. "To Juniper. We're glad you're in our life."

Juniper smiled. "I am blessed to know you both."

Bella took a sip, her nose wrinkling with the carbonation. "Jackson was married to your sister?"

If the abrupt change of topic surprised Juniper, she gave no sign of it. "He was twenty-one when he started dating my sister, Cathy. I was eight. When my folks died, they took me in. He was my brother-in-law, but that doesn't come close to describing him. He's my brother in every sense of the word."

Bella could tell by her mom's cool expression that she wanted to know more about Jackson. Bella kind of did too. "Why did they get a divorce?"

Mom's eyes widened. "Bella, not your business."

"What?" Bella said. "Is it a secret?"

"It's no secret," Juniper said. "Jackson and Cathy had a little girl. Cloe. She died of leukemia when she was eight. Her loss was too much for their marriage."

Bella dropped her gaze to the top of her soda can. Jackson was quiet, but he never looked sad. "Do you have a picture of Cloe?"

"Bella," Mom said, her tone carrying a warning.

"What?" Bella said. "I don't stop talking about Dad because he's dead. Why should it be any different for Cloe? When you don't talk about them, it's like they die twice."

"I love talking about Cloe. I just don't get a chance very often." Juniper pulled her phone from her back pocket, scrolled through pictures, and then turned the screen toward Bella. "That's Cloe."

Bella studied the smiling couple holding a little girl who looked a little like Jackson but mostly like her mother. In the picture, Jackson's broad smile made him look younger, lighter. Bella wondered if her face had changed in the last four months.

"She's pretty," Bella said. "They all looked super happy."

Mom glanced over Bella's shoulder and stared at the picture. "A very lovely family."

This had to be weird for Mom, knowing Jackson had had a whole happy life before she met him. Juniper glanced at the picture before closing the phone and tucking it in her back pocket.

"It sounds lame, but I'm sorry," Bella said.

"It's not lame at all," Juniper said. "Especially coming from you." She laid the beef and veggie burgers on the grill. They sizzled. "You get what it feels like."

"I do," Bella said. Her throat tightened with tears, and none of them said anything for almost a minute.

Juniper cleared her throat. "Who wants cheese on their burger?"

"I do," Bella said. "Want me to cook them?"

Juniper laughed. "Do you know how to cook veggie and beef burgers?"

"Sure. I cooked them in Dad's restaurant kitchen a lot. All the customers always gave me good feedback."

Mom's head cocked. "Your dad put you to work in the kitchens?"

"Sure."

"When?"

"Just about every time he picked me up on Saturdays." She accepted the spatula from Juniper. "Don't freak out. I never got burned, but Dad said not to say anything because he was afraid you'd worry."

Mom pursed her lips, clearly silencing words of caution and maybe anger. Finally, her big smile reappeared. "Did he teach you anything else?"

"I can make pasta and a really good tomato sauce. The last batch I made all on my own." Bella adjusted the heat down.

Mom sipped her soda. "Maybe you should take over the cooking in our house."

"Sure." Bella was tempted to lift the beef burger and check for doneness, but Dad had always said to be patient. A good sear made a burger juicy, whether it was beef or veggie. "I get tired of pizza and bagels."

"Me too. You should ask Ivy for a job in her food truck," Mom said.

"Could I?"

"You can ask. It's between the two of you."

"But I was going to help you in the gallery," Bella said.

"Which would you rather do?" Mom asked.

"Cook."

Mom smiled. "Then you better have a conversation with Ivy."

Bella, satisfied all the burgers had properly seared undersides, flipped them. "Do you think she'd hire me?"

"I don't know. That's part of making your way in the world, kid. You have to chase your dreams."

"Bella," Juniper said, "if you have this, your mom and I will sit down."

"I got it under control." It felt good to be cooking. She felt closer to her dad.

"I heard from Jackson," Juniper said. "He's inspected his client's boat and is ready to set sail. He'll be back here for our kayak adventure, and then he'll be off."

"Why is he coming back just for the kayaks?" Bella asked.

"Because he said he would," Juniper said.

"How long will he be gone once he sets sail?" Mom asked.

"Several weeks, a month, depending on the weather."

Mom set her soda down. "I didn't realize it was going to be that long."

"He's sailing the vessel to the Florida Keys, and then I think he's staying down there to meet with several new clients."

Mom fingered her soda can's tab. "I know he must be in demand."

"He has a long wait list. The last few years, he's been on the water nonstop. The silo and house renovations were a nice change of pace for him."

"He did a fantastic job," Mom said.

Bella pushed the spatula under each burger and placed them on the clean plate. She covered the grill and closed the air vent on the top like Dad had showed her. She set the plate in the center of the picnic table.

They each grabbed a roll and a burger and chose condiments. Bella liked extra ketchup and sweet relish. Mom went for the savories, like mustard and onion. Juniper loaded all the toppings on hers.

"Matthew would approve of your burger, Juniper," Mom said. "He always said a good burger was enhanced by all the toppings. It drove him crazy that Bella was strictly ketchup and I'm full on mustard."

"He said between the two of us, he could find a properly dressed burger." Bella was thinking about the first letter she'd written to her father. She'd been pretty angry. Maybe when she wrote the second one, she could focus on the good memories. "I won't ever forget my dad."

"I know you won't," Juniper said.

Bella sipped her soda. "Does Jackson like my mom?"

Mom froze. Juniper hesitated, her burger inches from her lips. "I'm sure he likes her. She's a lovely woman."

Bella's eyes narrowed. "Not that kind of like. Boyfriend-and-girlfriend kind of like."

"I haven't asked," Juniper said.

Mom took a big bite of her burger. Her cheeks glowed pink.

"I've caught them staring at each other," Bella said. "They think I don't see, but I do."

Mom picked up her paper towel napkin and carefully wiped around her lips. "Bella, too much information."

A smile tipped the edges of Juniper's lips. "Amazing what the young people see."

Mom didn't say it in words, but Bella knew Dad was the only man she had ever really loved. She might like Jackson, but he wasn't a "keeper," as Grandma said.

CHAPTER TWENTY-EIGHT
DANI

Monday, June 12, 2023
8:00 a.m.

Dani and Bella loaded their kayaks into the back of her SUV and were on the road by eight. When they arrived at the camp, Jackson was already on-site, unloading his four kayaks. He wore board shorts, a white T-shirt, and flip-flops. His hair skimmed his shoulders, and his suntanned skin set off his white teeth when he smiled. She wondered how his client meeting had gone. They hadn't texted since Saturday. He'd be leaving soon. What had he said about the water? It was freedom?

Bella and Reggie greeted the other kids. Her child actually had a smile on her face. She pulled the kayaks from her vehicle and set them down. Grabbing the bow handle, she pulled the first to the shoreline and then retrieved the second. As she stood at the water's edge, she stared at the sky's pinks and blues blending with the steel hues flecked with silver.

"It's a beautiful day," Jackson said.

Turning, Dani looked up at him. Her heart thrummed faster in her chest. "Yes, it is."

"Mom, can Reggie and I ride on the same kayak?" Bella shouted.

"Get the life jackets out of the car," Dani said.

"It's not that deep," Bella countered.

"Nonnegotiable," Dani said.

"Ahhh." Bella paused. "Hey, Jackson."

"Bella."

The girl dashed off, and Dani leaned in and kissed Jackson quickly. "Hope your trip went well."

"It did. How was dinner with Juniper?"

"She's great. Very funny." Images of Jackson with his wife and daughter had lingered all night.

"Pure at heart."

How many times had that phrase or a version of it been linked to Juniper? She didn't have to wonder where Jackson would be if Cloe hadn't died. He would've been with his first family. She shouldn't feel like an outsider in his life, but she did.

A whistle blew, and Juniper stood by the water's edge. "You all ready to paddle?"

"Ready to go?" Jackson asked.

Bella ran up to her mother. "Seth needs a partner. Can you stay?"

"You sure? I thought you wanted me to leave."

"You can stay," Bella said.

"Good thing I wore my board shorts," Dani said.

Bella introduced Dani to a boy with blond hair and glasses. "Seth. This is my mom. Mom, Seth."

Seth glanced toward the water. His face was tight with fear as he huddled under his life vest. He adjusted his glasses several times.

"I don't see very well," Seth said. "I'm nearsighted."

"So am I," Dani said. "I think between the two of us we'll figure it out."

"I'm afraid I'll drown," he whispered.

"The water's not deep, and I won't let go of you. I promise."

Lips pursed, Seth managed a jerky nod. "Okay."

Dani and Seth spent over an hour paddling on the shoreline, and even the children who'd been the most fearful were relaxing and easing into the morning. Bella was chatting easily with Reggie, and the two were smiling. Jackson had Billy on one kayak and Nick on another while he stood between them, guiding them along the shoreline. All the kids slowly relaxed, and by the end of the morning, they were paddling their kayaks and smiling.

Juniper called the kids to the shore, and they all turned their boats around and headed in. All the kids were chatting and laughing, and when Juniper announced the pizza had arrived, they all shouted with pure joy. It was good to see smiling faces. The sadness would return, but for now it was at arm's length.

Dani hauled her kayaks to her car and opened the back hatch. Jackson appeared and helped her lift them into the back.

"It was a good day," she said. "Thank you."

"It was fun for me," he said. "The kids are great."

"They're all lucky to have Juniper."

"And you."

"Me?"

"She told me you sponsored this."

She tied down the kayak. "Believe me, my contribution was very small."

"I'll have to disagree with you on that."

Not really thinking about anything other than him, she leaned in and kissed him. He pressed his hand to her waist.

"I'll never get tired of this," he said.

She chuckled. "Thank you for that."

"No, thank you."

"Mom!" Before she could react, Bella was running around the side of the car. Her smile had vanished. "What are you two doing?"

Dani and Jackson drew back slowly like teenagers caught by a parent. "I was kissing him," Dani said.

"Why?"

"I told you, I like him."

Bella folded her arms over her chest. Her lips flattened into a grim line as she tossed her backpack into the back seat of their car.

"Busted," Jackson said.

"I'll talk to her."

Bella glared at her mother, red faced and angry. "Does he know?"

"Know what?" Dani asked.

"That you're going blind," Bella said.

Dani stilled. "Bella."

"Did you *tell* him?" Bella pressed.

"Dani?" Jackson asked.

She turned toward her daughter. "I'll talk to you about this later, okay? In the car. Put your seat belt on."

Bella's face was flushed with anger as she plopped into the car and slammed the door shut.

When Dani faced Jackson, his expression was grim. "Is it true?"

She should've told him. When would've been the right time? She'd never identified the perfect moment, but it had passed. "Yes."

His brow knotted. "That was your doctor's appointment in Norfolk the other day. All the glasses you wear."

"Yes." She held her ground as she scrambled for reasons that would justify her silence. "At first, I didn't think what we had was serious, and then Matthew died. And then I just didn't want to ruin what we had. There was already enough going on with Matthew and Bella."

"I wish you'd told me."

"I should have. I would have." The words sounded as lame as they felt. "I'm sorry."

Jackson's brow knotted with disappointment. "I need to load the last of the boats on my truck. I'll talk to you later."

If he'd been angry, she'd have railed and not felt so terrible. But he wasn't mad. He looked hurt. Disappointed. Tears clogged her throat. "Sure."

"It's safe for you to drive home?" he asked.

"On a day like this, yes."

"Dani, we need to talk about this."

Jackson had been through so much pain and suffering. And for Dani to ask him to watch her go blind was too much. She couldn't. Wouldn't. "There's nothing to talk about."

He looked incredulous. "What do you mean? This is a big deal, Dani."

She could feel herself drawing inward. "My fight isn't yours."

"That's not how I look at it. Relationships are a team sport, and I thought we were a couple."

She'd stood alone for so long. The idea of depending on someone else terrified her. "You don't know what you're getting into."

His eyes narrowed. "Is this your way of telling me that you don't want this relationship?"

"I didn't say that."

"Sure you did. You've kept something very important from me, and now that I know and am willing to help, you're pushing me away." He shook his head.

"I don't know what to say."

"Dani, if you don't want to open yourself up to me and fully commit, then maybe I should leave."

Dani watched him turn and walk to his truck. She didn't go after him.

As she eased into the car, she was overwhelmed with shock and sadness; she could barely start the vehicle. Bella sat in the back seat, arms folded over her chest, her gaze turned toward the window. She was frowning.

Very slowly, she backed out of the lot and turned onto the main road.

When she pulled into the driveway at the house, Bella dashed out of the car and ran inside.

CHAPTER TWENTY-NINE

DANI

Monday, June 12, 2023
2:30 p.m.

Dani pushed through the front door to find Rosie anxious to get outside. Upstairs, Bella's music blared.

"Come on, girl," Dani said.

She followed the dog outside and sat on the front porch. Rosie sniffed around and peed. Dani glanced at her phone, hoping to see a text from Jackson. Nothing. Not surprising. She should've told him about her sight. She'd owed him a conversation. Her silence had supported an illusion. Whatever future Jackson had imagined with her had been rewritten by the truth.

She rubbed the tension banding the back of her neck. There was no way of knowing if she could work this out or not. But if she'd learned anything, each time she didn't speak, the life luggage she dragged along grew heavier.

She should've talked to him. Should have been honest. Tears welled in her eyes and spilled down her cheek. She looked at her moist fingertips and rubbed her thumb against her index finger. Tears. Real tears. She hadn't cried since her mother died. Even when she'd found out about her vision or when Matthew died, she'd remained dry eyed. And now she was crying over a man she'd known less than six months.

Rosie barked, ran up to her, and licked Dani's hands. "I'm fine. Don't worry about me. I know how to land on my feet."

She rose and, with Rosie at her side, stood as Dalton's truck and also Ivy's food truck pulled into her lot. She wiped her eyes, blinked away the remaining tears. She drew in a breath, summoned a wide grin, and waved as she walked toward the spot she'd had graded for Ivy's truck.

"Welcome!" Dani said.

In the back of the pickup truck were three picnic benches, no doubt seating for Ivy's truck. Her brother climbed out of his vehicle. From the back seat, he lowered Ivy's dog, Libby, and his aging Lab, Sailor, to the ground. Libby ran up to Rosie and, tails wagging, the two dogs chased each other in circles. Sailor looked vaguely amused by the antics of the younger dogs.

Dalton hugged Dani. "How is life on this side of the bridge?"

"It's coming along. We're getting settled." She squeezed him and then stepped back. After their mother had died, he'd hugged her close, and she'd clung to him, drawing strength he likely didn't have to spare.

She squeezed his arm. "Let me see this truck that Ivy refused to discuss." Beyond learning that Ivy's food would be a fusion of classic Outer Banks cooking and Italian, she had no idea what the truck looked like.

Painted a bright aqua color, waves rippled along the sides, crashing into the driver's cab. Written in bold letters on the side was RUTH'S CAFÉ.

Ivy shut off the engine and climbed out of the front compartment. "What do you think?"

Ruth. Dani smiled as she pictured Ivy's grandmother cooking in the Seaside Resort's kitchen. "It's amazing. It actually complements the silo's gray hues."

"Why do you think I kept asking about your design?" Ivy asked.

"It looks fantastic."

"Wait until you try the food." Ivy clapped her hands together. "This is going to be the destination pit stop for anyone driving to or from the beach."

"That is the plan." Dani summoned a smile but felt it wobble at the edges.

Ivy glanced toward Dalton. "What's going on with you?"

Dani could lie, but they'd both smell it. "I volunteered at Bella's camp today. We were on the water for hours, and I'm a little wrung out."

"Is that all it is?" Ivy pressed.

She smiled. "Yes."

"Even if it wasn't, she wouldn't tell us," Dalton added.

"Is it your eyes? Have they gotten worse?" Ivy asked.

"Basically, the same as the last appointment."

"That's good, right?" Dalton asked.

"It's good." Five years ago, she'd never have taken this level of vision as a win, but there it was.

"Where's Bella?" Dalton asked.

"Inside. A bit of drama at camp. Nothing that can't be fixed."

"How is camp going?" Dalton asked.

"Emotional. But that's been the main theme for Bella and me this year. Hoping next year brings calm."

"Is there anything I can do?" Dalton asked. "I could talk to her."

Dani shook her head. He'd always been a surrogate father. How many times had he loaded Bella's car seat in his construction truck and driven her around until she fell asleep? He'd said the trick was to drive over gravel roads or on the beach. However, whenever Dani repeated the process, it hadn't worked. Something about Uncle Dalton's truck had calmed the kid.

But no driving around or words from a favorite uncle were going to fix this latest pain. That was between Dani and Bella.

"Where's Jackson?" Ivy asked.

"He was at camp this morning, helping with the kids. Now he's prepping to ferry a boat to Florida. He'll be gone several weeks."

Ivy hooked a brow. "You going to miss him?"

"Sure. I like him."

"Like?"

Dani held up her hand in surrender. "Boundaries, Ivy. Boundaries."

Ivy laughed. "Okay. For now."

Dalton opened his truck's tailgate and tugged the first picnic bench toward him. Ivy came around and held the end up while he lifted the other side. They set the table on the gravel in front of the food truck.

"We've got six more picnic tables, but this is all that'll fit on the truck today. We'll be back tomorrow. There's a lot of setup between now and the eighteenth."

"Tell me about it." Dani met her brother's gaze. "And before you ask, I don't need any help. We're on track."

"You know who to call if you need anything," he said firmly.

"Will do."

They unloaded the second table and then the third as Libby and Rosie barked and ran in circles. Sailor settled down in a shady spot under a tree. Ivy grabbed her purse from the food truck and locked it up.

"Dalton, I had a random memory of Mom the other day. I guess Bella's camp is bringing it all to the surface. I remember a guy kind of boxing Mom's car in at a grocery store. She looked really afraid of him. As he was knocking on her driver's side window, another car pulled out, and she was able to drive off. Do you have any idea who that was?"

Dalton frowned. "Her first husband. My biological father."

The words sounded as if they were wrapped in barbed wire. "She must have told Dad, right?"

"She did. They never kept anything from each other."

"What's his story?"

"Paul Armstrong. Married Mom when she was twenty-one. I was about two when he hit her the first and only time. She packed me up as soon as she could and took us to the police station. There she ran into a cop who knew our dad. He called in favors, and Dad gave Mom a job."

"What happened to Armstrong?"

"Arrested for armed robbery shortly after she left. Did six years. Mom divorced him while he was in prison. He came looking for her after he was released. Dad never said, but I think he and a few of his friends convinced Armstrong never to come back."

This was the first she had heard about the man's fate. "He just left?"

"He was shot and killed in another robbery two years after his release."

Her brother was talking about Armstrong in such a detached way. "About the time Mom was getting sick."

"I always thought it ironic that she was finally free of that guy and then she dies." Dalton's jaw tightened. "Didn't seem fair."

"You've never talked about him," Ivy said.

Dalton shrugged. "Mom never talked about Armstrong. Dad was the one that told me about him after she died. Said I had a right to know."

Dani's mother had always been so positive and upbeat. There'd been no hints of this dark past. "Why didn't Dad tell me?"

"No reason to, really. It was all over and done."

Dani pulled off her glasses and cleaned the lenses with the edge of her shirt. "Her smiles hid so much."

Dalton arched a brow. "You're so much like Mom."

She drew in a breath. "I suppose so." She shook her head. "Bella's camp director has asked the kids to write letters to their lost loved ones. Bella has challenged me to write one to Mom. So far, I haven't been able to write a word."

"Why not?" Dalton asked.

"Mom was perfect to me. She never made mistakes. She never complained. Always smiled. For me to be any less than upbeat and positive with her feels wrong."

"Do you think Mom wanted you to carry this sadness all your life?" Dalton asked. "You don't want that for Bella."

"No, I don't."

"Then you'll write the letter to Mom," her brother pressed.

"Yes."

"You should do that, too, Dalton," Ivy said.

"What would be the point?" he said. "I've made my peace with the past."

"That's what I used to say," Dani said.

Dalton sighed his frustration. "What're we doing with these letters?"

"We'll put them in decorated mason jars and release them the last day of camp. There's extra room in my jar, if you want to write a letter to Mom."

"I don't know about that," Dalton said. "I've never liked digging into the past."

"Ivy, you could write one to Ruth and your mother."

Ivy nodded. "If you think they'll all fit in your jar, I'm game. It's solidarity for Bella."

Ivy was smart. Dalton, like Dani, wouldn't write the letter for himself, but he'd do it for Bella.

"When is this flotilla launching?" he asked, resigned.

"This Thursday at eleven a.m.," Dani said. "There will be pizza."

"I could bake cookies or cupcakes," Ivy said.

"I'm sure the camp director would be thrilled."

"We'll be there," Dalton said. "And I'll tell Dad. He'll want to attend."

She imagined Dalton had appointments to rearrange, but for Bella, he would. "Great. I'll tell Bella."

"We'll be there," Dalton said. "Now, time to get back on the road. We both have work waiting."

Dani hugged them both. "See you on Thursday."

Dalton loaded up Sailor and Libby in the back seat, and Dani held Rosie by the collar. Some of the weight pressing on Dani lifted a fraction, but as she turned toward the house, fresh burdens resettled squarely on her shoulders.

She released Rosie's collar, and with the dog on her heels, she climbed the porch stairs and pushed through the front door. Music blasted from upstairs. The song was "Save Your Tears." Ariana Grande and the Weeknd. Dani had heard the song at least a thousand times.

When she reached Bella's door, she knocked. Music pulsed. She knocked louder and then opened the door.

Bella lay on her bed, staring at the white ceiling. Dani crossed to the speaker and shut it off. Bella rolled on her side, away from Dani.

Dani sat on the bed. "I'm not mad. Sometimes emotions get all tangled up, and they burst out before we realize it."

Bella sniffed, said nothing.

"You're right. I should've talked to Jackson by now. What's going on with me is a long-term issue, and he has a right to know."

Bella rolled toward Dani, staring at her with bloodshot eyes. "Are you really, *really* going blind?"

"I am. It'll take years, decades maybe, but one day, I'm not going to be able to see well."

"What do you see now?"

"It's like I'm looking in a tunnel. Right now, it's wide and only blocks a little of my side vision. But as time goes on, the tunnel will narrow. In the end, it'll be like looking through a straw."

Fresh tears welled in Bella's eyes. "You don't act like anything is wrong. Why did we move here? We could've stayed in a house that you know so well."

"I realized if I didn't do it now, the day would come when I couldn't. You could've stayed in your life forever, and I'm sorry my need for change upset your life."

Bella sat up, swiped a tear. "I'm sorry I blurted out the secret."

Dani wrapped her arms around her daughter, feeling her heart squeeze as her body crumpled into her little girl's. It'd been a while since her daughter had allowed herself to be a child. She'd been chasing grown up for at least a year, and that all had accelerated after Matthew's death.

"It's okay," Dani said quietly. "My secret really can't stay hidden anymore. We all lose it from time to time."

Bella sniffed and rubbed her nose against Dani's shoulder. "You never lose it."

"I do."

Bella drew back, eyeing her. "When?"

"Last week. The movers were jerking me around, and I had stern words with them."

Bella sniffed. "But you didn't cry, shout, or say anything mean."

"No. But I was very, very direct." Her blood had boiled, and her patience for nonanswers had made her want to scream. She hadn't. But she'd wanted to.

"That doesn't count. You didn't melt down."

She'd cried today, but telling Bella would only add salt to the wound. "I was pretty upset."

Bella shook her head. "It doesn't count."

"Okay, if I feel a freak-out coming on, I'll call you. You can watch up close and personal. You can even record it on your phone."

Bella rolled her eyes. "Mommm."

A smile tipped the edges of Dani's lips. She loved that eye roll. Bella had been perfecting it since she was two. "Seriously. I'll alert you when I get upset."

"Has Jackson called?" Bella asked.

"No. But he's getting ready for his trip."

"Are you sad he left?"

Dani nodded slowly. "I am. But I'm going to give him a little time. A lot got dumped on him today."

"I'm sorry."

"Stop apologizing. I should've had the conversation before now. Let's put this aside. We have each other, right?"

Bella hugged her. "I love you so much."

She tightened her hold and held Bella close. "I love you, kid."

"Do you want me to call Jackson?" Bella asked.

"No. I'll talk to him."

"Will you?"

"Of course. I owe him." She slowly released Bella. "For now, I'll be in the gallery if you need me. Naomi is supposed to stop by with her art and review her contract."

"Do you need any help?" Bella asked.

"I always love your help, but today it all boils down to me."

"I want to write another letter to Dad for my jar," Bella said. "The first one doesn't feel right now."

"That's a great idea. You write your letter and find me when you're done."

Bella hugged her again. "Okay. I love you, Mom."

Dani squeezed her daughter tighter, trying to capture this moment so one day, when Bella was all grown up, she could summon the memory. "I love you too."

Dani left Rosie with Bella and crossed the lot to the gallery. She opened the door, staring at the empty shelves. She'd felt such excitement when she'd bought this place and decided to turn it into a new life for Bella and her. Now, the weight of her decisions pinned her under a heavy burden.

CHAPTER THIRTY
JACKSON

Monday, June 12, 2023
3:30 p.m.

Jackson stepped out of the shower and toweled off. His heart was racing as frustration ate at him. Dani should've told him. Christ. He'd opened up to her about Cloe, something he hadn't talked about in a long time. He thought by telling her, she'd understand that they had more between them than the sex. Damn it.

Her silence proved . . . proved what? That he had more trust in her than she had in him? His phone rang, and when he saw Juniper's name he cursed. "Juniper."

"Is everything all right? You looked upset when you left camp."

He pinched the bridge of his nose. "I'm fine."

"I know you, Jackson. Your expression didn't telegraph 'fine.' You looked like you'd been sucker punched."

He sighed. "It's okay. Really."

"Is everything all right with you and Dani?"

No, it was not. "I can't talk right now. I have to get my act together. I'm leaving for my trip tomorrow, and I'm not packed."

"You're always organized. And I know for a fact you're packed," she said.

He glanced at his duffel bag, chock full and ready to be zipped closed. "Not today."

"It is Dani, isn't it?"

Juniper had always been a pushy kid, asking questions and digging into sensitive topics that no sane person would've touched. "Kid, butt out."

She chuckled softly. "Clearly, you don't know me. I don't run from trouble, Jackson."

"You run toward it."

"You regretted running once, and you'll really be sorry if you do it again."

"I never ran from Cloe or Cathy."

"You saw Cloe and Cathy through the worst of it. You were there every step of the way. And then Cloe was gone, and the only thing binding you to Cathy was pain. That's what drove you away."

He'd been through hell and back with Cathy. Some people grew stronger in the toughest times, but when he and Cathy stumbled through to the other side, they'd both realized the loss of their daughter had broken them. And after the pieces had reassembled, they were different people.

That didn't lessen the guilt that had gnawed at what remained of him. He'd spent months second-guessing his decisions and choices.

Cathy had driven down to Currituck County to confront him. As they'd stood on the dock, the wind blowing her hair, she'd glared at him. "What's going on between us? Where do we go from here? Or is there even an us?"

He loved her so goddamned much. But he couldn't return to their house. "I'm drowning, Cathy. I can't live in that house."

"Then we get another damn house, Jackson."

When he looked at Cathy, he saw Cloe. It wasn't right or fair to her. But he couldn't shake the devastation he felt every time he saw her. "You keep the house, or sell it if you want to. Take it all. I don't want anything."

She stood on the dock, staring at the water as the breeze from the north rippled over the surface.

"I love you, Cathy, but I can't keep living with this pain that ate us alive."

Her eyes flared with sparks of anger. "I don't like how we are either. It's why I wanted us to get into counseling."

"I don't see how it'll help. It's not going to bring our girl back."

She faced him. "I've been to a counselor that Juniper recommended several times. It does help."

He shook his head. "You're stronger than I am." An invisible fist clenched his heart. "I can't."

Cathy stared at him a long moment. In the past, she'd never been afraid to push him, but she also knew when no amount of shoving or kicking would change his mind. "I want the best for you, Jackson."

He took her hand in his, rubbing his thumb over her gold wedding band. There'd been such promise and hope when he'd put the ring on her finger. "If I could wish for anything beyond bringing Cloe back, it would be to give you happiness. You deserve it."

Her gaze softened. "So do you."

"I'm not ready for it. I might not ever be ready for it. I feel like I'm in a storm and the waves have swamped the bow and dragged it under the water. No matter what, this ship will never be seaworthy again."

"You're saying we're not seaworthy again?"

"I'm saying I'm not."

She nodded slowly and pulled a mason jar from her purse. "I have something for you."

"What is it?"

"It's a grief jar," she said. "It was Juniper's idea. I've put a letter into it for Cloe, and Juniper wants you to do the same."

"Write a letter to Cloe?"

"It's not as easy as it sounds. But I felt better afterward. I'm going to leave it with you, and then you can release it into the sound."

"And then what? It won't change anything."

"It helped a little, and right now I'll take all the help I can get."

He took the jar but said nothing.

She kissed him lightly on the cheek. "Live your life, Jackson."

It had taken him a year to write his letter to Cloe. But when he gave the jar to the current, he panicked. He ran along the bank, jumping in the water before grabbing the jar. He needed to let go, but he couldn't. In that moment, he believed he'd never truly be happy again.

Eventually, he'd found solace in work, the water, and solitude.

Then Juniper had sent Dani on his path. And now he was in love with another woman who was headed toward difficult seas. It wasn't the challenge of the voyage that frightened him but his ability to weather any more storms. He wanted to help Dani but at this point didn't know how.

CHAPTER THIRTY-ONE
BELLA

Monday, June 12, 2023
4:00 p.m.

This stupid letter was the hardest thing she'd ever written. She'd tried to write it on her laptop, then on her phone, and then on paper. No matter how much she concentrated, the words didn't come. *I'm sorry. I miss you, Daddy. I wish you were here.* It all sounded stupid.

Tugging at her bracelet, she glanced toward her open closet door. The mason jar she'd found the day she moved in sat on the floor next to her favorite flip-flops.

She rolled off the bed and crossed to the closet. She lifted the jar, carried it to the window, and held it up to the light. The painted glass remained stubbornly opaque. She tried to open the top again. Stuck.

She slid on her shoes and, with Rosie on her heels, let the dog out. As soon as Rosie peed, she returned her to the house, loaded the jar in her backpack, and dug her bike from the side shed. She started riding down the road that skimmed the sound toward the waterway and Jackson's house.

Maybe it would've been a good idea to tell Mom what she was doing, but Mom would've said no, and then she'd have found a task to distract Bella. Better to just do what she needed to do.

The drive between her house and Jackson's took less than ten minutes, but the three-mile bike ride took a solid forty. The afternoon air was hot and sticky, and she could feel the sweat pooling between her shoulder blades.

When she finally turned the corner and saw his truck in the driveway, she breathed a sigh of relief. Coming all this way and not finding him would've been a waste.

At his front door, she raised her fist to knock when she heard the hiss of the blowtorch in his shed. Hoisting the backpack on her shoulder, she moved around the side of the house.

When she peered in the open barn doors, she spotted Jackson, a welder's mask covering his face. Gripping a blowtorch, he feathered its blue flame along some glowing red metal.

As if sensing her, he looked up. For an instant he stared at her, but the welding mask made it impossible to read his expression. He shut off the blowtorch and set it and the hot metal aside. He tugged off large leather gloves. Carefully, he removed his mask.

Even without the face covering, it was hard to tell what he was thinking. He always looked so serious.

He shoved his hair back. "Bella, what're you doing here? Is your mom okay?"

"She's fine. She doesn't know I'm here."

He grabbed a water bottle and took a long swig. "Why doesn't she know you're here?"

"She's getting the gallery ready. Meeting with a new artist. Business as usual. But not, if you know what I mean."

He remained silent.

"Let's face it. I messed things up this afternoon. I was upset, and I threw a grenade in the center of life."

Some of the frown lines around his mouth eased. "This is between your mother and me. Not you."

"That's basically what she said. She said she should've had the talk with you sooner. I could tell she was upset."

Jackson's jaw tightened, released. But he didn't say anything.

"Are you going to call my mom? Because, as you might have noticed, she doesn't talk about feelings very well. She never has. And knowing her, it could be years before she calls you."

He sighed.

"The house could be on fire, and you wouldn't know it by the way Mom calmly escorted Rosie and me out of the house."

More silence. He was not making this easy.

"If you could talk to her, she might talk back. She likes you."

He carefully set down the water bottle. "I'm not sure what I'm going to do."

"Is it because she's going blind? Because she only just told me a couple of days ago. Only Grandpa, Ivy, and Uncle Dalton know. But again, that's Mom. She doesn't want anyone to think she's not totally in control."

"I wish she'd told me."

"Me too. I might not have been such a brat about moving here if I'd known. I thought she was being selfish. But like she just told me, she was afraid if she waited any longer, she might not be able to make a big change by herself." She tugged at her bracelet, and this time the tie holding the ends together broke. The broken pieces felt heavy in her hand.

"Twist tie fix?"

"Yeah. Not super effective, but I like the bracelet. My dad gave it to me."

"I have wire. Won't be a pretty fix, but it won't break."

"Yeah, that would be great." She dropped the two halves into his palm.

At his workbench, he selected a thin strand of silver wire and threaded it through the links. Using needle-nose pliers, he twisted the ends tight and snipped off the excess wire. He tugged both ends, testing the strength. It held.

Bella accepted the bracelet back. She barely noticed the small strand of wire. "Thank you. This looks great."

"Sure." He reached for his keys and wallet on his workbench. "Let me drive you home, Bella. You shouldn't have ridden your bike here alone." His gaze grew serious. "You did ride your bike, correct? You didn't accept a ride from anybody?"

Bella rolled her eyes. "I'm not stupid, Jackson. And I have my cell phone."

"I'll put your bike in the back of my truck and drive you home."

"Before you do that, I need another favor." She set her backpack down, unzipped it, and fished out the jar. "I found this mason jar in my room."

He studied the jar, his jaw tensing. "You found this in your room?"

"In my closet. It's like the darn thing is following me around. Every time I put it away, it ends up back on my desk, in the kitchen, or on the closet floor by my shoes. Weird." She tried to remove the lid, but it didn't budge.

He said nothing.

"I can't get the top off," she said. "I thought about breaking the jar with a hammer because I really wanted to know what's inside. But I don't want to destroy it. I figured with all your shop stuff, you could open it for me. I think it wants me to know what's inside."

He didn't accept it immediately but finally reached out and took it. "I've been through every inch of that house. I never saw it."

"Well, it was there. And like I said, no matter how many times I put it away, it finds its way back to me."

He raised a brow. "You're saying it's following you?"

"Strange, right? It might have something to do with the ghost in the house. I didn't believe you, but there's a ghost. Her name is Anna."

"Anna?" He cleared his throat. "How did you come up with that name?"

"Ms. Nelson said she'd had a sister who died young. Her name was Anna. Very *Twilight Zone*. I don't want you to think I'm going crazy, because I'm not. Mom now thinks I made up Anna. But I've seen Anna and talked to her."

"Have you talked to Juniper about this ghost?"

"I did. We had dinner with her on Sunday. Juniper also thinks the ghost is me and I'm using Anna to describe my feelings."

"She said that?"

"Not in so many words. But I'm not stupid."

"Juniper doesn't think you're stupid."

"I can tell when grown-ups don't believe me. I mean, it sounds a little crazy to talk about a ghost and a jar that follows me around, but there you have it."

"And you thought I'd be okay with a ghost story?"

"You brought up the ghost in the first place."

"What if I was teasing you?" he asked.

Bella studied his face closely. "Were you?"

"I'm not sure. I heard a few things in that house when I was renovating it. But old houses make noises."

Bella studied him closely and saw no hints of teasing. "So, you believe me?"

"Who's to say? Life is full of the unexplained." He wrapped his long fingers around the top of the lid and tried to twist the top off. It didn't budge.

"Now I don't feel like such a weakling," Bella said.

He seemed almost relieved it didn't open. "It's good and stuck."

"Maybe you could use a blowtorch," she said.

"Let me work on it. First, we get you home."

As he set the jar on a worktable, her phone rang, and she glanced at the display. "Mom. I swear she has radar."

"Not much gets past your mother."

"No."

"Answer that while I load your bike in the truck bed."

"Right." She raised the phone to her ear. "Hey, Mom. On my way home."

"Where are you?"

"I went on a bike ride. I'm at Jackson's."

"Jackson's?" Edges sharpened his name.

No missing the shock and anger. "I asked him to open that stuck jar for me. He's going to work on it." She drifted away from the workshop toward the truck as Jackson came around the front. "He's driving me home. Want to talk to him?"

"I'll see him when you get here," Mom said.

"See you in a few."

Bella climbed in the passenger seat of Jackson's truck and slipped on her seat belt.

Behind the wheel, Jackson started the engine. "Are you always this assertive?"

"Mom calls it pushy," she said. "She said I've been running the house since I was born."

He put the truck in reverse. "I believe it."

Jackson, as people went, was okay. He'd been cool on the kayaks this morning and fixed her bracelet, and he didn't try to push or press the new-daddy status like the guys who dated some of her friends' mothers. He was just himself and didn't seem to care who he impressed.

Neither spoke on the drive, which was just fine because she'd run out of words. What else could she say to undo what she'd done? And how do you top a ghost story?

When they pulled up at the gallery, Mom was waiting with Rosie on the gravel parking lot. She was holding her phone and frowning.

"You got some fast talking to do, kid," Jackson said.

"Yeah, she doesn't look happy." Her mother crossed to the truck when Bella opened the door.

"Go inside, Bella," Mom said. "I'll have a talk with you in a minute."

Bella glanced at Jackson. A small, small smile teased the edges of his lips. She tossed back a quick grin before she hurried past her mother inside.

CHAPTER THIRTY-TWO
DANI

Monday, June 12, 2023
5:30 p.m.

"Seems my daughter and I keep inserting ourselves in your life." Dani's heart beat quickly as she scrambled for the right words.

He got out of the truck and unloaded Bella's bike. As he steadied the bike against a tree, his calm, steady stare settled on her. "I never had a problem with that, Dani. You and Bella have brought a lot into my life."

"We've brought activity, noise, and problems that aren't yours to handle."

He didn't speak, but his gaze didn't waver.

"I should've trusted you with the truth. You've been nothing but kind, and not telling you about my vision screams lack of trust. I'm sorry I didn't tell you."

His eyes narrowed. "Why didn't you?"

"In the beginning, a serious conversation like that didn't make sense. I wasn't sure we'd last beyond this project. I thought you'd sail off into the sunset."

Her words loosened a sigh. "And if I'd said I planned to make this area my home base, would you have told me?"

She fingered the hem of her shorts. "I'd like to think I would. But I'd already dumped more on you in the last few months than anyone had a right to."

"I've been through a lot worse."

Unshed tears burned her throat. For the first time in twelve years, she'd met a man she wanted to bring into her and Bella's life. And the timing couldn't be worse.

"How can I lay my burdens on you? You've put your life back together, and I know how hard that is. I can't take away what you've fought hard to regain and turn you back into a caregiver."

A muscle in his jaw pulsed. "What I can or can't handle is for me to decide."

"Beyond Bella, my dad, and my brother, I've never cared about anyone who came and went from my life. Retinitis pigmentosa is more than I can handle myself some days. And it's too much to ask of a guy you've known less than six months. A guy who's already been through hell."

He cracked a knuckle. "And when I told you I left Cathy, that magnified your fears."

"My fears don't need amplifying. You've been great. But it's a lot to expect of anyone. I don't want to deal with it, but I have to."

Slowly he shook his head as he stared out across the property before his gaze shifted back to her. "Dani, I admire the hell out of you, but as I've said before, you're closed off, don't trust anyone, including me. You're like your silos. A system unto itself. It's been hard to get to know you. The only time you come close to letting your guard down is when we're in bed." He shook his head. "I'm not blaming you. Hell, I'm not too different. I've been walled up for a long time. But two silos standing side by side, closed off to everything around them, don't do anyone any good."

She was pounding against the walls she'd built up around her, but her blows barely made a dent. "I've been building barriers for decades. I never noticed or really cared about it until I met you."

"Maybe whatever we had was what we both needed, and it's served its purpose. Run its course."

Her chest squeezed, constricted around her heart.

"I'm leaving in the morning," he said. "My client asked me to spend extra time in Florida looking at boats, and I've agreed. I'll get in touch with you when I'm back."

She desperately wanted to hold him and press her cheek against his chest and feel his heartbeat. But pleading wasn't in her DNA. And this moment was destined to arrive at some point. "When will that be?"

"I'm not sure. A month. Maybe more if I pick up more work." He got back in his truck.

She stepped back from the truck's door. No magic words to unravel this mess.

His expression was stoic. Was he unsure of leaving? Angry? Hurt? Maybe he just wasn't sure how to end this. A kiss. A handshake. A "be safe."

A county utility truck pulled into the gallery parking lot. The building inspector. Perfect timing.

"If he has questions . . . ," Jackson said.

"Don't worry about the inspection," Dani said. "I've got it covered."

He shifted the truck into gear. She stepped back and watched him drive off, a plume of dust chasing after the truck.

As Dani walked toward the gallery, her legs felt unwieldy, as if made of lead. She greeted the inspector and showed him to the interior stairs and the new wrought iron railing. The inspector climbed the stairs, shaking the banister as he moved. It didn't budge.

"That's the last of it." He pulled a certificate from his clipboard. "This is a temporary occupancy permit. The permanent one will arrive by mail."

"Terrific. Thank you."

After he left, she locked the door and climbed to the second floor, her fingers skimming over the railing. She sat behind her desk. Tugging a sheet from a skein of copy paper, she plucked a pencil from a mug Bella had made for her in third grade and sat down.

Dear Ruth,
You saved me. You reached into the storm, pulled me free, and gave me a safe place to live. You taught me how to draw, how to be an adult, and how to be a mother. I can never repay what you did for me, and I will always miss you. I'm forever grateful our paths crossed.
Dani

Dani folded the letter into thirds, sharpening the edges with her fingernail. She reached for a second sheet of paper.
Dear Mom,
She'd started this letter a dozen times since she'd promised Bella, but she'd never gotten past the comma.
Dear Mom,
Her freshly sharpened pencil hovered over the page. She reached for the page, ready to crumple it and toss it away, when she paused. Why had the letter to Ruth flowed so easily? Why did this letter refuse to be written?

Dear Mom,
I stay so busy every day because I still miss you so much. I learned somewhere along the way that the grief couldn't catch me if I kept moving. It's always close on my heels, but I've been able to remain a step ahead. I've allowed myself to mourn the loss of my best friend (who finally came back), my marriage (grief light), my little girl getting on the kindergarten bus (devastating, exciting), the death of that ex-husband

(sadder than I'd imagined), and the old life I'd lived across the sound (I still miss it and fear I've made a mistake).

But I've never allowed myself time to mourn you. Instinctively, I knew it would be too painful. So, I've used your loss to fuel me into overdrive. And by all accounts, it's worked like a charm. I have a daughter, a new, bigger business, and a refurnished house that wants to feel like home if I'll let it.

But if you look below the surface, centered in my core is loneliness. Matthew was right when he said I made it impossible for anyone to love me. I hadn't believed him. I certainly have let Bella love me, as well as Dad, Ruth, Dalton, and Ivy.

But now as I sit in my new office, all I can think about are Jackson's words. Beyond a very tight inner circle, I am closed. Just like the silos. Perhaps I've never been fully open to anyone.

The best man I ever knew just drove off and out of my life. Having him close made that loneliness a little (a lot) less painful. Maybe that's why he scared me. I felt happy—light, even, for the first time in a long time. And I was terrified of returning to my shell alone.

If grief can't burrow through brick walls, then neither can love. But I'll try to chip away at the bricks. I'll remember you more, and I'll honor your memory instead of shying away from it.

I miss you every day, Mom.

Love,

Dani

CHAPTER
THIRTY-THREE
DANI

Wednesday, June 14, 2023
5:00 p.m.

The last two days had been a buzz of activity. While Bella was at camp, Dani worked on the displays in the gallery. More artists arrived with their pieces, which required contracts, conversations, and a little hand-holding. Naomi had agreed to work in the gallery and planned to start next Tuesday.

Dani picked up Bella and Reggie from camp each afternoon, and the girls worked in the gardens by the gallery, planting and watering yellow and blue annuals, walking Rosie, and just sitting on the pier and being kids. The custom sign SILOS BY THE SOUND, made in the same script style of the original NELSON'S sign, arrived and was installed. It was all coming together.

She wanted the girls to enjoy their summer. Downtime. A little peace from the grief that had knitted into their DNA. They needed the space with their loss, and if Juniper had taught them all anything, it was that it was okay to talk about their lost loved ones. But she hoped that grief didn't stalk the girls for the rest of their lives like it had her. It might be too late for her, but not for Bella or Reggie.

There'd been no word from Jackson, but she hadn't expected him to call. She'd hoped, a lot, but hadn't presumed.

Now Bella, Reggie, and Dani were making dinner, as they had each night. Tonight, Bella made the tomato sauce, Reggie baked cookies, and Dani boiled water for the pasta.

"Mom, did you write your letter?" Bella asked as she passed the bowl of pasta.

"I did," Dani said. "One to Ruth and one to Mom. Do I put them in my jar?"

Reggie nodded as she swirled noodles on her fork. "That's exactly right. And then seal the lid."

"Do you want to read it, Bella?" Dani asked.

Bella considered the question. "No, that's personal. Between you, Ruth, and your mom."

"Okay."

"Can we watch you put your letters in the jar?" Bella asked.

There was her little doubting Thomas. "Don't trust me, kid?"

Bella shrugged. "Can we watch?"

Dani rose from the table and walked up to her room. She grabbed the letter from under her mattress. As she turned, she glanced at the picture on her dresser of Matthew, Bella, and herself. Beside it she'd put another picture, one her father had texted. She'd had it printed and framed. It was Dani and her mother. "Love ya, Mom."

Unable to open it or reread her shaky handwriting, she carried it into the kitchen, waving it at them. She crossed to the kitchen windowsill, where her jar had sat empty ever since Bella had brought the jar back from camp.

"Pay attention, ladies." She waved the letters again. "Now you see them, and now you don't." Dani carefully put the neatly folded letters in the jar. As she settled the lid, a jolt rocketed her body. It was grief, love, and relief all rolled into a surge of lightning. Her body stilled, and her breath slowed. The knot balled in her chest eased.

"See, that wasn't so hard, was it?" Bella said.

"Seriously?" Dani said. "Was your letter easy?"

Bella ladled more sauce on her noodles. "No. And I wrote two."

"How did you feel?" Dani asked.

"When I wrote the first or second letter?" Bella asked.

"Both."

"Sad. Happy. Sad."

"What about you, Reggie?" Dani asked.

"The two letters were easy to write, but putting them in the jar was really hard. It was like I was letting go of my mother forever."

Dani set her jar on the counter and walked to the little girl. Tears glistened in Reggie's eyes. "You aren't letting her go. You aren't. She'll be with you forever."

"There are times when I can't remember the sound of her voice," Reggie said.

Dani wrapped her arms around the girl. "Anytime you want to write her, do it. Anytime you want to talk to her, do it. I promise you, she's there right behind you."

The tears rolled down Reggie's cheeks. "Does it ever get better?"

"It never goes away. Most days, it does lose its edge, but every so often, when you least expect it, grief cuts. And maybe that's not so terrible. That jab is a reminder that you loved her very much."

Bella sniffed. "Do you think Daddy's here?"

Dani nodded to the pot of tomato sauce. "Did I teach you how to cook?"

Bella rolled her eyes. "No. Daddy did."

"Exactly. When you cook, he's here with you." She sat down at the table and took a bite of rolled noodles. "Though Daddy did oversalt his sauce."

Bella giggled. "I know, right? I used to tell him that all the time. But he said it was perfect."

"This sauce is perfect," Dani said.

"Can we do a selfie with our jars?" Bella asked. "That way we'll always remember what we looked like when we did this."

"Sure," Dani said.

The girls ran upstairs and reappeared in seconds with their jars. Dani stood behind them, held her jar with one hand and her phone with the other. "Say cheese."

Bella shook her head. "Not cheese, Mom. It's lame."

"What should we say?" Dani asked.

"We love you," Reggie said.

"Perfect for me. What about you, Bella?" Dani asked.

She shrugged. "Yeah, that works."

Dani framed the image. "On the count of three, say 'I love you.' One. Two. Three. *I love you!*" Dani snapped the picture.

"You are two lovely young ladies," Dani said, showing them the image.

"My hair looks weird," Bella said.

"And my smile is crooked," Reggie said.

"Can we do it again?" Bella asked.

"No," Dani said. "It's perfect. Besides, the point was to capture the moment."

The girls looked at each other. "Okay, fine," Bella said.

"Send it to your father, Reggie," Dani said. "He'll see the beautiful young woman I see. Bella, why don't you send yours to Dalton, Ivy, and Grandpa. Knowing Ivy, she's going to print it and mount it on her refrigerator." Dani texted the picture to each girl's phone.

"Ivy wouldn't put the picture on her refrigerator," Bella said.

"Why not? I am. In fact, I might get several copies made. I bet Reggie's dad would like one."

"Mommm." But the girls were grinning.

Dani and the girls cleaned up the dishes, and when the dishwasher was humming and the counter and tabletops cleaned, she found the girls in Bella's room watching a movie on Bella's laptop. "I'm headed to the gallery. Call if you need me."

"Do you think Jackson is ever going to bring back that jar I gave him to open?"

"I'm sure he will, honey," Dani said.

"Love you, Mom," Bella said.

Dani crossed the room and kissed each girl on the head. "And I love you both."

Dani made her way to the gallery and spent the evening unpacking the art, including Naomi's five pieces, and arranging them on the shelves. Several times she thought she was done, only to return ten minutes later to rearrange the entire collection.

Tomorrow was family day at Juniper's camp, and everyone was supposed to place their jars into the sound. Dani worried about releasing her jar. The grief sealed inside had been her partner in life for so long. It had fueled her, given her the drive to open the first gallery and move here. What would happen to her if heartache wasn't humming in her chest?

Like it or not, she had to find out.

She reached for her phone, selected Jackson's number, and attached the selfie she'd taken with the girls. Her fingers hovered over the keyboard. She'd disappointed him. And he'd left with no promise of return.

Ready for tomorrow. We miss you. I love you. The last line arrowed through her body. Too much? Too far? *Screw it.*

Dani hit send before she lost her nerve.

"Okay, Mr. Cross, I have uttered the *L*-word. If you need another reason to run, there it is."

During construction, he'd always texted back quickly when she had a question. This time, nothing.

Likely he was on the open water, where Wi-Fi was spotty. She grabbed a large flashlight and headed out the front door to the farmhouse. Even as she moved over the graveled lot, her steps were easier, a little lighter. Her life wasn't perfect. Certainly not the one she'd envisioned as a kid. But it was the one she had.

And she would make the best of it. Somehow.

CHAPTER THIRTY-FOUR

DANI

Thursday, June 15, 2023
9:00 a.m.

Ivy, Dalton, and her father arrived ready to join Dani and the girls in the final ceremony. Bella asked if she and Reggie could ride with Dalton, Grandpa, and Sailor.

"That works," Dani said. "Ivy, Libby, and Rosie can drive with me."

"Great!" Bella said. "Can we ride in the bed of the pickup truck?"

"Nice try," Dalton said. "Back seat. Seat belts."

Dani and Ivy, with Libby and Rosie in between them, followed Dalton down the side road toward the campsite. "You, Bella, and Reggie look very fetching this morning."

Dani had chosen a crystal-blue sheath dress, a long gold chain, and hoop earrings. She'd also selected a collection of beaded bracelets on her left wrist and light-brown thong sandals. The girls each wore white. Bella wore shorts and an embroidered top, and Reggie had donned Bella's ivory dress with small pearl details around the collar.

Dani grinned as she pulled into the camp's parking lot. With the dogs in tow, she found Dalton, her father, Sailor, and the girls waiting.

"Bella and Reggie, you look amazing," Ivy said.

"Thanks, Ivy," Bella said.

"Yeah, thank you," Reggie said.

"I've always told you, you must dress for success," Dani added. "When will you ever learn, Ivy."

"When you learn to cook," Ivy said.

"I suppose we all have our shortcomings," Dani said easily.

"You have no deficiencies," Ivy said. "The gallery is stunning. I never would've believed it was possible."

She had never doubted. She'd seen the reimagined silos clearly.

"Can we go see the other kids?" Bella asked.

"Yes," Dani said. "We'll meet you at the dock. Why don't you take Dalton and Grandpa and show them your camp? The dogs can stay with us."

As the girls ran ahead, her father hugged Dani. "Good job, kiddo."

"I'm glad you could make it. It means a lot to Bella. Thank you for texting the picture."

"Been a while since I've been through the old pictures. It was nice to see Becky again." He cleared his throat. "Are Matthew's parents coming?"

"I invited them. But I think this is all too much."

Pete's jaw tightened slightly, but he nodded. "Sure. I get it."

"Come on, you guys!" Bella shouted as she waved her arm.

"Coming, peanut," her father said.

Rosie and Libby barked. Sailor yawned. Dalton and her father followed behind the girls toward the growing collection of families. Lord, but she loved her father and brother. They'd been the cornerstones of her life.

"Where's Jackson?" Ivy asked.

"He's delivering a ship to a client," Dani said.

"He won't be here for the grand opening?" Ivy asked.

"No." He'd still not responded to her text, a fact she was trying not to obsess over. "I like him."

"I sense a 'but.'"

"It's complicated."

"Why?"

"Long story short, I didn't tell him about my vision loss. Bella did it in a fit of anger over something else."

"Oh."

"Exactly."

Dani handed Libby's and Sailor's leashes to Ivy and, with Rosie, walked toward Juniper, who today was wearing a white peasant-style dress. Her red hair curled around her face, and on her head, she wore a fresh crown of daisies.

"Welcome!" Juniper said.

"This is terrific," Dani said. "My family is out in full force."

Juniper rubbed Rosie's head. "I can see that."

"This is my friend Ivy."

"Terrific job, Juniper."

"Thank you."

"I brought cupcakes," Ivy said. "Hope that's okay."

"It's fantastic!" Juniper said.

"That's my brother, Dalton, and my dad, Pete, with Reggie and Bella," Dani said.

"I'm glad they all could be here." Juniper smiled. "Will you excuse me. More families to meet."

"Of course."

Dalton strode toward Dani. "Is there room in that jar for another letter?"

She looked up at her brother's stoic face. "There sure is." She unscrewed the top and watched as he tucked the neatly folded letter inside.

"Could I get a little of that real estate as well?" Ivy asked.

Dani grinned and held out the jar to her. "For Ruth?"

"For Ruth and my mom." Ivy shoved her letter, written on the back of a restaurant's paper place mat, in beside theirs. "I'll expect you two on the dock with me when we put this in the water."

"I'll leave that to you," Dalton said.

"No way," Ivy said. "Remember, Bella is watching."

They looked at each other, sighed.

Dani hooked her arms into theirs. "If it were easy, everyone would be doing it."

The parents, campers, and siblings gathered around, each family unit standing behind their child. Dani, Bella, Reggie, Dalton, Ivy, Pete, and the dogs were their own unit.

A truck rumbled into the lot, and Dani turned, half thinking it was Jackson. It was Seth's father. He looked like an older, wearier version of Seth. The poor man had lost a son. So much sadness and loss. She looked around at the other families. Everyone was doing their best to find the joy in this day. The ceremony wouldn't wash away all the sadness, but maybe it would soften it for a while.

Juniper beckoned everyone to the shore's edge. "I know this has been an emotional two weeks. But I feel like I've gotten to know you all so well. Thank you for sharing your journey with me."

There was a general rumble over the crowd, each adult and child thanking Juniper for her help.

The children, holding their jars, along with their families with them, walked to the end of the pier. The campers held out their jars.

"It is your choice. You can release it into the water, or you can keep it," Juniper said. "The choice is yours because this is your journey."

Reggie was the first to walk to the pier's edge. Dani FaceTimed Reggie's father, who answered on the first ring. He was sitting in the cab of his truck, and in the background were mountains.

"Here we go," Dani whispered.

Dark circles hung under Ronny Bailey's eyes, but he'd shaved and combed his hair. "Ready."

Dani flipped the camera around and nodded to Reggie that her father was watching. Reggie knelt, kissed the top of her jar, and then settled it in the water. It bobbed back and forth before the current caught it and carried it south toward what they all hoped was the ocean.

Reggie hurried back to Dani, who handed her phone over to the girl. Reggie moved down the pier, talking quietly to her father.

Several other children set their jars in the water, each walking back to a parent, grandparent, or loved one who hugged them close. When it was Bella's turn, she didn't move.

"Mom," Bella whispered. "I don't want to give my jar away."

"Then don't, honey," Dani said.

"Are you mad?" Bella asked.

"No, honey. Why would you say that?"

"Because you made all this happen. And now I'm not letting go. I want to, but it's too soon," Bella said.

"That's okay, Bella," Dani said.

"But that's the point of all this, right? To let go."

"There's no right or wrong answer. Just the fact we're here is a huge deal. You don't want to forget your dad, right?"

"No."

"Then we talk about him. We recognize our grief. That's what this is about." She tucked a stray curl behind Bella's ear. "And it's all fine."

"What're you going to do with your jar?" Bella asked.

Dani glanced at the container's bright colors, sketches, and flowers. She felt the very familiar weight of her losses as well as Dalton's and Ivy's in the small space. It was time for them to move forward.

"I'm going to let it go. But I've carried mine for a long time, and I need to release it," Dani said.

"Do you want me to hold your hand?" Bella asked.

"That would be lovely."

Dani and Bella, along with Ivy, Dalton, and Pete, walked down the pier. Dani knelt, felt her family's energy gathered around her, and drew in a breath. She lowered her jar toward the water. The current splashed up cool droplets on her hand as a breeze brushed her face. She held steady for a moment and then let the sound take it. The jar settled into the water, bobbing up and down, before it found the current. Very slowly the jars floated away. Tears welled in Dani's eyes, and for the first time she let them fall freely.

When she rose, she hugged her brother, her father, Ivy, and Bella. Reggie returned to her side, and Dani wrapped an arm around both girls, squeezing them close. She kissed them on the top of their heads. "Thank you, girls. I couldn't have done this without you. I'm so proud of you."

They all walked off the pier onto dry land toward the warehouse's large sliding doors, which were wide open. Juniper had decorated the shelter with white balloons, streamers, and a banner that read LOVE. The tables were decked out with white tablecloths and mason jars filled with candles.

The dogs barked as Pete led them to a patch of grass. Ivy and Dalton opened the back tailgate of his truck and removed a cooler. They carried it to the shelter, where Ivy unloaded what looked like the most amazing collection of cupcakes she'd ever seen. Each was decorated with flowers made of icing and small hand-blown sugar mason jars.

Several other parents unpacked hamburgers and hot dogs, which they set on the small grills by the shelter.

"I wish Jackson was here," Bella said. "He would've liked this."

"Me too," Dani said.

"Will he come back?" Bella asked.

"I don't know."

CHAPTER
THIRTY-FIVE
BELLA

Monday, June 19, 2023
7:00 a.m.

Yesterday had been Father's Day. It wasn't fun. She looked at pictures of her dad on her phone and cried. The air was crisp and clean after an overnight storm when she sat by the dock, half expecting Anna to show up and say something that would make her feel worse, but the ghost girl was nowhere to be seen.

Her phone had dinged with a text from her mom. It was a picture of her dad. He was making a goofy face, and when Bella saw it, she laughed.

Bella had texted back a heart emoji.

Seven a.m. Monday morning, Ivy, carrying bags of groceries, arrived and went directly to her food truck. She opened her window at 10:00 a.m. to an empty parking lot.

Dalton showed up at eleven to deliver the last of the picnic tables. Bella and Reggie hung out with Ivy in the food truck while Mom manned the gallery, likely rearranging already perfect displays.

Monday was a low-traffic day. Most tourists had already traveled to the Outer Banks over the weekend. Mom had said she'd wanted an easy opening to work the bugs out of her system, and that's exactly what she got.

Sure enough, they didn't have a lot of people, but that was good because the Wi-Fi went out, meaning credit card sales couldn't be processed. Ivy couldn't find her favorite spatula, and the back burner of her stove didn't fire. Rosie and Libby chased one of the three customers they had, and the public bathroom backed up.

But Mom never got upset. She wrote down credit card numbers for her first sale, retrieved her own spatula for Ivy, and unclogged the toilet. (So gross.)

Bella and Reggie were eating grilled cheese sandwiches made by Ivy when an old brown truck pulled up. Bella thought maybe it was a customer, but then she recognized the driver. She jumped up from her picnic table and ran to the driver's side window.

"Jackson! I thought you were sailing a ship somewhere," Bella said.

"I am. My boat is parked at the Coinjock Marina. I knew today was the big opening."

"We've had three guests," Bella said. "But Mom's not worried. It's like a preview before a play."

He got out of the truck. His hair was ruffled as if he'd run his hands through it a million times. "I get it. Your mom is hard to ruffle."

"We missed you at the camp celebration. Reggie and Mom put their jars in the water, but I didn't."

His brow creased. "Why not?"

Bella shrugged. "I don't know. Didn't feel right."

He knelt down. "I get it. Not as easy as it looks."

"No. It's not. I keep hoping I'll wake up ready to let it go, but nothing so far."

"Don't push it, okay?"

"Okay."

"Where's your mom? She in the gallery?"

"Yes. I think she's closing early today. She wants to evaluate what went well and what didn't. She called it a 'debrief.'"

A grin tugged the corner of his lips. "No doubt."

He reached into a bag on the passenger seat. "Here's the jar. I finally loosened the lid."

"Did you open it?" Bella asked.

"I didn't."

"Why not?"

His gaze dropped to the jar, his expression tightening and then releasing into a smile. "Cathy made the jar. It took me a year to put my letter inside. And I swore I'd never look inside again."

"That's your jar for Cloe?"

"Yes."

"How did I get it?"

"I have no idea," he said. "Maybe your ghost, Anna, put it in your path."

"Why would she do that?"

"Maybe she figured you'd be the best person to give me a shove."

"I don't think anyone can shove you if you don't want to move. And just between us, Anna hasn't been around."

"You okay with that?"

"It's not exactly normal to have a ghost for a friend."

He chuckled. "For the most part, that's true."

She held out the jar. "You should take this back."

He shook his head slowly as he stared at the container. "No, I think it's for you."

"Why is it for me? I didn't make it. You did."

"Like I said, it found its way to you for a reason."

Bella tested the lid. It twisted easily back and forth.

"I don't think I'm going to open it. I think it should stay sealed."

"Agreed."

She rattled the jar, heard the crinkle of paper inside. "Can I show Reggie? We won't open it."

"Of course. And if you two decide to look, go ahead. Show Rosie if she'll sit still for it."

Bella hugged Jackson, and he wrapped his arm around her. He smelled different from her dad, and his hug was a little lame, as if he were out of practice.

"You should check on Mom," Bella said. "She could use cheering up."

"Is she doing all right?" Under his deeply tanned skin, dark circles ringed his eyes.

"She's going full steam ahead, like she does. Always smiling. Cheerful. Basically, a code red."

"I hear ya."

He crossed the lot in long strides, moving with purpose. He wasn't her dad. Never would be. But he made her mom happy, and she kind of liked him.

"Good luck, you two crazy kids," Bella said.

CHAPTER THIRTY-SIX
DANI

Monday, June 19, 2023
2:00 p.m.

As far as opening days went, this one didn't really rate. Three customers and one sale. Not setting the world on fire. When she'd opened her art gallery in Duck ten years ago, she'd made $1,000 on opening day. Today, she'd made $150. Ivy had had eight customers and sold ten meals. She might even have outearned the gallery.

But they'd both known traffic on a Monday would be light. A soft opening. How many times had she said that today? They'd used this time to fix the bugs. That was a good thing. All her instincts told her this concept was a winner and she would make money here.

As Dani repositioned a vase, the bell on the front door chimed, and she felt a gaze settling on her. Another customer? Wouldn't it be nice to end this day with a sale? Smiling, she turned toward the door.

Her heartbeat accelerated when she saw Jackson standing in the doorway. A week in the sun had streaked his hair with gold and deepened his tan. He looked leaner, and his angled features had sharpened.

Broad shoulders filled a blue T-shirt tucked into khakis that skimmed worn docksiders.

"Hey there." She clung to her smile as she made herself move toward him until she was only inches away. "Is everything all right? I thought you were on your way to Florida."

"Delivered the first boat, flew back to Norfolk, and now transporting the second." He slid his hand into his pocket. "The second boat is docked at the Coinjock Marina. I borrowed a car so I could stop by and see you."

"How has the sailing been going?" She took another step toward him.

He stood his ground. "Engine troubles on boat number one. A storm off the Florida coast. Business as usual."

She drew in a breath. Putting herself out there again wasn't easy. "I missed you. I missed you a lot." The words rushed over her as emotion welled in her chest. "Did you get my text?"

"I did." His body stilled.

Instead of prodding him for his thoughts, she said, "You missed quite the show the last day of camp. Dalton and Ivy came with their own letters and put them in with mine. We let it go. Reggie released her jar as well. Bella didn't."

He frowned. "She told me."

"She's not ready. I think she's afraid she'll lose her dad completely. It took me over twenty years to ease up on my grip. Apple . . . tree."

"I understand that." Energy radiated from him. "Letting go of Cloe was like severing a limb."

"That jar Bella found at the house. Who did it belong to?"

"To my ex-wife and me. Juniper had us create it. Cathy put it in the water, but when I saw it float away and then get caught in the weeds, I panicked. Almost like Cloe was reaching out, begging me to hold on. I fished it out of the weeds. Cathy and I argued, and I told her it was better we take a break from each other. A year later we were divorced."

"How did it end up in the farmhouse?"

"I have no idea. Last I saw it, it was on a shelf in my workshop."

"Could Juniper have put it in the house?" Dani asked.

"If she did, she'll never admit it. She'll insist it was the universe. Or the ghost of Anna."

"Losing a child . . . that's your life. I don't know if I could've released it." She refused to link Bella's name with death or loss.

He cleared his throat. "Maybe one day I'll do it."

"There's no clock on this. Look at me. It's been twenty-two years since my mother died."

"But you did it."

"I've been grieving for a long time. It controlled everything in my life. I think loving you was the first time I'd felt anything beyond Bella. Grief has a way of feeding off of other emotions, so it's easier not to feel anything."

He captured a strand of her blonde hair. "Did you say 'love'?"

"I did. I also wrote it in the text."

"I noticed that." His gaze bore into her as if he was searching for validation.

"You didn't respond."

"I'm here now."

She drew in a breath, pushing past the resistance wrapping around her heart. "I'm not sure when I realized that I loved you. But I knew when I took that picture, I kept thinking you should be there." She smoothed her hands over her thighs. "A partner with low vision is a heavy lift, Jackson. I wouldn't blame you if you realized it's too much. It's too much for me sometimes."

"Why don't you let me decide what's too much," he said. "I've got broad shoulders that are used to heavy loads. Cloe made me a better and stronger person. I see that now."

Tears stung her eyes. "But I don't want to end up being a burden to you or anyone."

His head tilted. "Do you really see yourself becoming a burden?"

She dabbed her fingertip under her eyes. No running mascara today. "No. I do not. But it could happen. It won't. But it could."

He arched a brow. "What if I got sick? What if I was in an accident? Would you leave?"

"No," she said quickly. "But those are all what-ifs. My diagnosis is a certainty."

"Duly noted." A smile tipped the edge of his lips. "Is there anything else I need to know? Any bombshells I should be aware of?"

"No. I mean, I only made a hundred and fifty dollars today, and I could be hurtling toward financial ruin, but other than that, it's all good."

He cupped her face and kissed her. "I've missed you so much."

She leaned into the kiss, savoring not only the physical touch but the salty scent of his skin. Her heart ached as it opened in a thrilling and frightening way. Now there was another human on this earth who carried her heart.

"How long are you in town?" she asked.

"Twenty minutes. As soon as I gas up the boat, I've got to get going. I'm on borrowed time. I'll be back in ten days."

She smoothed her hand over his hard chest. "Feels like forever."

A muscle pulsed in his jaw. "It never did before, but it does now."

"Sail your boat, and be careful. I can wait as long as it takes."

He kissed her again. "This is the first time in a very long time that I'm looking forward to coming home."

Outside Rosie and Libby barked as Bella and Reggie shouted that they were officially closed for the day. "As long as you're not looking for peace and quiet."

"I've had plenty of quiet, and in all the noise and chaos, I've found peace."

"I'll remind you of that."

He chuckled. "I'm ready for it."

She kissed him, wrapping her arms around his neck. "I love you."

Jackson held her tight. "And I love you."

EPILOGUE
DANI

Saturday, July 1, 2023
5:00 p.m.

"When is he going to be here?" Bella asked.

"He said he was ten minutes out," Dani said as she locked the door to the silo gallery. Business at the gallery had been steady and growing as the tide of tourists ballooned. Dani had ordered extra lights for the parking lot so that when fall came and the sun set sooner, her lot would be fully illuminated. Ivy had hired an assistant to keep up with the tremendous demand for her fried chicken and fish. And Naomi was turning out to be a gifted salesperson.

"That was an hour ago," Bella said.

"It was five minutes ago. Jackson said he'd be here, and he will. It's Saturday, and the traffic, if you haven't noticed, is heavy."

Bella gripped her and Jackson's jars tight. "Because if he does not come, then I'm not going to do it."

"He'll be here." They walked across the parking lot and paused as Ivy was closing up her truck. "How did the day go?"

"Terrific. Who'd have thought this space would attract so many customers."

Dani shrugged. "Never doubt my visions."

"Duly noted." Ivy looked up. "There he is."

Bella turned. Her shoulders slumped. "Uncle Dalton."

"Don't sound so disappointed, kid," Dani said.

"I'm not."

Dalton and Sailor crossed the lot and reached Ivy as she stepped out of her truck. He kissed Ivy and whispered something in her ear, and she laughed.

"I'll remember that, Mr. Manchester," she said.

Dani was happy for her brother. But seeing him with Ivy reminded her how much she missed Jackson. He'd called daily and texted often, and even Bella had started sending him pictures of Rosie, Libby, the water, and the customers at the gallery.

Jackson's truck pulled into the parking lot. He quickly got out of his vehicle, and his long, even strides ate up the ground between them. His hair was even more sun streaked, and his face was deeply tanned. A smile played on his lips. He shook Dalton's hand and nodded to Ivy, but with multiple sets of eyes on him, he didn't kiss Dani.

"What took you so long?" Bella asked.

"Plane was delayed. Traffic in Norfolk. All the nonnegotiables were in play today," Jackson said. "Short of sprouting wings, I couldn't get here any faster."

Rosie and Libby ran up to Jackson and barked. He scratched both between the ears.

Bella handed him his jar. "Did Cathy have her baby?"

"She did. It's a boy," he said.

"They are both healthy?" Dani asked.

"Yes." Relief, sadness, and joy drifted behind his gaze. "Juniper is with them now."

"I'm putting my jar in the water today," Bella said. "I'm giving you back yours."

He studied the mason jar's darkened glass, still covered with sediment from the sound. "Are you sure about letting go?"

"Yes," Bella said.

"Have you seen Anna lately?" he asked.

Her eyes widened. "No. Not a sign. I think she's happy."

"Maybe I should do the same. I wouldn't want to upset Anna."

"That's probably wise," Bella said. "But if you don't want to, you don't have to let it go. Juniper says there's no deadline here."

He glanced at the jar and for a moment stilled. Finally, a breath he seemed to have been holding for years released. "I think I'm ready."

Not caring about their audience, Dani kissed him on the cheek. His hand came to her side, and she could feel the energy radiating in his body.

"Let's go!" Bella shouted.

"Where's Reggie?" Jackson asked.

"She's with her dad today. Mom said she'd take pictures so I could text them to her."

"Sounds like a plan."

The five of them walked out to the end of the pier. Rosie and Libby chased the small waves lapping under the pier's pylons. Sailor yawned.

"Who wants to go first?" Bella asked.

"Ladies' choice," Jackson said.

"I'll go first." Her voice carried a solemn weight. "Ready, Mom?"

Dani raised her phone. "Good to go."

Bella knelt at the end of the dock and lay down on her belly. Her bracelet dangling from her wrist, she suspended her jar above the water, said a few words to herself, and then dropped it in the quick current. She watched as it floated away.

Dani videoed the vessel until it bobbed out of sight. She sent the video to Bella. "I wish Reggie was here. But it's good she's spending time with her dad."

Bella's gaze trailed the jar's trajectory. "What if the jar comes back? What if it gets stuck on the shore?"

"The point is you let it go," Dani said. "You're not carrying the weight."

"But what if it *does* come back? Does that mean I'm not ready? Does that mean I'll be sad forever?"

"Then you put it back in the water. Letting go can take a lifetime," Jackson said.

"I can do it as many times as I have to?" Bella asked.

"As many times," Jackson said.

"Your turn," Bella said.

He knelt down and gently dropped his jar into the water. It bobbed on the surface, trailing after Bella's. He watched it drift away and finally out of sight. When he stood beside Bella, Dani laid her hands on both their shoulders.

"I'm proud of you both," she said.

"Juniper's camp was your idea, Mom," Bella said.

"It was her idea. I just helped her make it happen," Dani said easily.

"I never would've done it without Juniper and you," Bella said.

"And I wouldn't have done it without you," Dani said.

Bella's phone buzzed with a text. "It's Reggie. She said, 'Good job!'"

"Ladies and gentlemen, I have lunch in the food truck, if you're hungry?" Ivy asked.

Bella nodded, a given since the kid was going through a growth spurt and could likely eat her out of house and home. "Can you help Ivy and Dalton with the food, Bella?"

"Sure."

As Dani watched the girl and dogs run toward Dalton and Ivy, she slipped her fingers into Jackson's. "I've missed you."

He tugged her toward him and kissed her on the lips. "I feel like I'm finally home."

She smiled and wrapped her arms around his neck. "I like the sound of that."

"We need to talk about your eyesight," he said. "I want to understand what's going on medically. I can't help you if I don't understand."

It was her least favorite topic but one she couldn't ignore. "Of course. You can meet my doctor if you'd like. But for now, my sight is relatively stable, and it could be years before it degrades too much. It's going to be a gradual process."

"As long as you're honest with me about what you're going through, then I'll be fine," he said clearly.

"Back at you, Jackson. If you ever need to talk about Cloe, know that I'd love to learn all I can about her. She's part of our family."

He smoothed his finger along her jawline. "I love you."

"I love you too."

"Come get the fried chicken while it's hot!" Bella shouted.

Jackson chuckled. "Ivy's food truck is going to fatten me up."

"You have no idea," Dani said.

ABOUT THE AUTHOR

A southerner by birth, Mary Ellen Taylor has a love for her home state of Virginia that is evident in her contemporary women's fiction. When she's not writing, she spends time baking, hiking, and spoiling her miniature dachshunds, Buddy, Bella, and Tiki.

Made in the USA
Middletown, DE
01 September 2023